BATTLE FOR THE STARS
THE EMPIRE WITHOUT ENDS

JOHN DELEO CUSTER

iUniverse, Inc.
Bloomington

iUniverse books may be ordered through booksellers or by contacting:

iUniverse
1663 Liberty Drive
Bloomington, IN 47403
www.iuniverse.com
1-800-Authors (1-800-288-4677)

Because of the dynamic nature of the Internet, any Web addresses or links contained in this book may have changed since publication and may no longer be valid. The views expressed in this work are solely those of the author and do not necessarily reflect the views of the publisher, and the publisher hereby disclaims any responsibility for them.

ISBN: 978-1-4401-6613-6 (sc)
ISBN: 978-1-4401-6614-3 (ebook)

Printed in the United States of America

iUniverse rev. date: 8/5/2009

A SYNOPSYS

ONE INDIGENOUS PLANET, ONE moon of a lone star was the constant principal in the universe. A universal network of colonies was established known as the Dominion. A matrix grid of crosslink hyperwaves ensured free travel and unity throughout the galaxy.

As in any society there are those who may wish to rebel against the enacted laws set forth by those of authority. These brigands posed a threat. To protect the colonies the Colonial Legion was created to serve as a custodian of peace.

Kreed, an ex-legionnaire, managed an unexpected escape from the penal colony of which was orchestrated by the brigand fleet. Kreed was a reptilian humanoid and clairvoyant like all of his kind. He was the General Commander of the Legion during the Colonial Wars. Kreed was sentenced to hyper-genetic freeze for the illegal torture and execution of prisoners.

Because of his knowledge of military strategy and the Dominion's defenses he became the willful leader of the brigand raiders. His band of outlaws followed him to the end with the hope that he knew the whereabouts of a secret weapon, kept hidden from the legionnaires. Perhaps seduced by his cognitive powers they believed this weapon to be a mobile attack base, a concenter, which had the capability to navigate on its own power. With the station at their control they can unleash a chain of surprise attacks against the colonies.

A veteran legionnaire, Joshua Hollands, was First Marshal of the Colonial Legion appointed by the Consulship. He served as law enforcer for Central Command headquarters. Central Command's primary outpost for their operations was the Regalia starbase. The Regalia was positioned near Kwidon's orbit, the birthplace of the Dominion. The marshal must embark on a mission to find, apprehend, and bring Kreed back to justice before all will be lost.

SPACE WAS A VAST frontier of star regions and alien unknowns to be discovered. Cosmic forces danced in splendor in the openness of the evolving universe. Some phenomena could be scientifically explained but most were mysteries.

Amidst the interstellar horizon a United Star Systems, Wisdom, hung like a shadow overlooking the infant planet below. It was an infant because it was newly formed; a wondrous aftermath left behind by cosmic dust from the wake of a supernova explosion. Popularly known as a cosmic fireball throughout the galaxy. It was hell reincarnated but for a curious team of scientists it was heaven.

The U.S.S Wisdom was a science consort and held a stationary position at a safe distance above the hot planet. The shifting tides of liquid rock generated enough heat to equal that of a small sun. The magma's composition is what the scientists aboard the science lab wish to spectrum analyze and learn from.

Wisdom was generally a floating research laboratory. It had a whale-like structure with double horizontal fins at the stern. The bulky trunk of this flying fortress had many decks. Each deck was assigned to various branches of research such as radiology, geology and so on. The back quarter had many panels of harden glass windows. Behind the glass you can see many specimens of plant life growing in their artificial environment, this was obviously the greenhouse.

The senior officer stood beside his ensign aboard the bridge, "What do you read on the spectrum display."

"Standard composition for this class of planet, huge amounts of iron," the younger subordinate said sitting down at his station, facing his hologram computer.

"The building block of life," the senior remarked.

"Yes sir."

As the senior straightened from his leaning position he ordered, "Well, continue observations and record what you can. The S.M.I Corporation has their own time tables to keep."

"Yes sir."

A matrix of light appeared in a form of a flash accompanied by a shotgun sound, which was followed by a ship darting out of it. The ship was an intergalactic fighter, the Killwing. The Killwing was a Dominion gunship armed with double recoil thermal laser cannons, a favorite among legionnaire pilots.

Commandeering the IF-7 was First Marshal of the Colonial Legion, Joshua Hollands, a handsome middle-aged man who serviced the Legion since he was old enough to enlist. Equipped with his hand-held pulse gun, and his quick thinking, he was a well-seasoned soldier of whom you would want on your side if danger arises.

"Assembly One, this is Hollands reporting in," he said using his ship's transceiver. He was relaying the message to the commanding mining freighter, which was leading an industrial convoy.

"Acknowledging your transmission. It's good to see you marshal. I trust centralnet brought you to us safely." The dispatcher continued, "How was your flight?"

"After twenty years of service I still can't get used to molecular breakdown," Joshua responded, "Traveling through curved-space at unknown speeds."

"After twenty years you should be use to it."

"I'm old school," the marshal remarked. "How soon before your ready for launch?"

"We're bringing in the last payload now. My men are still out there."

"Copy that," Joshua understood.

"By the way, where's your squadron? Did they get lost?"

Before Hollands had the chance to reply a small fleet of legionnaire IF-7s made the jump out of the light-curve dimension. As the fleet of Killwings slowed to a halt in a standard cover formation behind the marshal's ship, "Say again dispatch."

The S.M.I workers were suspended in space protected by environmental cyber-suits. They were within safe distance from the orbital gravity of the infant world, which lay beneath them.

The primordial planet was active with shifting tides of the magma. This river of flared fury had a fusion mix of many mineral agents, but with the largest concentration of iron. This epoch of evolution was the precursor of life, which will one day flourish on the surface land and in its seas.

Suspended and protected, they were proceeding with the final steps of their mission, which was to retrieve a pod-and-launcher craft away from the orbital field of the planet. The podal craft was a tool used to extract material from places dangerous to humans.

Using thrusters, which were built into their robotic armor, they briskly moved backwards toward the astrotanker that was near mission proximity. Following their lead, the podal craft orbited away from the intense heat from the planet, steadfast. Using transmitter pads the craft was remote controlled. The controller pads faced near their eye level and were attached to short arm boom supporters, which hugged around their lower torsos.

Off-loading the contents onto the astrotanker, the Rogue, was the final stage. On minimal thrust the cybermen moved backward, swiftly but carefully, as the pod continued to shadow their lead. When the pod was within close enough proximity to the tanker they switched off their transmitter frequencies to allow their centralnet computer to take over.

Meanwhile, aboard the astrotanker, "Ready to off-load the rest of the cargo."

"Let's get this over with, Freighter Command is hasting us to fall in," the bridge officer responded.

They were both eyeballing holocam monitor observing as centralnet begun to do its work. Because the computer was piloting the craft at the moment everybody, involved in the task at hand, had nothing to do but wait.

Joshua ordered his squadron to assume their gunships into patrol positions, to encircle the convoy. Episcopes and acoustics were turned on to probe the unknown that might pose a threat.

"All fighters listen up. You know the drill, take your defensive positions," Joshua commanded while he took the lead.

The cybermen waited at a safe clearing while the pod proceeded with the transference of its contents. Their faces showed signs of sweat and fatigue. Floating aimlessly in space they look forward to walking the corridors aboard their freighter, even if it was artificial gravity that kept them grounded.

With centralnet handcrafting the mission, the podal craft positioned itself so that the rear exhaust was facing the freighter's intake antechamber. At the distance required, the launcher kicked on its retros creating a backward thrust. When the craft was close enough to the intake the launcher released the pod while, in the exact amount of time, retros disengaged. These actions caused a force of momentum to self-propel the pod toward the tanker's interface lock and funnel.

Very slowly the pod's tapered fitting end slipped, in slow procession, into the tanker's shallow outer clamps. When the pod's tapered bridge made contact, and with an echoing slam the pod came to an abrupt stop. The pod than made a half revolution of a turn to initiate the locking mechanisms, the pod was now safely docked.

"I'm in position now," Josh said while he flew his gunship in front of the chain of freighters.

"I copy you. We're just about done here," the head administrator said through dispatch.

"Take your time. I still have to re-cool the symmetry drive and chart our destination," the marshal replied back.

The pri-mass ore was being drawn into the tanker's hollowed structure for safe storage. Off-loading was accomplished by the use of turbine-powered vacuums mounted within the air-sealed chamber.

When off-loading was completed the pod made another half turn, but this time in the counter-direction. The counter turn caused the pod's tapered end to separate and unlock from the antechamber's interior rings. A tremendous force of internal thrust spurred the pod to draw out and away from the antechamber and back into open space.

While the pod drifted freely the launcher ascended upward

from underneath, with one to the other, preparing to make contact. In smooth harmony the two superstructures unified with the slamming sounds of hydraulic clamps making a confirmed lock.

The colonials than maneuvered the craft toward the hangar bay doors, which was located just below the intake at the stern. "Open hangar bay doors," one of them said. And soon after the control personnel, at the bridge, complied with the dispatch. By electrical impulse the door lift opened, so that the craft could make a safe entry. The entrance had a magnetic field to keep the bay pressurized.

In addition to their transmitters they also had mapping relays, which were customized into their control pads. This could guide the podal craft by any one of them at a distance, but the pod was now under singular control by one man. Using his digital map he steered the craft toward its designation where it made a successful descend.

Mission fulfilled, "Well let's go home," the most eager of them said. At a quickened pace the three propelled themselves toward the main entry hatch, which was located at the front end.

As the men made their way to the bow Arakiis, who was one of the trio at the rear, suddenly had a malfunction in his left thruster. With only one thruster on charge he hurled out of control, the unequalled pressure caused him to gyrate and thrash uncontrollably. His harrowing screams could be heard through his built-in transceiver.

The miner who was second from the leader, Obec-tong, was alerted and turned to see what was happening. A grim shock of disbelief showed on his face when he realized what was transpiring. "Bridge control, we have a situation critical. I say again dispatch, critical," he said in a panic. Obec rushed toward his distressed friend to attempt a rescue. The other one, who was closest to the front-end hatch and further away from the other two, as he turned to look, realized to what was occurring and he followed close behind.

Without a moment of thought or hesitation Obec made a futile try to grab onto him when he was within arm's reach. Disoriented and confused Arakiis whipped his arms and legs about in a spastic frenzy. He was trying, with no success, to maintain some of his posture. Obec quickly threw his hand out to snatch onto him, and as he did, Arakiis' foot shot out from nowhere kicking Obec back. His pressure helmet was slightly cracked but not breached. The blow threw him back in zero gravity and was caught in the arms of the leader, who was behind to meet him.

A feeling of hopelessness sickened their hearts as they watched. In a split second the victims' backpack thruster exploded causing him to catapult out of control. Nearing the fireball's orbit he became trapped in the gravity's pull. His two friends watched as Arakiis plunged to his death.

"Conventional thrusters are shut down, ready for matrix," Joshua said anticipating a launch.

"Marshal, this is convoy leader. We have a problem," announced the dispatcher.

"What's the problem?"

"One of our S.M.I units had a faulty thruster, it was fatal," said the convoy leader in disbelief.

"Stand-by, I'm coming aboard."

"There's no need, there's nothing you can do anyway."

"I'm sure but I'm coming aboard anyway, prepare for embarkation," was Joshua's finale transmission.

As Joshua discontinued his communication link, for the time being, he swerved his ship around and begun his thrust toward Freighter One. Since he took the lead position as escort he didn't have to go too far to get to the hangar bay, it was right behind him.

Freighter One stood still awaiting the arrival of their unanticipated passenger, with his own intrusive inquiries. Or compassion, the marshal might simply be reacting to his own heartfelt concerns.

Joshua's Killwing closed in toward the bow's main entry hatch. "Ready your ground crew to flag me in."

"Copy that. Docking pad 84," said the landing coordinator.

The door lift opened as the marshal's gunship pierced through the magnetically shield opening. The ground crew, who were geared with reflective jackets and signaling flares, motioned the Killwing toward its assigned designation, as it moved in and away from the wide entrance.

Reaching docking pad 84 he than, once aligned atop, he hovered down in a precautionary fashion. A discharge of ionized exhaust slightly fogged the surrounding area as the ship made a complete landing.

Before Hollands could dismount his ship he had to wait. The ground personnel had to first delouse his ship with a decontaminant to neutralize any possible radiation. Now, instead of ionized exhaust, it was this gas that clouded the parameter.

After the decontamination was done, and the gas cleared, "Copilot, dismount," Joshua said to his ship.

After which the ship's computer responded, "Thank-you marshal," and the cockpit hatch swung open. He than stood up and swung himself over and stepped onto a security ladder, which had just been attached to a retainer bolt by a crewman. He than climbed down until his feet was firmly on the ground.

"Where's the superintendent," Josh asked the crewman nearest to him.

"The equipment depot," the crewman responded.

Knowing this Josh walked over toward the propulsionlift, which was within his range of sight a few yards from where he stood. When he reached the lift he motioned the revolving door to open using the palm activation panel, which was motion sensitive. He than stepped inside the lift as the door slid shut behind him. Speaking out loud to the comspeaker he commanded, "Equipment depot." A slight sensation of g-force hinted he was on his way.

The system's branch computer quickly brought Josh to his desired destination. His mind was slightly paused by emotion; he knew he might not like what he was about to find out.

As the door opened he exited, and looking around for a moment, he saw two men standing side by side. One of them wore an insignia, which identified him as the one in charge. The other one was Obec; he was already stripped from his cybersuit and dressed in his standard uniform.

"Hello," Josh announced himself to the two individuals as he waved and walked over to them.

"Is that your report," Josh inquired.

"Yes marshal," the superintendent said holding a descriptor as he pointed to Obec. "This is the one that witnessed the event." The superintendent was retelling what he put in his log, or at least the general of it. "The man that we lost was Arakiis, he had no family that we know of."

The marshal than said as he gazed at the one who was directly involved during the accident, "Did you determine the cause."

"A minor circuit burnout that caused thermal failure in his left thruster," Obec said in dismay.

"Damn S.M.I," the marshal protested, "They care too much about fulfilling their quota and not enough concern about maintaining their most basic equipment."

"I agree, the Sovereign Mining Industry needs to balance their own interests with that of the commonwealth," the super sided with the marshal. "But now's not the time for a political argument."

The marshal's exasperations were replaced with a sudden sadness, "I agree," he said as he looked down to reflect on their loss.

"By the way, welcome aboard. I'm the dispatcher who spoke to you through transceiver," the super said as Josh looked up at him. He soberly greeted the marshal with a handshake.

As pleasant greeting were made Josh reached out to affectionately place his hand on Obec's shoulder, to show his sincere condolences. Obec returned the affection with a slight nod and than he just walked away.

A PINK-REDDISH HUE OF methane ice covered the entire landscape of Jahdiir. This was a world hostile to any living thing that may wish to damn themselves by setting foot on the planet's surface. Jahdiir was isolated and cut off from the inhabited worlds of the Dominion.

At a distance the planet seemed to serve no useful purpose an ignorant observer might assume. But because of its seclusion Jahdiir was very useful, as a penal colony. The barren terrain and lack of port bases made escape impossible.

The terrain was generally smooth, just slates of jagged ice that stretched out into the starlit horizon. Small pockets of craters were visible and scattered in numerous amounts, an after effect from meteor collisions through the passed ages.

A massive super-crater stood out from the rest because of its size and depth. One would never of known such a crater existed there since it was hidden over by a manmade fortress, polygonal in shape. The structure had a flat top roof and jagged sides with the same pigment as the terrain to blend in with the landscape.

This was the confinement facility for Dominion prisoners. The method of imprisonment was the use of hyper-genetic freeze, the process in which the inmate at the cellular level was suspended in frozen animation.

Near the prison building were human-like statuettes scattered around, a good number of them. These statues were not at all inanimate but were once living and breathing people, convicts from a long ago past. They were condemned to exile; cast out from the safe refuge of a temperature-controlled environment, to the merciless conditions of the outside. This was a form of cruel punishment before barbarism gave way to science. Their once living bodies were frozen and crystallized.

There were no side entrances, only accessor doors from the flat top roof allowed entry and exit. The inside had an industrial appearance. The walls, floors and ceilings were constructed from fusion metal with no paint or décor to soften the tone, just a pigment of discoloration. Survival gear and other types of machinery cluttered the inner chambers. Temperature gauges and monitoring devices were mounted on the walls near every exit. These devices were used as tracking aids for the sentry guards, to assess the station's environmental status and the staff's duty roster.

The detainment sectors were equally crude appearing but with one difference, refrigeration units that looked like caskets, which were set in column formations. And the noise, which came from the cooling generators, was more strident than in any other facility.

Caskets were a term not far from the truth since the occupants within were in a state of near death. Inflicting extreme cold upon them increasingly slowed their metabolic rate. Their nanocell implants kept them sustained and life support airlines kept them breathing. In addition to oxygen tanks bio-scanners were mounted on each cryogenic tube for the doctors to monitor them from time to time. On occasion you would notice these doctor, dressed in their physician's garb, performing their routine rounds on their inmate patients.

The sounds of screams echoed in cellblock 23A. A contemned man was sentenced to life of incarceration, which they all were since nanocell implantation was irreversible, and he was about to meet that fate. Fear was evident in the man's eyes and it was either cold or dread, or the combination of both, that made him shiver. His attire was ruffled and torn during his time at a labor detention.

"Don't worry son, it'll soon be over," the doctor said as he held a laser pen keeping a log.

"Please, God, don't do this," the convict cried out.

Ignoring the man's desperations, "Lay him down." After the doctor's order was given his two assistants clutched onto him and forced him on a nearby gurney. The doc pitched in, it took all three to literally pick him up, but once this was achieved they immobilized him with security straps. Using a hypodermic gun they sedated him, the sounds of his pleads quieted as he drifted into sleep.

"What's his blood type," asked the doctor waiting for a reply.

"Blood type O," said one of the orderlies as looked at the convict's chart.

"Good, a universal donor," the doctor replied sounding pleased. It was common practice to save extracted normal blood for public transfusions.

The process of hyper-genetic freeze was about to commence as one of the two helpers walked away and returned quickly with an intravenous module, which rolled on wheels that he pushed. The module had inner compartments where pouches were emplaced, which held the artificial blood that was compatible. The artificial blood had micro robotic cells, called nanocells, in the mixture. These nanocells have the strength to endure extreme cold to keep the patient alive. One orderly stuck a hypodermic needle into the patient's main vein of his right arm, and the same for his left with a secondary needle. As the prisoner's natural blood was being extracted the artificial kind was replacing it.

"Any rejection from the bio-scan," the head doctor asked.

"Negative, heart rate and brain rhythm read normal," responded the assistant. "It's by the book perfection."

When the transfusion was successfully completed the doc, using a side control panel, electronically situated the cryotube in a horizontal position as the shield covering opened. They adjusted the height of the gurney so that it was perfectly aligned with that of the tube's inner flat bed. After the orderlies untied his bonds they slid him inside, as the doctor stood near to supervise. As soon as the prisoner was in the cryotube they secured him against the inner bed with a broad security strap, which lay close sewn to the bed's fabric. The broad strap was stretched and pressed against the convict's chest to keep him immobile and secure, for the repositioning of his tube. Once he was secure inside the shield canopy was than closed. Again the doctor tapped the command keys on the master control, but this time to reposition the cryotube back into its normal vertical stance.

Intake lines were already attached and locked as they activated the freezing procedure. The convict was instantly flooded with cryogenic gas, the sounds were like escaping air from a balloon.

Before they almost had the chance to draw their next breath the inmate was frozen.

A glass plate on the canopy was at the prisoner's face level, so that the prisoner can be viewed. Although difficult to see since the gas turned to frost when the temperate dropped, coating the interior. But the doc and his orderlies looked through the glass at the prisoner, even though obscured, and were satisfied enough.

"What does the bio-scan read now," the doctor asked.

"Still showing normal parameters," the orderly responded as he glanced at the feedback. "These tiny little robots adapt quickly, their sustaining him."

"Note, the time of hibernation at 8.3/5th hours startime," the doctor said as he noted the log.

The monitoring center was equally dark and crude but more organized. Enough lighting was produced from the initiator lights, which emulated from the control paneling, and from a small plasma lamp near the entrance. Three controllers sat at their posts, each doing their own assigned duties. Their separate tasks, working in conjunction, was to track inbound and outbound traffic within Jahdiir's airspace.

"We got newcomers. The prisoner barge made their allotted ETA, close to orbital entry," one of the controllers said to the other.

"Yea, bet their anxious to get here," the response was as he plotted a safe trajectory.

"I have them on scope. Scanner detects them approaching at a steadfast orientation," the scan controller replied ignoring the other's sarcasm.

Nearing Jahdiir's orbit the barge descended. The freighter's fuselage was bulky and had several decks. The funnel exhaust ports were high tailed at the stern spewing out thermal drive. And the bridge, controlling the craft, was above at high deck overlooking the stars.

"Ground station, dust off the landing zone. We're coming in," the main pilot transmitted.

The barge made a steady orbital entry, following computer command, the barge descended modestly. The planet's gravitational forces caused heat friction on the ship's exterior but the heat suppressant shielding was able to withstand it.

Breaking orbit the freighter was now gliding through the atmosphere. As the prisoner ship cruised several kilometers above the ground the pilots viewed the awesome spectacle. Admiring its awesomeness and beauty, of nature's creation, at least from a stopover standpoint.

Approaching within visual range of the prison camp the barge hovered over the flat top. "Open accessor doors," the pilot dispatched to the landing controllers. At almost that instant the door's internal locking latch released separating the dividend hatch, making a clear opening for the freighter to lower for entry.

As the prisoner transport progressively descended, through the ingress, and passing its magnetic field, the accessor doors above began to close. Automatic magnetic conducers were put to good use when reacting to the doors' opening, keeping the harsh outside elements from flooding the inside.

With repellors initiating a downward push, for proper craft control, the transporter generated a deafening sound. The several decibels of the engine's roar were too penetrating for ear defenders alone, hand pressure also had to be applied.

The barge slowly met the landing threshold and as it did the exhaust clouded the bay. While the barge was close to a stop landing a small column of sentries stood nearby, still clenching their ear defenders that they had on.

Once near the ground the freighter's main power was turned off and the bay was again quiet. Only a slight hum from the underbelly repellors replaced the sound from the main engine. The barge was anchored a few meters off the ground now by an even current of its turbine counterthrust.

The sentries stood at attention near the starboard side of the barge and their CO stood in the same fashion in front of them, awaiting the new arrival of prisoners to dismount to be processed. They were dressed professionally in their uniforms with their ear defenders now collared on their necks.

They waited but not for long when the hydraulic exit ramp opened, slowly with a low pitch sound. As it lowered to an incline toward the floor a hinged step-off lip plate flipped over, flush to the floor, to give the ramp an added extension for an easier walkway. When the gangplank was finally fully extended the entry hatch, at the top of the incline, sharply snapped open.

Testing the CO's patience several minutes had elapsed as the barge stood still with no one coming out. Curiosity beckoned the senior officer, "Maintain posture," he said to his patrols as he decided to approach the barge to investigate the delay.

Cautiously he walked up the ramp's incline nearing the hatch. But before he had the chance to fade into the darkness of the inside a sudden blast of laser fire ripped through his midsection. The blast, like a streak of lightning, caused his body to catapult off the ramp to drop solidly to the floor.

Shock and dismay unnerved the sentries as they broke out of formation and grabbing their side arms. They were stunned again when a group of brigands stormed out of the barge, well armed with repeating pulse rifles.

The guards were slow to take the defensive because of the element of surprise, but they soon had their weapons aimed with a show of force. Bolts of laser fire quickly congested the threshold bay. The pace of the fighting increased and became more desperate as the seconds wore on, but fogged by smoke as an aftereffect from the discharging weapons.

"Tylus, Talmond, Corin, get to the monitoring center," a man said, who was dressed in coarse padded fatigues and seemed to be the leader. "Extract the prisoners' profile charts, the rest of us will hold 'em off here."

The two gentlemen, accompanied by a young female, obeyed the command while the onslaught of laser fire continued. They disappeared into the smoke, wasting no time exiting the bay, with their guns cocked and at the ready. The brigand leader, and his ragged band of marauders, seemed sufficient enough to keep the sentries busy while the three departed without a scratch.

With the penal station on full alert Tylus and the others arrived at the monitoring room. In a futile attempt to open the hatch they realized the lock was probably blown off from the inside. Whatever the number of operators that were inside they more than likely barricaded themselves as soon as the general alarm went off.

"Step back," Tylus warned as he placed an explosive charge and than jumped back himself.

Inside the monitoring room, "Central Command, we are under attack," one of the specialists transmitted through hyperlink. He squeezed his interlink transponder's switch and spoke with desperation, "We need reinforc-," his mayday call was abruptly interrupted by a sudden explosion.

The hatch was blown and the force of the explosion ripped the door inward from the bulkhead and into one of the other specialists, who stood near in its path. He was knocked unconscious to the floor before he had the chance to react against it.

As the three infiltrators barged in the room they quickly held the upper hand. "Don't move," Tylus barked out to the two other specialists who were left standing. The one lying face down on the floor, still out cold from the blast, was bonded to for security purposes.

"Let's speed things up, this place is losing it," Corin said anxiously.

"Calm down Jackie," Tylus leading the pack insisted. "The commander is well capable to handle any resistance. Besides, Jahdiir is cut off from the main network, it'll take some time before the distress call reaches Central Command."

"Damn it," Talmond cursed.

"What's wrong," Jackie turned to him to ask.

"They locked the system. I can't get in," Talmond griped. He right away turned his attention away from the computer console and to the captives, the two standing behind from where he was sitting, "Where's the access key?" Talmond asked them with an anxious tone in his voice.

The two guards, now prisoners, stood defiant and unresponsive when Talmond addressed them. Even though they were at gunpoint it was standard policy not to negotiate or give in to terrorists.

Terrorists they might seem to the general Commonwealth but as far as the brigandeers believed, they were freedom fighters.

"I can make them talk," Talmond said, as he was about to stand up to approach them.

"No, don't bother, I got a better idea," Tylus cut in, "I can by-pass the security system."

Crouching down near the terminal junction he tightly held on to the panel fitting and, with a solid grip, he snatched the front covering away from the metal casing. Once the panel guard was free, and thrown back, he took an analytical close-up view of the inner circuitry. Finding what he was looking for he grabbed on to two pieces wire and than he stripped the sheathing from the tips. When he stripped a little bit of the insulation from the tips he coiled the exposed metal wire together. By doing this he tricked the computer into thinking the access key had been inserted.

The beep from the computer indicated a read-out, access granted, "I'm in," Tylus informed the others feeling a sense of accomplishment.

He than touch-screened the computer to access the main menu. Once the main menu was projected he retrieved the profile charts, which gave him a list of names accompanied by their identification numbers. When he saw the name on the list he was looking for he tapped it. Responding to his touch command the name's profile chart flashed across the screen, extracted from the data storage.

"Here we go, cellblock 81 section 4. Identification number, 10-10-91," Tylus said in a hurry. "Lets get movin."

As the men prepared to leave, to head toward the given location, Jacqueline Corin glanced at the computer screen. "Amandus Kreed," she said as she than turned to look at her compatriots. "Why didn't anyone tell me it was him we were after?"

"You didn't ask," Tylus replied impatiently. He was anxious to complete his task so he could leave; a penal station wasn't his fondness place at the moment.

"He hung thousands by their scalp," she said as a chill ran up her spine. "Why free him?"

"Relax Jackie, we need him," Tylus said before he was about to exit. "He's the only one that knows the Dominion's defense network. Besides, I'm sure he still holds a grudge to those who put him here, which could be useful to us." Jackie sensed there was something else that he was holding back, if the rumors she heard were true, but she still didn't like the idea of Kreed's escape.

After Tylus' quick conviction he left the room while Talmond made sure that all three of the specialists there were tightly bond and gagged. When he was assured that all three, including the one lying dormant on the floor, were secured he himself left in a hurry following Jackie.

The fighting at the threshold bay slowed down and the smoke, from the discharging weapons, dissipated somewhat. But there was still some sporadic fighting left but most of the sentries were beaten. The barge was still hovering motionless by the repellors, keeping it suspended, as it waited for its newest passenger.

The brigand leader, knowing he had the situation pretty much subdued, stood without cover and snatched his interlink. "Tylus report, did you find the prisoner's location?"

"Yes sir, we're on our way now," Tylus transmitted back. "Stand-by."

Tylus, and his team, rushed through a few corridor links to get to cellblock 81. They were following location markers, indicated on the wall in bight yellow at every turn, to avoid making the wrong turn. Corin was hesitant but she followed close behind the other two.

Finally they approached 81 at section 4 and Tylus, who made it to the entry first; quickly palm activated the hatch to open. As fast at the hatch opened they all three darted inside. Jackie, who trailed behind, made sure the hatch was slammed shut behind them once she herself scurried inside.

Quickening their pace they searched through the walkways between the columns of cryogenic tubes. Jackie shivered a bit because of the low temperature setting. To her, being scantly dressed, it was like being inside a refrigeration unit. Steam from their breath was formed when their warm breath met the cold environment. Dark and dreary, this place gave Jackie the creeps; this whole penal station was like a mechanized graveyard.

The three made quick glances as they passed by each tube. Identification numbers were assigned and marked on each cryotube, placing them in numerical order. ID number plates were beaded on the front for easy search and monitoring. Even though Jackie was involved in the search her willingness was clearly hesitant.

"There it is," Tylus brought to their attention. "Quick, you guys get the moderator tank while I disengage the freezing processors."

As Jackie and Talmond complied Tylus disengaged the unit. Once 10-10-91 powered down, using the control panel, he manipulated the tube up and over into a horizontal position.

"Ok, ready guys," he asked the others. Jackie and Talmond hurried in response as they rolled the tank close, and in proper alignment, with that of the cryotube. "Opening the shielder now," Tylus said as he initiated the tube's opening sequence. "We only have seconds before his body goes into thermal shock."

Once the shield canopy was opened, wearing insulated gloves, they grabbed onto Kreed's frozen body and slid him off the tube's inner flat bed. They than closed the tank's canopy as soon as the prisoner was secured inside.

Tylus punched in the tank's command codes, "Turning control sequencers on, initiating melt-down."

"Ok, he's being thawed out," Jackie remarked with a nervous tone in her voice. "Now lets get out of here."

The bay was now quiet and completely under brigand control. The fighting was long over and the surrendered sentries were forced into kneeling positions with their hands placed behind their heads. Their captors seemed to have the advantage over them as they kept their weapons aimed at the guards.

The quietness was disrupted when Jackie and the other two rushed into the bay, rolling the moderator tank along with them. Tylus led, with his pulse rifle tucked under his arm, while Jackie and Talmond were at opposite sides of the tank pushing it toward the barge

"Hurry up, take it aboard," the brigand leader said.

As soon as they were at the lip of the ramp Tylus turned around to grab the front of the tank as Jackie stepped aside. With a firm grip Tylus heaved the tank up the gangplank as Talmond went behind to assist, pushing it up. While they were boarding the tank Jackie stayed behind, near the side of the ramp, with her gun raised to cover the rear flank.

Once the General Commander, which was Kreed's last given title, was safely aboard the remainder of the hijackers started boarding as well. One by one they ran up the ramp's incline; occasionally checking behind them to see if the guards weren't making any sudden moves.

But as they continued to mount up Jackie made sure that wasn't the case as she kept her weapon aimed at the guards, to thwart any resistance. Jackie's gaze was behind directed at the guards while the hijackers were looking in the opposite direction, which was the topmost point of the gangplank, toward the barge's entry. With Jackie covering their rear they were more confident boarding the safe refuge of the barge for a clean getaway.

After everybody was aboard, "Jackie, com'on," Tylus poked his out the entrance and yelled down to her. "Time to go."

"I'm not coming along on this trip," Jackie insisted looking up at him.

"We don't have time to argue."

"I mean it, I'm not taking orders from him," she meant Kreed. She was completely clueless as to the reason of his breakout, or that it was he to begin with, who would probably be their new leader of the brigand resistance.

"Forget this, ur coming with us," Tylus demanded, as he was about to jump ahead down the ramp after Corin.

"Stand your ground," she said as she jerked her weapon in his direction. Tylus abruptly stopped, not even half way down the ramp, as he stared down at the barrel of Jackie's pulse rifle. He not dare approach any further to her as he sensed her conviction and willingness to fire, with him at the crosshairs. "Besides," she tried to reason, "you need someone to stay behind to open the accessor doors."

"Damn it Jackie," Tylus cursed. No more time had to be wasted, especially on quibbling nonsense; he quickly turned and disappeared inside the barge.

The sentries, who were still holding their positions of surrender, felt a little more cocksure when Jackie stood alone. But their boldness was reduced when she redirected her aim in their direction. Keeping a keen eye at her captives she made a quick dash toward the control booth, as the barge's gangplank raised.

When she promptly reached the control booth's hatch she still kept her weapon aimed at the kneeling sentries, and maintaining a fighting posture. Keeping her defense readiness she carefully, without taking her eyes off the guards, opened the hatch behind her and she went inside. Once she was inside, and the entry hatch shut, the guards stood up quickly to try to retake control of the station.

But suddenly the barge's main engines turned on, after the gangplank was fully raised and locked. The ear piercing sounds from the engines immobilized the sentries as they clenched their ears, bowing down a little from the pain, as they tried to seek cover. But the high decibels of pain did not reach Jackie's ears since she stood behind sound resistant glass inside the control booth

The thrust from the repellors increased pushing the barge upward as Jackie opened the accessor bay doors. After there was a clear enough opening the prison barge, now a getaway vehicle, was freeing itself from the threshold bay.

Jackie stood motionless next to the control panel as she watched her fellow troops escape to freedom. She totally ignored the sentries, who were scrambling from both the deafening pain of the engine's roar and thermal push of the ascending vehicle. Their preoccupation of trying to take cover, and the fact she locked herself in, she felt no immediate threat.

Jackie stood, almost in a daydream state, staring at the barge as it reached further away from her. She was fully aware that she was now a prisoner and she was also fully aware of what evil now existed aboard that ship.

THE INDUSTRIAL CONVOY WAS only a few minutes away from jumping into curved-space. The freighters were moving majestically slow with legionnaire escorts at their patrol positions. Freighter One was also ready for matrix but the crew aboard was waiting for a passenger to depart.

Joshua was still aboard, the convoy leader, extracting information concerning the recent tragedy. He was at the computer system's branch office downloading data, which was relevant to the unfortunate accident. Each function or branch of the Dominion, which stemmed from the mainframe computer, was centralnet.

"Marshal, we just received a message from Orath station through hyperwave," a voice announced through the marshal's interlink, "Their inquiring about our delay."

Reaching to his side he grabbed his communicator, "Tell them we're going to jump launch any minute now." After saying that he put his interlink back to its retainer clip hoping that reply will get them off his back for a while.

Getting over the distraction he resumed his data research as a young man approached him, "Sir, we received a message-,"

"I know, I know, I know, you can tell those damn corporate execs to hold on to their comet tails," Joshua broke in. "We'll leave when I'm ready."

"No sir, its Central," the cosman apprised.

"Central?"

"Yes sir."

Joshua contemplated for a while and than spoke out, "Patch it through to my ship." Curiosity now confounded his previous thought as he made his way toward the propulsionlift. Whatever the message may be, if Central Command dispatched it, it couldn't be good news.

The Killwing was poised and ready for take-off on pad 84, presently cooled and idle from its previous flight. The docking bay was still active as before. The entire crew and staff were at their general quarters expecting a launch very soon. Those who were stationed at the bay had to make preparations before the jump; as in making sure everything was tied down and secure, the present delay gave them added time to do so.

Hollands stepped off the lift and moved quickly across the bay toward his ship. Why would Central be calling him, he thought, and the more he thought about it the quicker his steps were.

As he drew closer to his ship he slowed down to a moderate pace, to raise his wristband and enter his password. The effect of this activated the ship's camlock; a small automatic camera mounted within the hull with nothing but a small lens showing, at the pilot side of the ship near the canopy. As he drew closer to the IF-7, and a faint click sound from the lens, meant his picture was taken. Within seconds, when he was almost upon his ship, his picture was instantly scanned and compared to the one his ship's computer has on file. After measuring his entire body's physical structure, which was individually unique like fingerprints, the computer announced, "Silhouette-scan identity check confirmed, welcome."

"Thank-you," responded Hollands as though he was responding to a human counterpart.

The ship automatically opened the canopy as Joshua climbed up the security ladder and jumped into his pilot seat. Once inside he clicked on the vidcom's transponder switch while looking directly at the monitor near his lap.

An image projected on the monitor's view screen. It was an image of an elderly man dressed in a white loose garb. The blue insignia at his lapel ranked him General Commander, the supreme commander who was known as Murius. "Sorry marshal for this abrupt transmission," said the General Commander. "I would not have contacted you if it wasn't urgent."

"Of course Commander," Joshua understood. "What's the problem?"

"We had a security breach on the 10-Alpha-C colony."

"If I recall, 10-Aplha-C is a penal colony on the Jahdiir system."

"Correct. From the information I gathered the brigands have hijacked a prisoner barge and used the verification codes to infiltrate the colony," the Commander continued, "The infiltrators broke into

24

one of the cryogenic tubes and released a prisoner. An Amandus Kreed I believe his name was."

"Your predecessor."

"Don't remind me. He was the General Command until we caught him breaking every war crime in the book," the Commander felt a little uneasy when he thought about it.

"Why would they go through all that trouble to break him out?" Josh wondered.

"That's your job to find out. Travel to Jahdiir and gather the intelligence you need to re-apprehend him," Murius ordered. "The guards caught on of their accomplices. You might be able to get some info out of her."

"Her?"

"Yes, a Jacqueline Corin, one of their mercenaries. There's no guarantee she'll be cooperative."

"I'll see what I can do."

"You do that and keep me informed. End transmission," Murius said as he signed off.

Joshua's thoughts focused on the converse he just had with his boss. Since he was one of the inquisitors at his trial, he remembered the name Amandus Kreed right away the moment it was spoken. There was no love lost between the two, if there was such a thing when it came to Kreed.

After a few seconds of thought the marshal snapped out of it and focused on the situation at hand. "Randon," the marshal said through transceiver, "I have a priority mission from Central Command. Your in charge of the escort," the marshal giving his last orders before he departed. "Take these boys safely to the Gontaris system and keep the communication band open, just in case there's trouble."

"Understood, be careful out there," Randon voice went through the marshal's transceiver speaker.

Once all parties were aware of the situation the marshal prepared his IF-7 for take-off. "Clear guiding platform," Josh transmitted to flight control.

A voice announced through the bay's loudspeaker, "Clear guiding platform 84."

As soon as he was clear for launch Joshua initiated his repellors causing his Killwing to hover a few meters off the floor's surface. Suspended in midair, like an apparition, Josh punched the stern exhaust thrusting his ship across the platform toward an opening overhead hatch. Quickly passing the magnetic field the ship shot out into the starry horizon.

The prisoner barge stood still away from the matrix grid to avoid detection from other ships that might pass by. The static position of the bulky freighter might indicate there was no activity aboard; but there was, which directed the pilot's attention away from the navigation controls.

The spacious corridors were dimly lit and warm vapor from the combustion pistons clouded the surroundings. The environment was dreary and the mechanical sounds in the background were penetrating enough to cause, at the least, annoyance.

The cargo bay was just as ominous looking. Storage racks were columned off to the sides, where the prisoner's clothing was kept, neatly folded. And storage tanks were also present resembling hollow cylinders, which was where the food was stored.

Nobody was aboard the barge except for the brigand hijackers who all seemed to be congregated at the cargo bay. They were gathered around the moderator shielder, fixated upon it, while the occupant was still secured inside it.

"Initiating melt down and I-V heat," said Tylus to keep his fellow brigandeers appraised. While looking at the bioscan monitor he spoke again, "Body temperature slowly rising to normal parameters. Cryogen biofrost dissipating," he said as he read the read-out. "Vital signs stabilizing."

"Stand-by men, our new commander is awakening," Tylus ordered. After he alerted his crew he reached over, to the shielder's control panel, to open the canopy. The hatch slid open abruptly as warm vapor escaped from the airtight chamber.

The men crowded around the chamber and stood uneasy. You can sense the nervousness they felt as they stood at attention, for they knew Kreed's reputation of being merciless and barbaric when he wants to be. And they also remember his past deeds during the Colonial Wars, which was capitation or hanging by scalp, his favorite form of execution. Sadistic hanging was just one of his atrocities that led him to his frozen tomb.

Kreed was wrapped in cloth, which was now wet and soiled from the defrost sequence. Because he was shrouded in cloth his appearance was difficult to distinguish. Some noticeable features were his long tail, his snout, and forked tongue. He was obviously humanoid but not entirely human.

Complete silence took over as the brigands stood motionless their minds were somehow drained from thought by an unseen force. Reptilians were famous for their extra sensory abilities, and those abilities were presently being demonstrated.

After a few moments had elapsed Tylus, who hadn't moved from where he stood when he opened the canopy, finally broke the silence. "120 degrees starboard, 10.1 kilo light-years distance. Alpha quadrant, time intervals of 22 parminutes, static pulse."

Tylus felt a sense of psychological rape as the rest of his brigandeers stood puzzled. "It's ok people, reptilians are telepathic." He sighed a relief as though a big weight was lifted off his head, when Kreed finally severed the mindlink between them. Tylus explained now under his own cognizance, "Navigator, go to the bridge and punch in those coordinates. Those coordinates should take us straight to the hidden outpost while avoiding grid detection," he ordered. "As for the rest of you, command your posts."

A bright flash of energy disturbed the stillness of space. Joshua's Killwing shot out from the light, like a bullet, as the ship's retronic jet streams slowed his ship down. "10-Alpha-C, this is First Marshal Hollands," he said through transceiver. "Clear threshold bay and have the administrator standby to help aid an official investigation."

"We copy that marshal. Your coordinates are being processed to you now," the dispatcher said at the receiving end.

"Understood."

It didn't take long before Joshua's on-board computer system had the coordinates. On autopilot the IF-7 flew toward Jahdiir's orbital gravity. Descending, the Killwing followed the same passage the prisoner barge took. Josh felt strong turbulence as he entered the planet's atmosphere. His safety harness was securing him to his seat as the ship shook roughly. But he endured the tremors as though he was aboard a surface-tension mobilboat in still waters. For the veteran legionnaire enduring the rigors of travel came with the job, he was used to it.

Faintly visible amidst methane clouds the Killwing flew toward the surface. The violet color of the night sky was dull and foggy but the roar of the engines broke the tranquil surroundings. In such a short time the IF-7 flew horizontally from its angulated entry. A mere few kilometers from touching the surface the Killwing flew toward the penal station, passing over slated rock and ice.

As the Killwing approached the station, by an extra push in the rear thrusters, the ship swerved upward and than over, aligning itself atop the accessor bay doors. Coordinated by the centralnet computer the doors opened once the IF-7 was ready to lower through it. Synchronized by the network computer, as soon as there was enough clearing, the Killwing hovered through as its repellors kept the ship stable during the marshal's descent. The computer guided the ship downward at a slow approach and made a soft landing, Josh couldn't of done better himself he thought.

The threshold bay was still in ruin after the assault; the infirmary was caring for the wounded, and the maintenance crews were cleaning up the mess made by the discharging weaponry.

"Good marshal, we've been waiting for you," the warden said as Joshua dismounted his gunship.

"What's the assessment," the marshal inquired as they both walked toward each other.

"Just getting things back in order," now they were standing toe to toe.

"Your security was poor, how the hell did they manage this," the marshal was both shocked and displeased.

"I wish I-," the warden's attention was redirected when a corporal was about to pass them. "Corporal, bring the prisoner here."

"Yes sir," the corporal complied.

As the corporal was halted and turned around, heading back in the same direction he came from, the warden finished what he was about to say earlier. "As I was saying, I wish I knew," the warden seemed just as astonished as the marshal was. "I'm hoping you and your boys can answer that question."

"First I need to log all this in for my superiors," the marshal said staying focused on his intent. His voice, almost being directed at himself as though he was thinking out loud, "Gather clues and evidence, whatever it takes to bring back Kreed where he belongs."

"Do you know what their motive might be for this?" the warden asked.

"Unfortunately no, but Kreed's knowledge of our defense and military tactics could prove to be dangerous if in the wrong hands."

"Sir," the corporal broke in with Jackie at his side, but this time she was in shackles.

"So this is the unlucky one that got caught," the marshal said but Corin stood unresponsive. "Why did you stay behind? It's a big sacrifice for your pirate friend's," again she stood unresponsive always eyes forward, showing no emotion or reaction.

"You were told she might not cooperate," the warden reminded.

The marshal was beginning to get impatient, "My ship was only built for one. Do you have a shuttle?"

"Yes."

"As soon as possible transport her to Central Command, I'll get what I need from her there," Josh than took one last glance at the prisoner, "You should've left with the others." He attempted to antagonize a response from her but she still remained inexpressive, before the corporal took her back to her detention cell.

A digital beep suddenly came from Joshua's interlink. He reached for it instantly and brought it to his mouth to acknowledge the transmission, "Hollands here."

"Sir, they came from nowhere," the dispatcher shouted out excitedly.

"Who?"

"The entire brigand fleet," Randon said screaming incoherently through the static.

"What's your status, can you read me, over?" the marshal shouted back.

"They caught us by surprise, the defense net was not alerted," the marshal's squad leader shouted back still muffled by frequency noise. "We lost several patrol ships during the fight."

"What about the Rogue?" the marshal needed to know.

"They're attempting to hijack it," his voice was still barely understandable. "We can-," the crosslink eventually severed.

The marshal quickly through his emotions aside and he faced to say a few words to the warden. "I gotta leave right now, remember your orders," he said as he clipped back his interlink. Growing weary Josh turned to board his ship again. He climbed up the ladder as the canopy opened and than throwing himself into his pilot seat, and than he prepared for take-off.

Gontaris, a planet of rough terrain but rich in titanium deposits, was dead and barren because of its closeness to the sun. The atmosphere was polluted with sulfur dioxide and nitrogen fumed by the numerous volcanic activity. These characteristics made the planet's surface hot enough to incinerate flesh.

The battle was now obviously over, given the absence of laser fire, all that was left were twisted pieces of shrapnel, which were drifting near the planet's orbit. Some pieces were still sparking and discharging smoke, from severed electrical wiring, of what use to power Dominion gunships.

Some of the bigger pieces of fusion metal, remains of the barge, seemed to be drifting toward the continent below. A continent, difficult to see on a map because of the nonexistence of water, but it was surrounded by broad reservoirs of sand that characterized it. And any shrapnel collision to that continent seemed to be a potential tragic reality since the Orath station was on that land mass.

In the line of the pieces' trajectory were three IF-13 short- range fighters, slowing and preparing to maneuver into their positions.

After they punched through Gontaris' orbital field they flew closer, nearing the colliding chunks of metal.

"Control station, we're approaching target sight. No visual on enemy ships," the sentry leader dispatched to his superiors below.

"We hear ya, everybody down here is on alert status," was the control station's response. "Position your ships in a triangulated kill zone and make damn sure those flying debris fragments doesn't break through." After the order was given the dispatcher inserted, "We have a lot of scared people down here."

"Understood," the sentry leader discontinued dispatch. "Ok men, you guys know the situation. Assume the gauntlet," which was there preplanned tactical position.

Knowing their mission they complied with the order. Like pieces on a checkerboard they created a north, southwest, and southeast gauntlet. As the deadly fragments drifted closer toward the kill zone they laid out the pilots readied themselves.

"Activate targeting systems and ready your thermal cannons," the leader ordered his patrols.

As a piece of shrapnel drifted close enough to fire upon, "Hollanec, this one is yours. Fire at will," his leader invited.

"Firing," Hollanec said as he took aim. When the first fragment reached his line of fire he powered up his main gun. A thermal laser bolt discharged hitting the side of the fragment. The impact was hard enough to break it into pieces, which than scattered away into clear space.

"Good shot," the leader commended.

A few pieces of remaining fragments were still trapped in orbital gravity. If the battle remnants continued their present course, without challenge, the colonial city below will be in peril. The people of Orath hope that they would complete their mission with the utmost success.

As another piece of metal chunk reached the firing trap Joshua's IF-7 shot out from the matrix field just about the same time the north fighter was ready to take it out. The marshal's retronic jet fire slowed his propulsion, and without hesitation, his Killwing shot the fragment into tiny little bits before colliding into it.

"Report," Josh transmitted after his surprise appearance.

"Identify yourself," the sentry leader demanded.

"Marshal Hollands."

"We heard you were coming," the leader acknowledged. "Keep clear, we gotta make sure none of these pieces reach Orath."

"Roger that," the marshal ended transmission and waited.

Only a couple of pieces remained and Joshua kept his distance allowing the patrols to do their job. Josh knew, as they did, if any fragments reached the biosphere city below the outcome would be disastrous.

The next piece approached nearing the gauntlet and the southeast fighter fired his thermals when it got close enough to his range. His energy bolts shattered the piece in half, which separated and drifted apart, out of harm's way.

Very good shooting the leader thought as he took aim at the last piece, or at least the last piece that could cause significant death if uninterrupted. When he saw that the fragment was within his firing range he triggered his gun. The blast only chipped off a piece from the back quarter; perhaps he pulled a little on the firing arm when pressing the trigger or fatigue blurred his vision. The leader reminded himself to stay focused as he took aim and fired again. This time he made a direct hit, obliterating the target into harmless smithereens.

"Good shot," Hollands complemented the leader.

"You lost your escort," the sentry leader finding it almost difficult to say.

"I can see, what the hell happened. Where's Alpha One?"

"I don't know sir, but I don't think anyone survived," the sentry leader said expressing his sympathy.

Knowing that he kept half of his men back at the Regalia starbase; no need to bring a whole squadron for a mere escort detail, "You mean I lost half of my squadron," the marshal said stunned.

"We were under attack by the brigand fleet," the head sentry explained. "They came out of nowhere and hijacked the Rogue," and than he expressed his sympathy again, "I'm sorry about your men."

"Why wasn't the defense grid alerted," the marshal said making a valid inquiry. "They obviously made an illegal jump, centralnet should've put us on alert status immediately," Joshua said to the leader and also to himself. "The whole of the Colonial Legion should've made preps to intercept them before they even reached these coordinates."

"If your looking for answers from me I don't know what to tell ya," the leader said as he finally switched off.

Joshua was saddened by the events that took place during his absence. The hum from his engines droned slightly as he maneuvered his ship around the other fragments, what was left of his squadron and prisoner barge. The drifting pieces that were left posed no threat but it still invoked dread in Joshua's mind. If Kreed was with the brigandeers now he must be leading them, for only he would know how to avoid the matrix grid.

Nearing his portside bow the marshal saw what could have been Randon's ship so he flew in for a closer look. Steadily his ship moved along side of the wreckage. Sparking and spewing smoke; Randon's ship was now just twisted metal junk, which drifted aimlessly like the rest of the carnage.

Hollands had to snap out of his present state of thought because he knew he had to report the situation to Central. So he directed his attention to the ship's control panel but before he had the chance to utilize the transceiver, the transmission beacon lit up. Message coming in from Central he thought to himself as he turned on the vidcom.

The view screen lit up; it was the General Commander, "Marshal, our matrix grid detected a small band of brigand ships and a familiar signature, which quite possibly is the Rogue." The General continued, "I've dispatched your Alpha One reserves to pursue them," the Commander said hoping to conclude the matter quickly. "Your in charge to lead the attack and bring back what was stolen from us. Centralnet is feeding you the coordinates right now," and than Murius insisted, "You are to engage immediately."

"I only have half of Alpha squadron, my so called reserves," Josh had to report the sad news. "My escorts were wiped out trying to defend the Rogue."

"What!" Murius was shocked, "My deepest regrets."

"All for a tub of rocks, it doesn't make any sense," the marshal was grieved and bewildered at the same time.

"I know you can never replace your men, you guys had a tight camaraderie."

"We were like family," the marshal pointed out to Murius.

"But you know your mission, I have a sense there's more to this than we know than just typical piracy."

"Understood."

"End transmission," Murius signed off and than the vidcom screen went blank.

Without wasting anymore-precious time Joshua piloted the nose of his ship away from the planet, and the brigand attack's aftermath. "Orath, you seem to be out of danger." The marshal wondered if he should call in legionnaire guards just in case their brigandeers visitors return. "I'll bring back the astrotanker, I promise."

Once this was said the marshal disengaged his conventional thrusters and activated the symmetry drive. The Killwing's underbelly matrix crystal, emplaced within of what was called an orifice, lit up. The pulsating light eventually engulfed the ship, and after a shotgun sound, the illuminated ship disappeared into curved-space.

ANOTHER SHOTGUN SOUND BROKE the tranquility of the celestial heavens as Joshua's IF-7 exited the matrix field. Moving at high velocity, the ship's retronics kicked on to slow its propulsion to manual control. Once the marshal regained piloting he joined a small fleet of legionnaire gunships nearby, which were waiting for him to take the lead.

"Jon Darvus," the marshal dispatched after his ship neared to a stop.

"Yes sir."

"I'm placing you in command," the marshal found it difficult to say. "Congratulations, you've just been promoted to squad leader."

"I thought Randon was first lieutenant," Jon seemed puzzled.

It took a while to respond to Jon's inquiry eventually he just repeated himself with a firmer tone in his voice, "Your squad leader."

"Yes sir."

"Have you pinpointed the enemy target, distance and bearing?"

"A small brigand fleet 15 astronomical, they're within sensor range," Jon advised the marshal to do an extended sensor sweep.

Josh had to know the precise numbers of the enemy's strength so he, reaching to his instrument panel, configured his photoscope and acoustics to do a long range scan. His scope emitted an invisible light wave that would bounce back to his ship's relay and project an image on his vidcom, if there's anything out there, he would see it.

"They seem to be well grouped together," the marshal said as soon as he received the sensors' feedback. "But keep your heads up, HEL-bombers usually attacks from above with depth charges," Josh informed all his fellow pilots.

After his warning the marshal sharply maneuvered his Killwing to take the lead. After which he commanded, "We're going on conventional thrusters." At high velocity the Killwing fleet was ready to close in on the brigand HEL-bombers. "Keep an eye on sensors, make sure they don't flank us," the marshal warned.

The stars seemed motionless giving the impression he was also but in fact he was accelerating very fast. Impatiently waiting for eye visual the marshal would periodically glance at the read-outs. "5.2 astronomical and closing," the marshal announced to his pilots.

Anxiously to physically see the brigand raiders they maintained a keen eye but all they saw, still, was the emptiness of space. Propelling rapidly through particle friction extreme turbulence was induced, which stressed their ships' outer hulls. The pilots held on to their seats, figuratively speaking, while they endured the rough ride.

"Stay focused," Joshua reminded everybody again.

Suddenly a bright star-like energy object appeared dropping from above, near Joshua's gunship. Dropping near his bow and than disappeared into an implosion, a sonic boom pulsated as a result, but the drop was far enough not to cause structural damage.

Practice what you preach Joshua thought to himself as he sharpened his attention and said out loud, "Depth charges." Josh made a quick evasive turn to port as he shouted the obvious, "HEL-bombers, HEL-bombers, all fighters pull up."

The surprise attack left the pilots disoriented; they made evasive actions in disarray as they frantically tried to avoid the bombardment. One by one the depth charges dropped and detonated, like echoing shotgun sounds, targeting the evading fleet with almost precision. The pilots were trained well enough though to pull away from the attacks and toward the HEL-bomber positions above.

The marshal had the first opportunity to fire as he pulled the nose of his Killwing up, straight up, until his first target was in his sights. "Switching probe and nonessential systems to targeting," Joshua said out loud through transceiver. The marshal, and the same for the rest of his squadron, left their communications' transponder switch open so they could keep tabs on each other.

Josh only saw a glimpse of the enemy HEL-bomber he was about to fire upon so he pulled up even more as he zeroed in on the kill. As he neared his first target he glanced at his targeting computer, "Com'on baby, come to papa," he said as he waited for his targeting to lock on.

The g-force was tremendous as he propelled upward almost

vertically. The distance between Josh and the enemy ship was getting shorter, until; finally the HEL-bomber was finally within his kill zone. A beeping sound transmitted through Joshua's targeting, which implied that he was now clear to shoot.

His hand clenched the steering arm as he thumb pressed the firing button. The Killwing's assault guns recoiled several times as they discharged a barrage of laser blasts. The energy bolts made direct hits causing the HEL-bomber to explode upon impact.

Joshua quickly steered away to avoid flying debris, "One down," the marshal almost cheered.

After some time had passed, from the start of the brigand sneak attack, the pilots regained their composure as they pursued their attackers. The lieutenant was ready to claim his first victory as he zeroed in on his target; pursuing an enemy ship in vertical flight, he experienced the same stresses. Just as the HEL-bomber's crystal emitter lit up, which was the main bombardment weapon, Jon was ready to shoot.

"Watch out lieutenant," Joshua shouted over the carrier waves. An enemy-attacking fighter was about to flank behind Jon's ship, the brigand fighter prepared to lock on. The marshal quickly flew past Jon's Killwing, from over head, and fired. Joshua's blast obliterated the bomber before it had the chance to fire and make Jon a ghostly memory.

For a moment Jon lost partial control of his ship as he tried to avoid his close call toward destruction. Descending straight down for a few seconds he than was able to level out and regain manual control of his Killwing. "Thanks marshal," the lieutenant said as he wiped the sweat off his brow.

The other fighters were in the same predicament, destroying or evading the enemy. Surrounded by a swarm of HEL-bombers, one of the Killwings made an unlucky maneuver as he piloted his way into an enemy's flight path. A collision of fire and smoke the two ships smashed into each other almost head-on, the legionnaires had their first casualty.

"Alpha 10, enemy ship at your .45 degree position," the marshal warned as he looked on. Ten quickly steered his ship to his left as the enemy swooped down from just above his starboard. Beep,

beep, beep, the targeting computer sounded as the brigand moved into Joshua's line of fire. Both thermal lasers discharged from his recoiling guns. The laser blasts destroyed the enemy before it had the chance to fire on its intended prey.

"Thanks marshal, I owe you one," the Alpha Ten pilot praised.

The enemy sustained several losses, the legionnaires only a few, but the battle wasn't over yet. The few remaining HEL-bombers that were left were determined to fight on.

Why fight to the end, Joshua pondered considering the odds against them. "Good job boys, but don't relax yet," the marshal reminded. "We still have three to go."

The marshal made a ninety-degree turn banking away from the dogfight. Once he was at a safe distance he powered down his engines and initiated static mode, his ship hovering still. Keeping his Killwing motionless he kept a watchful eye on the fighting ahead, through his main cockpit window. He kept his senses vigilant as he switched his targeting systems to sensor spread.

"Their stalling for time fellas," the marshal eventually informed his squadron. "The astrotanker on scope is now 7.9 astronomical from us, these HEL-bombers are buying escape time."

"Marshal, watch out," his fellow pilot warned.

The pilot's warning abruptly startled Josh, "What the-," the marshal said as he swung his arms up over his face excitedly. An enemy bomber was bearing down on the marshal's gunship. His Killwing remained motionless and defenseless as the bomber locked on to him. The Killwing pilot, who dispatched the warning, flew past Joshua's fighter, almost a hair width between, and fired. The energy blast crippled the bomber as it closed in on the marshal. Josh quickly made evasive maneuvers to avoid an inbound collision, the bomber barreling down on him above at his portside. Swirling out of control and in flames the enemy ship self-destructed by its own heated exhaust, the marshal's evasiveness scantly avoided the shrapnel that rained down.

"Alright-alright, time to get nasty," the marshal said angrily as he switched back to targeting.

Joshua through himself back in the fighting but the battle was nearly over. The two remaining HEL-bombers attempted hit and run attacks against the Killwings. One IF-7 was hit but sustained only minor damage. Joshua ascertained that the enemy was trying to draw the legionnaires together to facilitate more bombardment of depth charges, to produce as many legionnaire casualties that they could muster, knowing the odds were against them.

The damaged ship stayed clear from the fight since it lost some of its steering power, but the other fighters were determined to destroy each other. Idling down and keeping clear the legionnaire pilot had no choice but to tend to his maimed ship and view the activity through his windscreen.

Part of the acrobatic display two of the Killwings pursued one of the bombers. The HEL-bomber swerved up to position itself for a depth charge drop. As the two Killwings chased the brigand ship, shooting up almost vertically, the legionnaire pilots were surprised when the bomber made a full twist and turn into their direction.

The brigand bomber was now heading back in the same trajectory but in the opposite direction. The bomber fired and made a lethal hit on one of the Killwings, in mid-chase, as it collided in the pursuant other. The two colliding ships were destroyed instantly leaving behind an exploding fireball in their wake. The Killwing that was struck by enemy fire dropped away at a short distance, from its terminal infliction, until it eventually exploded as well.

"Damn," the marshal cursed to himself after his eye caught a glimpse of the destruction.

The last of the bombers continued to fight instead of retreat. The marshal was impressed observing such courage, from his side and theirs. These brigands were probably ordered to stand their ground and fight till the end. Even though the last brigand pilot was alone and out matched, he seemed to blindly follow that order through, as though an unseen force was pushing him to be without relent.

Playing cat and mouse the bomber tried to out maneuver his foe. Blue streaks of energy shot out across the void and missed with each discharge as the IF-7 pursuers attempted to terminate him. Twists, turns, and verticals, the bomber flew like an angry hornet. Tracing the HEL-bomber's exhaust the Killwing pilots tried to out flank and draw the remaining brigand fighter into a trap, Joshua threw himself into the engagement.

The other legionnaire pilots were already engaged as they continued to fire their thermals and having not much success. Even though IF fighter can out gun most of anything HEL-bombers were small, fast, and maneuverable. A HEL-bomber's maneuverability compensates for their lack of firepower.

A few moments of time elapsed but the Killwings were still trailing the brigand's exhaust. Unnecessary for a half, of Joshua's squadron, to take out one bogey a few of the legionnaire pilots decided to break away and fall back on the fleeing astrotanker.

The roar of the HEL-bomber's exhaust sounded as it flew diagonally down and jerked thirty degrees away, from an approaching IF-7, at the same time firing his thermal lasers at it. As the HEL-bomber banked to port its lasers maimed the approaching Killwing by hitting its starboard wing. Unable to counterstrike, the wounded gunship stayed back allowing his other companions to even the score.

Soon after the brigand made his thirty-degree turn he quickly realized the maneuver was an error in judgment, when his alert beacon lit up, and sounded, he realized he was locked on. A laser bolt from Alpha Thirty-four's cannon ignited the brigand ship into flames; the remaining pest had been terminated, for now.

But there were more enemy rodents to exterminate, HEL-bombers escorting the Rogue were still gaining distance away from them. The marshal hoped Kreed would be among them, to end this with one final stroke.

Switching back to sensor spread, "The astrotanker is now 10.9 astronomical, and gaining distance from us fast," the marshal replied. He than said, "Get the lead out of ur exhaust pipes boys, let's take back what was stolen from us."

"What if they jump into matrix," one of the pilots questioned.

"They might find that hard to do. Centralnet restricted their online entry, the won't be able to logon to plot a course," Joshua assured.

Without wasting anymore-valuable time he powered up his thrusters generating five kps (kilometers per second) of push.

Joshua's Killwing shot out ahead and his squadron followed close behind. Having to endure another brush with acceleration the pilots were beginning to feel a little fatigue and battle weariness kicking in.

Josh, with his back press against his chair and his hands clenching the steering arm, was growing weary to. While his body was sustaining punishing forces of speed he grown impatient as him and his fleet continued to play their cat and mouse game.

"Enemy target, now 7.5 astronomical," the marshal said out loud numbering down the distance. The IF fleet followed Joshua's lead in an ever going manner, closing in, "6.8 astronomical," Joshua, still maintaining crosslink communications.

Still traveling fast through the stillness of space the pilots kept track of their target, as Joshua was, through the physical view and sensors. They couldn't wait to catch a glimpse of the tanker with their own eyes though so that they could carry out with their assault mission.

"5.2 astronomical and closing," the marshal's voice carried to all the fighters to hear by dispatch. Surrounded by the black starry quietude the Killwings continued to chase the renegade tanker. "3.7 astronomical," the marshal persisted his count down.

As Joshua counted down, through transceiver, the pilots kept their weapon systems on standby with their thumbs positioned close to the firing buttons. They already had one surprise encounter, and to avoid re-experiencing another, they made sure they were well enough armed and ready at all times.

"2.1 and closing, keep your eyes open gentlemen," Joshua warned as he himself stayed focused. As he, and the rest of his men, speedily approached the fleeing brigands the marshal's mindset was prepared for a fight. "1.1 and closing, this is it boys, " the marshal said to his legionnaires with growing anticipation. "1.0, 0.9, 0.8, 0.7." Droplets of sweat begun to twinkle down his cheeks as he attempted to relax his own tensions. "0.6, 0.5, 0.4, be ready to slow down on my mark," Joshua informed. He had the intention of both keeping his squadron informed and to keep them working together, like a fine oiled machine. "0.3, 0.2, 0.1, decrease push-off, now."

The Killwing fleet, almost in perfect unity, slowed decreasing thrust. "We're now a thousand kilometers from target," the marshal announced.

Since the Rogue was still some distance away it was difficult to make out, but as they drew closer their visibility of it became clearer. The astrotanker was eventually in their sights and the legionnaires' purpose grew as they were almost upon them. Another dogfight seemed eminent when they saw, to no surprise to them, the Rogue being escorted by four HEL-bombers in two by two cover formations.

The Rogue, still moving at its highest velocity, was not attempting to slow down. "I'll try to knock out the main exhaust," Josh said as he aimed his cannons at the tanker's stern. "The rest of you, keep your eyes on those bombers," the marshal cautioned his fellow pilots. "If they move, take 'em out."

Gazing at his targeting computer Joshua homed in on the tanker's stern anticipating a clear shot. Beep, beep, beep, the computer sounded, "Here goes nothing, firing." A laser bolt shot out from one of his twin cannons and made a direct hit. The stern exhaust ports blew apart fro its interior clamps and drifted away; only smoke was left where the exhaust ports used to be. The Rogue was now dead in space losing all acceleration and maneuvering control.

Responding to the Legion's first strike the escort bombers reacted, two at the bow and two at the tail end of the taker. The brigand pilots' awareness jumped into attack mode, they maintained their positions for a stark moment.

One of the bombers swerved down and away from the Rogue and unleashed a repetitive barrage of laser fire, which caused no injuries as yet. The barrage was a mere reflex reaction from the marshal's assault, the brigand pilot didn't have a chance to make deadly aim in that split second.

Counterattacking, one of the legionnaires shot back but only nicked the HEL-bomber's wing. Damaged by the energy blast the brigand bomber turned again to take another offensive. Prowling like a wounded bird of prey, the bomber took a .0-degree position atop the Killwing that wounded her. When the brigand fired the legionnaire pilot was in a state of temporary shock, which hesitated his reflexes, but he quickly snapped out of it with just enough ample time to dip his wings to avoid the blasts.

Though small a HEL-bomber was still deadly in its firepower, even if it did not carry the kind of metastabilizing power for its weaponry as a large IF fighter was equipped with. But not wanting to be at the receiving end the Killwing pilot was able to avoid the laser bursts.

Turning the nose around again for a secondary attack the brigand bird of prey looked wrathful as it made another run at the evaded Killwing. But before the brigand had the chance to fire an IF-7 snuck up behind it and fired, turning the HEL-bomber into stardust.

"Thanks Alpha Thirteen, good shooting," the grateful legionnaire transmitted.

"Nothing doing, we lost enough men today," Thirteen responded.

The three remaining HEL-bomber escorts were engaged in their offensives as well. Alpha squad decided, and than maneuvered into, a single column formation. As the IFs quickly piloted into a tight wing-to-wing column the HEL-bombers begun to climb to a .0-degree on top of them, to unleash their depth charges.

The Legion pilots accelerated up to meet their positions, and as they did, they picked them off one by one with relative ease. Ease because the legionnaires anticipated the brigands' objective, and as the bombers reached their firing lines they made easy targets. Now nothing remained, except for the astrotanker of course, and any resistance aboard her.

"We need to get inside, prepare for space walk," the marshal said as he unfastened his seat harness. "Expect heavy resistance, arm yourselves with the usual hardware," the marshal meaning repeating pulse rifles.

Most of the IF-7s' underbelly hatches opened, breaking the magnetic seals and allowing artificial air to escape. Once they were able to step out they did, with their cybersuits on and their thruster jetpacks ready. Armed with Dominion issued weapons they fired up their jetpacks propelling themselves cautiously toward the Rogue.

Following the marshal's lead the team of commando pilots made their way toward a small accessor hatch, which was at the portside stern of the astro. Joshua communicated his intentions through the mind interlink grid, "[There's a hatch near the exhaust ports, follow me.] Those words were projected across the team's helmet visors, near the lower rim so as not to block their visual, they complied with the order.

Once the marshal was within arm's reach of the hatch he gripped the valve release with both hands. With a firm grip he turned it in the usual clockwise direction to release the locking bolt. When the hatch was free to open he did allowing his team to move in first. Positioned off to the side, the marshal levitated motionless, as his team moved in on thruster control. "[They better increase my combat pay for this,]" one of the men thought to himself as he passed by the marshal.

"[Keep chatline clear, communicate hostile intentions only,]" Joshua transmitted through his thoughts alone, to project those words to everyone. "[Safeties off, fire short control bursts.]"

The last member eventually made his way inside, boarding the Rogue, and than Josh followed in behind. With another firm grip, as soon as he was still hovering but inside, Josh pulled him self back with a little retro thrust slamming the hatch shut to lock it.

A loud humming sound echoed throughout the chamber, which was mechanical in nature. "[We got gravity, power down,]" the marshal's thought relayed another command. Complying, the team gradually powered down their thruster packs, and by doing so, they descended to the floor.

"[Communications on MIG only and stay together,]" the marshal relayed to his team. "[We gotta get to the bridge.]" With cautious steps the team made their way toward another hatch, which was at the opposite end of the decompression tunnel, from where they stood.

One of the team members was fidgeting and sweating uncomfortably and decided to remove his helmet. Shutting off his oxygen lines and unlocking the helmet screws he took his helmet off, throwing it over his head and resting it under his arm. Scratching his neckline where his tight pressure suit made him itch, he was negligent to the dire consequences he may face.

"Bowan, put your helmet back on," the marshal had to transmit verbally. "That's an order."

Bowan stood confounded as he stared, curiously, at Josh. An expression of inquiry showed on Bowan's face as he wondered why he was being shouted at. Behind Bowan Josh caught a glimpse, through a window at the opposite end of the corridor, of an individual showing suspicious behavior.

"Put your helmet back on," the marshal shouted louder as he ran toward the bewildered legionnaire.

Too little too late when the lights dimmed red in the chamber. When the lights dimmed, and an alarm siren startled their nerves, a computer voice announced, "Decompression sequence commencing, environmental suits must be worn." When the announcement was over the same message repeated.

As the chamber's counter-pressure dissipated and the artificial gravity generators deactivated the troops, within their confined hall, lifted off the floor in zero gravity. Bowan, in a state of agony, long relinquished his helmet and grabbed his face as his blood begun to boil. Levitated like the others, but in pain, he wished he could have benefited from the marshal's warning.

Bowan's blood rushed through his arteries as his veins enlarged and his cells exploded. Blood oozed out from the corners of his eye sockets and seeped out from his ears as his eardrums also exploded. His face rippled as blood rushed through his head.

Knowing he had no time to spare the marshal quickly slung his tethered rifle to firing position. Levitating himself he took direct aim at the hatch and fired, triggering a blast of energy. The intense heat of the laser bolt melted the internal welds and blew the hatch open. The unknown assailant stood behind the hatch as it blew. The metal emplacement shout out from the blast and impacted the assailant with tremendous force knocking him into the far wall.

Breathable artificial air flooded the decompression tunnel once again and the situation returned to normal, including gravity, which dropped the occupants to the floor without retros from their thrusters to slow their fall. The remaining team members, adhering to the lesson from their fallen comrade, kept all pressure insulators worn and fastened. Bowan wasn't so fortunate, he was sprawled out on the floor where he had stood, convulsing and gasping for air.

The marshal stood up, from where he had fallen, and rushed to Bowan's side, "We need a medicorp, quickly."

Jon quickly approached and stood behind the marshal with interlink in hand, "Sentry post, we need a medicorp unit in a hurry. And prepare for evac." Once the dispatch was given the legionnaire clipped his communicator back to where he had it as Joshua tried, futilely, to console his injured man. "Help's on the way," he informed the marshal.

"Watch over him lieutenant," Josh said as he quickly joined the rest of his team.

The rest of his commando team, with the exception of the two, took the defensive outside the decompression hall. With their mental senses acute and their fingers on the triggers they scouted the surrounding parameter for their imposing enemy. A sense of security eased them, somewhat, by keeping their backs to the wall. With cautious steps they begun to maneuver through the corridor and eventually they fanned out, through a labyrinth maze of other corridors, in order to commandeer the freighter.

The brigand warriors heavily guarded the bridge, the area was on full alert with sirens roaring and warning beacons flashing red. The loud sirens muffled the sounds of the men as they screamed out commands and pranced back and forth on the catwalks, gearing and readying themselves for combat. They grabbed any weapon they could get their hands on to fight off the Legion's infiltrators.

Outside from the bridge two sentries stood guard on a suspended platform protecting the entrance from a colonial breach. As they stood with their hands on the butt ends of their rifles, barrels up, an unexpected laser bolt flashed from below them and made a hit killing one of them. The other, startled from the sudden attack, realized too late who the attackers were. The colonials quickly vanquished the other sentry with another fatal shot, which ripped through his midsection. The sentry's limp body draped over the guardrail from the shot and than dropped off, from the platform, crashing to the floor below.

"[Let's move in, I'll take point,]" Joshua transmitted still using his MIG utility. "[The rest of you watch my back.]"

From their squatted positions they proceeded, with hurried but cautious steps, toward the stairway. Joshua took the lead with his pulse weapon ready to shoot if need be, and the men behind, followed him toward the top of the staircase landing. Since the landing was not spacious enough to accommodate the entire squadron a few of them stood on the spiral staircase protecting the rear.

"[They bolted the hatch,]" the marshal transmitted, "[Charges,]" he commanded. And so his First Sergeant complied with the order, quickly handing Josh time-delay bombs. "[All of you back down, I'm blowing this baby off its hinges.]"

His team needed not to see his order twice scroll across their visual, they immediately distanced a few feet away down the stairs. After the marshal affixed one more charge to the metal hatch he cleared away to. After fifteen seconds elapsed an awakening explosion erupted leaving behind smoke and tiny fragments, and now an opening giving the infiltrators a clear passage.

"[We're in, lets go,]" the marshal commanded not able to voice his eagerness through the MIG, but surely they all were.

Meanwhile in the decompression hall, the lieutenant continued to watch with concern over his injured buddy. Jon was in a kneeling position, near Bowan's side, resting his hand on the rippled body. While trying to keep Bowan conscious a warning alarm startled the lieutenant as the space was being opened. The magnetic shield was activated, excluding their previous entry, to keep the artificial gravity intact. The pilot, who opened the hatch, stood away to the side to allow for an unobstructed passage for an automaton.

Out from the depths a medicorp 'maton moved into their view as it entered the hall on propulsion thrust. Adhering to its programming the 'maton glided, like a ghost, as it moved in toward the wounded body. The 'maton's stern thrusters spewed out a colorless gas leaving a trail of transparent irregularity. As the 'maton approached its triangulated tractor wheels swiveled down, so that the flats of them were facing the floor, as the automaton descended and its thermal thrust deactivated. Moving on drive-wheel control only the medicorp machine was now at Bowan's feet.

The lieutenant backed off as the 'maton initiated a bio-scan. A blue beam of light probed the entire body as the diagnostic data was being programmed into the 'maton's memory banks. Once the severity of the injuries had been ascertained by the robot it deactivated its bio-scan and than the 'maton's utility appendagers extended to commence treatment.

The bridge was filled with laser fire and blinding smoke as the battle ensued. The quick advance gained the legionnaires the advantage when the brigandeers were caught not as prepared as they hoped, and a few of them lost their lives because of it. Like armored destroyers, the infiltrators stood in a semi-circle formation trying to move in to encompass and overpower the brigands.

The colonials fired in short controlled bursts, as ordered, and made several successful kills. One colonial was gunned down during the procession but the rest continued to fight until the brigands surrendered, they would grieve later.

Avoiding laser blasts the colonials continued on as they tried, with much struggle, to seize control of the bridge. The colonials also had to bear in mind that there was more brigand resistance at the bridge's lower level landing. Laser bolts flashed up at them that the commando infiltrator team had to dodge and duck from. Although the brigands, below, were heavily armed they had the obvious disadvantage since the colonials held the higher ground.

Across from where the colonials stood two brigands held the advantage over them, taking a stand and taking cover on an elevated catwalk. They were determined to maintain the upper hand however futile it may be, since they were outnumbered and pretty much out in the open. They each unleashed repetitive bursts of laser fire at the colonials. One barrage of fire made a kill causing the colonial to throw himself back; as his hand released his weapon, he than dropped to the floor. His fellow pilot as payback shot the attacking brigand, who made the kill, through his heart. The brigand who stood next to his fallen comrade continued to fight but this time he squatted down, to avoid getting struck down as the one, who fought beside him, did.

The astrotanker was dormant and the same was true for the Dominion gunships while the activity aboard the Rogue persisted. Most of the gunships were unmanned, except for two. These two pilots remained aboard their IF-7s as sentries, watching out for possible enemy reinforcements.

No movement was evident until the tanker's main cargo hatch, at the stern, began to open. After the hatch was fully opened a podal craft exited leaving the Rogue behind and making a clear getaway. Kreed sat at the pilot seat at the bridge to pilot the craft, even though the vehicle was mostly manipulated by remote it can be manned as well. His web claw-like hands were at the navigation console as he finger tapped commands into the navigational system.

"Sergeant, we have a pod-and-launcher craft exiting the freighter," one of the IF-7 sentry pilots transmitted. "An escape is in progress."

"I'll try to dampen their plans," the other pilot said as he began to engage.

But before the pilot had the chance to pursue the fleeing craft Kreed swerved the nose of his escape vehicle, away from the Rogue, and than he initiated his conventional thrusters on full power.

"Don't engage, the marshal ordered us to stay here," the other pilot reminded. "There might be some more unfreindlies that might pop in to join the party."

Gaining distance and speeding away from the freighter it would appear as though Kreed would be successful in his escape. As they watched the podal craft leave the sentries probably didn't realize that it was Kreed aboard that fleeing escape vehicle; if they did they would've most likely pursue to apprehend, since that was the marshal's main mission.

Still in a squatted position the brigand, who was across from where the legionnaire attack force was, continued discharging his weapon. The Alpha squad, while trying to subdue the brigand, was also trying to avoid laser fire from below. By sheer discipline or luck the last brigand, who remained on the catwalk, was still alive and fighting. But his luck must of run out, when a laser bolt penetrated his body of which the impact threw him into the walk, his life ended.

Fully realizing that they have lost the battle the brigands, on the lower level, quickly surrendered by relinquishing their arms and throwing their hands behind their heads. Alpha squad kept their helmets on until they were reassured that security, aboard the astrotanker, had been established. The colonials clearly showed who was in charge as they kept the brigands encircled and at gunpoint. The brigand raiders, knowing that they have lost this time, threw themselves into submission.

"Marshal," the word came from Joshua's interlink, "all stations had been swept and secured, the vessel is ours."

Josh grabbed his communicator, after removing his helmet, and spoke, "Thank-you lieutenant," and than inquired, "Have you found Kreed?"

"Negative, a pod-and-launcher craft exited the freighter during the fighting, Kreed might have been on board."

"Damn," was all he could say.

"Sir, a message came through from Central Command," one of his pilots said to him as he approached.

"Yea, what is it?" the marshal asked as he looked up at him.

"Your presence is required at Central immediately."

"For what reason?"

"They didn't say."

"Well, I need to report to them anyway. Sergeant, I'm relying on you and your men to keep this vessel safe. Your new lieutenant is now in command, follow his orders like you would follow mine," the marshal insisted.

"Sir," the sergeant snapped at attention after the marshal's last words.

The marshal than looked away to speak into his interlink, "Your in charge of the fleet now," the marshal reminded Darvus who he had just recently promoted. "Make sure this property gets returned safely to the Gontaris system and report to me right away if there's any trouble."

"Yes sir," the lieutenant transmitted back.

"You got what's left of my squadron, take care of them," Josh said keeping his emotions in check, "Don't take any unnecessary risks, just get this tanker back where it belongs." Clipping his communicator back he than looked around, and than nodding his head, he expressed a satisfied look knowing that everything there was under control. He left with these final words, "Looks like I'm coming home."

A CITY AMONG THE stars, vibrant yet peaceful for it was peace for which it stood, the Regalia starbase. The station resembled a giant spinning wheel. The metallic frame had a slight curvature, like an umbrella, covering a metallic sphere emplacement, which was underneath at the hub. Like the spinning wheel it revolved generating a sense of artificial gravity for the occupants within.

Kwidon was the one world in this solar system capable of sustaining breathable life. A global biodiversity of species and plant life generated the perfect balance in the planet's ecosystem. Neighbored by the sun, the Syberon moon, and the hovering Regalia fortress, this system stood apart from the rest.

A major metropolitan city was constructed in a region less mountainous, in a world that mostly consisted of mountains and river streams. The metropolis was called Central city. Filled with life, industrialization, and commerce, Central was the heart of the Crosstar Trade Union surpassed only by the Regalius merchant colony. The majestic architecture of the pagodas and pyramids were built with the intent to fuse technology with the natural elements of the surrounding landscape, which symbolized the Dominion's power.

An orchestrated fleet of VECTROF and IF fighters made maneuvering exercises near the Regalia accompanied by Spearhead transports. Faintly visible by the naked eye, starcarriers were positioned in the background monitoring the activity as part of their many functions. An occasional turbocraft flew passed the convoy transporting goods to the Syberon lunar station. This was all but routine for the pilots and crew but for the novel observer this was a spectacle to adore.

A shotgun sound with a blinding luminous, after which, Joshua's Killwing darted out of the light making him known, followed. After his retronics slowed his velocity he radioed in, "Central, this is Hollands," he informed the Regalia. "Prepare landing crew, I'm coming in."

"I hear you marshal, your clear for entry," the dispatcher responded. "Welcome home."

Flying near and than below the Regalia Joshua initiated the

boarding sequence determined to do his own maneuvering without centralnet interference. The space station continued to revolve as the sphere's central hatch opened. Josh than began to ascend toward the opening. The Killwing was the size of a spec compared to the enormity of the Regalia. Still ascending, Joshua succeeded in his entry as he passed the magnetic shield; his ship was now within safe abode.

Now that he was boarded he decreased repellor thrust and waited for further instructions. "Hollands, your designated landing pad is CQ-2," the dispatcher announced. "Your pad's been dusted and cleared."

"Copy that dispatch," the marshal acknowledged. "Thank-you."

CQ-2's coordinates had been filed into his ship's branch computer and Joshua had no choice but to allow centralnet to complete the sequence. Even a veteran legionnaire like Hollands, who had been through the familiar surroundings a million times, would get lost in the numerous towers of platform pillars. Once again he was ascending but this time centralnet was piloting. The ship's repellors and stern thrusters catered Josh toward his assigned landing pad.

After clearing the fifteenth level he was near the end of his destination. Once he had spotted CQ-2 he no longer needed centralnet aid, and thus, he regained manual control. Two flight coordinators stood on the pad, away from the landing zone, and watched as the marshal was about to approach touchdown. Joshua's repellors decreased as his ship descended even closer to the pad until finally touching the surface.

Once his engines were quieted the two flight coordinators dusted his ship with delousing fluid to decontaminate possible stellar radiation. Joshua had to wait a few moments while this was being done. As he gazed out his cockpit windscreen he barely made out the activity of the two men, all that he had seen was a foggy mist of the anti-radiation solution.

Once the fog cleared a clamping sound, from the security ladder, had been fastened to a retainer bolt, which indicated to Josh he was safe to dismount. "Copilot, retract canopy," the marshal verbally commanded his ship's computer.

"At your command, thank-you," the computer voice responded as the canopy slid open.

As the two flight coordinators wedged metal stoppers against the landing gear and coiled the gas lines Josh climbed out of his ship and than searched for the propulsionlift. With the exception of Joshua's Killwing there wasn't much else, as far as obscureness goes, so the lift was not hard to find. He made his way toward it casually. As soon as he was there he palm pressed the revolving hatch to open, after which, he stepped on. When the hatch slid closed behind him a slight sensation of g-force was felt as the lift accelerated to the lower level, by wind tunnel suction.

He didn't have long to wait when his lift stopped and the hatch opened, making visible, the open ground outside. Spacious enough to walk around freely. The towering pillar supporters, which supported the landing pads, did not impede anyone's or anything's mobility because of the station's enormous size. As he exited the lift his name was called out. When he jerked his head in the direction of the voice he saw his commanding officer as he approached, General Commander Murius. As he reached out his hand to greet his superior a sentrycam, also known as a floater because of its ability of free flight, hovered like a pest close to his ear. A small spherical shaped 'maton, with a camera built in, that Josh chased away with his hand as though it was a mosquito.

"Marshal, welcome back," the General said as their hands met in a handshake.

"General," the marshal responded as his hand met the General's. "What's your latest findings on the computer glitch."

"Right now the situation is unknown. I dispatched a regenalt to investigate," the General continued. "He'll plug into the mainframe computer and extract the necessary data."

"How long will that take?"

"As long as it takes, he'll dispatch a communication link when he completes his mission," the General assured. "In the meantime you need to file a report and show up for a briefing later on."

"There's not much to report, I tol-," Josh was abruptly interrupted when a youngster, inattentive, bumped into him. "Hey champ, where's the fire." The boy was startled at first and than head shy, he made no remark. "What's your name?" The boy, again, kept silent and than he scurried away disappearing at a distance.

The marshal looked puzzled as he asked, "Who was that?"

"An orphan that one of our scavenger drones picked up in the Calabor system I think," Murius explained, "some far off run down colony."

"Does he have a name?"

"He didn't have any ID papers or markings on him but DNA tracking came up with one, Randella," Murius answered the marshal's inquiry. "He seemed to be left parentless at the end days of the war, both of his mom and dad were members of the separatist revolt."

"Do you know what came of them?," Josh inquired.

"No, they were supposedly killed but no bodies were found. We're temporarily keeping him in custody until Juvenile Holding arrives with an escort." Murius thought to himself for a while and than said, "This will be the third time he escaped from my patrols, which reminds me," the General than snatched his interlink from his belt and spoke into it, "Sentry patrol, this is the General Commander. Whoever's responsible for babysitting our young guest, he's loose on the ground level. Someone, please, retrieve him before he hurts himself," the General said with annoyance as he signed off.

"I see you have your hands full," the marshal said while trying to hold back a grin.

"You'll be surprised," the General responded as they both went their separate ways.

Flashing red lights in the darkness were beacons, in place, to caution piloting crafts of an object beyond. A massive metallic object, pass the red beacon zone, which was the parameter station, which resembled a super-cylinder ring. In the center of the parameter station laid centralnet station, a massive computer satellite with an array of antenna towers.

Wishing to approach, a dwarf shuttle moved in and than came

to a slow stop. The shuttle was the size less than any ship known in the Dominion's fleet arsenal. From the looks of it, it looked spacious enough for the driver to just lay flat without the comfort of a little wiggle room inside.

No human can pilot such a craft with even moderate maneuverability in such a confining space, but the occupant was only part human. For he, or it, was a cybernetic, a machine powered by its human brain. A regenerative alteration, or regenalt for short, are tools crosslinked into centralnet's mainframe computer and programmed to perform certain tasks, some of which their human counterparts cannot.

Not wanting to pass the beacon emplacements, the regenalt waited for the green light, from the parameter station, so he could continue on with his assignment. Centralnet was designed to emit an array, or matrix grid, of hyperwaves. These waves were crosslinked to thousands of ongoing spacecrafts, linked to their ships' navigation controls, which were all computerized that controlled their trajectories during interstellar flight. The regenalt had to navigate through the matrix grid while avoiding jamming interference with any of the crosslinks, which spread out like an invisible net within central's parameter. The staff aboard the parameter station had to dispatch, a good to go, through his ship's transceiver so he waited.

"Shuttle, you are clear to approach," the dispatch controller announced.

After a few minutes of patient had elapsed, on slow propulsion, the shuttlecraft moved in passing the red zone. He proceeded at a sustained speed following the downloaded coordinates that were given to him.

Once he cleared the beacons the shuttlecraft was, again, in empty space but only for a moment. After that moment passed he moved in close toward the parameter station and toward the station's ingress. The ingress was a tunnel-like opening of which ships can enter or exit through. There were much such ingresses constructed and spaced apart throughout the super-ring. The staff members aboard the parameter station observed carefully as the shuttle commenced entry.

The super-ring had several observatory windows, wide and clear, not even a smudge was evident for they kept all areas clean at all times. These windows were there for any one of the staffers to keep watch of passing ships, mostly maintenance vessels toward the satellite, or to simply adore the cosmos. So clean and transparent the windows' insets were that you could see clearly, even at a distance, people walking through the ring's corridor.

With casual steps, an individual walked through the corridor fulfilling his tasks. Occasionally he'll glance out through the screen of windows still taken aback by the awesome power they possess, a massive responsibility, no matter how many times he looked out or thought about it. Looking around the entire super-ring was composed of fusion metal with hardened glass windows, with mounted electronic equipment. The unknown staffer continued to walk through the single circular corridor until he entered one of the navigation control bunkers.

Chattering and mechanical beeps were the only sounds being manufactured by the activity, inside the bunker. The navigation controllers observed their monitoring equipment and observed, through the glass coverings, as the regenalt continued to make his entrance.

"looking good," one flight coordinator said to the other.

"Yea, regenalts have no need for a computer to hold their hand, they're on the same wavelength," the coordinator responded in jest.

Continuing on minimal thrust, the craft passed through the ingress. The ring's opening, large enough for a Spearhead transport to pass through, was like a huge polygonal access way reinforced by metal plates. The regenalt wasn't acting independently as he piloted his craft for he was crosslinked with centralnet, they talk to each other, almost like a remote control.

Once he was within the ring's parameter he was again in empty space, but only for a moment. As the shuttle approached closer toward its destination centralnet, itself, came into full schematic view. Centralnet resembled a giant satellite dish with towering antenna arrays mounted within the center. At a distance it looked more like a metropolitan city than a deep space computer satellite because of its enormity. Centralnet controlled the Dominion's interstellar aviation and long-range communications.

"Pilot, what is your purpose?" the controller dispatched, "Over."

"Acknowledge, situation deemed classified, end transmit," was the regenalt's style of converse responding as he approached even closer toward the satellite fortress. Never slowing or stopping, an observer had a better sense of the sheer magnitude of the fortress as the shuttle closed in toward it; the craft was a spec of dust in comparison.

In the cockpit metallic fingers operated the control panel. The regenalt pressed the necessary keypads to activate the outside viewing camera. A picture, of the outside, was transmitted to his view screen so he could keep track of his progress. He looked at the screen with his optics not knowing the progression of time the way his human counterparts might perceive it, he didn't have to endure the emotion of impatience.

By optical illusion the ship got smaller and the station enlarged as the shuttle approached it. Once he was a fraction of a hair close to centralnet the shuttle positioned itself near the super-generators right below the base of the dish. These generators pumped surges of subatomic particles into the machine's component make-up.

The regenalt moved in to attach the craft's data power outlet to one of the station's inlet attachment rings. Once the craft was close enough the regenalt made a half spin maneuver so that his stern was facing the inlet connectors, he than made the connection. A shuttering sound from the craft indicated to the cybernetic that he was now plugged into the satellite's diagnostics and inner workings. Cybernetics were able to speak binary, hence, the regenalt was able to communicate with centralnet's program, known by name as Steel Prime.

He keystroke his control panel but this time he did so to view the satellite's internal diagnostic schematics. While viewing his screen he would, on occasion, cross-reference his findings to catch any glitch or defaults. After he completes his task he'll have to report his findings and bring that information to his superiors, back at Central. He kept his power coupling plugged into his shuttle to keep the crosslink open, reason being, to talk to Steel Prime in binary code while he was doing his diagnostic sweep of the system.

The entertainment lounge rested atop the Regalia fortress. This was a place for civilian and non-civilian alike to rest and enjoy the amenities during their off time. Computer games, and island bar, and music kept the people joyfully occupied. No music was playing presently, just boisterous chatter and drinking. The dome lounge had many windows plus the skylight above. If someone had no one to talk to he could simply sit by a window and lose himself in his thoughts as he viewed the stars.

Which was what Randella did as he sat at the table with his arms folded, rested against the flat surface of his table. His chin was buried in his arms as he looked steadily into space, lost in a daydream.

Randella," a feminine computerized voice called out, "Remember, you are allowed here only if you behave yourself." The computerized voice was coming from a regenalt as she looked down on him. That particular regenalt was programmed in home economics, currently; she was babysitting the young boy. She spoke out again, "It will be my metal hide if you run off again." She continued, "I've been commanded to watch over you until your authoritative escort arrives."

"I know," Randella responded with annoyance. "I'm bored, I think I'll go back to my room," Randella said as he thought about making a clear getaway.

"Please don't run off on me," she warned. "The only reason why you're free to wander around the unrestricted areas is because I've been charged to watch over you." She continued, "Do not disrespect their generosity."

"I'm only going to play," Randella rebutted.

Randella, casually and unsuspicious-like, walked toward the hatch and exited to the outer corridors. As he walked through the main corridor, heading toward his living quarters, his regenalt chaperone moved very mechanically as she followed behind.

Once at his bedchamber he opened the hatch and was about to

walk inside when the cybernetic unit was about to follow him in. "Wait a minute, you can't come in," the boy protested.

"But I've been ordered to watch you."

"You can watch me just fine from out here," Randella tried to reason.

"But I-."

"Where can I run off to? I'm in my quarters," Randella broke in.

"But I-."

"Belle," was the regenalt's given name.

"Oh, very well," the cybernetic submitted. She than turned around, facing the other way, and stood guard. Randella than entered his chamber and closed the hatch once he was inside, all seemed well.

A ragged and dusty planet but rich in metal properties Gontaris stood like an eye sore, an eye sore, except for the refinery shareholders who were vastly getting rich from the planet's source. The manufacture and distribution of fusion metal filled their moneybags of regal payments.

Entering the planet's atmosphere the Rogue was being escorted by the IF-13s on a precise heading toward Orath, the astrotanker arrived home. Pushing onward they commenced a sensor spread behind them to scan their rear flank, just in case they encounter any more surprises.

As the pilots looked ahead they saw, through their cockpit windows, the Orath colony. The gleaming biosphere sparkled, like sunrays dancing off crystals. The intense sun reflecting off the super-dome's interwoven glass fibers induced the glitter. Even though the polyglass was dense and thick it was still transparent enough to see the city through it from the outside, if close enough.

Being towed even closer the Rogue was about to move into an ingress. Pressurized to keep the harsh environment outside, outside, the Rogue entered. Passing the magnetic shield the tanker traveled through the tunnel-like opening. Noise emanated from the ventilators, which forced air in the short entryway, to blow off any dust or debris the ship might have picked up during its short traverse to the city. As the Rogue snaked through the tunnel the city drew nearer, the pilots could make out features of Orath as they looked ahead.

Once the tail ends of their sterns were free from the ingress they were now completely within the biosphere dome. The volume of the city's mass was breathtaking. Hovering a thousand kilometers high the Rogue, and its two escorts, were slightly above the highest tower.

Moving onward, still at the same altitude, they passed many refinery manufacture plants. Orath was generally a metal processing colony that manufactured fusion metal for a variety of uses, anything that of industrial strength demanded. Titanium and other deposits made Gontaris the ideal choice for this outpost.

Passing the gothic appearing industry behind the astrotanker, and its IF-13 escorts, approached their landing platform. When they were eventually over the platform the Rogue's repellors were activated as it prepared for a careful landing. Since the short-range escorts fulfilled their task they flew by and away, as soon as they were assured the tanker was under proper remote landing. The Rogue's repellors continued their downward retro thrust, but decreased a little, as the tanker made soft anchor just a few centimeters from touching the platform. All engines, except for the repellors, were than shut down when the Rogue was at the end of its landing sequence.

The astrotanker spewed ionized exhaust; which came from the toxicity converters, releasing harmless spurts of vapor, as the tanker hovered still. The tower platform loomed over the city's smaller structures. Elevated transit rails spiraled in the background as the shuttle trains raced across on them, like bullets, transporting people.

Scurrying across the platform the specialty technicians, carrying and rolling heavy equipment, made a quick approach to the Rogue. Verbal commands were issued as the personnel hooked up their equipment and prepped up a workstation. Diagnostic technicians, who were accompanied by regenalt second assistants, boarded the vessel as the men outside linked their scanning devices to the tanker's micronic systems. They were mostly interested in the components responsible for this vehicle's navigation.

One of the specialists, outside the Rogue, eyeballed his computer monitor while doing an overall system's check. Waiting patiently, expecting to find nothing, he stretched out his arms to relieve the kinks in his neck.

Waiting for some feedback he had to wait no longer when a mechanical beep signaled from his computer. The computer completed some of the overall analysis and a readout displayed across his computer. He leaned forward as he straightened his glasses. Looking at what the computer found he made a curious discovery. "Sergeant, you better take a look at this," he said getting the sergeant's attention.

Aboard the Regalia, the female regenalt continued to stand watch outside Randella's room. Turning her head periodically she became suspicious when she heard no sound, within Randella's quarters, for some time. "Randella, are you all right," she said as her metal fist knocked on his hatch. "Randella, please, are you ok," she said again as she waited for a reply.

Belle heard no response so she begun to panic, "Oh my, if anything happens to that boy it's the metal heap for me." She immediately palm pressed the hatch open and she hurried inside. Looking around ferociously, panic stricken, she called out his name, "Randella, Randella!" Searching in every corner she came across a laundry chute, which had the sliding cover wide open. "Oh dear," she said knowing that he escaped.

Joshua, holding a scanner, was busy extracting information from the system's main database to help aid his report. He had to file all incidences; from the death relating accident, at the primordial expedition sight, to the time he got called back to Central. His report had to be filed expeditiously for his superior.

While he was pressing keys his interlink beeped, which indicated a transmission. Josh lowered his scanner and raised his communicator, "First Marshal Hollands."

"Marshal, this is Murius. Word just came through from the centralnet station."

"Ok, you got my attention. What's up?"

"I'll fill you in, come up for a briefing," the General Commander had a critical tone in his voice. "It's top priority."

"I'm on my way," the marshal concluded the dispatch as he looked for the nearest propulsionlift.

The lights were dimmed creating a pleasant environment in the General's quarters. Pinewood finished covered the walls and the aroma of green foliage, emanating from the potted plants, interpreting an earthlike atmosphere.

The main entrance hatch snapped open, after which, Joshua entered. Noticing his superior, who was standing at the other end of the chamber near his desk, Josh spoke out, "General sir, I hope you solved the mystery."

"Not entirely, but we have an idea where you might find your fugitive. Come, sit yourself over there," the General said as he pointed to the circle of chairs facing a projected blue laser screen. "By the way, maybe you remember your old copilot, now reinstated."

Stepping into Joshua's line of vision, making himself known, a reptilian humanoid moved away from the shadows. He was of the same species as their fugitive, Kreed, from their Murian home world. He greeted the marshal the only way he knew how, indigenous to his kind, with telepathic affection.

"Jagaba, my old friend," the marshal said after he gotten over the shock. "Yes, its good to see you to," reading Jagaba's thoughts and feelings.

"And a new member of your recon team, Crimson," the General made the introduction as the Regenalt made himself known as well. Crimson walked behind Josh, at the moment of introduction, and he tapped the marshal on the shoulder hinting Josh to step aside so he can pass. "He's your new navigator."

"Recon team?," the marshal inquired.

"That's what we're all here to discuss," Murius responded. "Now, let us all sit and I'll bring everybody up to speed on the situation."

As all the members in attendance, found their seats and made themselves comfortable, the speaker of the assembly stood next to the hologram screen computer. The projection unit was a TASC, Touch Access Screen Computer, which was touch screen operated. The General prepared his briefing by touching one of the keys on the screen to illustrate his findings. Touching one of the command function keys a stellar chart appeared.

"Lights down to seventy percent," the General directed his voice to the environmental computer. After the General's order was given the computer complied dimming the lights, making the blue laser screen and its images more pronounced.

"We found the missing piece of the puzzle, or some of it," Murius continued while everybody else stayed silent. "Our S.M.I men probed the Rogue's navigational system and found these coordinates," the General said as he touched the screen again to zoom in. "120 degrees starboard, 10.1 kilo light-years, time intervals of 22 parminutes on static pulse in quad sector Alpha." While he was announcing those coordinates out loud he saw his audience's perplexing looks, as he pointed to the location.

"As you can see, Alpha quadrant is outside Dominion territory," Murius explained. "Once you reach the outer rim you must travel the rest of the way on static pulse. IF-18 probe ships will accompany you during the flight."

"Do we know what's waiting for us at the end of those coordinates," the marshal had to question.

"Supposedly, the brigand's hidden outpost," the General answered with his best assumption. "We still have your prisoner, maybe she can tell us more."

"I'll do better than that," Josh stated entertaining a thought, he dare not share it with the rest right now.

A bright plasmatic light, from above, illuminated the detainment chamber and the surroundings had a dull, metallic, atmosphere. The chamber was almost bare except for a table and a couple of chairs, which were arranged in the center.

Jackie sat impatiently for hours waiting for her interrogation to begin. She'd been neglected for some time and she grew enraged. Inside there was quite chilly and she wasn't exactly dressed for the occasion. She had on black interlace straps and buckles covering her pelvic and bosom, but showing enough femininity to make the coldest heart melt.

"Good morning, I hope you slept well," Joshua said after he

entered the chamber and approached. "I'll ask the questions. Answer me honestly and to the point and we can make this as painless as possible," the marshal said as he pulled out the other chair to sit himself down.

"I don't know what else I can tell you guys, they never did trust me anyway," Jackie said annoyed. "I'm sure they kept certain information from reaching my ears." Jackie pulled herself up from the slouched position she was in. Her body grew fatigued from sitting for hours it seemed to her in her cold metal chair. "You locked me in this freezer for all this time for nothing."

"I sorry you feel that way cause I was about to hire you."

"Hire me?"

"You're a mercenary aren't you," the marshal than picked up her dossier, which he previously dropped in front of him. "According to this you served a couple of tours in the War as a scout."

"Where did you get that, I thought most of the war records were lost or destroyed," she asked being both impressed and confounded.

The marshal continued, "You were in the white brigade earned the combat star for bravery," he than looked up at her, "above and beyond."

"What would you have of me?"

"You know the brigands' strengths and numbers," Josh finding it distasteful asking an outlaw for help, he sat a little uneasy.

"How much will you pay me?"

"Your freedom," the marshal said daring her to refuse.

"And if I refuse?"

"Than your going to find yourself back at that penal colony only this time you'll be the one in deep freeze." The marshal continued, "And I seriously doubt anyone will go out of their way to break you out."

For a few seconds Jackie paused and said nothing, she would find it easy to lash out at him but she held back. She pondered the notion of masquerading as an ally and than, maybe when nobody was looking, she could make a clean break. She than looked back at the marshal and made a slight nod, she'll do it.

On docking pad CC-92 a transport sat vacant waiting for

passengers to fill in the vacancy. Outside, near the hydraulic entrance ramp, a line-up of young boys stood in a haphazard formation. While the sentries kept their eyes on the young lads the shuttle was being revved and programmed for a launch.

"Hey sergeant, we seem to be missing a body," a young patrolman apprised. "Randella."

"Do a quick sweep of the area, he probably scurried off again. He couldn't of gotten far," the sergeant responded. "But don't take too long, these young gentlemen have a schedule to keep."

As the patrolman did his quick search the sergeant led the rest of the group, up the ramp, and into the transport shuttle. Hesitant to board, the boys had to be nudged along as they mounted.

A few flights down, at docking pad A-29, a light-gray clad starcruiser stood ominously. A wing-class vessel, the entire ship from wingtip to wingtip was triangulated and slender in shape. The cockpit was spacious and had a long arrowhead-like windscreen above the nose. The ship, with all its implements and armaments, was designed for quick infiltration and evasion.

Murius stood by the starboard side, supervising, as Jagaba commenced an exterior safety check. The cruiser had to reach certain standards before the upcoming mission, or any mission.

While the ship was being checked Joshua, accompanied by his new enlistee, exited the propulsionlift and casually approached. They both stood-fast when they gazed upon the ominous design of the cruiser. Even Jackie, who wasn't impressed easily, was awe inspired. Their reaction was understandable since the ship was the first of its kind, a prototype.

"What is this?" Joshua said finally as he neared the Commander's side.

"The Cauldron," Murius said proudly. He was the one who endorsed the design fresh from the blue prints. "This is your ticket to Alpha quadrant."

"Very nice," the marshal complimented. "What's the armament?"

"This ship is armed with your basic thermal lasers," the General Commander said as he pointed to the areas he was specifying.

"One on the starboard wing, one on the portside wing, and the ball turret at the stern."

"Nice."

"That's not all," Murius than described in detail, "On-board the ship comes equipped with a reciprocal outlink station. Crimson can plug in and talk to the ship's computer and work in conjunction with one another."

"Impressive," Joshua said honestly.

"Indeed," Murius than explained, "You will need that advantage when traveling at static pulse, if off by a second picking up the carrier probes' transmissions your ship will be redirected off course."

The Commander, and his marshal, than briefly walked around the ship to do a once over check. And since this is the first time Josh saw Cauldron maybe Murius was showing it off as well, his prized possession.

Once the brief tour was over they were now back from where they started when they noticed Crimson walking up the ramp. Impeded by his mechanical parts he still made good time as he walked up the incline and boarded the Cauldron.

"Your regenalt will help you navigate safely through the uncharted space," Murius pointed out again, "IF-18 probe ships will take the lead and you'll rendezvous with them at the outer rim."

"Understood," the marshal said as he made his way toward, parting from his superior, and up the gangplank.

"And good luck," Murius voiced his well wishes as the marshal disappeared inside the cruiser.

The Cauldron's inner compartments were darker in color, comparative to the exterior structure, only the light indicators from the control consoles and the overhead blue plasma lamps added the extra lighting. Most sections of the ship were congested by sophisticated equipment, some not yet installed, since the Cauldron was a mere prototype and hurried into service. Most of anything they would need was at their disposal.

The same was true for the bridge but more prepped and organized, all the systems were properly fitted and functioning. The brightness of the outer bay could be seen through the forward windscreen, its wide-angle spread gave the pilots a complete visual of anything they faced.

The marshal wasted no time after entering the bridge, and the hatch snapping shut behind him, when he sat beside Jagaba at his pilot seat. Jagaba had already initiated the ship's repellors and thruster sequencers before Josh had the chance to order him to.

Crimson also sat in his place as well, far behind the other two, in his reciprocal station, handrails hugging the backrest. After he buckled in he reached behind to grab and pull his coupling cable from his built-in backpack. Once his cable end was free he plugged himself into the ship's navigation system, turning it a little clockwise to tighten the cable end to the power valve.

"Strap tight everybody," the marshal said as he maneuvered the Cauldron toward the free zone to make his departure.

Once the cruiser was free from the platform and suspended the Cauldron hovered down as the central hatch, underneath, opened. Passing the elevated platforms and catwalks they slowly descended toward, and into, outer space.

"Escorts, you may start your launch," Joshua transmitted. The two probe ships, which he was speaking to, were on standby waiting for the order. "I'll see you guys at the outer rim." The two IF-18s, long after they disengaged their conventional propulsory systems, imploded into bright matter/anti-matter lights as they made their jump into matrix.

The small task force, aboard the Cauldron, was now free and gained distance away from the Regalia starbase. The smooth hum of the engines purred as the cruiser flew into position.

Joshua than initiated the symmetry drive, forcing matter and anti-mater into a controlled collision. The ship's underbelly crystal orifice lit up as colliding opposites of pure energy unleashed, safely within the crystal chamber. The energy, like a bright flash from a cannon, engulfed the ship, and by immeasurable velocity, the Cauldron jumped into the distant.

BLUE ARCS OF JET fuel shot out from the ship's retronics after the Cauldron jumped out of the matrix field. The two probe ships were awaiting their arrival. In the dark starry background was, at a distant, a faintly visible blue mist of nebulous gas. They have reached the outer rim and the unknown beckoned them from beyond. But, for the moment, something else did.

"My God, what was that," a violent jolt startled the marshal. After he grabbed hold of his senses he realized what just occurred. He jumped out of curved-space and into a swarm of space junk. Flying debris littered this section of space, refuse from the Dominion.

Only the pilots' quick reflexes kept them away from disaster. To get to the other side, to continue on with their assignments, they would have to navigate through the swarm. Like three ballistic missiles they charged through the various scrap heaps using their thermals to punch their way onward. Old and abandoned satellites, and other refuse that can't even be categorized, were blown up. Just about anything that got in their flight path, which would hinder their mission, was targeted.

With thermal lasers on full power Joshua fired blowing up a small weather satellite. Creating a stunning fireball he flew through the dust and shrapnel, which was all that was left. Josh voiced out a war cry in delight. This was his idea of fun, an emotional release, to ease his tensions unaware for the moment he still had a job to do.

Over confidence doomed one of the IF-18 pilots as he blasted one of his targets and did not make a quick enough evasion to avoid the aftermath. The larger piece of shrapnel slammed into his portside wing. He was abruptly jerked off course with a damaged wing. The IF-18 swerved; nose down, into another piece of metal shrapnel. With a deafening explosion the ship was lost.

Damn it, the marshal thought to himself when he witnessed the collision. But he had to focus on the mission at hand or he'll meet the same fate. In his line of sight was an object he couldn't even describe and he was heading right toward it. A spiraling funnel was the best he could come up with. Distracted by the recent loss of his fellow pilot he couldn't avoid the huge funnel shape, whatever it was, so he decided to go through it.

Unyielding, the Cauldron shot through the hollow funnel. It seemed big enough for his ship to travel into and out the other end, or he hoped. Piloting blind, once he was inside the drifting mass, he navigated. With only faintly visible starlight at the opposite end to guide him, he snaked his way through the cone as he held his breath. The ship shot out so fast it was a mere blur; he eventually made it. As he did he blasted another piece of junk, which just so happened to be there, waiting for him at the exiting end.

Now that they were free from anymore-dangerous matter he assumed a position at a safe distance. Joshua's nerves settled as he threw a sigh of relief. The IF-18 probe ship took point while the Cauldron stood behind. Carrier probes would have to be launched since beyond this point was uncharted territory. A digital map would have to be laid out if they were to successfully navigate through whatever it was out there. Joshua, and his team, could do nothing more except wait for the probe ship to do what it was designed to do.

"Amazing, this heap has cadence tracking," the marshal was impressed. "Turn it on my old friend, we can see what's out there."

Jagaba was impressed as well as he initiated the tracking system, which was integrated into the ship's sensory systems. As the lights in the cockpit dimmed a laser image appeared in the form of a stellar chart. The chart was graphed in degrees and longitudes that would give a detailed description of their trajectory, once the probe markers were in place.

"Very stealthy," the marshal was impressed. "We can probe the entire universe and nobody would know it." Joshua was excited that he held all this technology at his fingertips and he cherished this new prototype craft as though it was his own. "Now we have to wait for the IF-18 pilot to do his job, the ball is now in his court."

As the reptilian fidgeted a little, slithering his tongue and ripping his tail about, he inquired. "Yes, I hope it doesn't take too long either," Hollands responding to Jagaba's mental telepathy.

A hatch in the bridge snapped open bring in unwanted light from the outside chamber as Jackie entered. Consequently Joshua reacted angrily, "Close it."

"What's going on?" Jackie asked ignoring the negative tone in the marshal's voice. She walked casually toward the marshal and rested her arm on the back support of his chair, looking over his shoulder.

"Nothing right now. Beyond this point we'll be out of range from centralnet station," Joshua continued, "In a few minutes our probe ship will launch markers throughout the quadrant to give us safe passage."

"And than what?, Jackie questioned as she stood cheek to cheek with the marshal.

"And than we just follow the coordinates given and get your hair out of my face," the marshal said with sharp annoyance. He was about to take leave perhaps because of her female presence, "Here, take my seat," he said as he stood up. "I'm going to check up on the rest of the ship, do a diagnostic sweep." The marshal than removed himself from the bridge as Jackie filled in his vacant seat.

Leaving behind the darkened bridge he worked his way through a cramped corridor, with a scanner now in his hand. Trying to make good use of his free time he did a diagnostic sweep on the ship's harmonics. Before he would continue on his mission he wanted to know, if the unexpected debris he had collisions with, had not damaged his extraordinary cruiser.

He eyeballed the readout display on his sensor device as he pressed keys and waved the device within arm's reach proximity directed at the surrounding equipment. With harmonic computations in his head, as he read the sensor readings, something abruptly shifted his attention. A disturbing shuddering came from one of the smaller compartments to his left. Nothing on his device would explain the sounds so he approached the compartment to investigate. Pressing the eject button the compartment door swung open and, to his surprise, revealed the source of the sounds. What popped out was a young boy who was hidden in the small storage compartment, pressed against the door cover. The marshal took a step back as the young Randella fell to the floor. The marshal recognized him thereafter.

"What on earth are you doing here? You picked the wrong ship to stowaway in," the marshal said as he snatched his interlink. "Jackie, I hope we got room for one more cause we have a passenger."

"Marshal, the markers are almost in place," was Jackie's response to the marshal's transmission. "We're getting close to the launch window."

"Copy that," after which, Joshua clipped his interlink back to its retainer while looking down at the intruder the whole time.

When the marshal made it back to the bridge Jackie gave up his seat and he retook the helm. The cadence tracker continued to operate and showed the probe markers, which were recently launched. The markers emitted transmission signals, which would bounce back to display any obstacle they may face along the way.

"Doesn't seem too far away," she observed. "Should be no problem."

"Yea, no problem," the marshal replied with a tone of sarcasm. As he explained he pointed to the various marker beacons, "All we have to do is avoid this binary star cluster and, this here, nuclear drift."

Once the ship's computer had the tracking coordinates a red light indicator emitted, accompanied by a high pitch/low tone alarm. "The coordinates are set, strap yourselves in," the marshal said as he buckled himself down with his chair's safety harness. "We launch in fifteen seconds."

Crimson, still affixed in his reciprocal station, had the task to crosslink the transmitting signals to the navigation system. Traveling through interstellar space, especially uncharted space, was not an easy task. The regenalt, who served to augment the ship's technology, would make sure no errors were made.

After fifteen seconds had elapsed the Cauldron was engulfed in light and than vanished within it. The ultra enhanced speed of a symmetry driven craft was too immense to follow by the naked eye. Even though they were traveling from point A to B the jump resembled more of an implosion than a ship covering distance.

The first split second of tranquility was broken when the ominous-looking grayish bird darted out of the matrix, which was followed by an explosive sound. As the retronics slowed their propulsion they knew they've arrived at their first marker.

A slight jolt of the ship unnerved them when the Cauldron skimmed across an unforeseen orbital field. They were a mere kilometer away from breaking orbit of a dark moon, its blue exosphere outline made it visible. They were in the midst of several dark moons and Josh realized this, with enough ample time, to pilot his craft away from a possible collision. A brilliant blue light emanated from a dense sun underneath the black cosmic bodies.

"Command sent, navigate through free space zone. Avoid orbital gravity," was Crimson's style of dialogue, the regenalt cautioned using his own computer language.

"Yea, thanks for the tip," Josh retorted as he tried to recollect himself. "Awaiting next jump, fifteen seconds."

Before Joshua would've had the chance to adore the magnificent display of the astronomical phenomenon they've encountered, they made the second jump into matrix. Disappearing into the light, they would have to make several such pulse jumps to get to their destination.

Jumping out of the matrix field, again, the ship slowed to moderate speeds, which was helped by retronic counter-thrust. The Cauldron reached the second marker.

Within the ship's path was a blinding white hole, opposite of that of a black hole, sucking in nuclear hydrogen of immense power. The swirling hole seemed to be feeding on it, sucking it in and discharging the ionized waste at the other end of this vortex.

"My God! Have you ever seen such a thing?" Joshua said as he gazed upon it. He was spellbound by the exhibition.

"The radiation that thing is generating could be lethal if we're exposed," Jackie quietly warned.

"Don't worry," Joshua said as he tapped the control panel. "The light circuits tells me the microbe filters are on and working," Josh assured. "That stuff should seep right through the outer vents like a sieve."

"We have ten seconds before the finale jump-," a distracting sound beeped from the control terminal before Josh had a chance to finish his sentence. "We have a power supply failure," he said as he stood up. "I'll have to reestablish."

"Jag, you got the helm. Abort launch," the marshal issued the order. "On my command, resume count down." The marshal could sense the worries in his copilot but Josh dismissed it as he vacated the bridge.

Exiting the bridge he reached the sub-chamber and than made it to the next hatch, which led him to the passenger lobby. Along the way he quickened his steps wanting to waste no time. Once he was within the lobby he headed toward the maintenance bay passing Randella, who sat Indian fashion on the floor. Entering the bay, which was another small sub-chamber cluttered with mechanical parts, he entered a central stairway. The spiral stairway led below deck to the propulsion drive pit.

Going down the chain of steps, he skipped a step, making a short jump unto the landing. He than leaped over the handrail, from the low elevated landing, to the floor. The drive deck was spacious and non-assuming and was surrounded by gray walls and floor, and overhead, junction cables and pipes snaked along the ceiling.

The symmetry drive was emplaced within a pit and fused into the floor's structure, in the central portion of the deck. The symmetry was an elongated piston generator, which had mounted modules and binary antenna links. These links were affixed in pairs and emitted crosscurrents of energy, but for the moment, the symmetry drive was dormant.

Josh pressed the transceiver button, while still keeping his interlink attached to his belt, he spoke, "Possibly one of the binary links are burned out." Joshua apprised those who were at the bridge. The marshal's copilot and Jackie kept their ears open, as they heard Joshua's voice through the speaker's intercom, and they awaited further status updates.

Josh squatted down low for a closer look at the drive to analyze and isolate the problem, and hopefully fix it. Two meters long, and a half-meter in width, Josh searched for the problem from one end to the other. Not finding the possible cause of the malfunction he stood back up, to walk around the other side. He than squatted low as before to investigate further.

To his relief he found what he was looking for, "This is it," he relayed to the bridge. His interlink was still clipped to his side with the transceiver on, which kept his hands free to work.

"This is what?"

"One binary link severed," he relayed again, "possibly from the stress of jumping and stopping, sequentially."

"How do you plan on fixing it?" she transmitted back.

"Looks like there's enough wire, I'll just twist the two ends together."

Doing as he said he slid the bent wire between his finger to straighten it and than, taking the binary half of the antenna, he twisted both ends together to form a connection. Once this was achieved he stood up and backed away, "Ok, we're go for count down."

"Roger that, we go in fifteen seconds," Jackie relayed back as Jagaba complied.

After an elapse of only two seconds a sudden acceleration of the Cauldron propelled his body back and to the floor. As he hit the floor, a few paces from where he was at, his entire surroundings turned bright white as though pure energy was taking over. And than, at an instant, nothing existed but broken down atoms and molecules. They were now within the matrix field.

Only a micro second passed and their destination had been reached. As the ship, again, returned to normal space the surroundings, within the drive section, also returned to normal. Joshua raised himself up from his fallen position. The pulse jump was so instantaneous he felt almost unaware that any trajectory took place.

"Marshal, are you alright," Jackie transmitted from the bridge.

Joshua's interlink received Corin's transmission but he was still a little bit groggy, from the fall, to answer right away. While he tried to shake loose the proverbial stars circling around his head, and bring himself back to his senses, he replied, "What happened to my fifteen seconds?"

"You might want to see this," Jackie responded.

"What's wrong?"

"Just come here."

Finally to his feet he thought to himself, what else could go wrong? Contemplating that question he made his way back up the spiral staircase and than he followed the same path from which he came from.

As soon as he was back at the bridge he viewed what was ahead, the Cauldron was facing a gigantic nebula. Joshua pondered over it curiously as he continued to view it through the windscreen. Jackie relinquished his chair as he approached allowing him to retain position as captain. He must decide his next course of action.

"There's no outpost, just a gaseous cloud," Joshua said in dissatisfaction. The marshal felt bitterness toward himself, following orders that seemed to have led him to this dead end. Disheartened as he thought about the lengths he went through, not to mention the loss of life.

"According to the sensor readings there's something in there," she said as she tapped on the console. "The carrier probe reports a central star."

"Most nebula occurrences have a central star that emits ionized gas, hence, you have your nebula," Josh remarked.

"I don't need a cosmology lesson," Jackie snapped back. "The coordinates, which were extracted from the Rogue's navigational system, led us here." She continued, "There might be something else in there, a planetoid maybe."

"A planet shrouded within a nebula," he marveled at the idea. "Well I don't plan on going back empty handed, lets find out." The marshal than reassumed the helm controls.

Deciphering the logistics between them and the carrier probe the marshal had begun the ship's forward momentum. Periodically he'd glance at the tracking screen as he steered to keep the Cauldron on the correct course. As the marshal followed his routine Jagaba kept his watch on the ship's sensors in case of an ambush. And Jackie, the only one without the distraction of activity, sat behind the other two with nothing to do but think of the possible dangers that might be ahead.

On slow and cautious procession the starcruiser moved straight forward as they entered the white cloud of the nebula. The white cloud, which should be logged and categorized as the Angelica Josh thought, seem to spread out limitlessly. The Cauldron, with its wide wingspan, almost seemed to be gliding rather than being driven by engine thrust. Driven not gliding, this awe of illusion persisted onward approaching closer to the carrier beacon's point of emission.

They could see nothing through the windscreen except for the gaseous mist that surrounded them. Their only eyes was the carrier beacon from their onboard tracking device, which transmitted the frequency they were following. The beacon signal grew more intense the closer they got and everybody aboard hoped for the best, as their alertness intensified as well. Jagaba continued to observe the sensors while keeping all weapon systems armed and ready but so far nothing critical was at hand.

"Nothing but a foggy mist," Joshua worried. "This thick blanket of gas makes a good covering for an ambush." Jagaba was equally worried and he sent a mindlink that expressed that emotion to his old friend and senior pilot, "Yes Jagaba, I don't like surprises either."

Their hopes of non-resistance were distinguished when a laser bolt flashed out of nowhere. The bolt skimmed across the exterior surface of their ship, causing no damage, but sent shock waves up their spines. Like cloud formations in a blue sky there were irregular pockets of space, which showed the starlight and their aggressor as the brigand moved in for another shot.

"HEL-bomber," Joshua shouted out. At an instant the marshal made an evasive maneuver steering portside down to avoid an incoming assault. The laser bolt passed by his below deck, which came near to impact. "Turning ninety degrees to stern," Josh announced as he maneuvered in such a manner.

"Too much excitement for me," Jackie said feeling somewhat disconcerted. "Kill the bastard."

To protect his rear flank, the nose of the Cauldron was now pointing in the direction from where the HEL-bomber was last detected. The long wingspan maintained the same aura effect as it glided through the nebula while they searched out their attacker.

Pushing forward they would occasionally encounter a clearing in the nebula with the hope that they might spot their assailant.

"Initiating EMP spread," Joshua apprised the rest of his crew. "I'll do a sweep on the parameter. If we're lucky, we can neutralize his circuitry and weapon systems."

"We don't have time for this," Jackie grew weary.

"We don't want him to flank us from behind and taking a pot shot at us," Joshua expressed what he was thinking.

The prism emitter, which was mounted underneath the forward helm, unleashed a transparent blue beam of electromagnetic pulse rays. As it did it swept a clear path while the Cauldron maintained its slow momentum, scouting out the enemy craft. "Now, lets see where you are," Joshua said to himself as he looked onward.

Doing a forty-five degree sweep and probe with a pulsating spread of laser light, which looked like a triangulated band instead of a streak, the Cauldron followed behind through the safe passage. Everybody aboard bore in mind that the chance of neutralizing any target blind was not much better than searching for a needle in a cosmic haystack. Understanding the odds they suddenly encountered a pleasant surprise as they approached a pocket in the cloud.

"There it is," Joshua said to his relief. "The EMP seemed to have done the trick."

The HEL-bomber seemed to have lost all maneuverability, it drifted without a surge of power or spark of life. The Cauldron moved in toward it, as though it was a carnivorous bird moving in to capture its prey. Once the starcruiser was within a dominating reach of the disabled ship Josh disengaged his thrusters. The cruiser was now at a complete stop overshadowing the smaller vessel.

"Well, what are you waiting for? Blow him to hell and lets get this mission over with," Jackie's anxiety overwhelmed her a little.

"Why waste the energy?" the marshal commented. "He isn't going anywhere and he lost life support, he's dead anyway. He can't even dispatch a distress signal for help."

The HEL-bomber was literally dead in space and the marshal quickly dismissed it from his mind; as he spun the Cauldron a hundred and eighty degrees, to head back toward the carrier probe's position. As soon as the half revolution was made the Cauldron stood fast and than, when the marshal exerted the fuel injectors, they lunged ahead.

The swirling effect of the Angelica clouds would be of great strategic importance, reason being, most sensors would be unable to penetrate this cosmic mass. Good for an ambush, as Joshua stated, but also good for concealment.

As the crew of the Cauldron slowly approached the center of the nebula the gas gradually dissipated to show what might have been hidden, if anything. Conceal what, was a question they need not answer, because they now stood before a lingering solar system.

The perfect concentric balance of alignment of the celestial bodies, meaning the sun; moon; the planet, engendered life. A single sun accompanied a larger planet. The sun's ultraviolet rays pierced the planet's thick ozone layer with just enough heat to sustain the living, if such a living could exist there. The white sphere revolved on its axis, which indicated the planet was alive with its own heartbeat generating gravity and the cycle of the seasons. Only partial heat, radiating from the sun, reached the planet's surface that allowed life to live but in an extremely arctic environment.

"Kahlidan," Joshua murmured.

"What?"

"Kahlidan, I've read in the mythological books of such a planet," Josh recalled back to his school days. "Hidden behind a veil of clouds, I think this qualifies as such."

Joshua snapped out of his awestruck state and redirected his attention to his immediate concerns, "What does the spectrometer read?"

"Atmospheric composition, comparable levels of nitrogen and oxygen to our own," she than said looking up from the spectrometer display, "But slightly higher levels of carbon dioxide."

Jagaba seemed agitated since it was his duty, as copilot, to operate the secondary controls, which included reading the spectrum analysis. But his cerebral influence, even if undirected, gave Jackie the creeps but she tried to dismiss it and kept her distance.

"This is incredible," she continued looking down at the sensor readings again, "According to these readings there's an abundance of life on the surface, more than I've ever seen."

"Well, than we're safe to do a little sight seeing without environmental suits," the marshal wondered. "Jagaba, punch her into gear. Prepare for orbital entry."

From being idle the thrusters ignited. Jagaba continued to watch the sensory systems while Josh piloted the Cauldron toward the undiscovered planet, which lay ahead of them. Everything within their parameter seemed normal and unobtrusive so they continued steadily; but they were attacked once so they continued with caution.

"Jackie, go to the back and break out some thermal gear, we're going to need them," Joshua spoke out. He picked up the reptilian's thoughts as easily as if Jagaba spoke verbally. "Jagaba says there's a storm front moving in directly below us," the marshal was simply reminded. Without the storm it would be well below zero anyway and they would need the proper insulation if they were to venture out. "Lets hope we don't have to land there, even with the proper clothing we would have to wait until the storm passes.

"Ok," she acknowledged and than turned and left.

Randella was awake from his previous catnap as Jackie entered the lobby. As a typical eight year old would he was unsettled and toying with just about anything at his reach that struck his fancy. Presently he was intrigued by a gyrocompass he just so happened to find.

"You break it kid and the marshal will have your hide," she said as she walked passed the youngster.

Her hands met the equipment lockers immediately, which was at the opposite end of the lobby near the hatchway. She quickly retracted the bolt locks and swung open the doors. She expeditiously took out, throwing it to the ground, insulation coats and head gear.

With an arm full of survival attire something unbalanced her. Something from outside the ship, like an external blow, shook the ship and the instant jolt threw her off her feet. The pile of clothes she threw to the floor cushioned her fall.

"What the hell was that," she protested.

"Jackie, buckle in," the marshal shouted the ship's intercom. "We got company."

"Buckle in kid," she barked out as she grabbed hold to Randella's lapel. She roughly led the bewildered boy, almost throwing him to his seat. She than grabbed both ends of the seat's harness and than fastened them together, no time for her to be gentle. As she pulled the slack straps tight the possibilities of what might be circled in her head.

"It's too tight."

"Not now kid, we're in trouble," she said as she sped off to the bridge.

"What's up?" Jackie asked as she rushed to Joshua's side.

The marshal was still at the helm when he replied, "Another one."

Momentarily ago they received a hit but the Cauldron's repulsion shields deflected the laser blast. Another shudder, caused by an incoming blast, jostled all who were aboard. Jackie held on to the backrest of Joshua's seat to keep her from falling a second time.

At least four enemy fighters were spread out in attack formation as they prepared to engage the battered starcruiser. Fortunately, for the crew, the Cauldron had a well-powered defense system or the crew would be experiencing a lot more than just a rough ride.

One of the brigand fighters swerved in on an attack run. Instantly the enemy's target finder locked on as the Cauldron stood still, but ready to react. Once the HEL-bomber's targeting system indicated an affirmation to fire the brigand unleashed a barrage of it.

The cruiser's evasive maneuver was made as the bolts of energy shot out toward it. Dipping the starboard wing down, the Cauldron was almost in a side vertical position, as the first couple of laser bolts skimmed its belly and the last few missed entirely. The brigand did a flyby and than maneuvered around to prepare a secondary attack.

"I had enough of this," the marshal said. "Jagaba, maximum thrust."

"Wait a minute, let me-," Jackie was cut short when a tremendous amount of g-force was suddenly induced. Joshua decided to engage the enemy with as must force as he could muster; which made Jackie drop on her butt again, but this time the chair behind softened her fall.

The Cauldron shot slightly up starboard toward the brigand, to counter the assault. Like a knife, the starcruiser cut through a two bombers' attack positions destroying one of them by thermal as the Cauldron flew between them rapidly. The Cauldron's single thermal blast ignited the doomed brigand fighter into fire and smoke. The other brigand was thrown away to his starboard side by the sudden percussion. The brigandeer, when he regained control of his steering, cleared away to avoid flying fragments.

Harnessed securely to her seat Jackie gripped onto the strap that was across her chest. Sitting directly behind the marshal she almost had her eyes shut as she was being bounced around. "Talk about your rough ride," she managed to say.

"Jackie, assume the ball turret," Joshua ordered.

"I feel quite safe right here."

"Don't argue with me," Joshua snapped back never taking his eyes off the forward view. "You need to make sure they don't flank us from behind.

After she reluctantly unfastened her safety harness, cursing her disapproval to herself, she fumbled her way off the bridge and toward the lower deck. Percussion, particle turbulence, and acceleration force made walking unstable so she had to brace herself against anything solid along the way.

The surrounding space parameter, near Khalidan's orbit, was still congested by laser fire. The larger triangulated-winged cruiser received a few hits but the repulsion shields were still holding and their bird sustained little damage.

Still playing the evasive strategy the Cauldron recognized the right time for another offensive strike. As another HEL-bomber maneuvered in from behind the starcruiser the marshal revolved 180-degrees to face it. An instant flicker of an energy blast was unleashed, which shot across and sliced through the imposing attacker. More fire and smoke was caused in the aftermath from another doomed brigand gunship.

Jackie just recently commandeered her turret chamber. The cruiser's 180 maneuver forced her body to the extreme side, throwing her against the chamber's armor plating.

"Next time warn me when you make a maneuver like that," she dispatched her exasperations to the bridge.

"Keep alert Jackie," was the marshal's response.

Her body was, again, thrown to the side when Josh maneuvered in the same 180 turn as the cruiser prepared for another engagement. When Josh made his turn the tail gun instantly had the line of sight to a target; Jackie took advantage and fired. At an instant a third brigand bomber met ill fate as it blew up into tiny fragments.

"How's that for being alert," was Jackie's quick response.

The Cauldron search out for the last of the assailants, the nose of the ship in the direction of the planet below. The starcruiser held a static position while Jagaba scanned for another possible encounter, hopefully their last.

Jackie kept her attention on their rear flank. "Where is he?" she whispered to herself looking out.

Another laser bolt suddenly shot out from overhead, catching them by surprise. Joshua dropped the wing portside to evade but the blast skimmed across the portside wing, the evasion wasn't quick enough. The last hit was too much for the Cauldron to handle and the repulsion shield's depleted some of the ship's energy supply.

"Engage at maximum," Joshua commanded.

Their bodies were suddenly pressed hard against their seats as they endured more g-force. The HEL-bomber swerved downward passing the Cauldron from overhead. The starcruiser's conventional thrusters burned excessive amounts of fuel to keep up with its smaller foe.

In an almost vertical position the Cauldron made an acrobatic move. Pushing the thrusters to the breaking point the cruiser swerved upward and than over and than banked vertically for a descent. Maneuvering downward with the starboard wing tilted they propelled like a ballistic missile, in pursuit of the now evading attacking ship.

"There he is," Joshua said to himself.

The HEL-bomber than turned into the direction of the Cauldron as the brigandeer prepared for another assault. The marshal triggered his forward guns to end the battle quickly. The thermal lasers streaked across toward the attacking ship. The HEL-bomber, increasing its speed, attempted to avoid the laser blasts by banking into a complete vertical position. The brigand did not have ample time though to make the evasion soon enough. The cruiser's fire bolts struck an unessential part of the HEL-bomber, maiming not destroying it. The brigand flew pass the Cauldron from overhead; again, leaving a trail of smoke.

After he performed his half somersault maneuver, and than ending with the Cauldron's starboard wing down, the marshal engaged the enemy again. After he hauled up, around, and turned his ship the marshal lunged ahead. The bow section was facing their point of destination, Kahlidan.

In addition to the white/blue planet the Cauldron's crew were also facing their broken down enemy craft; near the planet's thinly blue layer of the exosphere. The HEL-bomber was still discharging smoke, from the stern, which was where the impact met. Sparks spat out from the damaged power generator, which resembled a swarm of fireflies in the night sky. The brigand ship made very little momentum, if any at the moment, as though the pilot lost all navigation control or he was trying to decide what to do next.

Eventually deciding death rather than surrender the bomber reestablished an attack mode, with some fight still left in her. Unable to engage at maximum thrust the brigand used as much power his ship had to offer. He turned and aligned his main gun in the direction of the cruiser. The Cauldron had no intention of being fired upon so the marshal executed the first move, before the brigand had the option of doing so. The Cauldron's thermal cannons fired unleashing more lasers as the guns recoiled within their housing. As the brigand moved in even closer for a kill strike his ship, unexpectedly, banked its wings to avoid the Cauldron's fire. Unable to avoid the blasts completely the laser bolt grazed across the surface beneath the HEL-bomber's starboard wing. The blast caused damage to the wing's piston jack incapacitating the bomber's guiding fin. Because of the manner of the blow it caused the HEL-bomber to commence a rifling effect, spiraling like a projectile.

"He's attempting to ram us," the marshal shouted as he begun to exert his ship's steering.

To avoid collision Josh utilized his ship's repellors to create a downward thrust. Like an aerolift the Cauldron attained vertical flight by lifting up as the HEL-bomber spiraled even closer, and gaining speed. Like the brigand ship, unable to avoid being hit, the cruiser was unable to thwart a collision entirely. The HEL-bomber rammed into the starcruiser's lower fuselage, not mortally inflictive, but bad enough to hinder flight capabilities. The spiraling enemy ship continued outward into space, after hitting the cruiser, until it eventually exploded by a breach of its fuel cylinders.

A red light fire alarm blared as smoke crept through the crevices of the hatch. The smoke was beginning to accumulate heavily in the bridge and the marshal, and his lizard friend, knew they had to respond quickly. All alert systems lit up on their console as Josh jumped out of his seat to take action.

"Jackie, get out of that metal encasement and go to the drive pit. You have a fire to put out," Josh transmitted as he had his own fire to put out. "Jagaba, keep her steady. We'll have to make an emergency landing."

With a closed fist he hit the accessor button and the hatch snapped open. Without delay he entered the passenger hold, coughing and choking on the thick blanket of smoke as he did so. Heat emanated from the terminal's wire conduits, which ran up the wall and into the terminal's junction box. With a quick eye he saw a medium size fire developing, spreading and growing to be a larger one.

Before he lunged ahead to eradicate the flames he heard, faintly, coughing originating from the young boy as he gasped for air.

Overwhelmed by the fumes and smoke Randella tried, to no avail, to free himself from the seat's harness of which was still strapped across his chest. Without undue wasted time or action the marshal quickly helped the boy. Randella frantically pulled and tugged at his harness as the smoke blinded him; he was completely at the mercy of the circumstance. Anxiety took over that kept him from freeing himself on his own.

Joshua had to attempt a rescue so he hurried to Randella's aid. Getting in close to see what his hands were doing, the marshal pulled buckle lever back to unlock and separate the straps' hold on the boy. Quickly, after this was done, he forced Randella underneath the chair where the smoke was less dominant.

"Stay there boy, keep your face down and your eyes closed," the marshal said with a critical tone.

With Randella safe, for the moment, he concentrated on the fire he had to put out. Josh snatched a nearby fire extinguisher from its retainer to quickly dampen out the flames, which grew more intense with each passing minute. Unwilling to get too close to the heat he forced himself to do his utmost. Squeezing the initiator release he triggered the fire retardant to the main spread and vital areas. The fog of CO_2 consumed and suffocated the flames, fire needs oxygen to feed on and Josh denied it that.

While he was fighting the fire he slapped, which was off to his side and close to him, the intercom button and than he spoke, "Jackie, report."

The propulsion drive section was saturated with carbon dioxide coolant, which absorbed the fire. A burning stench, like charcoal, was in air from the burning of wire insulation. The electrical circuitry was scorched beyond repair, which explained the unpleasant odor. With the fire extinguisher still in her hand Jackie seemed to have the situation under control.

"I made quite the mess," Jackie transmitted back through the intercom system, "but the fire's out." As she spoke waving her hand about she fanned the foggy remnant away from her face, choking a little on it.

"Copy that, good work," the marshal said as he continued to fight off his predicament. .

Joshua calmed down a little though after he stifled out what was left. There were still some surfaces, in and along the piping, which was still hot to the touch. A new fire could ignite, which was what Josh took aims to prevent. He went over those areas again with the coolant gas to be assured that the fire will not rekindle. When his suspicions were no more he released the initiator as he held his breath. He tried to refrain from choking on the fire absorbent fumes.

Joshua lowered and eased his arm with the fire extinguisher still in his hand. He choked a little on the remnant aftermath, which was slowly dissipating. The emergency had bee quelled, or so he thought. He suddenly and abruptly felt a solid presence, which he perceived to be solid, but in fact it was an intrusion in his mind, telepathic in origin, it was a warning.

"Jackie, find yourself a seat and strap yourself in," Joshua spoke through the intercom as he quickly threw aside the fire extinguisher. "We're going in on a crash landing."

Before he had to troubleshoot his next emergency he quickly snatch the boy, from underneath the seat, and threw him into the chair. "Strap yourself in kid," the marshal advised helping him. Once the marshal was confident the boy would comply he sharply made his way to the bridge. The ungentle treatment implemented by the legionnaire caused bewilderment in Randella's emotions.

Joshua assumed his pilot seat once again while sensing the worries in his copilot. Jagaba tried, with all his might, to steer the craft toward a safe landing zone of the hostile planet below.

"Thanks for the warning," was all Joshua had time to say as he took over the helm. Jagaba fidgeted and sprung out extrasensory emotions, which were erratic, which Josh was puzzled to decipher. "Yes, I'm worried to."

G-force and atmospheric friction strained the structural integrity of their ship. They're now breaking Khalidan's planetary orbit while Josh asserted himself to keep the bow slightly elevated, for a hopeful smooth landing. During the course of the marshal's intent Jagaba was attentive to the ship's diagnostic rendering. They both strived to make sure no further damage will be inflicted anymore than need be.

Now they entered the stratosphere and the marshal was still exerting his strength to control his ship. Jagaba was prepared to engage the ship's retronics to slow their free fall; since the marshal had his hands full at the moment, he eventually made the engagement. Now within the planet's troposphere they were now enduring weather-like turbulence and strong crosswinds.

"I can't see anything," Josh exasperated. "The weather conditions are interfering with the ship's mooring guidance system." The Cauldron's retronics slowed their descent, at least a little. "Extend landing gear," Joshua ordered with a pressing tone in his voice.

As the landing gear lowered the bow section elevated slightly more while it was swiftly reaching the ground. The marshal strained less on the steering but his mental stress was still overpowering. Turbulence and crosswinds decreased in intensity but it was still strong enough for the crew to discern that they were within a dangerous storm procession. Suddenly a giant jolt stunned the pilots as their bodies dropped frontward, their chests pressed against their harnesses. Shocked by the quick impact but their security belt straps kept them safely affixed to their chairs, they have reached land.

"**Huh, what a rush,**" Josh showed signs of fatigue and sore muscles. "Jag, are you ok?" Jagaba seemed dead for a while and than abruptly showed movement, which meant he was alive. "Good." The marshal than swayed his attention to his other crew member as he leaned in close to the console, "Jackie, are you alright? You still have all your vital parts?" the marshal spoke through the ship's intercom.

"Yea, just barely," she said as she waved the dust and smoke away from her face. She sat beside Randella in the passenger hold; quickly reacting to the marshal's advice she entered the hold following the Joshua's departure to the bridge.

Finally relieving himself from his harness the marshal took an analytical view of their situation, "We seem to still have power," Josh said as he looked upon the terminal. He was now at his feet, leaning against the encasing, still checking over his control command center. 'We've landed right in the midst of the storm," he continued as he observed the digital relays. "We have hurricane-like winds and the chill factor is 80 below." Even the thought of those unforgiving weather conditions caused him to shiver a bit. "That's cold enough to peel the skin off your face." As he spoke Jagaba was still in his seat but the marshal was mostly thinking out loud. "I guess we have to wait for the storm to pass before we can venture out," now his voice was directed toward his crew.

Hollands than shifted his attention to the back of the bridge as he turned to look behind, "Crimson, are you still operational?" As he asked the question openly he walked over to stand beside the regenalt.

"Acknowledge," Crimson responded with his usual computer mannerism.

Looking in close at the reciprocal's intricate link-ups and bolting mechanisms Joshua knew that he knew nothing about cybernetic technology. His hand on the regenalt's shoulder, and looking in for a close see, was more of a show of concern for his crewman. But he took the regenalt's response as a truthful one, "I hope so, we need your help."

The marshal's gaze shifted back to the reptilian, "Jag, take a scanner and check the rest of the ship and give me a damage report." Jagaba complied by unfastening himself from his chair, "and I'll check on our stowaway." Joshua exited through the hatchway to the passenger hold, and soon after, Jagaba vacated as well to carry out the order given.

"Kid, are you ok?" the marshal asked the boy as he rested his hand behind Randella's neck. The young lad simply threw the marshal a blank stare and than nodded slightly. "Good," the marshal replied.

At this point in time Jackie unbuckled herself from the long bench, her clothes were ruffled and she was showing obvious signs of weariness. "If the rest of the mission is going to be like this drop me off at the nearest shuttle station," she said, exasperated. Standing near and facing each other Joshua responded with a cocky grin.

While the marshal, and his mercenary cohort, conversed Jagaba entered the lobby and walked passed the three. Moving steadily and ominously, his clawed feet scraping the floor, which left a faintly visible trail of scratch marks. His tongue slithered, which gave him bearing like an antenna, and his tail whipped behind him giving him balance as he moved. His slender, muscular, and prehistoric features resembled a carnivore; from ages lost. The awesome presence of the reptilian was enough to turn heads, which Josh and Jackie did, but than they went about their conversation as Jagaba took leave.

"The meteoptic relays indicate we've landed right in the outskirts of a massive snow squall," Joshua explained. "It's too cold to go out on a reconnaissance."

"So what's our next move?"

"Well, Jagaba is going to probe the ship for any damages that needs repair," Josh continued, "and I'll go to the cargo bay to prep the equipment."

"And what about me?"

Joshua threw her another cocky grin as Randella scurried pass the two, "You're on watch detail, make sure our young party crasher doesn't get into trouble."

"I haven't agreed to come with you to baby-sit."

"Until the storm subsides we have no use of you." When Jackie was about to rebut the marshal stopped the conversation short, "I'm not in mood to hear it, just stay out of my way for now," was the last thing Josh said to her, emotionally unaffected, as he walked away.

The cargo bay was quiet except for the eerie whistling sounds from the turbulent winds coming from outside. The bay was situated the closest, to the outside elements, within the Cauldron's fusion metal exoskeleton. All the stored equipment and vehicles were inactive and no other sort of movement was evident, until, Joshua entered the bay through the ingress.

He was preparing to scavenge through the stockpile of equipment to see what supplies he'll need. There were a few bulks of something, which were covered and tied with tarps. The marshal approached one of them, as though whatever was underneath would be of great necessity to him. Bound to the floor by lace ties he casually loosened the ends of them. Once the tarp was loose and free to be removed, he did so, revealing what was concealed. A hover propulsion vehicle known as a scudder craft, which he'll need to skirmish the outside terrain.

With an eight-cylinder turbine engine, thermal laser mounts, and a refueling cell near the front cowling; the scudder was ideal for recon. There was enough room in the occupancy seats and the side standing planks for a four-crew reconnaissance team. Josh walked around the scudder as he slid his hand across the outer covering with fanciful admiration. While he circled the hover vehicle he imposed a quick examination, making sure everything was in good working order.

His attention was diverted, from a slight collision, which came from behind. As he peered over his shoulder he saw nothing, and than another thud, he looked down and discovered what it was. It was a mechanical unit, stubby and square in its appearance. The medical corporation, for combat medicine and survival aid, programmed the medicorp unit. The machine moved into sight on two small tractor wheels and than stood still before Josh, as though it was greeting the marshal with a personality all its own.

Unlike regenalts, who were crosslinked to centralnet's mainframe database, these so called 'matons run on independent programs.

"Hey midget, nice to have the company," Josh acknowledged the 'maton's presence.

The marshal approached and squatted near the medicorp unit to examine it, "Nothing seems broken," he said as he looked over its electrical cords and component makeup. From being motionless the 'maton moved again, to the darkened corner where it previously kept itself. "I think you need some snow treads," the marshal thought. No response came from the 'maton since it was not equipped with vocals, it only initiates after voice commands, but the automaton would comply with silence and occasionally make jerk and sudden moves to indicate a response.

"A 'maton," a voice from behind alerted the marshal. As he jerked over his shoulder he noticed whose voice it was, his female companion.

"What are you doing here, you're supposed to be watching the boy," the marshal pointed out.

"Don't worry, he's right there," Jackie said as she pointed to the ingress. Randella was a little restless and wanted to join the two, "Stay there," Jackie told the boy, as he was about to step over the threshold.

Disappointed he was not allowed to venture in and around the bay, "Man, I can't do anything," Randella cursed. Since the grown ups were in charge he had no choice but to abide by their rules.

Jackie than shifted her attention away from the boy and said, "You seem to be well stocked," she realized as she looked around the vicinity.

"Yea, this stuff must of cost a fortune in regal currency, but I can't do the job without it," the marshal agreed and stated.

Randella was play-like and making childish noises and than tripped over the threshold, falling to the bay's floor on his elbows. "I don't have time to chat, I got preparations to make before the storm breaks," the marshal said and than fell silent. His brain detected a mindlink, which had to be originating from the only telepathic source aboard, a message from the reptilian. "Jagaba needs me at the propulsion drive," the marshal ascertained. "Take the boy back to the passenger hold and keep him there, he's getting on my nerves."

As the marshal walked down the spiral staircase his thoughts were flooded with concerns, what other problems must he deal with now? Once he was at the landing he maneuvered around a cavity in the floor, which was where the symmetry drive was emplaced.

Josh finally reached Jagaba's side, at his beck and call. They were both standing near the circuitry ports to summarize over the problems they now had to solve. The reptilian, without a linguistic spectrum of speech, enlightened his senior pilot.

"I see old friend," Josh responded. "Not something I wanted to know." The marshal stood beside Jagaba, as he shook his head in disbelief, while they both looked upon the burned out components. Josh was developing a headache, not knowing if it was from the overall tension or the cerebral crosslink Jagaba was engineering. "About how long?" his headache grew more intense. "Ok, get to it and keep me apprised."

Nothing differed much than before within the passenger lobby except slightly more on Randella's behalf as an interactive tool entranced him, which was called the mindgrid. As Jackie sat still in her seat, not longing to be there and wishing to be somewhere else, she kept a watchful eye on the youngster. The mindgrid was an apparatus made up of a hologram projector screen, a neurotransmitter headset, and chair where Randella sat; feverishly preoccupied.

Fellowship and open dialogue, with a mutual conjoiner at the other end of the link, Randella befriended a little girl. Her name and origin was kept secret, but considering the mindgrid was widely used, she could be resided at the other end of the galaxy or in some other galaxy. Her image was projected at the corner of the screen and the boy took a fancy liking to her. No words came out of the boy's mouth since there was no need. Sitting in the chair with the headset on, his thoughts were transmitted by hyperwave to the girl's neurotransmitter. Randella would dispatch through his mental thoughts and the girl would respond verbally, and contrariwise.

"I wish to see you fully," the little girl said. Not having to say a word Randella touch-screened the computer to enlarge. From being just a small head and shoulder projection at the corner of the screen her image maximized to full figure capacity.

"Your kinda cute," she smiled. Randella, who really wasn't interested in girls as yet, couldn't help but be attentive.

"How old are you?" she questioned. With his neuro headset he responded, "Eight, you're the same age as me," she replied. "What's your name?" she inquired a second answer. "Randella, nice to meet you," she stated while also sensing a tenor of agitation in the boy's neuro signals. "I'm Auria."

"My parents aren't home right now, they work in the calithian mines," she said trying to keep the conversation going. "What about you, where are you now?" All this while Randella continued to sit in his seat, appearing to be comatose, as though he was a part of the apparatus he was hooked in to. No vocal sounds came from his mouth, it was strictly a cerebral crosslink as he interacted and expressed himself. "Top secret, what does an eight-year old know that could be top secret?" His response was, she sensed, he was not allowed to talk about it. "Your weird," was her reply.

"I'm bored, I should be going," she said deciding to end the conversation right now and then. "So long Randella, I think you're nice," was her final transmission. After she disconnected the neurotransmission of her image disappeared and the hologram screen returned to the blue contrast of the command window.

A way a child would, he dismissed the converse he just had with his newfound cyber buddy and pursued something a little more interesting; he embarked upon a computer game. The game, which he logged on to, was called evaders where the user operates a thought controlled virtual gun.

The object was to knock out the evaders, which had the shape of spinning 3-D hexagons, who were protected by the blockers. The participant must race against the clock to destroy as many of the evaders as possible to keep the attacking army from destroying you. The more evaders he obliterates the more points he'll obtain.

As Randella commenced his game he became ecstatic as he begun to test his mental reflexes through the process. "Yea, let em have it," Randella said unrestrained. The sounds of the make-believe laser fire, and the bright colors being exhibited across the hologram screen, excited his senses.

While the boy was being indisposed, playing his game, Joshua appeared after the hatch snapped open. Knowing the full extent of his present crises he now sought solace in the comfort of his bridge. The marshal had to be by himself for a while to alleviate some of the worrisome tension, which grown to intolerance inside of him.

After the accessor slammed shut Joshua continued on toward his desired end, the hatch to the bridge at other side. He stopped, momentarily, between the boy and the woman of which they were both still in their seats. "What's this?" Josh pointed to the young boy.

"You told me to keep him out of your way," Jackie reminded, "he's out of the way." Joshua simply released a slight smile as he left the two behind.

Entering the bridge, "Crimson, I almost forgot about you," Joshua said as he peered to his side. The regenalt remained at his trajectory booth still plugged into the ship's computer network. The regenerative alternant sat motionless and unwavering, not knowing the strains of fatigue or impatience.

"I need you at the cargo bay," Josh issued an order. "Clean and charge the armament. We need to be fully armed and ready after the storm clears, you're on the expedition."

"Acknowledge, start task," Crimson complied. With his cybernetic hand he detached his link from the bolt coupling. Once he was free from the encirclement of the booth he departed.

The young orphan was still playing the game while under Jackie's supervision. She grew more restless by the moment for she hoped she would be put to far better use than watching a pre-teen play computer games.

Computer enhanced animation dazzled his senses and sparked his imagination. The sounds of virtual laser fire triggered his inner needs for more, so he continued to play. He was able, which was almost a psychic ability, to out maneuver the blockers and make his direct hits. As his score increased, accumulating more points, Randella became more boisterous. His loud cries of amusement agitated Jackie a little, as the uproar pierced her ears she would look up at him. She thought about ordering the boy to quiet down but she declined, at least he's staying out of trouble she thought.

His body remained motionless except for his rapid eye movement as he tracked the animated objects for annihilation. That, which could not be seen, his mind was also active as he repeatedly commanded his virtual gun to fire. As he did so Crimson walked passing him from behind but Randella had no awareness of the regenalt, he was one with the machine.

Even after the cybernetic exited the lobby Randella was still at it, scoring points. The bright multi-hue projection depicted that his virtual army was closing in as his time was running out. His tension increased as his time decreased but his aim suffered little, the adrenaline of the moment kept his reflexes sharp.

As repetitive fire continued on, and the boy prodigy was close to destroying the last of his enemy targets, an overpowering cerebral link took over. He ceased all rapid eye movement and his present awareness submitted to some unknown force. His body chilled slightly and his skin grew pale when he felt the eerie sensation, like he was being drawn into a different realm of existence.

Through his mind's eye, he saw the glimmering stars of the many distant galaxies. He felt a weird feeling of g-force, pulling and thwarting his body, as his mind was being pulled across the infinite span of interstellar space. Many spectrums of cosmic gas intrigued him even more as his mind accelerated further, traveling beyond the unknown. The bright remoras seemed to dance as he rapidly sped through and pass the celestial entities. Worlds and their moons beckoned him as he continued to witness, and be awestruck, by their fathom existence. Fathom or not this experience seemed unreal to him, like he was floating through time and space.

Suddenly he snapped out of his fourth dimension and reentered his third-dimensional reality. Slight shivers made him shake a little as cold sweat permeated the back of his garb. Still affixed in his chair he looked around the lobby and saw Jackie who looked upon him during his ordeal, and unknowing to him, Jagaba observed as well.

"What happened?" Randella finally regained his mental focus to speak out.

"You were under a cerebral link," Jackie answered insinuating Jagaba as the culprit.

"Why?"

"He thought you might be curious," Jackie answered. "I doubt you'll see any of that at the detention center."

"That's great, but I lost the game," the boy's focus now shifted back to the holoscreen. No action was being displayed on the projection only a flashing game over. The virtual army seemed to have destroyed his game piece while he was under Jagaba's spell.

"No gratitude," Jackie ridiculed as she turned her attention elsewhere.

Jagaba averted his attention to his own doings, "What's that stink," Randella cringed. The boy's and the woman's sense of smell detected a reeking odor. Their eyes were now on the reptilian, which was where the smell seemed to be coming from.

Jagaba had on his person of what he would call food, live food. The scaly creature released to the floor, from his sack; vermin, carrion rats and vulturites. The small rodents twitched a little caused by both shock and a heightened sense of awareness by their sudden surroundings. Live prey were Jagaba's chosen cuisine, the enjoyment of the catch.

While one of the carrisons became curious enough to scamper away Jagaba, with his snout and mouth, snatched the little rat before the vermin scurried too far out of reach. Instinct took over as Jagaba literally snatched it, while it was in mid-run, swallowing it whole. As the vermin slowly reached his digestive tract the reptilian's rib cage contracted, crushing the rodent enough to be easily digestible. The first tasty morsel eased the rumbling in Jagaba's stomach but did not satisfy it as yet. Jagaba now targeted the vulturite as the small scavenger bird began to stretch out its wings.

"It's feeding time," Jackie said as she yielded to the smell of it. The awful smell came from the rat, carrion means rotten flesh and that's what it smelled like.

A slight flexing of the muscles and spreading of its wings indicated that the vulturite was prepared to take flight. The bird's hind legs pushed off the floor as its powerful wings generated enough force for it to take off and fly to a safe distance. But before the vulturite had the chance to fly away from its predator Jagaba, using his powerful legs, jumped up and snatched the bird from the air. From the blinding speed the sight of feathery remnants, which drifted to the floor, showed that the last scavenger prey was unsuccessful in its attempt to escape. The flying rodent was now in Jagaba's mouth for consumption. Once the vulturite met the same fate as the carrion Jagaba continued his feeding. As the last carrion continued to exhibit life the reptilian moved in for the kill, preparing to snatch that life away.

"Well, at least this is entertaining, I've never seen this before," Jackie was both awed and ill stricken. Randella only showed an expression of disgust as he reassumed his previous endeavor.

The plasma heaters kept the cargo bay dry and warm slightly above room temperature. Most of the field equipment had been tested and placed for ready use. Crimson had his part to do as well, inspect the armament.

With his optic visor he directed his steps straight toward the munitions rack. Once there he released the bolt lock and, took into his possession, the assault destructor rifles, which were to be issued to his reconnaissance team. The destructor was a high-powered, rapid fire, offensive rifle designed for guerrilla warfare. Because of the rugged terrain and mountainous regions they would have much needed use of them.

Grabbing as much of the rifles his mechanical arms can carry he turned to his left and walked to the power charger, which was placed off the side near the bay's main overhead hatch. When he was within reach he gently propped the rifles against the main hatch near the charger module. He than leaned in and attached the cord inserts, from the module, to the cross-feed ports of each of the weapons. After this was done he switched on the charger and than he straightened up and took a step back. Observing the digital gauge indicator, to verify compliance, he was reassured when the light emitting numeric jumped up to the time of which would be counted down to completion. A current of positive charged particles were now being fed through the cords and into the rifles' power cells, the weapons were now being powered up.

A few minutes would elapse before the rifles would be fully charged so he stood, like an armored statue, and waited. As he did so his sensory fibers, of his lower extremities, received a sudden jolt. When he looked down at his ankles to see what the collision was his optics detected the medicorp unit. The 'maton caught Crimson's attention, possibly to greet his mechanical brethren. The little medicorp unit made slight front and backward motions as though it was expressing a human personality.

"Command sent, inferior life form," the regenalt stated as he looked down at it. The 'maton, quickly in response, made faster front and backward motions and than it spun around as though it was showing agitation to the cybernetic's remark.

Exiting the bridge Josh had to do one more thing before the team could dismount the safe haven of their starcruiser, that is after the storm leaves. Before Josh left the passenger lobby, as he neared Jackie who was still stationed at her seat, "Jackie, the storm is clearing, I'll relay when we're ready," he than disappeared through the hatchway at the opposite end from the bridge.

Now that the weaponry had been fully charged Crimson laid the rifles inside the rifle rack, behind the pilot seat of the scudder craft. With the safeties on Crimson left them alone but ready along with their corresponding power clips, for possible recharging if they should encounter combat. After the armament was prepped and left securely the cybernetic stepped away and positioned himself nearby to the side to await further instructions.

Soon after, Joshua entered the bay and his first impulse was to inspect the rifles. Crimson stood near the cargo bay hatch as Josh approached the side of the scudder where the rifles were laid in. Grabbing one of them, the marshal held on to its handle and side grip. With the muzzle pointing up he retracted the breach to look inside the barrel to look for possible contaminants, there was none.

"Very good," the marshal said to his pleasure, "good work Crim," as he released the chamber back and returning the rifle from where he found it.

After he moved away from his first priority he directed his attention toward his second, "Rover One," the marshal commanded. The 'maton complied as it rolled to his feet, "Time for a little maintenance."

Josh walked behind and away from the medicorp unit, where it stood, and buried himself amidst the scattered equipment nearby. He needed the right essentials to equip the 'maton with some accessories and he knew what to look for and where. The machinery and tools were scattered and bunched in one area of the bay but his focus seemed not lost. Although the disarray did not confound him he knew he would have to make attempts to have someone, of his crew, to clean up this mess.

Revealing himself once again, away from the clutter, he found what he was looking for. In his hand he held a pair of tread chains and a wrench. As he walked around, from behind, Josh faced the medicorp unit and he ordered, "Rise up little guy, maglifts only." By magnetic force the artificial life form raised a few meters fro the floor. As it did so the 'maton's revolving tractor wheels spun 180 degrees so that the points of the triangulated fixtures were directed down. A powerful magnetic field caused it to hover; combustion thrusters could not be used. Josh would have to squeeze his hands in and around the axles and he wanted to avoid from obviously getting his hands cooked.

As he laid the wrench aside, for the time being, he took the first chain and wrapped it around one of the wheels. With his left hand wedged between the axle and wheel he attempted to align the chain properly. The cumbersome task made him feel like screaming out profanities but he kept his calm. Once he achieved proper alignment he grabbed the wrench, with his free hand, to tighten the slack. After the chain was tightly fitted against the wheel's treading he performed the same task on the other wheel.

Finally the 'maton had been equipped to handle Khalidan's snow covered terrain. As the marshal set aside his tool he recommended, "How's your new feet little one, take 'em for a spin."

The 'maton obliged the marshal's recommendation by

maneuvering around a little bit with, what seemed to be, excitement. Rover One initiated its aft thermal propulsion. The mechanical unit than implemented a circling maneuver or testing run, toward the ingress. Catered by its back thrusters the 'maton propelled up and over to an inverted position. It than spanned across the bay's ceiling; reaching overhead and than away from the marshal, where he kept himself in a squatted position to observe. Once the 'maton was within a few centimeters from the bay's main hatch it halted. The medicorp unit than revolved back to its upright position and returned, toward its master. As it neared Josh the 'maton decreased its propulsion as it hovered down while its tractor wheels spun back. In smooth harmony, as Rover One descended, the flats of its wheels touched the floor. The 'maton rolled back from where it took off, at the marshal's feet.

The passenger lobby quieted down during the elapse of time. Jackie was still situated in her chair, clutching her chin and keeping her right leg bent and resting on the other, she waited patiently. Randella who long lost interest of anymore computer games, fell asleep. During the boy's play his energy drained and he was left stretched across the cushioned side bench.

"Jackie, the storm cleared," the marshal's voice transmitted from the lobby's intercom speaker. "We're ready, Jagaba can stay behind to watch the boy."

Literally jumping out of her seat Jackie approached and punched the comm's initiator button and spoke, "I'm on my way." Soon after her response she departed the lobby, after hours of restless waiting, their mission was now about to begin.

THE STORM CLEARED AWAY allowing the brightness of the sun to shine down. The sun's luminosity reflected off the snowy white surface of which would have caused anyone, who might tread the landscape, to squint. This sector of the planet's time zone was high noon and nothing was visible except, at a faraway point, jagged regions of mountainous terrain. Flatlands, where the high inclines were absent, were spread out like a desert, a desert of snow. Wavy formations were sinuously spread out on the snow's surface, like ripples in a pond, which was the after effect from the previous gust of the winds. Except for the aforementioned phenomena nothing else was in sight, not even the Cauldron.

No movement, at the moment, was visible except for the moderate snowdrift caused by the mild crosswinds. The whistling wind had an uninviting tone of which seemed to declare the planet's isolation and desolation. When it appeared as though the frigid parameter was withdrawn from any activity, or life, a stirring movement occurred. Snow shifted and slid down a nearby slope. As the loose snow shook, like grains through a sift, some of the slope's accumulation caved in into a developing rift. As the rift enlarged to a tunnel-like opening hydraulic vapor was released into the air. This peculiarity was evident that the Cauldron survived, hidden underneath the snow's mass.

Out from the depth Joshua stepped out from the safe covering of his cruiser, just enough to gain a vantage point of the parameter. The titanic winds of the squall made an unexpected grave for the starcruiser, and quite possibly, the perfect camouflage. Josh had on his winter gear; boots, facial visor, thermulated fatigues, cap and cloak. As he stood still to observe the planet's environment, the dreaded unknown he might have to face, he braced himself. He dug his feet into a firm stance to keep the wind's momentum from offsetting his balance. His cloak fluttered as the wind's current pushed at him, but he stood unraveled.

He aim to acquire a better view of his surroundings by obtaining a higher ground. He managed his way out of the cave-like opening by climbing, hand over hand, to the top of the mound. Assuming another secured stance he surveyed the distant horizon. With his hand cupped over his eyes, to block out the sun's radiant beams, he imposed a analytical look in every direction.

"Josh," Jackie called out as she revealed herself from underneath.

"Look up," Josh directed her attention.

As she did she had to squint trying to keep the sun's rays from blinding her, she had to place her hand to her brow to block some of the light. "What do you see?"

"Nothing warm," Joshua answered with a tone of humorous sarcasm. Nothing warm indeed, Joshua thought to himself as he continued to probe the outstretch of land. The marshal wished he had something pleasant to say but he did not want to underestimate the conditions Jackie would have to endure, and the same goes for the rest of his crew.

As Joshua stood on top of the mound, to get a bird's eye view on the assessment, a faint humming noise echoed from afar. Obviously not too far away since it was within his ear shot and seemed to be heading his way, hence, Josh was alarmed. The sounds were mechanical in nature, and to his many years of experience, had a familiar tenor. The marshal became more apprehensive as the sounds grew more intense.

"Get in the covering," Joshua shouted to Jackie, "we got trouble."

With little regard to being placid the marshal threw himself into the rift while pushing Jackie back into the cargo bay in the process. After landing on his hands and knees in the snow he quickly jumped inside as well with the intension of staying hidden. Staying hidden from what Jackie thought but the marshal knew as he, not even taking the time to brush the snow off his garb, jerked her close to be still. Josh realized, all too well, what the incoming threat was but he hoped he was wrong. Without delay or taking a glance outside he quickly covered the bewildered mercenary with his cloak as the humming amplified louder.

"What is it?" Jackie inquired with a tone of agitation.

She disapproved of the ungentle way she was handle, or understood why, but Josh paid little attention to her feelings, "Just keep quiet."

As the sounds outside drew nearer to a deafening roar the origin of the disturbance flew into sight, it was a cyclodrone or aeroship. The cyclodrone was a vertical flight atmospheric transport with a main propeller at the top and had powerful stern thrusters. The aeroship sharply passed by the crew's concealment at low flight. The crew, aboard the enemy transport, were desperately searching for any remnants of the Cauldron. The cyclodrone's main propeller spiraled through a central ring, called a halo, as the central ring's rotary fins gyrated in the opposite direction. The ring had the same size, in diameter pretty much, to encompass the whole craft. To prevent torque, the ring's inner rotating fin action created counter-pressure for stability, as the aft thrusters propelled the craft at super-sonic speeds.

Only a few meters away the white-camouflaged brigand transporter, after passing the Cauldron's position, turned around abruptly to make another pass. While doing so the brigandeer pilot and gunner peered out their windows to examine, rather or not, if any tracks; metal fragments; or anything that might constitute a sighting of the downed starcruiser. The aerodynamic structure of the cyclo streaked through the atmosphere as the brigands continued their on-going search and destroy mission.

The cyclodrone cut through the air until it came to a dead stop, across from where the Cauldron was inconspicuously hidden. Keeping himself motionless as possible the marshal slowly turned his head, only to see the closeness of his predator. The legionnaires took a few steps backward hoping that the distance, and their snow covering, was enough to keep them undetected.

"Keep still," the marshal whispered to Jackie as they were huddled together.

The cyclodrone's two-man crew continued to survey the parameter for any traces of their foe. The sound of the engines blared less intensely since the stern's combustionators were on idle charge. But the engines, which generated the main propeller and repellor thrust, were still loud enough to keep its prey alarmed.

The brigand pilot, Josh detected, saw no signs of irregularities or disturbance in the snow-covered terrain. After a minute or two elapsed the brigand pilot powered up his stern thrusters, the sound of the cyclodrone's presence than intensified. Maneuvering the aeroship's body to a quarter degree turn the cyclodrone banked starboard and than navigated away. The brigand search team continued to scour the surrounding area and than further away, of the outlining regions, which was when the marshal heard nothing more than the returning silence.

After the outside element returned to normal status Joshua stood up. Jackie straightened up, still in her sitting position, after the marshal distant himself from her side. She stayed low to the ground awaiting the marshal's thumbs up that it was safe to move about.

Joshua took a couple of steps outside to look at the sky. Looking around in both directions, "I think we're safe," Josh was relieved, "but that was too close."

The marshal regained his nerve as he took a step back under the shading near Jackie; she was finally on her feet at that time. "Look, I need you out there to set up some sweepers around the parameter," he instructed as he walked further into the ship's cargo bay.

The suggestion caused her to feel apprehensible, "What do I do if I find anymore unfreindlies out there," she protested. "Who's to say there isn't an armored division of combatants and foot soldiers nearby?"

But the marshal didn't have the time to comfort Jackie because danger came with the job. "Take these, position these proximity probes around the ship," the marshal said as he reached out to extend the devices to her. "Crimson will be your point man just in case you encounter resistance." He piled four probing devices into her holding despite her objections. Joshua's dominance annoyed Jackie but she carried out his order, she took leave.

As she exited the ship Josh turned his gaze to the regenalt, who remained where he was before, to await his order, "Crimson, go with Jackie. Watch her."

"Acknowledge," the regenalt responded and than followed her trail.

After the two were out to tend their task the marshal turned his attention to the second item of his list of priorities. He walked toward his scudder's portside, which was the driving side, and once he was there he thumb pressed a push button at the control console to start the main ignition. After several tries the exhaust ports eventually ignited with thermal pressure. A discharge of transparent fumes, from the exhaust, polluted the air as the internal gases continued to burn. The correlated left and right engines hummed steadily, like a cat's purr.

As burning fuel fumed the cargo bay, keeping the scudder running to warm up, the marshal had to communicate his mission's plan to his copilot. He turned and walked toward the left side of the bay's hatch to use the comspeaker. "Jagaba, do you read," the marshal said to get the reptilian's attention.

Jagaba was still stationed below, at the drive section, making the required repairs. He was in the process of replacing damaged components with new ones when the marshal's voice transmitted through the intercom. He relaxed his hand, that held the circuitry, and he looked to his side at the speaker.

"Jagaba, we're positioning scanning devices around the ship," he continued as the reptilian listened, "so keep your eyes on the homing relays."

After the marshal discontinued communication Jagaba stepped in close toward a sensor monitor to activate it. The monitor was near the intercom, embedded in the bulkhead, so Jagaba need not had to stray too far. With his forefinger, he pressed upward the initiator switch to turn on the gauging monitor. The monitor lit up relaying a digital recording chart, which, thus far, projected only a center-point along with two markers. The two markers were the two proximity probes that Jackie had already established. After Jagaba observed the monitor, for only a few seconds, the reptilian communicated a positive transmission to the First Marshal and than he resumed his duties.

The temperature was dropping slightly as the day wore on but Jackie was dressed and equipped for the condition. She kept herself balanced at the lower end of an incline as Crimson stood guard at the top of the ravine. To brace herself she jabbed her left knee into the snow, which supported most of her weight, and positioned her other leg, outstretched, beneath her. Her outstretched leg was positioned parallel with the incline with the toes of her foot pressed against the ravine's slope.

She was emplacing a third probe, of four, into a scanning position. Jackie made an extra effort to keep the marker device embedded deep enough into the snow to keep it secure and upright. The probe resembled a mini-satellite, which had two discs, one above the other. The top transceiver disc probed the upper parallel plane, scanning for any possible air raids, while the bottom disc would scan the lower parallel plane, for any possible ground assaults. Once Jackie was assured that the probe was supported well enough, and will not fall over, she turned it on. Instantly the two discs made three-hundred-and-sixty degree revolutions on ball bearing joints, one revolving in the opposing direction of the other.

Now she was nearing the end of her task, she had one more crosslink marker to establish. Taking with her the last probe, which was safely tucked away in her backpack, she begun to free herself from the ravine. Tracking up the incline with her knees and hands, she pressingly ignored some of the snow that escaped into her boots. She recently put in crosslink markers at each point of the compass she thought; north, south, and east, now she must complete the encompassing safe zone.

Once she was free from the ravine's grasp she headed west. "C'mon Crim," she said sharply to her metal chaperone. As she headed in the western direction Crimson, hindered slightly by his metallic body, slowly followed her with his rifle in his grips.

The crosswinds were a little breezy and, unfortunately, were picking up speed as the afternoon progressed into the evening. The thick clouds begun to shift blocking out the sun, causing her shadow to fade away along with the sunlight. Her scarf, which was tightly wrapped around her neck, fluttered as the wind impeded her movements. Her thoughts were of leaving this discomforted environment but she pressed on.

Boulders of ice were around her and the snow she was treading through was ankle deep. The harsh elements caused her to slow down a bit but she continued on with steady momentum. Corin treaded through the flat, thick layered, snow until she came to a stop. She discovered as she looked down that she was standing at the top, at the edge, of a cave with a ten-foot drop below her.

A perfect place she thought to set up her last marker. She kneeled down to rest on her knees as she unharnessed her backpack. She than positioned the utility sack upright against a frost covered rock to open it. As soon as she opened her backpack she reached in to pull out the last remaining probe. Jackie performed the same set-up sequence as the one before it. She carefully positioned and than planted the last link-up into the crusty snow with the face of the mini-satellite facing outward, overlooking the ground below. After she accomplished this she turned the unit on to commence its spiral trip wire security sweep. Now that the Cauldron was guarded, at least not without warning, she stood up and headed back toward camp.

As Jackie saw the camp in sight she also saw Joshua standing outside near the pilot side of the scudder craft. Jackie approached him with Crimson taking the lead, the machine human completing his given order.

Still several feet away from the marshal's position, "All the markers are in," she continued as she drew nearer. "As long as you have a positive transmission you'll know if anything comes around," she was now at his side.

As Joshua made preparations to pilot the scudder craft Rover One, in its flight mode, was out in the open hovering toward the craft to join the other three. The 'maton had its thermal thrusters on at minimum but had enough force behind it to excite the snow, beneath, into a frenzy.

The group of four seemed to be ready to mount up to get their mission under way. As they begun to do so they would leave Jagaba behind to complete his ship repairs and keep Randella under his care.

The marshal looked at Crimson with an expression of annoyance, "You can mount up," he commanded the regenalt.

"Acknowledge," Crimson replied quite detached from any emotion, "start task."

Regenalts were programmed to respond, and only initiate after, vocal commands from their human counterparts. Even though cybernetics were only part human, cerebrospinal driven, they were designed and programmed to consider themselves inferior to their human masters.

But still Josh was annoyed that a member of his own team had to be commanded to do the obvious. But he shrugged off that problem for the moment, keeping a mental note that he could reconfigure Crimson's data banks at a later time. "Strap yourself in," Josh told Jackie, "we could be in for a rough ride."

Corin walked around to the passenger side and than she hopped into her seat. As the 'maton moved in from behind the stern she slid her belt strap across her waist; latched and than tightened it, she was snugged in securely. "Let's get goin," she said anxiously.

With its proportioned maglift underneath caressing the ground the 'maton catered its maneuverability. Rover One ascended up slightly over the rear fin to find a secure place, aboard the craft, to settle so as not to wobble during travel. Knowing its own location by its optics the automaton descended to a landing on a central flat surface, behind the front seats. When the 'maton touched down it than tipped its body over on its back by turning its triangulated wheels, at the axles, literally pushing itself back until its body dropped on its posterior side.

When the four-member crew were aboard and ready for launch they did so. Joshua, with his hands at the controls, ignited the stern thrust. The stream of thermal exhaust, which was forced through the tapered funnel exhaust ports, excited the scudder across the terrain and into the unknown landscape.

The overcast diminished, somewhat, allowing the sun to brighten the scenery once again. Shaded visors had to be worn to shade their eyes from the illumination, Josh especially so he will not be blinded during his present piloting. The time now reached the middle of the afternoon with wind speeds decreasing. The brightened day made the canyons, ravines, and flatlands alive and fresh. The flatland of cracked creviced slates of ice, which they were currently navigating above, seemed to spread out for miles.

The planet seemed barren and lifeless but where there was carbon compounds there was usually life.

The scudder skimmed across the flatland with ferocious velocity. The vessel rim of the craft was only a few meters from touching the surface, the underbelly maglift system kept the hovercraft elevated. The powerful hydrogen fuel thrusters propelled the craft like a ballistic as the navigator handcrafted the controls. And the passengers and pilot were securely locked into their seats as they traversed across the openness.

As they continued spanning across the wide-open terrain, rocks and boulders congested the icy planes as they narrowed in toward the canyons. They conducted their search according to what their sensors read, a carrier signal that could pick up other similar or identical wave patterns. Only the mountainous regions, that they were now entering, interfered with their tracking transmissions, but only slightly, they were still well on course.

The marshal increased the power to his maglift as much as he could to ascend upward even more to avoid hitting a rock, which they were about to collide into; fast. Hovercrafts weren't flying vehicles; they were only designed to ascend as high as their maglift systems would allow. Knowing that a collision would be unavoidable Joshua banked the craft to near vertical. You could almost see the diamagnetic stimulators at work as they shot pass the rock, almost flying over it, in a dodging maneuver.

"Corin, keep your eyes on those sensors," Josh raised his voice over the airstream and the scudder's loud engines. The marshal needed to be heard and his directions understood through all the noise. The loud roar of the engines and the crosswind turbulence deafened everything else, overpowering the sounds of their own voices. Check for any anomaly that might resemble an electrical circuit or life form."

The mountainous region, which they were in, became less maneuverable as the area around them shrunk in volume. Glaciers and icecaps were being appreciated by their awesome appearance as they entered a tight corridor of a ravine. Since the passage way was narrow and obstructed the marshal had to keep his pilot instincts sharp. The thermal exhaust discharge left a trail of snow debris in the wind while maintaining their current acceleration speed.

In the corner of his eye Hollands detected an ice formation in his path. To avoid another possible collision he quickly passed through a central opening of the obstacle, which was a giant icicle. The marshal, being able to tilt his craft's fuselage, was able to accomplish a clean brisk through the icicle sediment. No collision or butting presented a danger since Josh was able to keep the sides, and everything else, out of harm's way.

A bend near the end of the ravine showed the crew of the scudder, hopefully they thought, a way out from the tight squeezed enclosure of ice and rocks. The marshal, again, banked vertical to turn, following the corridor's path at the end of the bend.

Now heading in the eastward direction they relaxed a little for their surroundings present a lot more freedom to maneuver. After the scudder exited the ravine the marshal decreased his speed until he came to a halt, they were again on flatland. The recon team was relieved they were no longer enclosed in such a claustrophobic confinement. While the hovercraft was static Hollands and Corin took a short time to marvel at the breathtaking view. The far horizon was nothing but mountainous peaks, which elevated into the clouds.

"What do you see on the sensor readings?" The marshal took in the spectacle of scenery for only a second until his awareness returned to business.

"Nothing ahead," Jackie leaned to glance over the readout monitor. "But the readings detect some activities northwest from us."

"Than that's our destination," the marshal casually said as he lunged his machine toward the new heading.

Crossing another stretch of flatland the hovercraft continued climbing at top speed. The magnetic field beneath the hull was invisible except for a slight distortion, which resembled a colorless gas. The hover vehicle crossed over cracks of slated ice a few meters above it. The chain of mountains in the horizon seemed close but in fact, because of their enormity, they were hundreds of kilometers away. The size of the mounts, and their distance away from them, was misleading but they were pretty to see.

The flatland was cracked and creviced as the one before it, which was probably the result from the oscillating temperatures of the planet's environment. The sun still shined bright in the cloudy blue sky while its moderate heat perforated the icy surface. The yellow heavenly body was lower than before near the peaks of the distant mountains. Since the day was wearing down into the evening the crew of the scudder could spare no time to enjoy the scenic ride.

Hovering across the flat terrain the scudder slowly came to a stop as it cruised in close, near a drop, in the icy field. They were now confronted with a problem as they faced the edge of a cliff and the open air in front of them. The palisades stretched out a long way at both sides, a circumference, which forced the crew to decide their next course of action.

"We could follow the cliff line," the marshal stated. "We might be able to find a passage way or something that might lead us down there, but it'll take forever." He than turned to Jackie, "Have any ideas?"

"We could climb down."

"We should have some support cables in the back," Joshua reluctantly said. The marshal seemed to have no other options to consider, despite his reluctance he was forced to agree. "Dismount, except for you Rover One. You stay with the craft."

Jackie walked over to the edge of the cliff as Josh acquired the necessary tools his team would need. Standing before the edge she leaned slightly forward to look down, which gave her a scary feeling of acrophobia. The drop had a depth of a few kilometers to the ground and the bottom, at the base, was clumped and shard with uneven ice and snow accumulation. She cringed as she examined their current obstacle that they must prevail over.

After she took a step back, and took a deep breath, the marshal and the cybernetic joined her. "Here, you'll going to need this," the marshal handed her a security harness.

"We better renegotiate my payment plan." Corin felt nauseous but she remembered it was her idea as she carefully fitted the harness to her back, and than secured the belt strap of it around her waist. "I didn't think I'd be doing this when I woke up this morning."

"Your freedom doesn't come cheap," Josh sneered. "Your lucky your not doing life in a cryotube."

The three members of the recon team strapped on their support-feed harnesses. The body harnesses were strapped with the belt straps wrapped and fastened tightly across their chests and around their waists for a controlled safe descent. The miniature winces, which came linked with the harnesses, were positioned at their sides within their reach. Before they took the first step off the ledge of the cliff, together in a tem effort, they stretched out their cables to allow some slack before they would descend. After doing so they grabbed the ends of their cables and, using a bolt driver, they pinned the ends into the icy rock for a strong hold, to brace their weight.

Hollands tested the security of his support line by tugging on it firmly, "Ok, let's go," Josh said when he was confident enough. The other two followed his assurances, almost in unison, as they commenced downward.

In step with one another they turned around fronting the rock face as they begun to lower themselves. Trying not to lose their footing on the slippery ice, they slowly climbed their way down the deep decline. With a firm grip, they held on to their cables with one hand as they worked the cranks of their winces with the other. In close timing with one another, as though they've done this drill before, they descended as the pulley-wince system gave them proper leverage. As they continued to levitate down they hand cranked the spindle feeds. Slowly with care, as they lowered closer to the landing, their feet walked the smooth and ridged surface of the vertical rocky mass. One would think that the drop, which they were treading down against, was a giant iceberg, but in fact, underneath the thickness of the ice was nothing more than granite rock and petrified clay. The coming of the present ice age transformed the planet's entire landscape.

Approaching the landing they slid down their cables with relative ease. Crimson planted his feet into the ankle-deep snow first on the landing's edge, and than Josh and Jackie touched the surface quickly after. The cybernetic wasted no time discarding his climbing gear before the other two had the chance to do so.

After they unhooked themselves from their support lines they slung their rifles into their hands. They kept the barrels of their weapons pointed up, but ready with the safeties off, as a common safety handling.

Crimson stood out from the rest because of his reddish-pigmented body armor and his oval-shaped optic visor. His features made his appearance to be threatening, as he moved with mechanical awkwardness, but steady enough to keep up with the others. Joshua shook the snow off his cloak as he looked around to attain some direction. Jackie left her survival harness hanging with the others after she unfastened the belt coupling. Once Corin was free from any encumbrance she waited for Joshua to take the lead.

The day was still bright; hence, visibility was not a problem. The terrain underneath their feet was slightly hilly but otherwise free from any major obstacle. Their lower garbs, from the knees down, were drenched from the snow as they continued to negotiate through it. The sharp breeze of the crosswinds knifed through their skin, even though they had on proper thermal protection. The ends of Jackie's scarf fluttered as the wind drowned her optimism.

She pressed the scarf to her mouth with her hand, to keep her face covered, and while being attentive to the homing tracer she held in her other hand. Corin held on to the searching device, with her free hand, to help direct her fellow crewmen to their target. "We're moving in the right direction," she apprised. "I'm picking up circuitry current and metallic composites, straight ahead."

"Are you sure, we need to hurry back to base before nightfall," Josh warned.

"I'm positive."

"Well, I hope we get there pretty quick, Jagaba should be close to finishing his repairs," the marshal responded with a tone of self-discouragement.

As they trudged through the ankle-deep snow they maintained a firm grip on their weapons, with the exception of Corin. Jackie's destructor rifle was slung, dangling, over her shoulder. She had to have a hand on her tracer to direct the crew's heading, while she still kept her scarf pressured against her face.

They finally reached an embankment after they walked a few more meters from their last location. "We're facing something, fifty kilometers ahead," Jackie warned the others.

The embankment made a perfect hiding place from whatever may be beyond it. Joshua and Jackie relinquished their firearms, laying them against the snow bank, as they lifted their heads up above the mound to get a view. Crim remained standing, with his gun in hand, to add cover for his crewmen should they fall under fire.

Joshua examined the parameter and pinpointed their target, which was faintly visible. Knowing where the enemy was, without losing sight of the target, he lifted his visor to his brow. He than snatched his rangefinder, which was in his upper cargo pouch, and lifted it to his face to look through it. Manipulating the adjustment controls he zoomed in on his target and ascertained what he dreaded the most, a processing refinery, and Central's suspicions. At the base line of the internal lens, of his rangefinder, projections of digital coordinate readouts were displayed. Those readouts gave him the necessary information he'll need to help him contrive a plan.

The overall shape of the refinery was a flat top building, which was a couple of kilometers in length and a half-kilometer in width. Constructed in the central portion of the roof laid a giant metallic sphere, polygon in design. At the crown of the sphere, two exhaust stacks were put into place to serve as a filter of unwanted waste. The complete design and construction of this fortress, which stood before the stunned recon team, was magnificently built.

As the marshal continued to look through his rangefinder he spoke, "I think we have confirmation."

"What do you see?" Jackie finally questioned.

As he lowered his view-piece he answered, "A thermal-fusion processing station," as he handed Jackie the rangefinder.

She took the rangefinder to find out for herself what Joshua was looking at. She than said as she looked through the lens, "Incredible, what's it's purpose?"

"I would think it's obvious," Josh voiced his concern, "If that station's fully operational they can manufacture enough raw materials to create a small fleet."

Through the duration of their discussion Crimson remained in the same position as before, poised for defense. With both hands on his gun he looked around slowly, from side to side, to scope the parameter. The cybernetic was searching for anything that might be perceived to him as a threat. As Josh and Jackie pondered and spoke to each other the regenalt's sound receptors absorbed the data without much reaction to it.

"We can't engage them ourselves, we're outnumbered," the marshal thought out loud.

"What's are next move?"

"We need to call in the fleet," the marshal contemplated. "But first we need proof that this monstrosity exists."

While Jackie continued to marvel at the fortress the marshal reached at, in a separate cargo pocket, his camera. His digital camera was specially designed for reconnaissance; almost paper-thin but with a coiling protracting lens, which could zoom in from any distance, but was compact enough to be carried inconspicuously.

"We're going to need photos," he said as he aimed his camera.

"Hurry, we're losing sunlight," she said as she lowered the view-piece. "I wanna get back to the ship."

Joshua dismissed Jackie's wishes as he looked through the camera's sight. He first decided to take a snapshot of the overall view of the brigand's outpost. The viewing control mechanisms were located at the topmost part, within reach of his fingers, near the camera's side grips. He had the ability to manipulate the viewing by a trekker wheel and toggle thumbstick.

"Don't count on leaving," he eventually discouraged as he resumed.

The camera's viewing projection was digital and it had a targeting pointer, which was maneuverable by the trekker wheel, in the center of the viewing. For his first snapshot he decided to take a picture of the fortress in its entirety. Without moving the pointer he enlarged the station so that, from left to right, it would be in the photo-shot. When the full enhanced view of the fortress was in sight, but not to the point of distortion, he captured the pictured by pressing the push-button with his left forefinger.

"Take a picture of that," the marshal said to himself out loud, "and one more just for luck," as he clicked a second time.

He than, using the trekker, moved the pointer to the left-lower side of the station, after which, he enhanced that section to view it. Enhancement was possible by using the thumbstick, which was to the left of the trekker. He enlarged the left flank to a degree of clarity and he became astounded at what he saw. A group of white armored regenalts, known as footsoldiers, stood in a double-column formation near an accessor hatch.

"We've got trouble," the marshal said as he took another snapshot. "Footsoldiers, a lot of em."

He than aimed his camera to the right-lower section, without enhancing or manipulating the pointer. To his dismay he spotted two hover assault tanks, known as combatants, doing routine maneuvers near another bay hatch. In addition to the combatants, sentries were posted near the bay's entrance. The sentries were at their posts guarding the area.

"They're well armed and equipped," Josh stated as he took another photo-shot. The marshal made his statements out loud to keep Jackie apprised, and Crimson also absorbed the intelligence reports.

Once a sufficient amount of pictures were taken he lowered the camera to his side and than, turning around to sit, he rested himself against the embankment. "I saw a couple of HAVIC units doing exercise maneuvers near the base of the station."

"What does that mean?"

"It means we can't do anything until reinforcements arrive," he answered while facing her. "We better get back to the ship."

Using the embankment as cover they slowly withdrew, back to the dangling harness cables, to return from where they came. The cybernetic followed behind the other two while keeping his face toward the enemy. Crimson needed to take cautionary assurances that they were not spotted or being pursued.

The courageous crew of the scudder returned to their camp after their successful recon mission had been completed. The hovercraft approached, briskly, nearing the Cauldron's entrance ramp and than slowed to a dead still. This time the starcruiser was very much visible and a beautiful sight to see in their eyes. Jagaba had enough foresight to leave the engines running during the recon team's absence. The emanation of heat from the ship's thermal engines seemed to have melted the snow covering, the Cauldron was now unveiled from its snow burial.

Immediately after Joshua disengaged thrust he dismounted. "You might as well stay here," the marshal directed his voice to Jackie as she removed herself from her seat. "Crim, you get inside," he ordered the regenalt to comply. "You're needed at the reciprocal to help navigate the ship back to the outer rim."

The marshal was the first to walk up the hydraulic ramp and disappear into the shadows of the cargo bay. Once he was aboard, and on his way to the bridge, Crimson stepped off the scudder's side plank and followed the marshal's trail. After Crimson boarded Jackie was left standing by herself, leaning against the hover vehicle, accompanied only by the 'maton.

Jagaba sat in his copilot seat appearing to be in good spirits. From the sounds of the engines and the gleam of initiator lights, which lit up the control terminals, the ship seemed to be adequately repaired. The reptilian, with much relief to everybody, seemed to have mended the Cauldron's wounds well enough for take-off.

The reptilian was making last minute diagnostics on the ship's operating systems as Josh entered the bridge. As the marshal casually approached Jagaba's side he walked passed Randella. The boy was bored and growing weary from inactivity as he laid down, on his stomach against the cold floor, Josh almost had to step over him.

"Jag, take this," the marshal said as he placed the spy film in Jagaba's hand. "It reports a lot of trouble." As Joshua continued he could sense Jagaba's inquiry and hesitation but he ignored those sensations as he carried on. "Make sure Central Command gets that film and have them bring in the fleet, we have need of them."

Before the marshal took leave he issued one last command, "And take care of the boy, he better be in detention care when you're back."

When the marshal received a positive acknowledgement from the reptilian he turned around to exit the bridge. Midway to the accessor the hatch shot open and than Crim entered. The marshal passed by the regenalt but not even throwing a glance in his direction. As Joshua vacated the bridge Crimson managed his way into his trajectory booth.

Jackie was leaning against the scudder waiting patiently for her senior officer to join her. As he appeared out from the ship he made his way down the gangplank to Jackie's side. "Well, that's it," the marshal announced. "He's on his way home."

"What about us," Jackie replied as she watched the entrance ramp lift and close. She had a feeling of deep fear and apprehension, and the marshal sensed it in her tone.

"I guess we have to fend for ourselves and make do with what we have."

"Why do we stay, why can't we leave with them?"

"Someone has to stay behind to monitor enemy movements and keep an up-to-the-date log on their activities," Josh explained. She understood his reasoning although she didn't like it. Like it or not she had to grin and bear it for the sake of the mission.

The Cauldron's repellors engaged, which enabled the ship to levitate. The power from the exhaust current caused a whirlwind of snow and air, underneath the ship's hull. As the starcruiser lifted off Jackie shared the marshal's cloak, keeping themselves covered from the cruiser's dust storm. When the Cauldron reached several meters from the ground's surface the ship's landing gear retracted. With Jagaba at the controls, he discontinued downward thrust once the landing gear was safely pulled in its housing. After the backlash of flying debris eased a bit, the two on the ground, relaxed their hold on each other.

An outburst of stern exhaust caused the Cauldron to dart up and disappear into the clouds as the two on the ground watched. Marooned on the ice planet they contemplate the future. They knew they must endure without outside help for the time being. Equipped with a medicorp unit and a sufficient amount of survival gear, and their own wits, they brave the tasks that lay ahead.

The night quickly passed before daybreak giving way to another beautiful morning. The temperature rose as the sun did allowing the creature element to awake from their state of nocturnal sleep. Safe and warm shelter would have been necessary to acquire protective refuge from the bitter cold nights.

Safe and warm shelter was erected in the form of a makeshift tent. A thinly woven sheet of thermulated material was easily constructed up to allow for a dome-like covering as the two occupants slept inside. A self-inflating tent wasn't the only piece of survival gear Joshua had for his use but it was a comforting one.

As Jackie and Josh slept soundly through the night the harsh winds were beating against the tent's structure, the top overhang fluttering. The entrance flaps were sealed tight to keep the wind-chill out as the two absorbed each other's body heat. Although closeness wasn't Jackie's idea of a perfect night sleep it was the only way to get through toward the morning. Under such conditions personal sacrifices had to be made for the purpose of their survival and for a successful outcome of their mission, a team effort must be foremost.

The only movement was that of the occasional snowdrift caused by the random but moderate wind, still stirring. Except for that and the fluttering movement of the tent's exterior, no other activity was astir.

The quietude, within the tent, was broken as the marshal unsealed the flaps to welcome the new morning. Josh was first to emerge out of the covering as Jackie remained still, still in her sleeping sack. The marshal kept his winter fatigues on, which were slightly ruffled since he slept in them through the night. Only half of his body was out from the shelter, on his feet but in a squatted position, as he gazed upon the new day. The sun's rays struck down against the surface; as a result, the impact of the light upon his face temporarily disoriented him.

After he stretched the soreness from his muscles he withdrew, back completely under his shelter, to awaken his sleeping femme fatale. As the outer flaps dropped behind him he commenced toward his backpack to also repack his gear.

"Jackie. Jackie," the marshal said twice.

"What?" she replied, but slurred and groggy.

"Rise and shine," he said as he was nudging at her side. "We gotta make use of the daylight."

Corin slowly raised herself from her sleeping bag and than she stretched loose the kinks in her neck, from her long night of repose. Her hair was slightly frazzled, and her expression was as well, before she eventually snapped out of it and returned herself to a proper mindset.

"What's on the itinerary?" Jackie finally regained her alertness as she spoke out.

Joshua answered, "After we close camp we need to give this ice block a thorough search over." The marshal continued as he packed the rest of his gear, "If there are any life forms out there, besides the brigandage army, we need to establish some kind of communications with them."

Once Jackie unsheathed her body from her sleeping bag Joshua issued the first order of the day, "Pack everything, and leave no trail for the brigand scouts." After he fastened shut his backpack he gave a final remark, "I'll load up and get the scudder craft ready."

Immediately after Hollands exited the tent Jackie deflated her sleeping bag, reducing it to a mere nylon-like strip, to be retained back in its canister shell. She was wide-awake now and her reflexes were sharp enough to handle anything that might come to tread against her, she felt refreshed after her much needed sleep through the night.

Partial heat emanated from the sun above providing some comfort as Joshua threw his backpack behind his navigation seat. Fully insulated, his headdress and visor worn, to do battle with any weather condition that might be thrown his way. His garb made him appear strikingly much like a nobleman even though his attire were for practical uses. With his outer wear showing him to be of rank the brightness of the morning gave him an optimistic attitude.

With her hair combed and her cargo sack packed she straightened the creases out of her fatigues as she revealed herself from the tent.

She quickly joined Josh as the marshal initiated the scudder's aft engines. As exhaust fumed the tail end of the craft, the smell drifting to her senses, she wedged her gear underneath the passenger seat.

"Good morning Rover One," she greeted the 'maton.

The robotic unit remained stationed, its thermal coupling plugged into the charger, to keep its mechanical innates warm through the night. The 'maton kept itself static and lying dormant, not moving from where it was the day before. Although unable to respond vocally to Jackie's greeting it moved with a slight shudder, which was its way of acknowledging to her kindness.

"Jackie, tear down the tent," Josh asked of her, "I'll help in a minute."

As Corin turned toward the tent Josh observed the craft's control relays with a microscopic eye. After he was satisfied that his hover vehicle was running correctly he left the craft running to allow the inner gears to warm up to full cycle.

After all their tools were securely aboard they were now in the process of erasing any traces of their encampment. Josh turned to give Jackie a helping hand; his warm breath was visible as it met the cold air.

Jackie stood at the side of the tent near the pneumatic generator port, which was small in size and mounted. After she flipped open the port's panel covering she reached in and deactivated the air inducers, which had a slight drone sound when running. After she shut down the aerogenic systems the effect of this caused the tent to sag a little. After the generator was disengaged she initiated the air release, which caused the air to seep out through valve openings. As air escaped through small eyelets, at the base, the tent flattened to the ground.

Once the air was out from the pocketed insulation they were ready to fold up the thermulated material. As Jackie reached down, to her hands and knees, she pressed out the remainder of the air and Joshua lowered himself as well to do the same. At both sides of the stretched out material they were in their kneeling positions, to do a thorough patting down, while trying not to get in each other's way. Any excess air still trapped, within the canvas, had to be stomped out for easy folding.

After the air was ballooned out they both grabbed their respected sides. They picked up their ends, with both hands, of the round sheet of canvas and they walked toward each other until their sides met. Once the tent was folded in half they repeated the routine, long ways, until it was pressed over enough to be manageable.

And than Joshua stood up and took a couple of steps back so Jackie can finish up herself. She started rolling the tent up while at the same time keeping it neat and aligned. Once after the tent was completely rolled, to carry-along size, Jackie took the tie strings and wrapped them around tightly until finally compacted enough to be stowed away.

"Let's get a move on," the marshal stated as he faced the scudder craft again. He walked at a normal pace but ready to embark.

Jackie stood up from her squatted working position and flung the twenty-pound canvas over her back. She to walked at a moderate speed, hindered perhaps by the weight she carried over her shoulder. Joshua was long in his pilot seat as Corin tossed the rolled up tent aboard, in the back near where the 'maton was stationed.

After Jackie walked to the passenger side she boarded and buckled herself in, "Ready," she uttered.

With a sudden surge of thermal exhaust through the aft thrust the scudder was underway. Avoiding the clearly marked parameter of the enemy outpost they embarked upon another stretch of unknown territory. Using the on-board sensors to guide them they begun to survey the rest of the planet and find, perhaps, indigenous life forms if any.

The wind's turbulence pushed at their bodies as they sped across the terrain. Joshua manned the steering with a attempted effort to avoid any snow mounds or hidden boulders. As the scouting continued Jackie clutched the side of her seat as the acceleration force pressed against her ears.

After close to an hour of traveling, and searching, the scudder slowed to a stop. The hovercraft rested between two snow mounds with nothing ahead of them except more of the same, the same barren wilderness.

"The sensor scan is picking up minute traces of life slightly west from us," Corin stated as she kept her eyes on the readout. Jackie was more relaxed for the moment, now that the wind pressure was no longer stressing her.

Josh felt a little relief as well, while he rested for a few seconds, until he could decide what plotted course to set. "Human?" the marshal asked her.

"No, to faint to be human," she answered. "Could be a rodent or scavenger of some kind."

"Anything else?"

"In this environment? Looking for life here is like looking for a star in a cluster galaxy," she gasped hoping for an easier proceeding.

Josh thought to himself awhile as he leaned against the side, his left elbow resting on the yield guard. "Well, where there's life there ought to be more," he made his decision. "That's good enough for me, west it is."

The day was still young and bright as they again hovered across more ground. The turbulence and wind resistance pushed them back against their seats but they hung on as they continued to thrust onward. They reached a surrounding that was rough and rocky but Josh averted any possible collisions by his keen eye steering.

As the craft continued to zigzag in and around boulders of snow covered rock a carnivore stepped out from nowhere with an outstretched paw. No time to react to the surprise attack the snow leopard struck and knocked the scudder back, from its forward momentum.

Sensing the scudder's end Josh gave up his seat by throwing himself out and away from the craft, seconds before impact. The aft thrust smashed into the ground with the nose up, the weight pressing the aft into the snow smothered out the afterburners. Jackie was quickly thereafter thrown from the passenger side, but not voluntarily, as the tail end struck the ground. The sudden jar, from the crash, caused her body to lift from her mount and be thrown into a nearby bluff.

Rover One also made his escape, but only after its receptors detected the sudden jolt. The automaton propelled away, aided somewhat by the momentum of the craft's recoil. And in a split second after, in mid-flight, the 'maton maneuvered with thrusters and sped away to a safe distance. The scudder's nose eventually toppled down a moment later, giving way to gravity, as they were left stunned several feet apart from the wreckage.

Causing a hydrogen leak, smoke discharging from the back quarter, the craft was now fully rested on its underside. Knowing the inevitable the marshal reacted quickly. He presently felt naked without his gear and he knew he had to retrieve the bare tool for his survival. Josh jumped up from his fallen position to hurry toward his maimed vehicle, still stunned and disoriented, he stumbled a little in the snow along the way.

The beast was of humungous size with clawed feet and saber teeth on the upper jaw. The snow leopard was completely insulated with thick white fur and had powerful elastic muscle strength in the hind legs for jumping. By the creature's inherit habitat high jumping and biting strength would be necessary attributes for survival.

The creature moved in close toward the scudder wreckage, sniffing to investigate, and enticed by curiosity. The creature moved in ominous fashion, its size and strength was enough to deter predator and prey alike. It deterred Josh when he moved in close as he looked up at the towering beast, but the most of his concentration was on the craft. He waved the smoke away from his face as he tried to avoid choking on the developing fumes.

Once the marshal was at the foot of his hover vehicle he reached into his holster to draw out his weapon. But he did only to discover that his holster was empty; his weapon must have fallen out when he was thrown from his seat. Within danger's reach he quickly reached behind his seat to snatch his gear.

In prowling steps the leopard moved in closer to where the marshal was but the marshal had no time to take too much notice of. Once his backpack was in his hand he darted around the scudder to Jackie, who's limp body was at the base of the bluff. Seconds after Josh made his clearing an explosion of fire erupted, after which, the hovercraft begun to incinerate.

The percussion of the explosion threw the animal back; its four legs recoiled like a spring, reacting by instinct to avoid injury. As the explosion occurred, also reacting to instinct, the marshal threw himself on top of Jackie to provide her cover from possible projectile fragments.

The scudder burning the snow leopard was now several feet away from the aftermath, but now very antagonized. The animal was licking its wounds, minor abrasions by shooting fragments. Josh hoped that the explosion would have scared the beast off but now the leopard was even more infuriated than he was before.

Josh pushed himself up and rolled off Jackie to observe the burning rubble, Jackie still unconscious at his side. Most of their gear went up in smoke as he watched, the only tools they had were Joshua's missing side arm and his backpack he was able to snatch away. Rover One kept itself hidden in a rock crevice within the bluff, perhaps unnerved by the incident. As he kept his eyes fixed upon the blaze, the smoke drifting into the atmosphere, the sharp odor from the burning fuel and metal penetrated his sense of smell.

In addition to the blaze, which was quickly turning the scudder into embers, his attention shifted in the direction of the beast. With sudden quickness the leopard leaped forward, to his heading, its clawed feet gripping the surface as the animal approached. With its back arched and its body positioned low, the snow leopard stepped closer and closer toward the pair. Without wavering the predator kept its snout and keen eyes directed toward its prey as it prepared to move in for the kill. While the animal maintained its pace the leopard showed little other movement as though it was ready to strike out, like a snake, at any given moment.

The marshal's attention was thwarted momentarily when Jackie regained consciousness, and regained movement in her limbs. As she pushed herself up, but only to remain sitting, she looked up and noticed the leopard. "Oh my God," was the only thing that came out of her mouth.

Suddenly a human form leaped off the top of the bluff and landed on the beast's backside. With abrupt swiftness a third party introduced himself to the surprise legionnaires.

A muscular longhaired man, who wore animal pelt for clothing, was clearly some kind of tribesman native to Khalidan. His characteristics were very human, with a minor exception; his feet had deep vice-like arches in the mid-region, which would be ideal for supporting his body and for jumping on the planet's rough terrain. This unknown barbarian, which was how the two off-worlders perceived him to be, towered at seven feet tall, which still seemed to be an unequal match up against the carnivore. Unbeknown to Jackie and Joshua his people were called the tawaques, and by the look of the barbarian, they seemed to be the superior race that dwelled on the planet.

Still on the beast's backside, he quickly swung his body around, so that he was facing the same direction the leopard was. He than wrapped one arm around the leopard's neck to gain some control; his main vein rippled across his bicep showing his superior strength. He also held a spear in his free hand, which he'll use as an offensive weapon to slay the beast. The leopard tried to jostle and shake the tawaque off its back but some how he managed to endure it as he maintained his tight hold, with an almost superhuman ability. He kept his head close to the leopard's; and with his spear, tried to keep the beast's razor sharp claws from piercing his body.

But in the end he was unable to adapt to the leopard's reflexes and elastic strength. The leopard's right claw met the tawaque's cheek creating a nasty gash, which forced him to let go of his grip. He than, instantly, spun over and fell as the beast threw his weight to the ground. Both Jackie and Josh witnessed the struggle with a combination of wonder and fear as they both stood up and backed away slightly from the scene.

On the ground and facing up at the leopard the tawaque seemed to be at the mercy of the beast, as it prepared to maul and tear him to shreds. His face bloody, from the gash, his adrenaline took the place of his pain for the moment. The leopard now had its new source of food in a position of submission when it finally lashed out with its saber teeth. The tawaque's survival instincts accompanied his adrenaline, which ensued him to grab his spear. He drove the point of the shaft upward the very moment the beast lunged at him with its teeth. By the animal's own momentum, and the tawaque's strength, the sharp point of the spear pierced through the animal's throat. After a few convulsions and gurgling sounds the beast dropped limp, the snow leopard had been slain.

The tawaque stood up and away from the corpse while directing his gaze at the two new arrivals; leaving his spear deep embedded in the leopard's lifeless body. Mix feelings of curiosity and apprehension made him stare at the two but also made him keep a defensive distance from the strange visitors. Jackie and Josh also had those same feelings as they strained their neck muscles to look up at the imposing height of the land dweller.

"Meyti," a word of unknown linguistics came from the tawaque's mouth. "Meyti," the same word he barked out as he waved at them in an unfriendly fashion.

"What's he saying?" Jackie asked the marshal as she kept her eyes glued at the unique specimen they discovered, quite abruptly.

"I don't know, I left my translator at home," he said being facetious. "But the way he's waving us off I think he wants us to leave."

"Zua natev meyti," the tawaque said while he continued to wave them away, while maintaining his distance.

The tawaque than turned to look down at the corpse, his spear still left where he plunged it. Almost without thinking he grabbed and drew his spear out of the carcass, blood dripping from the flint stone point of his shaft. He postured himself as a proud hunter, and successful one, as he prepared to gut the animal.

"Let's not disappoint him," the marshal said encouraging her to leave by pushing her back with his arm.

He soon followed her path leaving with quiet steps, and not turning his back from the slaughtering. As both of them made their absence, taking slow steps back and away, they kept their eyes on the tawaque who was beginning to carve out his meat. But before they made a complete withdraw from the scene Joshua noticed his firearm lying in the snow, which he was relieved to retrieve. Eventually the two were completely vacated from the tawaque's presence, leaving the tawaque alone to cut and store his meal.

Out of sight from the land dweller the marshal and his cohort walked alone with little gear and foresight as to what to do next. It was late in the afternoon and the day was still young. The marshal had just encountered the first intelligent life form that he was counting on to draft into his service, he hoped. He had thoughts of returning to the bluff to establish some kind of communications with the specimen but he thought better of it, he left the tawaque to his doings as the tawaque requested. But still they were not here as tourists but they were here on a mission and Joshua distained the idea of letting the whole day fall to the waste side.

"What do we do now?" Jackie inquired.

But Josh had no answers so he gave her no reply as he stopped and stood still to contemplate. The marshal dropped his backpack, which was in his hand, and he put his hands to his waist as he looked around but he was still empty of any ideas.

"What about Rover One?" Jackie than asked.

"It'll find its way to us with its sensors when it feels safe to come out," Joshua assured.

After a few minutes of elapsed time, as the two stood still considering their options, Rover One appeared. Hovering toward the legionnaires with casual speed the 'maton seemed undamaged as it took its position next to its masters. Still continuing to levitate Rover One nudged and probed the marshal to see if any harm had come to him.

"Hey, do you mind?" the marshal said feeling pestered by the 'maton's prodding.

"Its just happy to see you."

"Its just a dumb machine following its programming," Josh said as the automaton backed off a little as he commanded.

Than Rover One sensed that Jackie had been hurt and it hovered toward her to tend her wound. The medicorp unit protracted an appendager to Jackie's forehead, which was where she received a mild concussion. An aerosol antiseptic sprayed out, from the needle-nose end of the robotic arm, to sterilize a mild cut near her brow.

Startled by the shooting mist, "Hey, do you mind," she said as she jerked back.

"Its just happy to see you," the marshal threw her own words back at her.

Suddenly they were both startled again by a thump sound of raw animal flesh, which dropped from the air between them. The sound was followed by another thump of tawaquan feet after the tawaque leaped off a nearby snow mound and landed, making a grand appearance. Landing into a solid squat, his arched feet cushioning his drop, he raised himself up to his full height as he observed the alarmed legionnaires, with as much marvel as they had for him. His sinuous muscles were displayed since his body was only partially covered by his animal pelt clothing; his thick skin insulated him from the cold.

The two kept their distance from the barbarian. The tawaque did the same as he observed Jackie and the marshal with wonderment and cautious curiosity. While they continued their analytical standoff with each other the tawaque made the first gesture toward breaking the distant silence they had. The tawaque plucked up the slab of meat, with his spear, and tossed it to Joshua's feet as though he was giving a peace offering.

"Vejot ote zuast," the primitive said using his own alien language.

"What does he want?"

"Well, from his interpretation I believe he's trying to make first diplomatic contact," Josh reasoned. The marshal thought to himself for a while before saying another word and than he spoke again, "I have an idea, tear a piece of your sash and give it to me."

"What for?"

"Don't argue, just do it," the marshal insisted. "Just a small piece."

Right away she removed her scarf, unwinding it from her neck, and tore off a small strip from it and than she handed the piece to Josh. She was just as inquisitive as the tawaque was as he took the piece and approached the primitive. When the marshal drew near the tawaque jerked back a little as he cocked his spear in a defensive manner, with the point in the marshal's uneasy direction.

"Shh, I'm not going to hurt ya," the marshal trying to relax the wary land dweller.

Josh looked around, while still holding on to the piece of material, until he saw a small flat stone for his needs. After he reached down to grab it he squatted low to the ground and placed the stone in plain sight for the tawaque to see. The tawaque leaned over slightly curious at Joshua's doings, unaware of the marshal's aims. The tawaque observed Joshua, as the marshal bunched the material in a tight fold, and than he placed the wadded up piece on the stone.

Jackie looked over the marshal's shoulder as he carried on. Once the piece was carefully placed on the smooth flat surface of the stone he reached in and drew out a small prism from his left cuff. After which, he looked up at the sun to gain its position and to make sure that his body was not blocking the line of light. He than, while looking at the tawaque and smiling, positioned the prism between the sun's radiance and the material.

Hollands steadily held the prism while the sun's beam was being directed and magnified through the optic, and against the piece of Jackie's sash. The marshal's demonstration generated heat-causing smoke to develop, which in turn, than made the material ignite into a small flame. A mixture of excitement and fear stirred the tawaque into a slight fervor as he witnessed the small event.

Josh than leaned close to the flame and placed his hand behind it, in a cradle-like fashion, to keep the wind from blowing it out. He than blew on the flame, with short controlled breaths, until the small piece of cloth was fully engulfed. When only ashes remained the small made fire eventually burned out but the demonstration was a success.

The tawaque was excitable and interested to see more of, what he perceived to be, magic. Now that Josh had broken the proverbial ice the tawaque drew even nearer to the marshal's side and smiled back, amazed at what he saw.

"Here, you want it," the marshal said as he attempted to give him the prism as a token of trust. "Here, take it," the marshal said as he extended his friendship.

The tawaque's hand seized Joshua's gift, which Josh was parting with, and the primitive became even more excitable. In the primitive's state of euphoria he started bobbing up and down while saying, "Nehod, nehod. Ahv-t nehod," in his own words.

While beating on his own chest the tawaque said, "Jepheth, Jepheth." Than the tawaque gave the marshal a hard pat on his chest, without the intention of being aggressive and said, "Zua esi."

"I think he's giving us his name," Joshua deduced.

"Friendly, isn't he," Jackie said with a tone of humor.

"Shh, not now," the marshal quieted Jackie to keep her from confusing the primitive. He than introduced himself while tapping on his chest, "Joshua, my name is Joshua."

"Josh-u-a," the tawaque slurred the name while trying to speak it. Jepheth than made pointing gestures to affirm his assessment, first to himself, "Jepheth," and than to the marshal, "Josh-u-a." After an understanding was reached the land dweller clapped his hands feeling he made a major accomplishment.

The marshal felt he made an accomplishment as well as he turned to Jackie and said, "I think we may have found a friend, and a guide."

INDUSTRIAL MIGHT WAS BEING carried out and displayed exuberantly back at the brigand's refinery station. The metal processing and manufacture sector of the station had white covered surroundings, but thus, you would not know of it. The brunt luminosity from the hot molten metal reflected off the white paint and hence the surroundings had an eerie red appearance. The combustionators, from the blast furnaces, caused an aftereffect of by-product steam, which spewed out from the variety of converter eyelets, fogging the backdrop.

The brigand workers, who were operating the line, wore white radiant suppressant overalls to protect themselves from the intense heat that emanated from the source. They stood by control modules to oversee the pri-mass ore being dispensed out from the over hanging blast chamber. As the fusionized magma left the chamber the pliable element dropped into rectangular long molds below, to be shaped and cooled. The super size spherical chamber used the process of atomic compression to reheat the ore; but not just to heat but to also fuse the properties into a single element, fusion metal.

The workers would, on occasion, check the read-out monitor to observe the time-delay coordinates to make sure the whole operation was running smoothly and in accord to safety specifications. One of the men, who stood nearest to one of the modules, glanced at the monitor and than to the other individual beside him and nodded assurances that the operation, thus far, was up to standard codes.

As the metal processing continued, without any signs of slowing down, the men continued to oversee the computer operated machine at work. As the two conveyor belts moved, at the same rate of speed, the long slab-shaped molds snaked across to underneath the blast chamber as the liquid ore was being shot into the casts by injectors. The molds were being filled to its specified capacity, as they moved below the injector heads, and than passed them by to the next step.

Once the molds left the above blast chamber they made way toward the chill chamber. The chill chamber was a big rectangular shaped refrigeration unit with small door openings, which the molds would enter into. Once the molds were inside the refrigeration doors would shut automatically; the timing was and had to be computer controlled throughout the process.

Only minutes would be needed to cool the metal into a rigid enough slate to be handled. The cooled slates than exited the chill chamber, through doors at the opposite end, to reach the final stage. A four-man crew, who were a few meters away from the chilling process, waited patiently until the casts were within their grasp. As soon as they were able to the men, two posted at opposite sides of both belts, readied themselves for the refinement stage.

As the two slabs of metal drew to a close the men, as the metal pieces coasted by, polished away any tarnish or inconsistencies that appeared. As the slabs moved pass them both, of the two-man teams, they would implement the following procedure. One of them would spray dissolvent solution on the slab's surface, with a small hose, while the other would do the polishing with a hand-held rag.

After the entire lengths of the strips were cleaned and polished they would free the finished pieces from their encasings. By flipping the molds upside down, and hammering the backside, they would empty the casts back to their hollow original state to be used again.

After the cleaning crew had done their job the two slates of metal struts reached the robotic units, called bipod loaders, to receive the slates for them to take away. The loaders resembled bulky machines with two mechanical legs and programmed only for the task at hand. Each one of the two bipods were stationed at the near ends of both conveyor lines, but off to the sides. Before the finished products had the chance to drop off the ends the loaders' sprocket-like wheels, which were giant gears built into their mechanical make-up they used as hands, would grip the slabs and carry them over into the loaders' arms.

The men paid no attention to one of the robotic machines as it moved, on hydraulic piston legs; to carry the pieces off to the depot. The loaders would remain at their station until their grips could carry no more, and one of them was up to its limit. In an ominous uncaring fashion the bipod moved on a heading toward the promag tube, an offloader able to hold and transfer a few tons at a time.

Nearing a compartment hatch the electric circuitry sensors, which were mounted within the wall above, opened it once the loader was at the threshold of the entrance. Entering the compartment room the loader approached the tube with its load of metal struts in its arms, as it did, more proximity sensors opened the tube's swivel-down accessor port. Using the same method as before the bipod rotated its sprocket grips, only this time, outward to snatch and snare the pieces over and into the tubular cell. After the cylindrical hold was filled the loader moved away, back to its station, and as it did the promag's swivel hatch closed. By propulsion magnetics the struts were drawn through the tube and toward the supply depot for offloading.

The hangar bay's surroundings did show the white of its coverings, from the floor to the ceiling. The bay was spacious and had several overhead accessor doors along the sides, which gave entry and exit from the station. Long columns of HEL-bomber attack ships were station side to side, recently assembled and had never been flown. The maintenance crew and brigand pilots were bustling around quickly arming the ships or implementing system checks.

In addition to the gunships a small squadron of cyclodrones, used for patrols, laid dormant near the backdrop of the HEL-bomber columns. The aeroships were startling to see because of their sleek design and armament. An intricate makeup of coils, bearings, and reinforced springs, interwoven with the superconductivity technology that turned her, the cyclodrone represented the awesome.

Tylus stood uneasy as he leaned against one of the aerolifts as though he was waiting for something, or someone, "Tylus," a man shouted as he approached.

"Quiblo, it took you long enough," Tylus said trying not to shout as his companion did. "Were you able to get the stuff?"

"Yea, but it wasn't easy getting it pass the sentries," Quiblo responded.

"We'll do it tonight but keep it quiet and try not to think too much. Remember, his clairvoyance is about as strong as his stench,"

Tylus said plotting. "Just do your assigned duties and tonight stay away from the sentry 'matons."

Inside a nearby chamber, located not too far from the hangar bay, the surrounding environment was abundant with plant life and the temperature was warm and humid; this was Kreed's greenhouse throne room. The plants were plotted in a feeding solution where it was grown; the process was called hydrobedding. Because the area was moist and damp the only few walkways that were there were wet patched and muddy. Anyone who was not accustomed to the humidity would have an unwelcome feeling in this sort of environment; but for Kreed it was like home.

Kreed sat at his throne with his head crest and body limp; his eyes were affixed to the empty space in front of him. But that empty space was fill as soon as a brigand soldier entered and stood before his lord and master. The soldier was apparently sweating from the humidity but he stood at attention without wavering, or reaching to wipe the sweat off his brow. Kreed had a strong telepathic influence over his men; he controlled what they felt and he knew what they knew.

"Yes my lord, everything is running smoothly and on a timely fashion," the soldier stated after he made cognitive adherence to Kreed's mindlink. After a few seconds had elapsed, during which their minds were still connected, the soldier broke the silence again, "Your wish is my doing." Before he snapped to an affirmative and bowed he spoke these final words, "Another storm is brewing, best to recall the scouts who are out on recon until the storm passes." After this was said the brigand soldier did an about face and left to carry out his duty; as Kreed remained where he was, his eyes straight and not flinching a muscle.

The day was now drawing to a close and the sun was beginning to set. It was .05 hours startime and the tawaque, along with his newfound friends, were treading through the snow for a destination yet unknown to the legionnaires. The tawaque was leading them as a guide; hence, he knew the landscape better than the others. Rover One followed behind the rest rolling across the snow covered surface on its tractor wheels, the 'maton's chain treads gave it good traction to keep up with the team.

"Eh tevusn," the tawaque shouted as he pointed ahead. He had to shout to be heard amidst the severe crosswinds that were developing. Besides the wind pressing against their ears the storm, which was materializing, was also pushing them back as they trudged ahead little by little. The sun, at that moment in time, was being veiled behind thick clouds.

Joshua, as he tried to endure the elements, looked ahead to see what it was Jepheth was pointing to. "Another snow squall," Josh shouted, the wind muffling his voice.

As they saw the culprit of this madness, to them, the squall resembled a giant whirling vortex, which were many kilometers in diameter. The gyrating entity was induced by down currents of north and south winds, which were colliding.

Jepheth seemed to have changed his direction; instead of going straight he turned to his right, perhaps to find shelter. "I hope he knows where he's taking us," Jackie responded. Not knowing what the two were saying the tawaque simply waved his arm up and in a forward motion, urging them to follow his tracks.

The thick clouds darkened the outside scenery, and the wind's velocity, stirred the loose snow up and around them, the snowflakes were like flying shards of glass. To protect themselves, Joshua had his scarf wrapped across his mouth and chin and had his cloak to veil his eyes. Jackie pressed up against the marshal as he lead her way, while she had her hand close to her face to deflect the snow away. Rover One showed no difficulty withstanding the punishing blows of the currents, hence, his body was metal and driven by horsepower. Even though it was dark and shrouded by snowdrift the 'maton's optic sensors helped the automaton to see its way clear toward the others, to wherever they were going.

Approaching a chain of rocky mass they decided to place themselves inside a cave for safe haven until the storm passes over them. In single file, with Jepheth leading the way, they hurried inside growing weary by each passing moment. Rover One was the last one to scurry inside; now moving kind of sluggish caused by the frigid temperature.

Relieved that they were now safe and sound under a shield of rock they relaxed their muscles and shook off the loose snowfall from their clothing. Rover One found a nestling place to rest near the rock wall where it remained unmoving. The other three made themselves at home and as comfortable as possible, hoping that their new abode was only temporary.

Their first priority was to find some sort of heat source to keep themselves warm. Jackie kept her arms folded as she rubbed the sides of them, while stomping her feet, in order to increase blood flow for added body heat. The 'maton's mechanical innates were beginning to freeze because of the frigidness, and it sensed a sense of lethargic.

The tawaque seemed to have developed a sense of anxiousness as he gathered some dried up twigs he found and than dropped them into a bunch. "Ahti zuaz nehod," the tawaque stated as he bunched the twigs tighter together.

"Now what does he want?" Jackie spoke out of sheer fatigue.

"I'm not sure, but I think he wants me to start a fire," Joshua guessed for himself as the tawaque pointed to the nest of kindling he had made.

"Sounds good to me, I'm freezing," Jackie said while still trying, with futile attempts, to keep herself warm.

"Ahti zuaz nehod," the tawaque said again. This time, though, he was waving around the prism the marshal had given to him as a gift. "Ahti zuaz nehod," Jepheth kept saying while jerking the prism in the marshal's direction, and, while pointing to the same spot.

"No, I don't want it," the marshal insisted while pushing the prism away. Apparently Jepheth appealed to the marshal to invoke his magic, with little understanding that it was a conjoining effort with the sun that made Jackie's piece of sash burn.

"Ahti zuaz nehod."

"No, it won't work, there's no sun," Josh said while still pushing the prism back to the tawaque's keeping.

"Try and work your way out of this one," Jackie grinned a little but still shivering.

"I have a better idea," Joshua responded to her, and the land dweller.

Joshua than stepped away from Jepheth's irritating insistence and he walked over toward, the soon to be, campfire. As soon as he stood before the pile of twigs he unsheathed his weapon and took aim. With one startling shot a laser bolt discharged from Joshua's pulse pistol, which ignited the bunch into a medium size fire, they now have their means to keep warm.

Once the fire was lit, which threw the tawaque back, Josh holstered his weapon and than squatted near the flame. Jackie also rushed toward the fire, after which, she to squatted close to where she could get warm. She than placed her hands close to the fire to relish the warmth. Rover One, sensing the heat from the fire, rolled over close to it to thaw out its inner circuitry.

"Just what the doctor ordered," the marshal sighed.

"You don't have to convince me," Jackie agreed.

One look at what Joshua was able to do Jepheth held the piece of crystal while looking at it and than threw it to the ground, like it was a tick, useless and bothersome. Not meaning to disrespect the marshal's gift but he knew where the power was; it was draped down the marshal's leg. Without any further thought of it he quickly joined the others, beside the campfire.

The tawaque nestled in close to the warmth hoping; as sure as the others did, that the storm would quickly pass over them. Even though his thick skin provided shielding against the cold a campfire was still a welcoming sight for him, it kept the predatory animals away and the added warmth was comforting as well.

In the meantime, while they were waiting for the squall to settle down some place else, they had nothing but leisure time to relax and to get to know each other. Specifically introductions were needed between the legionnaires and their tawaque escort, who they now know as Jepheth. Jackie was now warm enough to distant herself from the fire a bit, while keeping herself patient and calming her inner anxieties. As she laid on her side in a repose position Joshua laid his backpack aside and than gave Japheth a glance with hope to narrow the personal solitude between them, maybe even learn his native language.

Joshua than turned to the campfire and than pointed to it while saying, "Fire, this is fire." The marshal shook his finger at it and spoke again, "Fire."

"F-f-fire," the tawaque stuttered finding it difficult to speak the marshal's own words. But contrary to his lack of pronounce, and his primitive surroundings, Josh was impressed by the tawaque's fast approach at being coached.

"Goshi," Jepheth said while pointing his finger to the blaze. "Goshi," he said again while still gesturing toward the same.

"Goshi," the marshal repeated finding it much easier to speak his language than him his own.

Slightly excited as though he was accomplishing something the marshal turned to Jackie and said to her, "Well, now we know how to say fire."

"You got nothing better to do?" Jackie asked with a cynical tone.

"We can't go anywhere until the storm clears," the marshal replied. "Besides, the more we know about him and his people the better our chances of getting some help."

"If they'll help us," Jackie stated pessimistically.

Joshua ignored her last statement and resumed dialogue with his nomadic friend, with a little more optimism than his female companion. Now, at this time, Jackie laid completely down on her side to sleep for the night while Josh continued.

Once the word fire had been established, and understood, Josh stood up and stepped away momentarily. The marshal seemed to be contemplating something, his actions had purpose, but the tawaque stayed where he sat wondering what that purpose was.

But the tawaque's curiosity was short when the marshal returned, from a short distance, with a stick in his hand. At an instant the tawaque jumped up as he quickly grabbed his spear, interpreting Joshua's action as a provocative attack. Jepheth stood in an on-guard stance pointing his spear at the marshal while grunting unappreciative sounds.

"No," the marshal trying to calm the primitive. "No, I'm not going to hurt you."

The marshal relaxed his arms while spreading them apart, like he was going to embrace the land dweller with a hug, and while loosening his grip on the stick that he held in one hand. He than slowly approached where he sat before and kneeled down, "I wanna show you something," the tawaque now relaxed a bit.

Using the stick of dried wood, the marshal found in the darkened corner of the cave, he used it as a pointer to draw lines in the loose dirt between them to see. It would appear that Josh was sketching a course in the dirt; a representation of the direction they traversed, from the spot of their first meeting to where they are now.

The tawaque than laid his spear down, off to the side, and reached out his hand for which Joshua handed him the stick. He than held the stick in the center and, using the point of it, begun to draw additional markings in the dirt, an extension of the marshal's rough sketch map.

After the tawaque finished his drawing of the map he used the stick as a pointer, "Xi esi ji-shi," Jepheth said while circling the map with his pointer to indicate it. "Xi esi Ji-shi," he said again while pointing to a specific spot on the map.

"This is where we are, here?" the marshal gathered while pointing to where Jepheth was pointing. "Here?" he said, but this time stomping the ground with his fist to where he was sitting.

"Shishi," the tawaque responded while nodding his head.

"Shishi, yes?" the marshal interpreted while still thumping the ground. "Here?" making progress the marshal thought.

Than Jepheth moved his pointer to the other side of the map and than jabbed the ground there several times with his stick while saying, "Xi phif vu-hu ji-shi."

The marshal made the assumption that the curbs on the map were the mountainous regions they would have to cross, and the lines, represented the foot trail of their trek they would need to travel.

"Is that where we need to go," the marshal assumed the native knew the terrain better than he did. "There, we need to go there?" the marshal tapping his finger on the point given.

"About how long?" Josh asked, as if the native could answer right away.

"Pu," Jepheth said shaking his head.

The marshal than raised his hand up to his face level, fingers spread apart and his palm facing the tawaque. "How long?" the marshal asked again while counting his fingers for Jepheth to see and interpret.

"Shishi," Jepheth understood.

The tawaque than made slow up and down movements with his hand for Joshua to see and construe. Josh observed the hand signals he was making, but was confounded, but he knew the tawaque was trying to tell him something.

Sensing the marshal's frustration he quickly stood up nearly jumping toward the cave's ceiling. "X-jip vjii taup soy-tit epith tivi," he said pointing to where he estimated the sun should be.

Even though the clouds were still thick, which obscured the sun, Joshua was able to fit the pieces together. "What, the sun?"

The tawaque than jerked quickly to Joshua's front and kneeled before him. "X-jip vjii taup soy-tit," he said as he slowly raised his hand again to his face level in a shaking-like fashion. "Epith tivi," he than said as he turned his palm inward while lowering his hand. "Epith soy-tit," he than said as he raised his hand up again at face level.

Joshua made the deduction that the act of Jepheth raising and lowering his hand, and than raising it again, was his way of expressing the instance of the sun rising and setting and than rising again. "What, tomorrow morning?" Josh asked as he pointed to the cave's ingress.

"Shishi."

"Yes, tomorrow morning?" the marshal asked again. After the interpretation was successfully made Josh lowered his finger and smiled at the tawaque.

The tawaque smiled back but at this point the was ready to follow Jackie's example, to go to sleep. "Voni vu tmiquay," Jepheth said as he back away from the marshal and laid himself down to rest and than closed his eyes. "Tmiquay."

"Yea, time to sleep," Joshua said feeling kind of tired himself. But before the marshal prepared to snooze he crept silently toward Jackie, who was long fast a slumber, and than he gently nudged at her.

"What is it?" Jackie said as she was quickly startled from her state of sleep. Her eyes were slightly squinted when she looked at Josh but she was alert enough to be responsive.

"Sorry, didn't mean to wake you," the marshal was apologetic and knew than he really didn't need to wake her. "The tawaque insists we'll reach his tribal community in the morning, it's just over the next region."

"He told you that?"

"Yea."

"You can speak tawaquan?" Jackie looked at the marshal with a puzzled expression.

"Not exactly, just trust me on this," the marshal insisted.

As Jackie lowered her head again, to go back to sleep, Josh retracted back to where he was before. The night was almost upon them and the marshal knew that they would have an eventful day tomorrow. So he relaxed down on his back, and close to the fire, to do as the others did; he went fast asleep.

The refinery station drew short of activity when the workers and technical crew took rest for the night. The machines were turned off and were cooled to the touch from the many hours of blasting nuclear fusion against primordial matter. Even the loaders were dormant as they stood against the walls, like sentries; but they were not. The robotic bipods were simply stationary awaiting the next day's work schedule.

The only movement that was came from the sentry spheres, 'matons, as they buzzed by in midair patrolling the grounds. The mini spheres' sensors, which were integrated into the security alarm, would automatically sound off the moment they detected a threat breach. Any infiltration within the compound, or personnel not in their rightful place, would trigger the alert.

The dimly lit corridor stretched from end to end, bordering Kreed's throne room entrance hatch; only the nocturnal lights allowed for some illumination. All was quiet; hence, the walkway was absent from the reverberation of human steps or activity.

The only occupants were those of the two sentries, cyclops footsoldiers; standing erect on diagonally pitch jointed bipod legs. They were posted on both sides of the throne room's main entry hatch, standing completely stationary without a nuance of movement. That is except for their optics, which kept a vigilant spread on their surroundings.

The silence was broken as a couple of sentry spheres flew through the corridor while video surveying the parameter. The 'matons moved speedily, one behind the other, as the noise from their mini-thrusters echoed. The latter stopped abruptly and turned to the side toward a collection of storage drums, thinking that its sensors had detected something, shortly after the leading 'maton had vanished into the next sector. Sensing nothing the secondary 'maton disappeared as well to join its other equal.

The corridor was again silent until laser bolts shot out from between the barrels, which was followed by collapsing sentries; the streaks of energy met their targets. The first mortally wounded cyclops had no time to raise his repeating rifle since he was the first one targeted, and thereafter, he dropped to the floor. The second one quickly jerked his weapon straight as his single-eye laser sight emitted a blue probing beam to home in on their attackers. But it was too little too late to keep itself from getting hit, it was quickly terminated as well; the attack transpired in only seconds and it was over.

Out from between the storage stock Tylus and Quiblo revealed themselves, who were armed and moving with stealthy steps. In addition to his weapon Tylus also carried a small equipment sack as they both headed toward Kreed's ventilation vent.

"Hurry, before the sentries return," Tylus warned as they were now within arm's reach of the vent.

"About how long?" Quiblo asked.

"A small amount of this neural gas and he'll be in a coma within minutes, dead within hours," Tylus answered as he made preparations.

Using a bolt shear Tylus commenced to remove the bolt heads. The charger-powered tool was lightweight, easily held by a single hand, while the other hand remained free. The square retractable fin vent was held in by four bolts, one at each corner, and Tylus was eventually down to his last; while Quiblo stood behind as a look out. As Tylus trimmed away the last bolt head he held the opposite corner with his free hand to keep the vent from crashing to the floor.

Once free from the bolts, while still holding on to the corner, Tylus secured his cutter into his retainer belt and than he quietly laid the vent to his side, leaning it against the wall.

Afterward, both men slipped their gas masks on to protect themselves from the harmful vapors that might possibly escape out from the ventilation shaft. With his pulse rifle still slung on his shoulder Tylus than seized one of his toxin grenades, which he kept in his sack, and he pulled the pin. Once the detonator was unlocked, and free to be released, Tylus lightly tossed the incendiary gas bomb into the shaft's opening. Soon after the grenade was thrown, relieved that they had protection from the fumes, Tylus and Quiblo waited where they stood for the poisonous vapor to do its effect.

After a few long minutes, it seemed, had passed Tylus gave Quiblo an affirmative nod, the go ahead, to move in. His rifle was no longer dangling over his shoulder but was held straight, ready for his defense as he approached the hatchway to Kreed's chamber; Quiblo followed his trail.

They both had their backs to the wall; with their weapons poised and while looking side to side to make self-assurances that no one would stumble upon their scheme. While they both kept themselves alert, almost to the point of being on edge, Tylus reached for the accessor control panel and than he motioned the sensor to open the hatch. When the hatch snapped open they both hurried inside the throne chamber to avoid being exposed in the open corridor. As they entered the throne room they kept a watchful eye at their rear as they took steady and careful backward steps inside, before the hatch closed.

Now that they were safe, for the moment, inside Kreed's throne room greenhouse they commenced a search for a body. The cloudy white mist of the toxin gas made visibility difficult but they continued to seek out for Kreed, as time was running short. Their air-filtering masks kept them protected from the harmful toxin as they moved about the area slowly, never distancing themselves too far apart; so as not to lose sight of each other.

"We must hurry, before the breach of security sounds the alarm," Tylus warned but muffled, yet coherent, through his mask. Quiblo didn't counter the remark but he agreed with a nod, as he trailed behind, and peering through the dense gas.

As they both walked toward, and now only a few feet away from the throne, Quiblo broke his silence. "Wouldn't his ESP defenses signal the others for help," he questioned as he tried not to imagine it. "His mind control is powerful."

Tylus rebutted to reassure, and reassure himself, "Hopefully his brain is dormant along with his body." After his reply he thought nothing more of it, although, he would feel more comfortable if he actually saw the body to examine it. "Hopefully, if he's in his state of comatose, his cerebral link would be severed."

Suddenly sounds, like escaping air, distracted their attention as they looked around to find the source. Their focus was directed toward the ceiling, which was where the sounds seemed to be coming from. Air vents, a few at both opposite sides of the chamber, appeared to be sucking in and drawing out the toxins. Mounted within the walls, near the ceiling, the air vents were establishing normal environmental conditions, by environmental auto control or manually done was unknown to them. As they stood bewildered and surprised the surrounding area defogged and cleared to the previous state that it was earlier.

Once the toxigenic gas seemed to have depleted out into the atmosphere, through shafts leading to the station's outside air vents, the two men slipped off their gas masks. "What's going on?" Tylus asked himself after his mask was off his face and in his hand.

They were now breathing clean air but their self-trepidation took away their enjoyment of it, for they feared that they were caught in the act; and as the entrance hatch snapped open their fears materialized. Their fears took the form of a huge rectangular-shaped environ chamber and the two sentry guards, who entered and stood guard beside it. As the hatch snapped shut behind them Tylus and Quiblo stood and quivered, they knew the game was up.

The two cyclops sentries stood, at opposite sides of the environ-chamber, with the muzzles of their weapons pointed at the infiltrators. Knowing that further resistance would be futile, "Throw down your weapon," Tylus ordered his fellow conspirator as he did so. "We're finished."

Nobody, whom was present, moved a muscle until the environ hatch swung open, like a hinge door. The two, who were now captives to their surprise, flinched a little for they knew, and feared, what was in store for them. Although the environ door was opened electronically; the door weighed a ton, it opened slowly.

Precipitous steam escaped out from the mobile chamber as the hatch withdrew; and within, emerged the occupant. An unwelcome and familiar alien form; with head crest and bloodshot eyes, Kreed stood before the two assassins.

General Commander Kreed invoked a mind lock to the ringleader; Tylus found himself unable to move was the effect, as though his neurotransmitters no longer sent signals to his body. Kreed approached with such wickedness in his steps Tylus felt the need to drop down to his knees and beg for mercy but he was unable to, or even speak. When Kreed was within breath closeness to the main instigator Tylus cocked his eyeballs up at the towering reptilian.

With sudden quickness Kreed snapped his hand out snatching Tylus' throat, his claws pierced the brigandeers's skin; blood gurgling sounds were the only sounds he made. By superhuman strength, either it be from his natural ability or from the nanocell implants that still flowed through his veins, Kreed picked Tylus up to his face level; the brigandeers's feet were dangling a few centimeters from the floor's surface. Blood stained Kreed's fingers as he maintained a tight hold on the other's neck, Tylus gurgled and gasped for air.

With aggressive impact Kreed spat a neuro-venom at his prey and than threw Tylus to the floor, half way across the room it seemed. Tylus ended up sprawled out on the floor convulsing and twitching until he became completely paralyzed; in a few seconds he would die.

Quiblo felt a sensation of horror, which shot straight up his spine and through his senses, as he backed away from the display of cruelty he had just witnessed. No time to fear for his own life as one of the cyclopes speared his body with a laser bolt after the automaton triggered its pulse rifle. Quiblo didn't know what hit him as his midsection got blown away. As Quiblo's lifeless body laid in blood and fragments of bone the two sentries jerked at attention to face their superior, the two conspirators were now out of the way permanently.

After a perilous journey the three travelers had reached their destination; a tribal community, which spanned several kilometers across their focus horizon. A pleasant sight they probably all thought considering the many tribulations they had to persevere through. They finally made it to civilization, a primitive civilization, but a place anyway for shelter, and maybe, a warm welcome from the inhabitants.

They were all running ragged; sleeping in caves, enduring the harsh weather, and almost getting eaten by wild carnivores and they hoped they've been through the worst. Jepheth led the party with his spear in one hand and his pelt sack dangling over his opposing shoulder, his arms were outstretched as they neared the village to alert his fellows of their arrival. Josh and Jackie tagged with a less conspicuous demeanor, not knowing what their presence would stir. Rover One also tagged behind, but way behind and out of sight from the other three, it was safe for its databit processors to assume that these primitive land dwellers have never seen a machine of any kind before.

Nearing two hundred yards to the village the tawaque motioned the two, who were still following behind, to stand their ground while he preceded forward. As Jepheth approached even closer the villagers looked upon the new arrivals with a combination of curiosity and defensive paranoia. When Jepheth reached a modest distance from two of his known tribesmen, who appeared to be higher up in the social rank, the legionnaires assumed that their escort was attempting to calm some unsettled nerves. As the other tawaques uttered to themselves while studying the new comers Jepheth had his hand poised at the two while he talked in tawaquan; he tried to assure his chiefs that the strangers were friends and were not to be feared.

Once their nerves had been settled the two chiefs retreated toward the main group of onlookers, despite their apprehensions. As his associates moved away Jepheth walked a few steps toward the legionnaires' direction and than waved at them to come forth, "Duni-up ximduni," he said twice while waving his spear about in a come on in fashion. Jackie and Josh looked at each other, assuming everything was equable, and they relaxed a little as they approached his way.

They approached a wall carved stone of an igloo-like house, which was the vicinity of where Jepheth stood, but away from the concentration of curiosity seekers. Out of the cave or what resembled a cave opening; and at the far side from where the legionnaires were at, the occupants within gave up their abode for the new residence but with protest. Led out by one of the chieftains, he himself seemed to have grievances over the matter, but he submitted. Apparently a deal was struck and the villagers obeyed the chief's demands as they hurried out carrying as much as they could of their personal belongings, while quietly cursing in their native language. Neither Jackie or Josh, or even Jepheth for that matter, knew that the new homestead was theirs, temporarily, until the chief flagged them in. The two off-worlders looked at each other and deduced to reason that they now had shelter as the chief left them to their doings.

"I guess we're supposed to take up residence here," Josh figured.

"How accommodating," Jackie responded having reservations.

"Don't slap a gift horse in the mouth," the marshal reasoned, "at least it's a place to stay for the night." As Joshua observed the exterior structure of the dome he remarked, "It's not the Cosmopolitan Inn but it'll do."

"Gummux ni," Jepheth stated while hand signaling the other two to enter. The land dweller took the lead, leading the legionnaires toward the hut's entrance way. "Gummux ni," he said again while waving his hand in a forward motion.

Jackie and the marshal followed Jepheth around the side to

the front, as they felt appreciative to take advantage of the chief's offering. As soon as they were at the foot of the entry they intruded upon the vacancy of the hut; Jepheth was the first to disappear inside. The door of the entry was merely a covering of peltry flaps; a couple of hide material overlapping to allow some sort of trapped warmth.

As soon as they were within the modest size structure they immediately felt the heat emanating from a central campfire, which was still burning. A small opening directly above the fire, through the crown of the dome, allowed the smoke to be drawn into the outside atmosphere. The only light seemed to be coming from the fire itself, which gave the surroundings a serene and calming appearance. The dimness of the interior was tinted as the flickering lights of the campfire, reflecting from the shadows, danced giving a sensation of warmth and home-felt ease.

"Em-mh miewi zua pux," the tawaque's last statement was before he took his leave. The other two had no idea what he said as he walked out leaving them to their privacy.

They now stood by themselves looking around their new surroundings. The interior had typical furnishings, in accord with the indigenous habitat. A stalk mattress laid on the floor to the far side where husband and wife would sleep. Arrays of necklaces, made up of different colored feathers were displayed on the wall, possibly to declare the clan's stature within the tribal community. And other artifacts as well were prominent and displayed in an orderly fashion; including an abundant supply of fur peltry sheets folded and kept neat, not too far from the bed. A few spears and a bow, with arrows, were openly shown on stone retainers along with unrelated cutting tools that were also presented there. Joshua guessed that the male clansman was an adept hunter or mason.

A spinning wheel for manufacturing strong threading, for example laces to tie the spearheads to their shafts, was placed near the mattress as well. A primitive tool for a people with no accessible technology, the device was powered by foot pedal and crank only.

Jackie approached the device with a little gnawing curiosity,

"How quaint," she said as she slid her fingers across the stretched thread of textile.

"Don't touch anything," the marshal insisted, "our presence here is disturbing enough for them." He than said as he dropped his backpack to the floor, "I'm sure they don't want us fondling their stuff, leave everything as we found it."

She lost interest quickly in the threading device, as she walked away from it, trying now to feel comfortable in her new surroundings. Placing her hands to her waist and looking around she stated, "I hope we don't have to stay on this miserable block of ice too long."

"Feeling's mutual," Josh agreed.

"How long before Jag brings in the cavalry?" she questioned.

"It depends how long it takes Central to draw up mission plans and mobilize the fleet."

"It's been two days."

"You should see the fleet, it's a massive undertaking," Josh impressed upon her, "Not to mention we're outside of Dominion charted territory, the logistics alone will take time."

"I'm just anxious to go back to warmer climate," she said as she hung her arms down to her waist and walked over toward the mattress. She than sat herself on the bed and leaned back, her hands placed behind her to support her upper body, to rest awhile.

"I assume than you get the bed," he said with a look of not surprised agitation.

"Unless you plan on sharing it," Jackie cringed at the thought of it. "I'd rather sleep on the floor."

"Never mind, I got the floor, at least I'm closer to the fire," the marshal said as he walked toward the burning light.

He crouched down near the fire to absorb the warmth placing his hands in front of it, and while periodically, rubbing his hands together. He than stood up to grab his backpack from where he dropped it. Once his gear was back in his hand he than walked back to the campfire and placed it at a safe distance to unpack some of his essentials. One of the items that he took out was his interlink module, which he placed next to his pack. When the interlink was positioned upright he raised the binary antennas and he switched on, and left on, the transceiver code.

"I see I'm not the only one anxious to get off this place," Jackie smirked.

"When the cavalry does come their going to signal us," he said as he moved the interlink back a little bit further from the heat. The interlink was just one of his Dominion issued gear and he would prefer not to have the releasing heat, from the campfire, melt the internal wiring. "They can use our frequency to home in on our location."

"And when they do?"

"We'll be ready."

"I see we have company," she said as her attention was diverted.

Unannounced; Rover One snuck in through the flaps and flew into view by its aft thrust and than the little unit stopped before the two, once it made itself present. The 'maton seemed to have followed, using its audio sensors, the trail of the legionnaires' voice signatures. The automaton successfully snuck into the village, it would seem, without raising too much of a commotion among the residence. A few centimeters off the ground the 'maton turned off its aft thrusts when it was at Joshua's side but its maglift kept it aloft. Even though the two were please to see no harm had come to their friend they went about their business and made themselves feel at home.

Dome huts were made out of carved rock, to withstand the punishing weather conditions. And they were spread out unceremoniously allowing just enough patches of space for corrals to house their beasts of burden. There were no extravagances of any kind, only a humble village setting not exceeding practicality.

While the covert pair situated their belongings, and made their temporary outpost as livable for them as they can, the village was in a typical state of daily routine among those who resided there. The presence of the offlanders, however, did cause subtle excitement of the village inhabitants.

Subtle wind swept across the land as the noon sun shined down.

Jepheth had no thought, at least for the moment, to partake in the day's splendor since he was presently engaged. Jepheth stood before the two chieftains near a corral, which fenced in a small grouping of boadors. While the black saber-tooth creatures were eating from their troughs and/or moving about, Jepheth conversed with the two tribal heads. Judging by their scowling looks, and Jepheth's blank expression, all other distractions seemed inconsequential.

Jepheth stood face to face with the tawaques listening intently with a sedated look, as though he was submitting to their demands or suggestions. The two were expressing themselves in their tawaque language excitably, their words close to coinciding one against the other, before Jepheth had a window of opportunity to throw in a few words of his own, if or when he wanted to.

While the private meeting continued Joshua approached near their vicinity, but not too close to startle them or interrupt their conversation. It was obvious to the marshal that the issue of their debate was about him and his companion, but what about he could not decipher specifically. Josh only picked up on a few words of their native tongue and he didn't have time, or the desire for right now, to learn the lingo. As Joshua stood his ground with curious intent Jepheth spoke his mind as well whenever his superiors seemed to allow him to. Occasionally, with keen ears, Jepheth would glance over in Joshua's direction and than return his gaze to his own reckoning as their heated converse continued, not wavering because of the marshal's presence there.

After several long minutes the conversation ended and the two chieftains, the pair whom made their attitude clear, stomped away directing themselves toward other business. Jepheth, to, turned away but with a much more casual and understanding demeanor, as he neared toward the marshal. The marshal looked puzzled after the heated debate was over and he hoped that their intrusion wasn't too much a burden on them, particularly too much of a burden on Jepheth, who brought the intruders into their camp.

As Jepheth neared even closer Joshua took a couple of steps back, intuitively, because of the tawaque's size and built. Jepheth towered over the legionnaire and Joshua gave in to the superb specimen that now stood at reach.

"Fu zua japev," the words came from the tawaque's mouth as Josh looked up at him. The marshal had to strain his neck to make eye contact to the seven-foot behemoth; they stood toe to toe. "Fu zua japev," he said again while shaking his spear this time. The tawaque continued to play his game of charades, his intent unbeknown to the marshal.

It wasn't as though the marshal was unwilling to learn the native's language and customs but he was unable to because of a lack of time, he still had a mission before him to complete. "I have no idea what you're saying," Joshua shook his head while politely saying. The marshal felt a sense of hopelessness for his lack of comprehension; what else could he do but smile, cause he knew the tawaque's intentions were good.

"Ovet ula miv-ni tejux zua xejiv o-eh niep," the tawaque said as he shifted his spear to his other hand. He than placed his free hand on Joshua's shoulder, friendly-like, and than led the marshal to an unknown destination, as of yet the marshal thought.

They eventually approached, of what seemed to be Joshua perceived, a replica of what resembled some sort of indigenous mammal. The mock-up was a carcason, which were many and grouped in herds. They were harmless plant-eating mammals that roamed across the flatlands during migration periods; the mock-up resembled such a beast. Carcason skin was wrapped and sewn around padded stalk and supported by a post in the ground, to keep the dummy held upright.

Joshua could not possibly fathom what the thing was used for the moment he saw it; I mean to him it looked like a scarecrow. While the tawaque left his side and approached it he stood by himself and pondered over it, the thing of which had horns sticking out of it.

"Vishi qesed-evodi," the tawaque said with a loud and proud tone in his voice. "Vishi qesed-evodi," he said again while lightly tugging at the representation.

"What's that thing supposed to be?" the marshal shrugged.

"Vishi qesed-evodi," the tawaque said one last time as he removed his hand from the dummy. Without saying another word

Jepheth perked his spear up as he retracted back toward where the marshal was.

The marshal took a couple of steps aside as the tawaque positioned himself in the same proximity where the marshal stood, facing the dummy. As soon as Jepheth was in his preferable position he leaned back on his spear while standing in a half-straddle stance, taking careful aim at the dummy. With a mighty thrust he lunged his spear at the target, a slight whooshing sound Josh heard as the tawaque's throwing arm sliced through the open air, he made a dead center hit at the carcason facsimile.

"Target practice," Joshua caught on.

Jepheth turned to face the marshal with a proud look, "Vishi qesed-evodi." He than faced ahead again to walk toward his target and retrieve his spear. When he was within reach of the dummy he grabbed and shook loose his weapon with a firm grip on the shaft. Once his spear was back in his hands he walked over his own footsteps, in the direction of the marshal's waiting.

"Very good shot," the marshal nodded with a smile. Hollands shared in the tawaque's joy in his display of precision spearman-ship, which was the feeling the marshal tried to put across.

"Xejev," with inquiry he shook his head as he approached closer.

"Very good shot," Hollands said again trying to express a compliment.

"Vejepol-zua," the tawaque acknowledged as he smiled back.

Jepheth was quickly at the marshal's side now, but slightly behind, Joshua assumed what was next. The tawaque handed the marshal his spear and than took a step back.

"You want me to try?" almost laughed at the thought.

"Tejuav."

The marshal took that as a yes and than he looked down thinking to himself, I'd rather use my pulse gun. He inbreathed and than released while at the same time hoping not to embarrass himself. As the tawaque stood a foot away, hoping to see a fellow warrior at play, Josh felt ready to give it his best try.

He remembered and than utilized the same body technique he observed the tawaque perform, and he mimicked those movements.

Even though he never picked up a spear before, or anything that didn't have an energy bolt firing out the other end, he tried to look his best anyway as Jepheth supervised.

Joshua held tight to Jepheth's spear as he stretched his throwing arm back; positioning the spear into a cocking position, and distributing all his weight on his back leg for added power. He inhaled deeply, and when he felt mentally ready, he exhaled while releasing the spear with a strong thrust.

Unfortunately his aim was off cause he missed the target completely. The spear shot through the air, beyond the target, and into a nearby homestead, about fifty-yards further from the dummy. An elapsed time of only a couple of seconds when the spearhead struck the side of the dome and bounced off it, unable to penetrate through the homestead's solid rock structure.

The home's owner, who stood a few feet away, was alerted immediately when the spear struck. He was leaning packing his gear, which appeared to be hunting gear, into his carryall when he hear a thump from behind. The moment he heard it he turned around and saw the spear, to his displeasure, chipping the side of his home. He than directed his gaze at the two, who were responsible, with a dissatisfactory look, while at the same time, being thankful it wasn't his rear end that got gouged.

Jepheth restrained his laugh because, unaware to Josh at the time, there were other going-ons in the village and he was pressed for time. The homestead's owner looked away cursing to himself and resuming his business while Jepheth continued his.

"Zua natet, zua natet vesez eheop," the tawaque seemed to command.

As Jepheth quickly walked toward the homestead, to retrieve his spear, the marshal stated, "Wouldn't you rather have me use my gun, it's quicker," the tawaque grinned in response but had no idea what the marshal was stating. "And I promise you I won't miss."

Jepheth barked out a few words when he was within reach of his spear. He picked up his weapon from where it landed; the homeowner not looking back as Jepheth did so. When his spear was back in his hands, to be used again, Jepheth walked back toward the marshal as the marshal shook his head and feeling slightly pessimistic about retrying a second attempt.

Jepheth was back at the marshal's side again, but slightly in front, opposite of the marshal's throwing arm. "Zua natet fu ov so-hejiv," the tawaque, this time, seemed to want to pass on the proper instructions.

The tawaque handed Josh back his spear trusting that the marshal could hit his mark, with a little aid. As Jepheth gave the spear to the marshal he gave the marshal a gentle pat on the back while directing Joshua's aim at the target, which Josh interpreted, to try again. Josh was pleased that the tawaque had faith and confidence in him; though he had no idea why he was throwing spears around, but he proceeded anyway for his next attempt while trying not to make a fool of himself.

He took a deep breath, looked at his target, and assumed his firing position. After the marshal attempted to get in his throwing stance the tawaque jumped in to give him added suggestions. "Lioqa zuaz isem tev-iseov, imecux temoh-jev cipev," Jepheth said as he help lifted the marshal's hanging arm to the marshal's shoulder level. Jepheth seemed to be tugging and shoving the marshal into a proper position before he would allow Josh to execute a second try. "Imecux zuaz temoh-jev cipev," the tawaque said as he forced Hollands to bend the elbow a bit.

The marshal's hand was in the right line of aim between him and his target; apparently Jepheth wanted the marshal to use his thumb and forefinger as his crosshairs, to sight his objective. And one final note, Jepheth positioned the marshal's forward instep in a bit and the knee bent to give Joshua added stability and throwing power.

The marshal was finally in his position he needed to be in, which Jepheth tailored him into, and Josh forced himself to be mentally focused. Aligning the target with the v of his forefinger and thumb, and with his final out breath, he released his spear with a quick swiping action of his throwing arm. In a little more than a second the spear darted through the air and struck through the heart of the carcason dummy.

"I did it," Joshua expression both excitement and surprise.

"Wisez huaf," the tawaque said nodding his head and smiling proud.

"Let's do it again," the marshal glanced at his friend.

"Shishi," Jepheth said as he walked toward the target to fetch the spear again.

Meanwhile, Jackie had long established her new living quarters; settling her belongings and feeling more relaxed, that she finally decided to emerge out of the dome hut. She felt that she laid about long enough and that it was time for her to stretch her legs a bit, and to breath in the cold-crisp air, the day was still young and vibrant.

Looking around her parameter she noticed a lot of activity; a broad scale of villagers, mostly the men, packing equipment and forming some sort of orchestrated assembly. They were busy like bees, Jackie thought, but the women basically stayed out of the way so, so did see. Since all of the villagers, except for maybe the children, was twice her size she tried to keep herself on the sidelines to avoid being trampled. With all the commotion and moving about transpiring she felt like returning to the quietude of her hut; but she continued to explore the strange new surroundings.

A parade of boador-driven carriages was being moved toward the outskirts of the village. The children were helping their fathers and big brothers, playfully though, by pushing their carriages along or helping to carry weapons, or other items, toward the cavalcade line; like children typically were, they wanted to feel like they were part of the activity. It would appear, according to Jackie's observation, that the leaders were massing some sort of hunting expedition. Jackie stood, near the fence side of a neighbor's corral, and was at awe over the spectacle.

Hoping to find a safe clearing through the congestion she decided to walk around the back of the neighbor's hut, to look for her co-partner. Walking along the fence line and nearing the rear of the hut, she was abruptly startled by a presence, as she was about to snake around the corner.

A tawaquan woman, of lengthy proportions but very beautiful, appeared to Jackie's surprise, which took her aback while looking up at the encounter. The tawaquan woman, apparently the neighbor, had long frazzled black hair hanging down below her shoulders and had an athletic physique. She wore the usual animal skin coverings, but of thick black fur, and have a minor deviation from what most of the women in the village wore. Her appearance was very sensuous; she had on a heavy woven mini-skirt that hung down to her thighs, fatigue boots with the laces tied around her ankles, and a vest-like top to expose a little bit more of her feminine side. As they both stood, almost toe-to-toe, the tawaque's eyes gazed down sharply at Jackie, who still stood stunned.

"Excuse me," Jackie said as she backed away while still keeping her eyes on her. When she was finally a few feet from her she turned to look the other way, there was a sense of female rivalry or intimidation between them.

She decided to put the encounter way behind her as she left the vicinity and walked around the front. It didn't matter which way she went she would still have to feel her way through the crowd. She sidestepped crossing traffic and walked around a small group of children, who were carrying hunting utilities and food scraps for the beasts of burden. Once she was out in the open, the city square if you will, she recognized the full scope of the masses, a people of thousands. Where did they all come from, she observed thus far.

She would ponder over that dilemma at a later time but for right now she had to search for the whereabouts of the marshal, who was the mission's leader. Even though he wasn't her official superior they both had equal aims, which was to complete the mission and get off this ragtag planet.

"Jumef up vohejiv," Jepheth stated, which didn't mean much to Joshua's ears, as he held on tight astride a boador.

The tawaque seemed a bit hasty in his attempt at alien exchange of cultures with the marshal. Jepheth handed down a few quick pointers on proper spear throwing and handling; and now its back riding, on a creature not for the timid. Hollands couldn't understand why he was being coerced into doing these things but maybe the reasons for will be revealed, and soon he hoped.

"What are you saying?" he would rather fly a gunship he thought to himself, "hold on tight, sounds like a good idea."

They were both closer to the cavalcade line but still within village limits. They were at the village stable where they housed the main herd of boadors, the best kept and groomed for the village cavalry. The warriors took good care of their animals because they were their only means of transportation and their only hope to keep the men alive in such a hostile, desolate, environment.

Never engaging in such a feat, or anything close to being similar before, was the sensation Joshua had as he kept a solid grip on the beast's reins and stirrups. On the back of the beast he was being jostled a bit because of the boador's unsettling nerves; being as young as a year old, it was used to the weight on its back. Josh also popped some sweat while trying to steady the beast, trying also to present a good show against his lack of experience.

The average height of a tawaquan soldier was better suited to handle such a wild and strong animal because of their size, strength, and monkey-like feet. The underside of their feet had deep arches, in the middle region of the soles, which was perfectly designed to grip onto rocks and jagged bluffs of the terrain. This evolution in their biological make-up was ideal and beneficial since it gave these nomadic tribesmen great speed and strength; like for sprinting and jumping, or to pinch the boador's side to motivate the animal's steering and forward motion.

Joshua lacked such a physical attribute so he was given a much smaller, and supposedly, a much manageable mount. Easy to steer, yes, easily manageable, no, cause he was given a boador of adolescent age. Not as big as the average age boador would need to be to ride, but in Joshua's case, the more plausible since the younger ones were weaker and more sensitive to the stirrups; with a full grown boador Joshua hadn't the strength to control but with a yearling he might prevail. This year old boador was also hard to manage because of its high spiritedness; and because the young'uns had never been broken into to ride or to be the transporters of men.

The marshal tried to ignore the stench, which permeated the air from the stable, as he tried to keep the animal stationary. "Keep the damn thing still," Joshua snapped while he tugged on the reins.

The yearling kept wanting to steer himself back toward the stable, possibly, to eat from his mother's trough.

"Teviz xejisi zua esi," Jepheth shouted at the animal. As the young boador kept trying to retreat back to his mother the tawaque maintained a firm grip on the animal's bridle, or at least try, to keep him still enough.

"This is pointless," Josh said to himself. "Let go," the marshal commanded the tawaque, "let me get him broken into." Obviously Jepheth didn't comply with the order so Josh tugged on the reins where Jepheth had his grip and he said again, "Let go."

"Zua xepix vu vesiz vejot enupi," the tawaque said as he released his grip on the beast.

It would seem to Josh, maybe that did the trick. As soon as Jepheth released his hold the yearling calmed a bit. "That's a good boy," the marshal said trying to sooth the beast while petting his black mane.

"Eneb-epeh," Jepheth sounding stunned at the yearling's quick adherence to Joshua's tone.

Everything seemed to be under his professional control, or so he thought. After the tawaque released the beast it was calm, before it did a hundred an eighty turn back into the stable. Josh was self-assured that he had his way with the boador but when the yearling returned back to his mother Hollands pleaded, "No, no, where ya goin." The beast was unwilling to comply with Joshua's bidding and despite the marshal's pleads the animal retreated back to its warm shelter, the sight would have been funny to any onlooker.

This part of the village stable was no different than the rest, had a modest appearance and was partitioned by a corral fence. Only a mere overhang allowed some cover for the mother and her offspring from the falling snow or sleet. The interior was padded down with stalk, and underneath the overhang, a trough was placed for the animal's food and water.

Saddled to the backside of the yearling, while jerking the reins, Josh tried to steer the animal back out into the open but with little success. The year-old boador seemed hungry, which precipitated it back to his mother to be fed and to return to the comfort of the litter. The mother was lying about on her side and seemed to be slightly irritable, but tolerable, from her six little nestlings who were fidgeting and squeezing in to nurture from their mother's milk.

Joshua, to his displeasure, heard laughter in the background as his boador cub tried to squirm in through the other six to get his fair share of the sustenance. As he turned to look in the direction of the intruding sounds, "This is good, you make an ugly den mother," Jackie laughed irrepressibly.

"Yea, that's cute," he said as he looked away from her. "Not now, I'm kinda busy right now," he returned his attention to the problem at hand.

Unable to snuggle in for a nipple the mother abruptly, but not to hurt, kicked the yearling away. Maybe it was the fact that Joshua's boador was too old now to suckle from his mother, or maybe she had enough problematic young'uns to attend to, but none of the less she showed her authority. With that incentive only than was Joshua able to manipulate his young boador away from the corral and back to their point of origin. The marshal felt the animal's reluctance, and feelings of abandonment, but the animal eventually submitted to Josh as he steered the reins.

"May I ask you something?" Jackie asked as she moved in closer, "What's all this about?" now holding back her jeering but still expressing a grin.

"I'm not doing this for your amusement," Josh scowled. "But I think they're mobilizing some sort of hunting party." Joshua remarked as he looked at the multitude of people ahead, who were preparing to embark, "And I'm invited."

"What for?" she lost her grin.

"Maybe it's part of my initiation," Josh guessed. "But if it is, this might be an opportune time to win over their confidence." The marshal continued as Jackie listened, "After all, we can work better together as allies than strangers."

Jepheth was not too far away, he broke in, "Zua natev giof ov," the tawaque said as he grabbed the boador's bridle. "Ietez, fupev tediso ov," the tawaque uttered as Joshua dismounted.

"I don't know what he said but I think I failed the test," he said now standing on his feet beside Jackie.

A subtle momentum occurred ahead amid the cavalcade, they seemed ready to embark. Jepheth noticed the change and he turned to Josh and said, "Zua tevis jisi, hiv siefez," while motioning to the marshal to stay put. Jackie and Josh stood side by side as they watched Jepheth walking away toward the masses.

"What's up now?" Jackie questioned.

"How am I supposed to know, quit asking questions," Josh getting annoyed. They were still observing as Jepheth drew away, assumingly they thought, approaching to converse with the assembly leaders.

From a distance Jepheth was distinctively, but minutely, seen from the legionnaires' standing point. The tawaque stood beside the main concentration of his people as he exchanged talk with the others, who seemed to be the heads of his tribal gathering. Jackie and Josh stood still and patient as they watched, with analytical inquiry, to Jepheth as he communicated with his superiors.

After a minute or two had passed Jepheth turned away from his chiefs and walked a couple of steps toward the legionnaires' direction, and shouted from his distance, "Duni up, kuop at," he said as he waved Joshua to come forth.

"Well, looks like this is it," the marshal said as he mounted his ride. "Wish me luck."

"Why just you?" Jackie said with protest.

"Take a look for yourself, only the men are leaving," he said as he grabbed the reins while looking at the cavalcade. "Try and stay out of trouble, I should be back within the evening," were his final remarks before he shoved off toward the grouping.

Joshua's yearling moved with common jerkiness, but swift and fast. Josh had yet to learn the basic verbal commands, and gain enough experience of handling the animal's reins, but he knew enough to keep himself mobile. During the boador's long prance-like strides the marshal kept a firm grasp on the bridle, and his feet affixed inside the stirrups, for added security.

Within no time at all Joshua was at, and a part of, the cavalcade assembly. He positioned his ride near Jepheth; the others seemed to ignore or intentionally kept a social distance from the marshal, maybe because Josh had yet to prove himself among the other tribesmen.

Jepheth still remained standing until one of his fellow tribesmen handed him the reins of a boador for him to ride. With his very flexible arched feet he hopped onto his boador's saddle with little effort, his feet landed in the stirrups the moment his butt landed in the saddle. He held a firm grip on the reins with both hands the moment he was atop the boador's backside.

With his vice-like feet Jepheth pinched the animal's sides and hollered a command, which spurred the boador to move. Jepheth quickly turned to Josh though and said, "Jumef vohejiv, gumemax ni," after which he looked away to steer in the direction with the others.

"Yea, time to go," the marshal said as he kicked his boador to move as well. He tried, with success so far, to avoid getting trampled by the other riders and carriages as he moved with the flow.

Despite the hustle and bustle, and the tight grouping of the many joiners, the cavalcade eventually formed a single column. Josh kept a close distance with his guide and mentor, following Jepheth's every move. Once the single-line column was formed Joshua saw nothing but wide-open plains ahead, with a chain of mountains in the far horizon. With the sound of the blow horn the cavalcade commenced. They now picked up speed galloping their beasts of burden out toward the open wilderness, leaving behind tracks and flying snow debris in their wake.

From rapid speed the cavalcade slowed to a casual pace to allow sufficient time for the trackers to scout their prey. The noon drew to pre-evening hours, more than enough time to search and bring back wild game. At least that's what the tawaques were counting on, to feed and clothe their families. The marshal was also hoping for a good hunt and he waited patiently for the trackers to probe what might lie ahead.

Josh rode along side his only mentor, and for the moment, his only friend until he was given the chance to prove himself among the rest. As their beasts carried them across the rough wilderness their slow gallop kicked up snow debris and left a trail, among the hoof and wheel marks, which displayed a clear clue of the cavalcade's passing.

The hunting party, from the single column, broke down into small individual groups who were riding in close proximity to each other. Maybe it was because each of the individual clans, or clan alliances, wanted to be the first to make the first kill or be given the credit of leading the entire tribe on the right path. Competition was high but camaraderie was just as high, they demonstrated good sportsmanship and fellowship with each other.

As Josh and Jepheth rode together they were conversing but Jepheth did most of the talking, since Joshua only caught on to only a infinitesimal limit of tawaquan words. The marshal simply nodded to show acknowledgement, which expressed that he was interested in what the tawaque had to say. The marshal only looked away from the tawaque for a short time to observe a carriage, which was being driven in front of him. He quickly looked and smiled at two little boys who were aboard the carriage; they smiled back, after which, he redirected his attention to Jepheth's ongoing dialogue.

"Lioq huopeh, o piof vu dejidel up tuni-vejopeh," the tawaque said as he slowed his ride to dismount.

"Where you're going," he said as he slowed his ride as well. At this point he saw Jepheth being fully dismounted from the boador's saddle.

"Lioq huopeh," the tawaque said as he waved his arm to motion the marshal to keep going. The marshal continued his stride than while Jepheth removed himself, and his steed, away from the flow of traffic.

Curiosity confounded the marshal as he watched Jepheth separating himself from the marshal's side. Maybe his tawaque friend, Joshua thought, wanted an update on the trackers' latest findings, or maybe his boador was thirsty and had to be replenished, but whatever the reason the marshal continued his onward gallop.

His curiosity was, later on, replaced by a sense of adventure and sheer boredom, which beckoned him to go his own way. Not too far from the main group however but far enough to catch a glimpse at the landscape, to awe at and admire. Not wanting to impede the cavalcade Joshua steered his ride to the side and away from the main concentration of hunters.

The surrounding parameter was hilly, the parade of cavalcade riders were in the midst of gullies and bluffs but their line of passing was clear however. Furthering himself from the group Josh galloped his steed toward one of those gullies and saw, with humility, the awesome landscape. Making certain he was not too close to the gully's edge, so as not to slide down the incline, he succeeded to keeping his boador stationary and calm by talking soothingly to the beast and petting the yearling's mane.

He slowly dismounted, so as not to unnerve his animal, and he kept a firm hand on the saddle's pommel as he swung his leg around. "Easy boy, take a rest," he said as he finally stepped away from the beast. He than, once he was assured that his ride could be unsupervised for the time being, the marshal carefully watched his steps as he walked along the edge.

He thought to himself, what a perfect spot to stand, as his senses absorbed the aura of nature's tranquility but the serenity also masked the danger's, which also stirred and lingered out there. Taken aback by the peace and isolation he felt, his mindset was in a different place.

Suddenly he lost his footing when he miscalculated and stepped too close to the edge. The accumulation of snow, at the far edge, gave way from the weight of his body and he was abruptly at the mercy of gravity as his body fell. Eventually, after rolling and tumbling down the incline, he reached the bottom of which, to his dismay, was a basin. Basins were common and dangerous on the planet's surface, because of the oscillating temperatures and strong wind sheers, snow filled basins were like traps during winter thaw seasons. The loose snow at the bottom felt to him, like grains of sand in an hourglass, as he begun to sink to his ankles and deeper.

"Hey," he shouted, "somebody help me." "Jepheth," he than called out to his friend for assistance, "help me, please." He was now up to his waist in snow, which seemed to him to be like quicksand. "Hey can anybody hear me, I need help," he continued his frantic calls for aid.

The sounds of his screams brought about onlookers, small group of tawaque hunters who were close enough to hear the marshal's cries. But his calls seemed to be of no consequence to them as they stood, idly by, and watched his descent into the abyss. Maybe it was their instinct to fend only for themselves and their families, what nature would call natural selection, which kept them emotionally disconnected.

"Hey," he tried to reach his hand out to one of them. "I need help, please," he pleaded as he was now up to his chest in snow. The onlookers stood, like statues, as they watched the marshal slowly descend into his grave.

To the marshal's luck Jepheth appeared as he saw, to his impatient demeanor, his fellow tribesmen's unwillingness to help. "Fupev nuwi, on dunopeh fuxep," Jepheth shouted down to the marshal. The tawaque looked around, not sparing a second, to scope out the best way to retrieve his friend from the depths of disaster.

"Jepheth, thank the creator," the marshal praised as he was now up to his neck. "Hurry," he shouted as his arms were outstretched trying to reach up at him.

An idea quickly came to the tawaque and Jepheth, without wasting any more life saving time, took advantage of the tools that he had. "Fupev nuwi," he shouted down as he took action.

The other onlookers stood as before, detached from the present crises. Jepheth seized the reins of his boador and than he tugged the animal near the edge of the gully. The tawaque than looked around again and saw something else that might be of good use, a solution to the dire problem. He kneeled down and reached for an underground root, which was lightly exposed beneath and embedded just below the rim of the edge. Taking hold of the root he tugged at it, ripping it from the ground, while at the same time avoiding falling into the basin's trap himself. When enough, to his own assessment, was mustard out of the ground he took his flint stone axe with his free hand and than he slashed the root, which he could now use as rope.

Keeping the beast steady he tied one end of the vine to the pommel; making sure the knot would be tight enough to endure the stress of the weight. He than looped the slack of the vine in his hand so Jepheth could throw it down to the marshal with a good enough aim, for Joshua to reach it.

Once the vine was rolled up loosely in his hand Jepheth looked down at Josh and said, "En v-suopeh ov fuxep vu zua, devedij ev," as he threw the vine down to him.

Joshua was now sunken down to his shoulders with his arms outstretched scrambling to reach the vine. Unable to though, "I can't reach it," the marshal frantically made aware.

Cursing to himself the tawaque pulled the vine up, out of the depression, looping it in his hand again as he did so. And as soon as the entire length of the vine was in his hand, "Devedij ev," he yelled out as he threw it down a second time.

This time the marshal was able to grasp on to it after Jepheth tossed it down closer. The snow nearly caving in over his shoulders Josh held on tight to the end of the vine with dear life. "Ok, pull me up," the marshal shouted up at Jepheth.

Firmly holding on to the bit of the boador's headstall Jepheth, with a firm but low tone, commanded the boador to take backward steps. At the bottom of the basin Josh held on as the beast pulled back, guided steadily by Jepheth, pulling the marshal free from the snow covering.

The marshal was now completely free from the basin's trap swallowing, his feet away from the bottom's grip, as Jepheth and his ride continued to heave him up the incline. Not loosing his tight hold Josh was now midway up from the depth as Jepheth continued to walk his beast back. Eventually though Josh reached the top of the basin, still holding the vine, but now he was able to scramble his feet to climb up as he was being pulled.

With one last step, and hand-over-hand, he was able to step away from the incline and was now standing on flat solid ground. As Jepheth jerked at his boador to stop Josh was at his side again.

"Thanks," the marshal sighed, "I'll return the favor someday." The tawaque just responded with a nod, a big smile, and a strong pat on the marshal's back and than walked away to resume his business.

Meanwhile, all was less dramatic within the village as the women and children went about their daily activities. The children played, as a means of exercise and having fun, or to avoid their tedious chores placed upon them. The women however prepared for the safe return of their husbands from a successful hunt, they hoped. If, or when, the men bring in a good source of meat and carcason skins, to carry them through the winter, they need to prepare a feast festival, which usually follows such an expedition.

Jackie was musing over her thoughts next to an abandoned campfire, squatting down and scrapping the ground with a piece of charred wood. She might have been wondering on the whereabouts and doings of her counterpart, she had nothing else to do but contemplate these things.

As she was losing herself in idle quandaries a familiar presence approached toward her campsite, the tawaquan woman. The tawaquan woman, who neighbored Jackie's temporary resting place, kneeled in close toward the fire across from where Jackie was sitting and she looked at Corin directly with penetrating eyes and a stern face. Perhaps the tawaquan woman wanted to open up to the new comer and to help Jackie feel more at ease, or maybe she was just curious over the appearance of the offlander.

"Shenbora," the woman said as she pointed to herself. "Shenbora," which Jackie assumed was her name.

Corin faltered back slightly and not knowing how to react to the native's attempt for open dialogue. "Ok," she said hesitantly, "That's your name, Shenbora."

Shenbora smiled slightly, perhaps pleased she was making some progress, "Nez peni ot Shenbora."

Innocent laughter, Corin heard from her rear, as a small group of tawaquan women seem to be amused at Jackie's toil with their native language. But Jackie was neither insulted nor amused, she just simply wanted to break the monotony of sitting around doing nothing, she didn't even look back at them.

"Jackie," she said pressing her hand against her chest. "Jackie," she repeated but slowly.

Shenbora recited Jackie's name but with some difficulty but Corin gave her credit for showing initiative. Shenbora also seemed fascinated with Jackie's attire and when she walked over to her and reached to feel the material Corin shied away, after which, the tawaque retracted her hand.

Wishing to give the offlander a feeling of ease Shenbora removed her necklace, which was dangling around her neck, to give as a friendship offering. "Gus zua, gesum ni gus zua," she said as she gave an unthreatening hand gesture of good will.

Jackie thought, and felt, she had to show some sign of trust in counter-respect to the same, and without faltering this time, she allowed Shenbora to hang the ornament on her and the tawaque did so with gentle affection. As Jackie fondled the beads, which now decorated her neck, the tawaque felt, only for a moment's curiosity, the end strands of Corin's black-silky hair but Jackie didn't seem to mind.

Unobtrusively the moment was distracted as two boys, the age of mere toddlers, approached their mother and Jackie seemed surprised. Because Jackie hadn't seen her with a male significant other for a husband, and the fact Shenbora had siblings of her own, caught Jackie off guard.

As one of the young'uns sat on her mother's lap Shenbora embraced him with tender love and care. As Shenbora talked playfully with her son the other one stepped towards Jackie's side, the looking attentively at the offlander and her strange apparel.

"You have children?" she said as the boy, who stood next to her, snuggled in a little closer. "These are yours?" Corin asked as she loosely clung her arm around the boy's waist.

"Zit, nez tup'es," Shenbora responded while nodding to Jackie and glancing back at her beloved.

Continuing still on their scouting mission the tribal clan groups were scattered with the pursuant need of making a thorough tracking advance. Although daylight was burning they were sure of themselves that they could find the migrating herd, for their hunt, in plenty of time and to bring back a feast worth celebrating.

While the majority of the well-seasoned and experienced hunters were dusting the parameter for tracks Jepheth and Josh took a moment to gaze upon something that caught the marshal's interest. They both stood atop a bluff with their sight fixated at a large herd of macroderms, plant-eating mammals indulging on what vegetation they could find.

"Fu zua tio, otepiv ov nehepog-odipov," the tawaque spoke as he pointed to the spectacle. The marshal was impressed by what he saw and was humbled by their strength and size.

The macroderms were grouped in their respected families, the entire herd spanned across the flatland to scavenge for food. Their physical characteristics were strange and alien to the marshal or any offlander; bulky and muscular bodies supported on their front and hind legs, double humps located between the vertebrae and neck region, spiraled tusks, and long snake-like trunks to reach the topmost parts of the evergreen pines.

As Joshua looked on, from afar, he witnessed one of them availing himself to one of the earth-giving delicacies. With its ten-foot trunk it reached up, as the animal stood up on its hind legs, to grab and pull down the upper half of the pine. Falling needles showered the surrounding vicinity as its trunk clutched the thinner part of the tree, now on all fours, as his protruding lips snacked on the fresher pines.

"Enebopih, xi tejuamif hu," Jepheth said and than he turned around to rejoin the others. Joshua stood still for a few seconds to absorb the rarity one last time and than, he to, turned around to reintegrate with the group.

The interior of an unknown structure was dark and murky, the only light illuminated from hand-held torches and fire lanterns that were mounted along the rock walls. It would appear to the oblivious onlooker that these mazes of tunnels were deep underground, insulated from the wintry environment above.

Two familiar figures were walking through the main tunnel-way, Shenbora guiding the way as Jackie followed her steps. The flames of their torches flickered as they ventured through the subterranean abode, what was to Jackie, the unknown. Shenbora's torch illumined their forward momentum while Jackie marveled over the discoveries that she might find.

The temperature was rather warm, compared to the temperature topside, these underground tunnels seemed to shelter out the wind factor, and the heat from the torches and lanterns, also contributed to the warmth. While the mercenary followed close behind her guide she kept her scarf dangling as she perspired a little, probably from the tight fitting of her winter garb.

"Xejev zuas teviq," Shenbora said as she pointed the flame of her torch to one side and than the other. The tawaque might of said, watch your step, Jackie safely assumed but she really didn't know.

To her amazement Jackie discovered that this tunnel fortress was filled with cavities dug or carved out, each a residential chamber for a family or clan. Jackie looked to her left for a second to observe one such family. A couple, an elderly woman, and three of the family's children were all present inside that cave. They stared back at Corin, with a look as though she's invading their privacy, as Jackie walked by.

They were two levels within the underground enclosure that they now entered into, a lower level and an upper level sculpted out from the granite. Jackie, still at Shenbora's back, just emerged out of the narrow corridor she was in and found herself in the wide-openness of a central hub, from which, the multitude of arterial corridors centered on. Corin was on the upper level standing on a walkway, which was their version of a catwalk. As she looked down at the lower level she saw more dwellings and people living in them. It seemed to her, after her surroundings made an impression on her, that she had entered the main square of the tunnel fortress, and her thoughts told her, that this place was like an underground city.

"Vejot xez," Shenbora shouted. Shenbora was several paces ahead of Jackie standing a foot inside another tunnel passage, which was at the opposite end of the walkway from their entrance. Jackie looked around for a few seconds more and than she begun to exit the square as well, nearing in towards her companion.

Holding the torch in front of her, the light of the flame guiding

Jackie's steps, she was now within another narrow tunnel with the central underground city square, she observed a few seconds earlier, at her back. The tunnel passage, which they were now navigating through, was a continuous chain only broken by the excavated central square they had just now walked away from.

There wasn't much headroom for Shenbora, to stand erect, so she had to lean slightly as she walked on. Jackie, though, had plenty of overhead since the tunnels were fitted for the Paleolithic inhabitants, who towered in size compared to the new arrivals. Jackie walked straight and with ease, as she was relaxed and enjoyed the tour.

It wasn't long though before Jackie saw more of the tribesmen, not too far as she closed in toward them, who seemed to be going about a ritual of some kind. Their ritual, to them, had religious elements as they sat Indian-style near a rock wall and spit painting figures and shapes on the wall's surface. This sort of practice was very alien to Jackie, which invited much fascination in her as she watched, while she was standing behind them and looking over their shoulder.

The practice of painting pictographs to ornament the walls, Jackie assumed, was a means to keep their customs and traditions alive, and to pass the teachings down from one generation to the next. Jackie noticed, as she observed on, that the painted pictures seemed to be telling a story, maybe of their past and or maybe they were detailing their family tree or the history of tribal clans.

As Jackie kept a continuous gaze at them, while they performed their craft, she observed one of them and his technique as she stood behind him. He had with him several bowls, each one filled with powdery substances of some sort, which were spread out for him to reach. Each bowl contained a different color powder, which Jackie noticed was red and blue and a variety of others.

He took a wooden pint scoop, and with it, he scooped out a pinch of red powder of which he than took the powder into his mouth, but not to swallow. Doing this, Jackie assumed, he mixed and moistened the powder with his saliva.

After the powder had been moistened and dissolved into a liquid he than grabbed another wooden instrument, which was close to his side with an array of other such-like tools. The instrument that he held in his hand was a wooden stick with a flat shaped template at the end, He than leaned over to carefully place the flat-end of the implement flush against the wall at his desired point, thus, he was in the middle of painting a picture. He than spat the red liquid at the template, after which, he pulled the template back to reveal a shape.

Wow, that's how they do it, Jackie thought to herself as she took a step back and smiled. The tawaque, she observed, wasn't the only one doing what he was doing, the other four who were working beside him were performing the same. Splattering sounds were made as they spat paint on the wall while surgically placing the templates where there representations were to be put in place.

"Duni jisi," Shenbora said to her. Shenbora was a few paces from where the assembly of the four painters were seated, and from where Jackie stood. "Duni jisi," she said again as she waved at Corin to approach.

When she approached Shenbora's side the tawaque wanted to show her a few of the paintings, since she sensed Jackie's interest in them. The tawaque moved her torch in close to the wall to brighten the surface in order for Jackie to get a good glimpse at the array of pictographs. Jackie leaned in close, with the anticipated interest that she showed, as Shenbora begun to explain its meaning.

"Vejot teves deni vu at-eh nomemip-oanehu," she said getting the legionnaire's attention. Than she shifted her flame to the next pictograph; there were a series of pictures, like a chain, which told a story and Shenbora attempted to explain them one-by-one. But for a second only Corin was still focused on the first pictograph, to the best of her cognitive ability the picture resembled a star with a saucer shape in the center of it. After which she swayed her attention to the next pictograph that Shenbora was already focused on.

"Xiwi niv veji janepet ci'gusi," she said trying to explain the second picture. "Qiuqmi moli zua," she said as she pointed to Jackie.

To her amazement she was struck by the strong resemblance of the figure, which looked very human much like her. "We've been here before," she said as she gave a stunned look at the tawaque.

"Shishi," Shenbora acknowledged her deductions. Jackie assumed that the first pictograph, a star with a saucer shape in the center, was a spacecraft of some kind and she was able to correlate the two pictures.

Shenbora than swung her torch to the third pictograph and spoke, "Xi xisi exeov-opeh zuas dunen-opeh." After she spoke those words she pointed to Jackie again indicating her as someone relative to the third picture.

The third picture representation had the same saucer-star design but with a depiction of a bunch of tawaquan people sitting around it, and looking up at it. Jackie reached another conclusion as she turned to face the tawaque. "You people were awaiting our return," she said as she dragged her finger across the three pictographs, to indicate the sequence of the story thus far.

"Shishi," Shenbora acknowledged, assuming only, that Jackie understood.

The tawaque than swerved her focus to the fourth symbol and she continued to narrate. The fourth representation was an exact picture of the carnivore she and her marshal, to their distress, encountered a day ago prior. The picture suggested the carnivore attacking a tawaque hunter, trapped in the jaws of the beast as he dropped his spear.

"No need to explain this, I've almost been there," she grimaced while wishing not to revisit the experience.

Shenbora than shifted to the next scene and Jackie followed along, "Vejot ot zuas japev-opeh qeseviz," she said even though Jackie couldn't understand the words. Jackie didn't need to understand though because a picture speaks a thousand words and she could interpret the pictures on her own, Shenbora spoke as the narrator probably for her own pleasure of it. The picture depicted three tawaque hunters in the process of slaying a carcason, one of them thrusting a spear into the animal's throat.

"This is your source of food," she said to herself, "what you hunt." She touched the fifth symbol lightly with her hand while admiring the correlating colors and the artistic skill that was put into it.

Shenbora assumed Corin was able to follow along, and keep up, so she concluded to the end of the story by directing Jackie's attention to the final pictograph. "Uas genomez, uas womem-ehi," she said as she drew her flame close to it.

"Your village," she said since the picture was an exact copy of it.

"Duni, xi hu," Shenbora said as she tugged at the mercenary's side and than stepped away. Jackie guessed that her tawaque guide concluded this part of the tour and she wanted to leave elsewhere, as she noticed the tawaque leaving her side.

Before Jackie straightened up again, to leave, she wanted to take one last look at the fifth symbol. She placed her hand on the carcason drawing one last time and to envision what it would be like to hunt such a herd, at this point she could only imagine.

"Duni, xi hu," the tawaque woman shouted. Assuming Shenbora was calling on her Jackie left to rejoin her.

Two know figures kneeled in behind a hill, concealing themselves from unsuspected preys. Jepheth and Joshua cropped up their heads over the hill's topside and they peered out at an open plain that laid ahead of them. To their pleasure they found what they were looking for, an entire heard of carcasons. Simple looking creatures with long, flat, hammerhead-like snouts and their physique were slender but muscular supported on thin skeletal legs. The carcasons were scavenging for food on the snow-covered surface of the flatland, shuffling through the snow with their their hammer-head, using them like flat gardening spades, to dig up some hidden vegetation of which might be edible enough for them to eat.

"Duni, xi natev vemem veji uvejis-t," Jepheth said as he tapped Joshua's shoulder to get his attention. The tawaque gave Josh a thumb signal to retreat and he, without revealing himself to the herd, slowly crawled backward before he stood up and left.

"Yea, we must tell the others," the marshal said as he to crawled back and away to rejoin the group.

The cavalcade was spread out as before, and searching, oblivious to the location of the herd. Three of the chiefs, with the main hunting party in the backdrop, communicated with each other to plot their next course of action. Restless and anxious to find fresh game they looked around to triangulate, between the three of them, their last location where the trail was cold. They held their spears, and kept their throw axes slung, which were cleaned and sharpened waiting to be tainted with blood as they deliberated.

Their attention was swayed abruptly as Jepheth and the marshal paced toward them. When Jepheth reached comfortable vocal range to face the tawaque hierarchy, the marshal stayed back a little while his friend communicated their findings.

Josh could barely hear the words that were spoken but Jepheth must have relayed his discovery to their understanding, he assumed by their swift sudden action. Without waiting to see who would lead first, it was first come first serve, as the tawaque leader gave a holler to rally the cavalcade. The tribal hierarchy sprung up on their saddle mounts, and with a sound of thunder, they charged leading the hunting raid toward the herd.

The entire hunting party reached the hill, but from a disorganized and scattered assault. They eventually formed a single column along the edge across to the end of where the mound inclined. They saw, with excitement, the large grouping of carcasons of which they probably thought was the mother lode of all hunts. Jepheth and the legionnaire were on their back saddles, side-to-side, and they showed just as much enthusiasm as the rest of their party.

One of the chief leaders raised himself up from his saddle and gave a war cry while waving his spear in the air, which signaled the large gathering to commence the raid. The thundering sounds of galloping hooves, and the high-pitch squeaking sounds of the cartwheels, stunned the herd and they briskly begun to scatter and sprint away to safety. Jepheth and the marshal maintained themselves in the tawaques' disciplined column formation, the marshal struggling to stay astride but still managing to hold on.

Charging through the main concentration of the herd, and when the herd broke up to scatter in all directions, so did they. Each hunter aiming his spear, or holding it at the ready, waiting to strike and to make that first kill. Joshua was bewildered by the chaos, and with his spear in his inexperienced hands; he tried to look for an easier target.

One of the chariot riders, who targeted and navigated toward an escaping carcason, turned too sharply when the animal darted to the side. The chariot flipped over when the wheel was unable to sustain the pressure causing the axle to break. The rider was crushed by the weight as the chariot flipped around on all sides, and was almost trampled to death by his own boador drivers.

Despite some tragedies, with precision and skill, the riders lunged their spears and most were making good kills. But to the marshal this was almost a mockery; he had yet to initiate his first throw. Almost all around him the carcasons were dropping like flies, as the tawaques seemed to be monopolizing on the hunt.

Joshua than targeted a runaway carcason, a runt in size, easy prey he thought. From being motionless, and looking dumbfounded, he now seemed ready to achieve his first kill. His eyes were filled with determination and as he lifted his spear slightly while keeping a firm grip on the shaft, and with a bellowing command, he commenced his charge.

While he charged as fast as he could to intercept and hit his first target, he held on to his reins with one hand as though his life depended on it. The fast moving carcason sprinted to the left and than to the right as Joshua tried to stay on top of the animal's trail, as he tried to stay on top of his saddle. The runt darted to the side again, and even though the marshal seemed to be keeping up fairly with his prey up till now, he was unable to adapt to his ride's jerky and sudden moves and he was eventually thrown off his saddle.

As his boador bolted off, and somewhat excited from the marshal's inexperienced handling, Josh stood up and brushed the snow off his pants. To him this was a learning experience, attack something bigger he thought, it wouldn't be as fast as a runt.

After Joshua looked around for a while he found and picked up his spear, and than he looked around again, and saw nothing but dead carcasons littering his surrounding area. The marshal showed an expression of disappointment and exhilaration as he sighed and tried to control his breathing. He glanced out toward his right flank and saw his fellow hunters who were still engaged; stabbing his spear in the snow, he took the time to relax a bit.

While Josh took a moment to catch his breath the hunters, to the sweet smell of victory, continued the chase. Jepheth made charge after charge herding the stampede for the others to exploit. Affixed effortlessly to his saddle, unbroken from the erratic movements of his boador, Jepheth steered and reined supreme as a seasoned warrior.

The stampede was now being herded in the opposite direction and Jepheth found the opportunity to display his initiative. Still advancing, like a bat out of hell, he targeted one of the stampeding carcasons, which was within his tracks. He need not have to hold his reins; his vice-like feet gripped the sides of his ride, which gave him full use of both arms. He took steady aim while keeping his eye on the carcason's every move; he arched his spear back and than gave a mighty throw. A direct hit he was pleased to see as he retreated back toward it and retracted his spear from the dead corpse.

The stampede was long off when Jepheth retrieved his spear and than he plunged toward their direction, still astride and prepared for more. The tawaque's strength and agility was equal to his eagerness to continue.

Joshua was well rested now but disappointed, and slightly embarrassed, as he walked about feeling foolish as he searched for his ride. To his shock, as he looked up, the stampede was charging his way. Mindlessly he grabbed cocked his spear, in a defensive motion, as though it would stop the stampeding herd. Closing in, too close he thought, the marshal begun to back away, but before he had the chance to run off, galloping hooves surrounded him.

Jepheth closed in toward the sight and saw, with much concern, Joshua's predicament. Unable to get in near enough to help Jepheth approached as close as possible to ward off any more runaways who might be running in the marshal's direction. Hollering, and showing a sign of supremacy, the tawaque did his best to attempt a rescue.

The bodies of the herd seemed to be crushing him as they charged pass the marshal, him being sandwiched in between the advancing carcasons. He still held firmly to his spear as he tried to avoid being trampled on, but he was almost unable to move. Jepheth was a mere fifty yards from the marshal's location, and as the tawaque watched with despair, he tried to get in even closer to give aid.

The marshal still, as fear set in, tried continuously to remove himself from the unsettled position he found himself in. But eventually the strength of the stampede became to be too much for him and he was shoved down, and as Jepheth looked on, it appeared to the tawaque that the marshal was being trampled to death.

The stampede finally scurried off, along with the pursuant hunters, and all that remained was a dead carcason and the reposed body of the marshal. Jepheth seemed devastated, as though he had just lost a loyal companion, which impelled him to get to Josh quickly to check for any signs of life.

"Ov dep'v c'I," Jepheth said as he dismounted.

Jepheth slowly walked closer toward the marshal's limp body, which appeared to be lifeless. But before the tawaque had the chance to grieve he noticed movement and some breathing, the marshal was only stunned but alive.

"En hemef zuas ul," the tawaque said as he helped Josh to his feet.

"Yea, I'm fine," the marshal said as Jepheth padded him down to check for injuries. "No, I'm fine, I-am-not-hurt," Joshua said slowly to reassure his friend.

To both of their surprise they saw what laid at their feet, a dead carcason. The animal must of, with misadventure, advanced into the marshal's spear, Josh made his first kill. Jepheth gave the marshal a celebrative pat on the back, and as he uncoupled his axe from its sling, he prepared to skin the carcass. Not having the stomach for it Josh took a step back while scratching his head; he was still stunned but thanking chance.

Bringing the expedition to a close the gathering of hunters packed up their gear and the spoils of the raid. They kept the meat stored aboard their carriages and some they stored in their cargo sacks, which were harnessed to the saddles of their steeds, for safe transit back to the village. The carcason skins were neatly folded and kept separate from the meat, to avoid permeation from the smell of raw flesh.

Joshua stood next to his yearling as he packed in his share of the carnage that he was given credit for. As the marshal heaved to drape the peltry across his saddle Josh felt pride for himself and he also sensed the others bidding him with a little bit more with respect, in reference prior to the raid. Noting the marshal's inexperience Jepheth, most likely, skinned and gutted Joshua's kill, but it was his kill.

After the carcass hide was evenly folded in half and placed across the saddle Josh glanced around to see where his friend might of disappeared to. To the right of his rear he saw Jepheth standing among side his chiefs, to talk among them that seemed to have some relevancy to the marshal, the marshal assumed as he detected the tawaques looking in his direction periodically.

After a moment or two had elapsed the tawaque stepped away from his brethren to walk toward the marshal. Once at his side he said aloud, "Nez gesoipif, duni," as he made a gesture to the marshal to follow him. "Zua fof huaf, zua hion huaf," the tawaque spoke again as he roughly, but with affection, placed his hand on Joshua's shoulder.

"Yea," Josh sensing their exuberance of his successful outcome, "success."

"Duni zua netev qesuiwi zuas xusevijoz-pitet," the tawaque said as he suggested, with a slight pull on the marshal's arm, to follow his trail. As Jepheth and Josh walked together, toward a destination that was yet unknown to the marshal's quandary, the chieftains and the others smiled and expressed a sense of pride at the newcomer's proven courage.

As soon as their destination was reached they were followed and than surrounded by a large group of tawaques, which appeared to be the entire expedition party. They all congregated near a cliff line and they were exuberant and boisterous as they gathered close together, like spectators, spectators that seemed to be waiting for a display of some sort. The cliff was facing another of the same, like a deep ravine, with a mammoth trunk of a tree stretching across both ends. Between the two opposing cliff lines was a deep drop but the trunk seemed to be the centerpiece of the spectators' attention.

Jepheth was the first to advance toward the reposed tree, while he showed enthusiasm by raising his fists in the air and bellowing his war cry. Jepheth gradually distant himself from the marshal's standing as the marshal pretty much felt beside himself with questions. The tawaque participant continued to keep his fists raised as he shouted cheers to his people's pleasure. While Jepheth displayed his superiority the other tawaques crowded around the legionnaire with fervor and with joyous anticipation. The marshal was stunned by this sudden outbreak, and as they forcibly removed his cloak from his back, he was still besieged with questions but he also felt a sense of outrage.

Jepheth than lowered his fists, and his demeanor, as one of his fellow tribesman handed him a pair of padded truncheons. After Jepheth took these weapons into his possession he took a momentary stare at the marshal, after which, he looked away and headed toward the lying tree. With spring-like action he jumped on top of the tree trunk and he than walked across it midway, like walking across a bridge, being fully aware of the endless abyss beneath him.

Joshua, now with his cap and cloak discarded, removed his winter goggles and he threw them to the ground as he showed signs of hesitation. While the marshal looked on, at Jepheth as he easily balanced himself on the tree beam, one of the tawaques handed Josh a set of truncheons as well. The marshal accepted the weapons with some reluctance as he took hold of the sticks with one hand, and than examined them to ascertain the best way to utilize them. Judging by Jepheth's posturing, and the aura of competition that surrounded him, the tawaques seemed to be inviting Josh to a sparring match and Jepheth was his sparring partner. Joshua shook his head and smiled with disbelief as he thought silently that this was their way of giving an initiation test, to prove himself worthy of their trust or brotherhood.

The marshal followed Jepheth's trail, and once he was at the tree, he noticed that the topside was at his chest level and the marshal literally had to climb to reach it. As he kept a firm grip on both sticks with one hand he tried to pull himself up with both arms, as he hugged the side of the tree and grabbing whatever he could to negotiate the obstacle.

After he successfully made it to the top he now stood upright, above those who were still standing on solid ground. A partial fear of heights seemed to be keeping his feet glued briefly as he gasped and made short breaths to control his breathing, to eventually work up enough nerve to walk across to the point where Jepheth stood. As soon as he was in control of his fears, and his awareness, he took careful steps to balance his way toward his friend. The irregularity of the trunk made walking difficult but the legionnaire managed his way onward, forcing himself to avoid looking down at the drop beneath his feet.

As the marshal approached the tawaque stood still with his feet clasped firmly to the trunk, his truncheons held and raised at the ready. The marshal attempted steady steps as he approached his menacing sparring partner, but managed to keep himself balanced but almost nearly slipping off as he neared in closer.

nce they stood toe-to-toe and face-to-face, combative eyes affixed to each other and alert, it would seem that their friendly joust was about to begin. Josh hoped, rather, it was friendly as he looked up at the towering creature but given the depth of the death drop below he knew that this was serious.

"This is just a joust between friends, right?" Joshua asked Jepheth in all humility. And after those last words were spoken Jepheth lunged ahead at his beleaguered foe.

The tawaque advanced with a downward slice of his truncheon as Joshua evaded with a jump back, nearly slipping off as he did so. Even though the tips of the truncheons were padded with stuffed rawhide safeguards, because of the tawaque's strength and size, he could still inflict great injury against his smaller adversary.

After his first attempt the tawaque than lunged again with another downward slice with his opposite weapon, to try to surprise Joshua in a repeat of the same technique. This time though the marshal deflected the blow as he held his weapon to a face guard position. Jepheth's truncheon struck the marshal's defending weapon with enough force to nearly push Joshua flat against the surface of the trunk, from which he stood, because of the comparative larger weight that was put behind it. The marshal scrambled back and away, before Jepheth had another opportunity to advance upon him again, and to regain a proper fighting stance.

The tawaque made another advance, and than another, each time initiating downward cuts with his truncheons as his advances were made. Every attack technique Jepheth executed the marshal was able to successfully; but with some difficulty, defend against. The size and weight of the land dweller, which drove his hammering blows, forced Josh lower and lower against the barked wood he stood on.

Cheers and boisterous sounds of encouragement egged the two combatants on but the marshal silenced those calls in his mind, while he literally fought for his life. This time now, and suddenly, Jepheth executed a downward diagonal cut, which forced Josh to shift his defenses. Surprised by the change in the tawaque's offense the marshal averted such a strike by ducking back, which forced Jepheth to miss contact.

The tawaque leaped an advance again, following the marshal's every attempt of evasion. Continuing to strike side-to-side blows at the staggered legionnaire the marshal was clearly on the defensive as he maintained a combination of duck and deflect maneuvers. As one of Jepheth's attacking truncheons whipped toward the marshal's side the marshal would parry with his weapon, to force Jepheth to miss his intended target, while keeping his other truncheon held as a blocking countermeasure. After the tawaque recoiled, to attack the opposing side, the marshal would defend himself in the same manner.

The marshal was beginning to grow weary, and his arms were beginning to feel heavy, from continually blocking each incoming assault. As the marshal continued to struggle, to stay in step with his opponent, Jepheth shifted his offense again when he unleashed another downward slice. The unpredictable moves of the tawaque forced the marshal to think fast on his feet, and to adapt with his opponent's moves.

The marshal ducked again, and the tawaque missed again as his weapon struck nothing but air. After his last try Jepheth than executed the same offensive technique but with his opposite weapon. The marshal quickly side-jumped the downward cut, in effect causing the tawaque to miss again. In the process of Joshua doing so, to his shock and dismay, his foot slipped on some loose peat moss and he found himself, no longer standing, but clinging on to dear life.

The marshal's sharp reflexes enabled him to avoid disaster by snatching on to a twisted twine of roots; as was part of the tree's outgrowth, which snaked along nearly the entire length of the tree. The roots were strong and thick enough to support Joshua's weight as he held on to it, and while trying to wrap his leg around the thickness of the trunk. The marshal mustard all his strength to hold on as he attempted to swing his leg over once, twice, and than again but with little success to reach topside. He was too low from the top rim, and the trunk was too broad in diameter, for him to regain his original position that way.

Jepheth was almost as surprised as the marshal when he witnessed Joshua's tumble but because of friendship, fair play, or empathy the tawaque did not take advantage of the marshal's misfortune. The marshal was close to being completely concealed underneath, that when Jepheth leaned over to the side to check on Joshua's status, the legionnaire was barely visible.

The tawaque stood topmost, his stance well balanced, as he looked down straining to observe Josh's precarious position. The marshal did not want to slow his reaction time by looking up to discern Jepheth's next line of attack, given his higher ground advantage. The legionnaire tried to keep a clear mind as he held on, and to ponder for a moment, the best way out of this trap that he fell into. This was not the first trap he found himself in, the last one was when he unfortunately stepped foot within a basin, but this time he had to rely totally on himself and not his friend to come to his aid.

Still keeping a firm grip, with both hands, on the twisted twine he managed to hook his right leg on the same to better support his weight. Keeping his eyes alert and directed at his task, and being conscious of every position he took, he kept his gaze away from the far drop below. Wishing to shorten the time for Jepheth to advance an attack, even though the tawaque was waiting for Josh to regain equal standing, the marshal was not going to wager on that.

To make use of the tree's strong embeddings, which was abundant around him like a web, he quickly decided to retreat away to gain some distance from where the tawaque stood, his only advantage was that Jepheth was nearly blind to the marshal's doings. As he still held on with his hands he unhooked his leg from the roots, which he was now hanging upright. To gain safe distance away from the land dweller he begun to move, hand over hand, finding what he could to hold on to gradually heading toward the opposite end of the tree. His arm muscles begun to strain and hurt as he moved his way along the mammoth tree trunk. As he did so he would, of course, test the stability and strength of every protrusion he would use to shimmy across on. At times his hand, as he hung on with the other, would have to feel its way through a web of embeds but some how he still managed his way onward.

Now he was a few feet away from where he started at, and to the marshal's ease, the tawaque did not detect his present position. Jepheth; his weapons lowered and held loosely in his hands now, leaned to the side slightly attempting to view the marshal's progress. Joshua took short and controlled breaths and he made slow momentum so as not to alert his opponent to his position.

Josh felt that he was now near his window of opportunity, to climb back up and to re-engage his sparring partner. He was still clinging on to the same roots, his legs were still braced against the thick twine, as he inched his way. He than stopped, deciding he had gone far enough, when his left leg lost its grip on the embedding as his right leg still remained braced. He was only momentarily stunned by the slip but he was still safe from falling as he maintained a hold with all three of his limbs. Understandably he was growing drained from his strenuous task, at his present moment, as he exerted to lift his leg up for another bite on the twine to reinforce his hold.

Still holding on tightly he reached up and around to the side with his right hand to grab, what seemed to him to be sturdy enough for his weight, a root that he grasped at. He tugged on it first to test its strength, and when he felt confident enough, he than freed his legs from the intertwining roots. He was now supporting his weight with one hand as his legs and other arm hung down. Josh than struggled to reach up with his left hand to grab on to the same, with much vigor, to double the hold of his weight.

He than hung motionless for a second to catch his breath and than, while the tawaque was still searching for his whereabouts, the marshal heaved himself up. When his chest was finally pressed against the bark; his fists near his chest cavity, and still holding on, he quickly reached up again to grip and hold on to a small stump in the tree. As soon as his left hand reached the stump, and he grabbed firmly on to it, he gave himself another heave as he struggled to swing a leg over the cylindrical hurdle. His face begun to turn red, and droplets of his sweat begun to trickle down his cheeks, as he crawled up and over topside to safety.

He stopped for a moment to rest and to catch another breath, and to thank the stars he was able to pull himself out of harm's way. The marshal was now fully secure on top of the resting tree as he stayed, kneeled against the bark and with his head lowered as though he was praying.

Jepheth, with his back to the marshal, was clueless as to Joshua's locale, which gave Josh the opportunity to exercise a surprise attack. Not wanting to miss the opportune time to achieve this he sprung into a sprint toward his unknowing opponent.

Once he was within range the marshal quickly shot his leg up, between the tawaque's legs, and contacted a kick to the land dweller's groin from behind. The force, of such an impact, to such a delicate and vital organ caused shock, numbness, and crippling pain to the mighty Jepheth. The shock wave shot up, and through his body, as his hands relinquished the weapons that he held.

His weapons were lost forever, at the bottom of the canyon,

as the tawaque dropped to his knees. Now kneeling against the hard surface of the trunk, his arms sprawled open as he tried to cope, Jepheth eventually tilted nearing a fall off the side. But the Paleolithic specimen seemed to have had enough strength to snatch on to a thick twine to catch his impending fall before it happened. The tawaque was now dangling as he held on to the snaky vegetation with one hand; he now seemed to be facing imminent doom.

The marshal wasted no time to lend unrestrained assistance, "Hold on, let me help you," the marshal shouted down as he threw aside his weapons. Josh quickly kneeled in toward Jepheth, as he tried not to tumble off himself, he knew he had to think and act quickly to save his friend.

"Tevez cedel, eh dep neli ov neztimig," the tawaque shouted back.

The marshal took a quick assessment of the tawaque's predicament, which looked grim. When Joshua saw, to his horror, Jepheth's only lifeline giving way from the weight of his body, the twine snapping off from the roots, the marshal took immediate action. From a half kneeling position Josh took a couple of steps back and rested his belly against the trunk. As Josh heard the snapping sounds of the twine he saw his friend descending with each sound, descending by centimeters but enough to cause worry. Hollands slithered down closer toward Jepheth, as he kept his top arm embraced against the tree bark to anchor himself. Josh had detected another twine of roots, which seemed strong enough to facilitate the tawaque's pressing urgency, of which he than quickly took hold of.

After the marshal closed his fist around the twine he jerked on it, and than he tugged on it again to pry it loose, which he could than use as rope. As Joshua focused solely on the twine the tawaque made a sudden maneuver, which both surprised and amazed Josh.

With a tight grip on his lifeline Jepheth heaved himself up, with one hand, as he lifted his knees up toward his pelvis. He than, at this moment Hollands was unaware of the tawaque's doings, clasped the tree trunk with his feet. Jepheth than, using his arm and the strength of his legs, sprung up and over topside and landed solidly on his feet. As the tawaque performed that gymnastic feat Josh followed Jepheth's springing action with his own eyes, which caused a stunned look to show on his face.

From his lying position the marshal stood up slowly as his face showed an expression of awe. "Good move," he remarked as he balanced his way toward the Khalidanian.

"Zua jewi qesuwif zuas xusev-jeopit'te," the tawaque said as he smiled to show that he was pleased. "Duni nez gesoipif, miv at dismissive."

After no more was said they clutched each other's forearms, like a handshake, to salute each other like allies. They both heard cheers from the spectators who witnessed the entire progression of events; the tawaque assembly seemed enthused over the new alliance.

The day winded down to the late evening hours and the sun's luminosity begun to diminish somewhat as it prepared to set. But even though the day was decreasing the exuberance and high spirit increased as the entire hunting expedition party arrived back at their village. A good day's work; to keep their ration yards full with food and to keep their bodies warm with skinned peltry.

The triumphant return of the hunting party was met by a rally of excited villagers, who gathered and waited at the outskirts to welcome the cavalcade as heroes. Women; children, old folks, and those who just stayed behind, cheered and waved at their loved ones as the slow gallop of hooves paraded toward the village. Their fears, of the party's absence in the wilderness, was replaced with joy and anticipation for their up-coming festival celebration.

Joshua felt a sense of pride as he rode his yearling toward the central corral; his tawaque friend rode beside him. The corral was visible in the forefront several feet ahead when he noticed Jackie, as she stood waiting passively by.

The marshal tugged on the reins to stop as soon as he was beside her, as Jepheth rode off ahead. "How's things on the home front?" he asked as he dismounted.

"Bored, you look like you had fun," she smirked.

Josh responded directly as he stretched his legs, "It was strictly mission intent." The marshal responded to Jackie's remark, a woman's remark, without making eye contact because in his mind fun wasn't exactly the word he would use.

"I hoped to give them a good show to win their confidence, and I think I did," he said as he arched his back to stretch.

"What does that mean, will they help?"

"I don't know, we'll know tonight," he said as he grabbed his boador's reins. "They're going to throw us a party." The marshal than walked the rest of the way to the corral to lodge his ride, the animal seemed ready for much needed rest, Jackie walked beside him along the way.

The twilight had arrived and it was now early in the night. The only light sources that were came from the glimmering display of the stars above and from the lit torches and campfires throughout the village. The hard day's work had passed and now it was the time for the people to celebrate and to enjoy the results of their sweat.

The partying villagers were excitable, glad to see that their kin had made it back safely and with a victory to boot. The bulk of the partygoers assembled within the central town square. The vicinity was crowded with those who left the day's stresses behind them and to allow themselves, for that night's moment, to have some fun.

The sounds of kettledrum music and laughter created a joyous and almost addictive aura around them that you could not help but to join in and share the moment. A huge bonfire that they haphazardly built brightened the night's darkness. As the folks there sat around the heat source some pierced raw meat with their spears and held it near the open flame to cook it, like a skewer through meat. And for the others, who weren't preparing their night's supper, danced to the music or sat around to boast about today's exploits.

Jackie and Josh sat side by side on short logs, which had fur saddled across them to cushion their buttocks. They sat within close enough range, from the bonfire, to absorb the warmth and to breathe in the aroma of cooking flesh, which hastened their yearning to partake of the sustenance.

Rover One was at the back of the two hovering stationary with its maglifts on at minimal power. The 'maton was no longer in hiding since it was now thought of as something that was part of the group; any friend of Joshua's was a friend of theirs.

"Iev jieseviz," Jepheth said to Josh as he approached him. The Paleolithic man handed Joshua a cooked drumstick, from a long since dead carcason.

Joshua accepted the offering with gratitude and with a gnawing appetite, his Legion issue ration packs weren't substantial enough to quiet the rumblings in his stomach. "Thank-you," he nodded. He grabbed both ends of the humongous drumstick and than he took a huge bite out of it, bad etiquette didn't seem to matter much in that climate.

As Josh ate Jackie sat motionless with her eyes centered on nothing and she held an expression of placidity. Perhaps she'd forgotten her problems, for the time being, and she just wanted to take that moment to loose herself in the warmth and closeness of her surrounding new friends.

Jepheth hadn't forgotten about her though as he tore off a big portion of the breast, and than stabbed the big slab of meat with his flint stone knife, to give to her. "Iev jieseviz," the tawaque said again as he attempted to give her, her share.

The slab of breast dangled on the tip of his knife as he invited her to take it. For an instant Jackie looked bewildered, "I can't eat all that," she said as she threw Josh a wide-eyed look.

"Take it and smile, don't insult them," the marshal insisted to her. He looked away from his meal for just a second to criticize Jackie, hoping she doesn't damper the spirits of her hosts.

Feeling somewhat reluctant she reached out to receive her piece of breast meat. But when she touched it she quickly snapped her hand back, on account that it was hot. "Ouch, it's hot," she laughed a little at herself. She fanned it with her hand, to cool it, and than she withdrew the slab from Jepheth's knife.

She held the piece of meat sloppily in her hands as she readied herself to feast on it. She ate like a bird, tearing the skin with her teeth and than taking small bites and nibbles. As she swallowed small portions, and amazed that she liked it, Jepheth nodded with a smile as he turned away from her.

The background drum music continued its beat, as their two special guests ate, as though the music they were playing was a means to let loose as an award to themselves that they survived yet another day. After Jepheth snatched his share, of that night's delicacy, he sat between the two to eat hearty with them.

As Josh continued to work on his drumstick, biting and tearing big portions to digest, one of the chieftains, who sat beside him at his left, started to talk to him in tawaquan. The tawaque chief seemed excitable and non-timid in that night's festivities; to the marshal's sense it would seem that the chief was merely making idle chitchat.

"Shenbora, fepedi gus at," the chieftain commanded Shenbora, who was the same Shenbora Jackie befriended earlier that day. The tall, long brunette haired, tawaquan woman stood up on demand and as she did so the background music stopped momentarily.

The crowd silenced as Shenbora made herself visible for all and she prepared for something, which was yet, unknown to the two newcomers. She wore her mini-peltry skirt and tank top; exposing too much skin for Jackie's jealous nature, she sensed Josh looking upon her with adulation.

Standing near the bonfire, and the thickness of her skin, she was insulated enough to wear such skimpy clothing. As soon as she appeared ready the rhythmic beat commenced and she commenced to dance. She danced provocatively as she swayed her hips and aesthetically fanning her arms about, like the spreading of a peacock's tail. Her movements were consistent to the steady beat of the drums as Joshua stayed in his seat, looking almost seduced by her every move.

As Shenbora danced with splendor, and as her audience remained captivated, the chieftain turned to the marshal and said to him, "Tenuli vejot," as he handed Josh a smoke pipe.

After the marshal took it in his hands he inspected it with a combination of puzzlement and curiosity. It looked, to him, to be a tool of obvious application, and judging by the chieftain's demeanor, the marshal figured what he was expected to do with it.

"What is it?" Jackie inquired.

"I don't know, I think he wants me to smoke it," the marshal seemed reluctant though.

The marshal looked at the chief again, but this time with questionable eyes. "Tenuli vejot," the chief said a final time as he made a gesture to Josh to suck on the mouthpiece.

The marshal than shifted his attention back to the thing that he held in his hands. He accepted the chief's offering by inhaling deeply; of whatever organic substance he was smoking. Than Josh released the mouthpiece from his lips as he exhaled slowly. Joshua felt a sensation of extreme high and light-headedness, like he was the king of his domain.

"Mono-uthoran," the marshal recognized, "known throughout the galaxy as incense. It's a euphoric drug, it's supposed to make you feel like you're the center of the universe."

Josh than attempted to hand over the pipe to Jackie so she can have her turn. "I don't think so," Jackie refused.

"Take it," the marshal ordered. "He might take it as an insult if you decline." As Jackie, hesitantly, took the pipe Josh turned to the chief to give a nod and a smile of acceptance as a show of gratitude.

The tall and alluring Shenbora continued her dance to dazzle the crowd, with her beauty and elegance. Leaning down, while spreading her legs, she swung her head between her legs with the beat of the drums. Her long black hair whipping back concurrently as the crowd grew more enchanted. And as she shook her chest and shoulders in a beguiling manner she arched back, exposing the cleavage of her shapely breasts. Her flexibility was so elastic that her hands were behind her now, touching the ground, as she jerked her pelvis up and down as the beat of the drums progressed faster.

At that moment the incense drug was having its full effect on Jackie. She felt unlike herself as the drumbeats, and the alluring dance, intensified. Perhaps the dance was having an effect on

Jackie but in a different way, she felt aroused and the longing to be with a man.

Jackie than turned to Josh with orgasmic eyes and the marshal in turn, maybe it was his second sense, turned his head to catch those eyes. Jackie than creased a smile at the marshal, and when she did, she stood up to turn her back and than she walked off toward her hut, almost enticing Josh to follow.

The drug must of had an effect on the marshal as well when he stood up to obliged Jackie's invitation, who had now since vanished into the darkness. The assemblage looked on, inconspicuously, as the two disappeared from their presence, as though they were planning the courtship of the two from the beginning. As the two legionnaires excused themselves, for some privacy, the tawaque tribesmen cautiously laughed quietly among themselves, to be discreet. The 'maton stayed where it was; perhaps its design for human compatibility was so exact, it knew when not to intrude.

Jackie was the first to reach the sanctity of the hut, standing within the dimly lit serenity of her surroundings, as she waited for her male companion. Her winter thermulated fatigues had been discarded, to reveal her insinuating strap-and-buckle coverings. And that, which was not covered, she revealed the beauty of her tanned skin.

At that instant Joshua stepped into the faint light from the shadows and he saw, to his pleasure, Jackie wearing the same seductive attire she wore since their first meeting. His footsteps, as he approached, was as clear as a pin drop within the quietude of their surroundings. When she turned her head, but not her back, to Josh she begun to disrobe slowly.

They were obviously not themselves; noticeably they were under the intoxicating effect of the mono-uthoran, which spurred on their actions at the present. Jackie, without turning her back to face the marshal directly, unbuckled her top. Once her top had been unbuckled the one-piece strap overlays almost seemed to slip off by itself as it dropped to the floor to her feet to reveal the contours of her breast.

Joshua smiled to her as she seemingly, the marshal could sense, tried to lure him closer. With casual hands he threw off his winter garb and than he removed his shirt, as he approached Jackie, still with her back to him. When they were both close enough to touch she turned, the color around her pointed nipple faced outward while her other pressed against his chest. He gently placed his hands on her hips as she leaned back into the nest of her sleeping sack, and than they started the night out with a kiss.

Josh and Jackie slept soundly with each other, side to side, in the cradle of passion and warmth. Induced by the euphoric toxin or not they both, that night, seemed willing to share themselves openly. Maybe it was the fact that the hallucinogenic drug forced them to lower their guards to allow them to bring out their feelings for each other, which might have been within them all along.

The intruding chirps, and beeps, of a spheroid opened the marshal's heavy eyes suddenly, which hovered within arm's reach from Joshua. As Josh jumped up to a sitting position he thought to himself that his interlink's emitter beacon did the trick, it led it to his position. As a small token of surprise, for the ignorant observer, the spheroid robot spread opened its small hatchlet to expose a vidcom screen, and at that moment, Joshua knew that the cavalry had arrived.

A familiar image was projected on the small screen, "Marshal, I'm glad to see you're with good company," it was General Commander Murius.

"Sorry s-," Josh was stopped short.

"Never mind with that," Murius broke in, "The fleet is here and near orbit, but we have a problem," the General Commander continued while the marshal stayed silent. "We've received the intelligence photos from your copilot, and before this transmission was sent, we did a complete probe analysis of the target."

"What were your findings," Josh inquired.

"The entire parameter of the station is surrounded and protected by field guns. The moment any of our ships penetrates the EMR net they'll be instantly obliterated by the ground cannons," Murius explained.

"That could pose a dilemma, what do you suggest?" the marshal scowled at the situation.

"You need to draw them out somehow, like hornets out of their hive."

"How do you suggest I do that?"

"Either by baiting them from outside or sabotage from within, I'll leave that to you," Murius being decisive to his subordinate.

"I'm afraid most of our supplies were destroyed by an unforeseen force of nature," the marshal doubting the mission he was given.

"I'm sure you'll think of something," the marshal's superior being insistent. "I'll be waiting for your signal, end dispatch."

At that instant, after the transmission ended, the spheroid drew its small hatch closed and than scurried off in flight. Possibly the metal ball-shaped 'maton was programmed to return to its v-pod, to be retained back at the flagship, the U.S.S Coronation, after the transmission was complete. The starcarrier, Josh assumed and hoped, was preparing to assemble a strike force while he was commencing his own mission.

Slowly the marshal than leaned to his side, from his sitting position, to Jackie's side and he gently nudged at her shoulder. "Jackie, Jackie, wake up."

"What-?"

"Shhh, get up, the fleet is here," the marshal informed at a near whisper.

"What?" Jackie was still heavy eyed and groggy.

"The fleet is here, we have a job to do," the marshal being very formal now. "Get dressed."

After Joshua stood up to get dressed Jackie dropped her head back into her pillow with a very frown look. She now had to cope with a slight side effect of the drug she took, the night before, which gave her a splitting headache at that present morning. After she sat up, while holding on to her sleeping bag to modestly cover herself, she also seemed to be suffering from short memory loss. The marshal had a head start, and was pretty close to vacating the premises, as Jackie reached out for her clothing. After Josh left her to her privacy she wondered, what the hell happened last night?

It was 16.4 hours startime and the sun was burning bright, in the pre-afternoon hours, and the two legionnaires hoped that the good morning meant for a good outcome of their mission. But they both knew that the chances for success were slim as they stood near Joshua's yearling to do an inventory count of what little supplies they did have.

The little 'maton stayed clear from everybody's way to observe and provide medical service, if need be, throughout the mission. As the legionnaires attempted to workout some sort of mission plan Rover One's thrusters were idle, standing on its bi-tractor legs and its optics attentive to their doings.

"What do we have?" Jackie asked.

While Jackie waited for a reply the marshal shuffled through the contents of his cargo sack. "Interlink, compact scaling-wince, some primer paste, not much," the marshal answered, "I'll think of something."

They both turned their attention away from their problem, temporarily, to see if their tawaque companion and allies were going to assist them. They saw and heard Jepheth conversing with the village leaders, and by the tone in his voice and his hand movements, it would appear as though he was pleading with them.

"Are they going to help out?" Jackie finally spoke out as they both looked on.

"I don't know," Josh probed for an answer.

Josh asked himself, silently, that same question until finally Jepheth turned to walk toward them with his answer. Jepheth seemed desponded as he made his approach and Shenbora, who held a peltry sheet skin in her arms, accompanied him and they walked until finally the four were together within vocal range.

"Xi dep'veh hu xovej zua hu," Jepheth said in his blunt tone of voice. "Hu," his tone was a little bit louder as he waved them off.

"Doesn't look like they're going to help," Jackie was unsettled.

Jepheth than snatched the sheet skin out of Shenbora's arms and than gave it to the marshal as a gesture of appeasement. The tawaque, as he looked down on the marshal, placed his hand on Josh's shoulder and said again, "Hu," as he signaled them both to leave.

After Jepheth looked away from the two he pushed Shenbora to leave and the tawaque followed her behind. "I guess we're on our own," the marshal said disappointedly.

Josh tugged at Corin to step in a bit closer, as he held on tight to the saddle horn, he mounted. As soon as the marshal was astride he lowered his hand to Jackie to pull her up. Jackie, as she placed her foot in the stirrup, grabbed his hand and than threw her leg up and over, as Josh gave her a hoist. She now sat in the saddle mount sitting behind Josh, who was at the head to man the reins.

Once she was secure to the saddle, her hands to Joshua's waist, Josh waved a farewell to Jepheth and the others and than said, "C'mon Rover One, try to keep up."

Responding to his command the 'maton initiated its maglift, and readied its thrusters, until eventually it was several centimeters off the ground. The 'maton's thrusters were on standby as it waited for its human masters to take the lead.

"Hold on," Josh cautioned Jackie. Because of Corin's inexperience she felt both awkward and insecure, and after the marshal kicked the sides of his animal, they were off.

After shimmying down the palisade wall, with cord-and-wince, the two provided themselves with cover behind a snow mound. While Josh was looking through his rangefinder he was also contemplating a game plan to instigate; as Jackie and the 'maton remained low and under concealment, they stayed still and quiet. They had not the tools to provoke an outward diversion so they would have to attempt something more dangerous, infiltration of the refinery station.

"Looks almost deserted, just a few footsoldiers posted," he said as he looked through the optical range lens. "A couple of HAVIC tanks as well."

"Sounds like a walk in the park," Jackie was a little surprised.

"That's what scares me," Josh was a little apprehensive. "The General Commander said the parameter is surrounded by field guns. If they excavated the sedimentary or granite rock for that they could have artillery units and soldiers within these palisade walls," the marshal said as he lowered his viewing device.

"What do you have in mind than?"

Josh pondered over that question for a while and than he glanced up at his boador, which was in his line of view near the cliff line, and he said, "I have an idea," as he looked back at the open plains before him.

Four footsoldiers, two at each end of the hangar bay's overhead hatch, stood silently guarding their posts. The regenalts' white armor blended in with their snowy environment. If it were not for the black trim of their coverings, or their tinted-blue optical visors, they would have been easily overlooked by the white landscape. They held their pulse rifles erect to their sides; with their opposite hands holding the side handle grips, for snappy readiness if they perceive the slightest breach in security.

Several meters from the cybernetic sentries three hover assault tanks, or Hover Assault Vehicle Instant Combatants, scraped the ground with magnetic stimuli as they approached the hangar. The teeth on their tractor mounts, for snaring to crawl over hilly terrain, revolved as these machine combatants glided, like apparitions, toward their shelter. Besides the dreadful screeching sounds of their engines, and the guards manning their posts, nothing contrary to their routine aroused any suspicion.

A slight shift in the placid snow surface was so subtle that the sentries were not alerted to it, or maybe not as yet. From a distance it would appear to any to be insignificant, perhaps a snowdrift from the wind. But a closer look would tell that it was anything but that of natural occurrence. A fissure in the snow exposed a pair of eyes, whose eyes belonged to Josh as he snaked across the flatland with Jackie beside him. They kept themselves camouflaged with the white peltry sheet skin spread over them, with a little bit of snow fluff over them as well, as they crawled toward the hangar.

Intimidation grew as the tanks hovered pass them but they carried themselves undeterred as they drew nearer. Jackie was arm to arm close to the marshal, both were pressed to each other, and she moved along as he did. They were diligent in their concealment as they kept a pinch hold of their peltry sheet with their fingertips. The sentries, thus far, were ignorant of the impeding infiltration as the two intruders crept their way closer, underneath the snowy-wet blanket they held.

They were now a single meter away from the main access as the last tank, of the convoy, approached them. As the tank hovered over them they ceased their forward crawling pace, quickly discarding their camouflage, as they grabbed the underneath of the tank's exterior rim. Jackie was about to lose her grip before Hollands pulled her up, by her belt strap, so that she could regain her hold.

As soon as they were sure that they both held a firm grasp to the chassis they concealed themselves further by pulling themselves further in underneath by grabbing, whatever they could hold on to. The collision of like pole magnetic currents, between the magnetic generators and booster plates, made holding on difficult. The force, strong enough to levitate the tank, tended to push their bodies to the ground, they were not directly underneath the repulsion point so holding on was manageable. As they maintained their grip, keeping their faces turned away from the push of magnetic currents, they eventually made it passed the sentries and into the hangar.

As the tank's exhaust rudders manipulated the tank's direction, to park, the two infiltrators released their hold on the framework. As the third tank moved along side the other two the intruders scrambled to their feet to hide themselves. The hangar bay seemed empty of personnel, only a moderate staff, when Josh and his companion found no difficulty hiding away undetected. As they scurried to cover a penetrating, mechanical, screeching sound reverberated from the hangar's overhead hatch closing shut.

The parameter had an arsenal of tanks, cyclodrones, and air cruisers in modest supply but no starfighters seemed evident there. Josh, as he and Jackie stayed hidden behind the environmental power control manifold, appeared to be surprised at the relaxed showing of security. He stood behind the cast metal implement with his pulse gun raised and with Jackie at his back.

"I dread when I say this is too easy," he remarked while being careful not to be seen.

"Seems almost like they abandoned the station," Jackie seemed just as puzzled.

After the final tank joined parallel with the other two, merging into its own parking zone, the tank's tractor wheels lowered by pivotal arms and than descended as it powered down its engines. The HAVIC was now idle as the topside manual hatch swiveled open and the crew inside begun to dismount. A crew of three brigand raiders, or colonial rebels, emerged out from their metal encasing, to step off and away from their assault vehicle and to go about their other business.

Josh and Jackie waited patiently for the crew to vacate the hangar bay. After the rebels exited, through a hatch at the far side of the bay, the infiltrators were than free to move about.

"Looks like the coast is clear, stay close," the marshal cautioned. They both stepped away from the manifold with Joshua taking the lead and with his weapon raised. Since Jackie was the only unarmed of the two she felt the need to stay close behind the marshal's protection.

"Lead the way," she replied.

Assuming the tank drovers were off duty, and were on their way to the locker rooms to disrobe their battle fatigues, Josh had decided on a different hatch to venture through. The marshal's reasoning was that the locker rooms, and living quarters, would be unlikely near the refining and manufacturing facilities, but possibly at the other end from the primary function of the station.

Joshua detected another hatch, to the left and several paces from where the drovers exited. Looking around briefly with his gun drawn, to make sure no prying eyes were eminent, he darted toward his chosen hatch with Jackie tailing behind.

When he was just a step away from the threshold he stopped and threw his back against the wall, with his gun still held at the ready. Jackie was behind the marshal with her back pressed against the wall as well; if she hadn't lost her pulse rifle in the scudder explosion she'd be armed to, she felt defenseless.

They both kept silent as Josh reached toward the door's motion sensor to activate the access. With a quick wave-like motion, his hand swiping down across the sensor pad, the built-in laser eye detected the variance of which caused the hatch to snap open. Now that they had a clear entry they hesitated cautiously and than the marshal took a quick glance inside. When Josh was confident that no unfreindlies were at the opposite side of the wall they both jumped in to close the hatch behind them.

Dimly lit plasma lights kept the stockroom free from glare, which made the surroundings relaxing to the eye. The pyrogenic heaters were set near off, which kept the temperature just below room tolerance. Columns of skeletal frameworks of gunships filled the stockroom. The quietness of their surroundings probably meant that they infiltrated at the time during the station's off-duty hours, they hoped anyway because it looks and smells like it might be a trap.

"These works seemed to be abandoned," the marshal thought to himself out loud.

"What does that mean?"

"I don't know."

"Almost seems a shame," Corin stated having an eye for good workmanship.

Not stopping to adorn the fashioned metal the lady mercenary continued to follow the marshal's lead. She made silent steps as they both walked stealthily toward the other end of the chamber. Jackie felt naked without her weapon; she would have to rely on the marshal's handgun to ward off the unthinkable. They finally approached another hatch, and without looking back, they accessed it the same way they did the last.

They were now within the refinery sector and saw, with a look of impressiveness on their faces, supernova reactors near its twin conveyor lines. The reddish hue reflection was absent, molten magma and its sifted metal deposits no longer lit the surroundings, only a few scattered plasma lamps allowed modest light. The reactors, and the other correlating processing units, were cool and idle and appeared to be so for a good length of time.

"What now?" Jackie asked as she stood behind the marshal's back.

Josh stopped and stood still for a moment, to take a look around, and to fathom some ingenious way to do irrevocable damage to the station. This valley, within the palisade walls, was too well protected by the geography alone to also make a ground assault not feasible, his mind stirred as he thought to himself.

"I don't know yet," Josh answered. "We need something we can use as a detonator."

As Josh continued to stand motionless for a brief time, to look around for something that might be useful he saw something. Among the arrangement of modules, of the conveyor system, an idea came to him. The two conveyor belts, which makes the metal molds move to the different processing locations, had to be supported by secondary systems.

Such as the one that caught the eye of the marshal, "Jackie, see if you can find a utility compartment somewhere," he said. "Find something that I can use to make a fire." Without delay she quickly obeyed, not wanting to stay there any long than she had to.

While Jackie was undergoing the search the marshal walked toward the conveyor system's transformer tanks. He than casually, but with directness, rested his backpack on top of the system's control terminal. The terminal was elevated several centimeters off the ground and fused securely to a framework support. The topside of the emplacement was flat and smooth, which seemed to be ideal to be used as a worktable.

Thereafter Jackie approached, "I think I found something, an igniter," Jackie informed, "Would this work?"

"Yea, beautifully," the marshal seemed pleased. "Just hold on to it, I'll let you know when I'm ready for it." Corin stood patient, and ready, to give the marshal a helping hand whenever he asked for it.

The marshal opened his backpack, and after shuffling through the other contents, he took out his primer paste. The pliable plastic explosive, inside a squeeze tube, was designed to melt away metal brackets or locks. The marshal's options were limited by his lack of the proper supplies; primer was not meant to cause a large explosion.

He than removed the screw-on cap while he moved in close toward the liquid tanks. After he kneeled in close he positioned the tip of the squeeze tube against the tank's surface. A grayish paste-like substance dispensed out and stuck to the curvature surface, almost like glue and leaving no runs.

"What are those?"

"Transformer tanks," Josh explained, "they're filled with hydrofusion."

"To do what?"

"I'm not sure, I'm not a chemical engineer." Josh continued, "I just know that this much compressed incendiary will cause a pretty big bang."

"Enough to bring the station down?"

"I hope so," he said but not looking away from his effort.

He squeezed out enough paste he thought would be sufficient to do the job, and when he thought he had enough, he ceased compression as he drew the tube away from the tank. He than carefully screwed the cap back on while making sure not to lose any droplets of the unused paste, which dirtied around the tip of the squeeze tube.

"Hand me the igniter," Joshua called upon Jackie. While asking Jackie to do so, in his nonchalant tone of voice, he stuck what was left of the primer paste back in his back sack.

"Here," Corin complied.

The mercenary placed the igniter in the marshal's hands as he looked around, instinctively, to see if anyone was coming. The object is to set up a charge to bring the station down and get out unobstructed, without loss of life to themselves.

Josh pressed the igniter switch, which than sparked a blue flame. He than leaned in close to the patch of primer he laid down. Preparing for the explosive charge to do his bidding.

"How much time do we have to get out?" Jackie needed to know.

"Depends on the thickness of the tank's outer shell," Josh answered. "I average about five to ten minutes for us to leave this heap stand."

The tip, of the blue flame, ignited the primer causing it to burn but not explode. The paste was simply being used as a fuse to detonate the compressed hydrofusion, the source where the real damage will be resulted from. Smoke ensued and the volatile putty rapidly burned red hot, quickly burning its way through the metal encasing and inner shielding.

"Ok, it's time to leave," the marshal said abruptly as he tossed the igniter away.

Josh quickly stood up and turned and noticed that Jackie was well ahead of him as, he to, departed the same way he came. This time though he was following Jackie's lead, as he ran toward the hatch, which led him toward the stockroom. At that instant he could see Jackie running toward another hatch at the other end, which led them both to the hangar.

As the two were in a hurry to make a quick and clean getaway the primer continued to burn. Light smoke drifted from the heat and the smell of burnt metal, like charcoal, scented the area within a five-foot radius from the burning. As the primer paste slowly burned through the tank's shell small charred metal flakes fell to the ground, the liquid fusion tank seemed unnervingly close from being set off.

Exiting the chamber behind them and than entering the hangar bay laser fire erupted, which stopped them for only seconds. Joshua squatted low and fired back at the sentry guard as Jackie ducked her head down, she reacted without thought. Before she had a chance to bat an eyelid the sentry guard was down by Joshua's sidearm.

Without hesitation or wasted time they both hurried toward the main overhead hatch, near the manifold they hid for cover earlier. As soon as they were within grasp to their way out the marshal reached for the accessor pressure button, which had a keypad underneath it.

Josh punched the push button but nothing happened, the mechanism was locked. "We need an access code to open the overhead," the marshal said in a hurry.

"Circumvent the wiring."

"There's no time," Josh thought quickly, "but I have an idea. Get ready to fall behind me."

Before Jackie had the chance to stay mentally in sync with the marshal Josh punched the general alarm button, which was near the upper corner from the pressure button. At that instant the surrounding vicinity dimmed red as the indicator alarm flashers spun and as the loud alarm sounded.

When the deafening sound of the alarm continued to roar the infiltrators quickly stepped away from the control terminal and faced the overhead, waiting for Joshua's assumption to come into play. To Jackie's surprise the screeching sounds of the pulley drives retracted that caused the overhead hatch to slowly lift.

Apparently the marshal assumed that if the alarm was sounded the patrols, outside, would raise the overhead and rush in to investigate. His assertion paid off when the hatch was at their waist level and he was now free to make his move. The two ducked under and escaped out from the station's enclosure, being psyched for a fight. They were intercepted, only for a short while, by the four footsoldiers, as they appeared stunned by the sudden sighting of the intruders.

Before one of the four footsoldiers had the chance to focus its visoroptics on the trespassers he was shot down. The laser bolt, from Joshua's pulse pistol, struck through the sentry's facial armor blinding and killing it instantly. In quick succession another footsoldier was shot down as well, the laser penetrating the cybernetic's chest cavity.

It didn't take a second thought for Jackie to get into the fight; it was either fight or die, because the odds were not in their favor. Before the third footsoldier had the chance to fire, his aim was directly at the marshal, Jackie reached out with both hands and grabbed the regenalt's arms forcing the muzzle of its rifle up. With the footsoldier's chest exposed, while still maintaining a grappling hold, Jackie push kicked the regenalt in the chest. The blow pushed the cybernetic back and down to the ground while Jackie still held on tight, on the arms that still held the weapon. Corin forcibly spun the rifle around so that the muzzle was pointing down at the sentry and than she pulled the trigger, two shots to extinguish the life from it.

The last regenalt fired with aim that made a hit to the marshal's shoulder, only grazing the skin as Josh tried to dodge the incoming. Without delay Jackie, by a pump action breach, switched from single-fire to rapid-fire and unleashed a barrage of laser shots at the unexpected foe. The storm of energy bolts tore the regenalt down while Josh was down on one knee with his hand to his shoulder, nursing his laser burn that was inflicted. Ignoring the pain for a second Joshua smiled, now Corin was armed and no longer had to stay at his rear for protection.

Now that their path of escape was clear Jackie quickly helped Josh to his feet, he still coddled his shoulder. From where they hid earlier they both ran toward that snow mound to get as far away from the station as possible, they've wasted enough precious time they thought. They quickly gained distance from the station leaving the four corpses behind, since Josh only sustained an abrasion he was able to run on his own.

Brigand soldiers, dressed in their white battle fatigues, were on high alert as the alarm and flashers stirred their attention even more. The excavated network of tunnels, within the interior of the palisades, was bombardment proof by the dense presence of hard granite and other terra formations. Such tunnels and caves, as this one, were present around the station; the linking of the natural elements with the gun emplacements posed a formidable defense.

The gunnery crew had a bird's eye view of the two escapees, through a vantage opening near the gun mount. The brigand's wasted no time adjusting the cannon to ground/surface range; they did by cranking the range setter. The long, 5.1cm diameter, barrel protruded out from the excavated rock nearly two kilometers above the ground. Click by click the shaft of the barrel lowered to obtain aim at the two runners, while undoubtedly the gun operator focused his gaze on the cross hairs of the cannon's sight.

The saboteurs were running across the uneven, snow blanketed, plain as fast as their legs could carry them. They were unaware of the thermal field gun, which was emplaced over them, until it fired at them. The laser blast, which landed too close to Jackie's heels, turned the snow and the rock-solid ground underneath into flying shrapnel.

The sudden blast to the ground, which was followed by the percussion, caused Jackie to lose her footing and she fell, face first. Corin was just a few steps behind the marshal when she went down; and the shrill in her voice caused Josh to turn her way. Joshua quickly jumped to her aid, and after placing his hand under her armpit, he helped her up.

Her limping as she stood up led the marshal to believe that she might have received an injury, "Are you hit?" Josh asked her with concern .

"No, I'm ok," she said as her running again proved it to be true. That time she was lucky; the blast simply had a psychological effect on her, the marshal appeared relieved that that was all.

Their feet hacked through the snow as they were running, cutting a trail behind, as they frantically sought shelter. Blazes of laser fire erupted with near misses as they evaded the barrage. The thumping of their hearts forced adrenaline through their veins, as they continued to brisk across toward the mound, and as soon as they were within a foot of that they hurled over it. Shielded behind rock solid dirt and snow they poked their heads up over the mound to wait for the inevitable, or hopeful, explosion that they manufactured.

The point, of which the primer paste was planted, was still burning through the tank's shell and near to igniting the volatile gas. Flakes of charred metal were no longer dropping to the floor as the incineration process was reaching its finale. But the pungent odor was still sharp and lingering while the central point of the burn was red hot; melting a hole through the tank, like acid.

As the two were huddled behind the snow mound, and looking outward at the station, what they were waiting for came to pass. A shattering explosion followed by, what felt like a windstorm to them, threw the off-worlders back. The station's super-dome collapsed in on itself in flames and fragments; turning debris into flying projectiles, caused by the force of the explosion.

Josh and Jackie leaned forward, back into their kneeling positions, to look at the aftermath of what they've achieved. Rubble laid scorched, fire continued to burn, and smoke drifted upward into the atmosphere turning the blue sky into a black shade, which almost blocked the sun, from their vantage point. The saboteurs could see some of the occupants busting out of the hangar bay, which had not yet been completely demolished. Some of the survivors were engulfed in flames and others were trying to regain their senses.

"Looks like we did it."

"Yea," the marshal looked grim over the collateral damage he caused. "Let's get topside, I hope we drew the hornets out of their hive."

Leaving the inferno behind they were now sitting astride within the expansive plane of the flatland, a good and safe distance away from the palisade valley. Although relieved that they were away from the enemy's wrath, temporarily, they both knew that staying in the openness the way they were, without any means to take cover, was like two ducks in a pond during hunting season.

They were both astride on the marshal's saddle, Jackie sitting at the rear, while they took this time of inactivity to rest and gather their thoughts. Jackie fidgeted as she reached for Joshua's rangefinder, which was dangling on the clip of Josh's cargo pouch. As they both took time out, Jackie preparing to spot the horizon for enemy troops, Rover One was tending to the marshal's wound. The 'maton treated the marshal's burn abrasion with an antibiotic coolant spray; to prevent possible infections, and to ease the marshal's discomfort somewhat.

While the 'maton had its utility appendagers protracted Josh gazed out at the horizon, switching his attention from the medical attention he was receiving. So far he saw nothing unfriendly heading their way, but if there was anything specific out there it might be too far for the naked eye to see, and Jackie had the magnifying device. But Josh had a bad feeling that they were in the clear only for the moment; the brigand troops were probably out there right now scouting their tracks, Josh thought.

Jackie focused through the marshal's rangefinder, while he was being patched up. "What do you see?" Josh was almost afraid to ask.

Through the optic lens she saw, as she gasped, artillery vehicles and air-to-ground assault crafts accompanied an entire corps of combatants of which. As she continued to monitor the assault forces she answered Josh, with a tone of despair in her voice, "Your not going to like these odds."

Rover One was putting the final touches on Joshua's field dressing, lightly spraying on an adhesive to seal the sterilized gauze, which was snuggly wrapped around his shoulder. And after the 'maton retracted its wiry arms Joshua responded to her statement, "Well its not just the two of us, we have a quarter legion of forces up there."

As Jackie lowered the viewing device she remarked, "What are they waiting for?" not really expecting an answer.

The 'maton completely retracted its arms; the only things exposed out were its needle-like hands, resting on the apertures' flap hatches. "Have faith, some of them are my boys up there," he rebutted as Rover's flap hatches snapped up to hide its utility features.

As they waited, for what seemed to be an eternity, the sounds of galloping hooves and heavy animal breathing interrupted their thoughts. Their focus on the opposing resistance was waived when they turned their gaze to discover Jepheth was at hand to help them.

"Nez gesoipef-teh," the tawaque said loud and proud as he pulled on the reins to halt his ride.

"Well, its my boys plus one," the marshal smiled, pleased to have the tawaque's assistance.

"Zuas puv emupi," Jepheth said with a slightly lowered tone in his voice. His hand than went for the hunting horn, which was on a twine hung around his neck. He raised it and pressed his lips to the mouthpiece and he than blew through it. This action caused a penetrating, base-like, sound at the other end of the instrument.

The two legionnaires sat motionless, astride the yearling, looking stunned and puzzled as to the tawaque's purpose. Their inquiries slowly changed into the realization when, in the aftereffect, more sounds of galloping hooves responded to Jepheth's signal. All the warriors in the village came into distant view when they charged up a distant incline many kilometers from the three, who stayed where they were as the assemblage drew nearer. Even though they were at a visibly faint distance away they were close enough for the off-worlders to distinguish who they were, their newfound allies.

In a single column they were saddled on their charging boadors, with an expression of battle readiness on their faces. With their spears in one hand and their other on the reins they bellowed out warcries as they engaged toward the battle sight, with a feeling of indestructibility of euphoria. In addition to the cavalry boador-driven chariots towed the ballistae, which were hitched to the back ends. The projectile-throwing units seemed precariously unhinged as they were being propelled, speedily, across the uneven terrain, but they were quite secure. The entire wide view of the charging horde made quite a spectacle, which was both majestic and frightful.

To the legionnaires, and to their land dwelling friend, the sounds grew louder as the charging warriors drew nearer. When the concentrated force of tawaques reached a single kilometer, from where the three onlookers waited, the warriors slowed their charge to pacing speed but continued onward, closing in to take up battle positions. As the hastily approaching tawaque force neared Josh, Jackie, and Jepheth they looked at each other with mixed feelings of amazement and trepidation. What they lacked in technology they made up for in numbers; but Josh didn't seem to like the matchup, all but Jepheth who expressed nothing but confidence in his fellow warriors.

When the cavalry was now only a hair-width away to passing them the two legionnaires were slightly unbalanced from the saddle as the yearling fidgeted a little, from the sudden bombardment of new arrivals. The tawaque riders looked ahead, at the enemy's onward trudge, to form a battle formation ignoring the legionnaires completely as they passed them by.

"Tevez cijopef at, ximeh mief veji xez," Jepheth spoke to the marshal as he reached out and gave Josh a pat on the shoulder. And after camaraderie was made between fellow warriors Jepheth lunged ahead to join his brethren; but the two off-worlders stayed where they were, at the rear.

"Looks like we got more than enough help," Jackie remarked.

"Looks like," Joshua said, but under his breath. "C'mon guys, where are you?"

In space the cold, hard elements of the planet's environment seemed far away from the cold hard steel of the U.S.S Coronation, as it hovered to a stop just outside the orbital field. The eagle and star emblem was proudly displayed at the front, near the bow, painted in blue on the hard dock.

As the starcarrier maintained a static position the flight

coordinators made preparations to launch all fighters off from their flight deck. Within the Mission Operation Control Room, within the carrier's flight tower, professionalism with direct intent was maintained as the coordinators manned their stations. They kept an attentive gaze at their Touch Access Screen Computers, or TASC, to assist the pilots in safety checking their on-board equipment and to help the pilots plot their course to enemy positions after launching procedures.

A young ensign, who was a signal officer, sat at his console facing the three-dimensional hologram screen to perform his assigned task. His commanding officer stood nearby, looking over his subordinate's shoulder, as he augmented his detective eye with that of the ground crew. The signalmen, who were equipped with their plasma flares and environmental suits, were present on the flight deck to conduct the fighter pilots to their launching strips.

"The first squadron is ready to go, sir," the ensign turned to inform his lieutenant.

"Good, give them the green light," he authorized firmly.

Without hesitation he returned his directness toward the console and than spoke through the transceiver, "Squad leader One, you have a green light from mission control. I say again, you are clear to engage."

Saw "Copy that, we're ready," the pilot transmitted back.

Both men stayed vigilant as they kept their eyes focused on the concave of the hologram screen, to supervise their first launch of the mission. Digital surveillance cameras were positioned outside and directed at key points of the flight deck. The small cameras recorded in real time the outside activities in the form of mathematical equations; which was than transmitted, and interpreted by TASC, to form a moving image on the screen. The first lieutenant and the young ensign regulated part of this major military operation, and also ready to convey update reports to their captain.

Jon Darvus, leading the first squadron, will be the first one to launch to head the first wave of attacks. The signalman was several paces away from his Killwing and stood clear from the flight line, but close enough to the nose of the fighter craft to give Jon signal directions.

Lieutenant Darvus saw the signalman clearly through the canopy's windscreen as the signalman made gestures and waves with his flares, which were coded messages that gave the pilot directions.. Protected by an environmental suit, and anchored by a pair of magnetic boots he wore, the signalman proceeded in getting the pilots underway.

He first made backward waves, which instructed the squad leader to forward his spacecraft to the starting point. Rolling on its landing gear, when the Killwing was at the launching point the signalman crisscrossed his flares to resemble an x, which conveyed to the pilot to stop. He than made jerky flutters with his handheld flares, which meant attention. He than positioned his flares horizontally close to each other and made adjacent spins, which meant increase power to engines. With each of the proceeding steps Jon understood and complied as the final step was about to be executed. The signalman finally jabbed his flares outward in the opposite direction from that of the gunship, at the flight line's heading, which meant launch.

A second after the signal was given the Killwing's afterburners ignited and boosted the legionnaire pilot, across the flight line, and out into space. Once after the squad leader was off and away, free from the hard dock of the Coronation, he steered his IF-7 toward the planet, which loomed like a white pearl beneath him.

The signalman than quickly turned his attention to the next legionnaire pilot to launch him out. Just as before, the next in-line pilot followed the same signal language as he positioned his craft to the ready mark.

There were actually two flight lines, one angled slightly from the launching strip, to allow both take-offs and landings to occur at the same time if need be. While one battle detachment engaged the enemy another squadron could land, to refuel and rearm. But for right now no ships were boarding, the battle had just begun.

In a single column battle formation the tawaque warriors faced the advancing enemy. Astride on their boadors, armed with their spears or throw axes, they were determined to give a good showing of strength and courage. Between a few meters of increments their ballista chariots were positioned and poised in the deadly direction of the brigand raiders. The two legionnaires stayed on the saddle back of the yearling and at the rear of the formation; not knowing what will come of them, a feeble showing of tawaquan chivalry against an armed division of battle hardened machines.

"What are they doing?"

"A bad idea," the marshal made his opinion.

Jepheth had the honor of rallying his warriors by taking position ahead of their offensive line. He galloped briskly up and down the column line to both, keep discipline in their foothold, and to keep their morale high-spirited. A sense of over zeal swelled, as they appeared more and more eager for war. The single column of thousands, although armed with primitive weapons, had an aura of regality of which was enough to create a tremulous psychological effect to any enemy. Jepheth looked proud as he held his spear high, with one hand, and controlled his reins with the other.

"A bad idea," he re-uttered. The two legionnaires stayed affixed to their saddle and looked on as the warrior assembly faced the enemy in warlike fashion. Josh took his rangefinder away from Jackie and raised it to his face, to determine the brigand's proximity and status. Through the magnifying lens he noticed that the enemy was quickly closing the gap, and as he lowered his view piece, he knew lives would be lost today.

Suddenly, and with passion, the tawaques charged to do battle against the ongoing movement of the brigand spearhead. The ground shook as hooves were beating against it and the high-pitch axle shrieks, from the chariots, made a resounding echo of terror. Each tawaque warrior stayed in-step with the other, they did not break their column formation. The legionnaires were still where they were, sitting on the yearling's back and looking ahead as the tawaques left them further behind.

"Now what?" Jackie asked.

"Now nothing," Josh deciding not to answer. Instead he gave a commanding holler and a kick to the animal's side, which provoked his boador to jump ahead to join the charge.

The enemy was getting closer, and was now within crystal-clear visual, to the tawaque attackers as the two opposing armies were about to collide. The brigand cyclodrones, and mobile artillery, was beginning to achieve range enough to strike the tawaques as both sides quickly closed the gap between them. When the anticipation reached its climax the chariot drovers slowed to a still to take their offensive positions, but the cavalry continued their rapid advance. As the tawaques continued their thrust, to break the brigand line, the drovers prepared their ballistae for firing.

Pair of cyclodrones, like a pair of stalking predators, were the first to intercept the warrior charge and they laid down a barrage of sporadic laser fire. The deep base humming of their engines reverberated as they flew passed the land dwellers; and broke their column line into disarray. The repeating thermal blasts, of their front turrets, left death and destruction in their wake.

Heat of amplified luminosity drilled the cavalry down; except for those who were still lucky enough to remain on their saddle-backs, missed by mere fractions only. In a matter of seconds at least five cavalrymen were knocked off their saddles, some were dead, and some only their rides were hit. But for all, flesh and bone exploded as energy bolts penetrated their bodies. Some, who were not hit, trampled or tripped over the dead as they tried to avoid the bloody obstacle. At least one rider that stumbled over the dead ended up with his animal on top of him, crushing his body, until his beast of burden scrambled back up to scurry.

"Dismount," Josh hollered as he jerked on the reins for a dead stop. They both jumped off the saddle with their weapons in hand. "We'll provide them cover here, just start shooting," Josh ordered Jackie to do so with urgency in his tone.

They both made use of the yearling as a shield, facing the bulk of the fighting, and they commenced firing at anyone who wasn't wearing animal skin clothing. Jackie was to the animal's rear with her pulse rifle, a weapon that she seized from a sentry guard earlier, and Josh was closer to the yearling's head with his pulse pistol. They both fired unhesitant at the brigand raiders, taking concealment as best they could. They saw the ongoing march of the white clad army of the brigand line, and they yearned for the legionnaire help they were promised.

They cyclodrones made another run as they swerved around and accelerated again at attack speed, pointing their nose turrets in their direction. "Here they come again," Josh shouted. Jackie need not wait for his warning, they both ducked low to the ground to avoid getting struck by one of their thermal discharges.

Low to the ground, near the boador's belly, they waited and preyed until after the two aerial gunships would fly passing them overhead. At low range, near or at five meters from the ground, the aerial gunships unleashed their hell. The rapid chain of laser blasts struck the ground continuously and approaching ever so near to the legionnaires.

As the barrage drew closer, the not so stupid yearling, decided it wanted no part of this so it sprung back up, on its feet, and dashed off to avoid approaching injury to itself. Now that their only shield had ran off, to safer ground, the legionnaires were now facing the birds of prey head-on. When the two were within the range of the gunships they jumped out of the line of fire ducking to the ground again, but this time they were lying flat on their bellies across from each other, as the repeating blows to the ground passed between them.

"Jackie, you hit," the marshal rushed to her with a loud but concerned voice. He placed one hand gently on her shoulder, and the other gently on her back, and checked for any laser burns to her body she might have sustained.

"No, I think I'm ok," she felt nauseous of being constantly threatened by danger as she pushed herself up. Not knowing if she'll survive through this battle she did have the experience enough to know not to lose her grip of her weapon.

Josh also had his pistol in hand as he said, "C'mon, lets get back into this fight," as he quickly pulled her to her feet. "We won't be safe anywhere without air support, but we need to stay alive a little while longer," the marshal said as he coached her up. Without saying another word they lunged ahead toward the crossfire, of the opposing sides.

Those who were not trampled to death, by their own rides, were still sore and dazed by their fall but still strong and eager enough. Now that at least a couple of the tawaque warriors were now ride less their fellow compatriots rode in, with outstretched hands, and pulled them up to the back of their saddles and re-engaged.

As the tawaques assembled again, to form a secondary assault line, a line of cyclopes marched offensively ahead, ahead of the brigand armored divisions and infantry. The cyclopes destroyers emitted a continuous wave of their laser-sighted beams, which were used to home their weapons in on their targets. Their single eye was for rudimentary optics but their optic amplifier lens, which overlaid the other like an eye patch, was adjoined to the robotic head covering and integrated into its brain. When given a neuron signal a harmless beam could be projected at acquired distances. Streaks of blue hue visual lasers made direction controlled moves, like pointer sticks, to scour for the enemy.

The tawaque war chiefs were shouting out commands, and their warrior subordinates, followed them as they positioned their ballistae. The chariot drovers pulled their chariots, which their ballista units were hitched to, a hundred and eighty degrees so that the crossbow sections were facing the brigand advance. The drovers, who were dismounted held on to the headstalls of the boadors and slowly backed them to rear the ballistae into firing positions. As the ballista handlers cranked the elastic strands of the cross-sections the tawaque infantry took positions behind, to attack when the signal was given, after the projectile spears diminished the odds against them.

The streaks of blue, range finding, lasers bounced off the tawaque warriors leaving wounded and death in its absence. The cyclopes, each one marching in step and with six meters of spacing between them, kept their pulse weapons aimed and fired them in controlled bursts. They fired with deadly precision, each energy bolt shot along the range-finding line of sight. Moving on piston jointed legs, and programmed to kill, their half-human counterparts allowed them to spearhead through and disorganize the tawaque resistance.

At one instance a few of the lasers that were discharged from the cyclopes killed one tawaque and injured another, as they attempted to load their ballista. After two of their comrades were put out of action two more took their place to finish loading a heavy spike into the release track. One of the replacements threw aside the corpse as the wounded victim coddled his injury and staggered away, while his replacement retracted the bow.

The second wave of attack ships were about to disembark and the mission seemed to be in full swing. The flight mechanics detached the underbelly access shafts from the fighters and the flight lines had been swept clean from debris, so more launches could quickly get underway. A superlift, in the background, could be seen elevating more fighter crafts up from the hangar bay below. But the superlift seemed oblivious to the Killwing pilot who focused most of his thoughts on last minute equipment checks before he'll receive the green light to launch out.

"Control tower, I finished the check list. Operating specs seem to be in order," the pilot announced through dispatch.

"Second squad leader, you are clear for launch. Good hunting," the flight coordinator dispatched back.

"Roger sir," the squad leader responded. "All fighters listen up, we have a green light for go. Prep main throttle for full thrust and follow my lead."

All of the starfighters waited in column for the squad leader to propel off the launching strip. Their afterburners revved as ionized exhaust discharged from their aft cylinders, waiting idle before they engage the internal injectors to augment power to the exhaust for thrust. Their converter engines remained on standby until they had their turn in line. First the squad leader will make his departure and than the next one in the column line, eventually all the fighter pilots will launch out in turn, like a continuous chain.

The second squad leader nudged ahead, his thrusters intensified with the needed kick to push forward. The signal operator, after he received the go-ahead from the control tower, signaled the pilot leader to coast forward and engage. With the added momentum needed the first Killwing pilot raced across the launching strip, from the amidships, and than quickly off the bow.

Within the cockpit the squad leader viewed his compact

holographic TASC topography chart, at his lower right side, which gave him a digital picture of his approach. He piloted his Killwing at a fast angle of decent, navigating consistently with the plot coordinates given by his computer, as he attempted breaking orbit. "The terrafinder is picking up some severe storm activity, but several kilometers from theater of ops."

Motioning his flares to the second pilot, for alert readiness, and than after the following signal was given the ground crewman granted the Killwing for launch out. With the same ferocity the second pilot sped across the flight line and off the bow.

Just before second squad leader was about to enter the planet's exosphere, and before particle friction took root, a laser bolt from an unknown location grazed across his portside stern. The origination of the blast puzzled the pilot until he saw an enemy ship looming down on him.

O damn, brigand HEL-bombers," the squad leader became tense. "All fighters, engage them with extreme prejudice. Let's take out this rebel trash." He diverted his attention for a second, enough to say, "First squadron will have to make due by themselves for the time being."

At this moment most of the starfighters were off the flight deck and were now engaging in battle earlier than they have thought, or want. There was no battle formation in practice here, no organized strategy, except to kill each other. All of the fighter crafts, brigand and colonial alike, were in a swarming frenzy, the colonials took a second to get over the surprise from the sudden ambush.

With deadly precision a brigand ship veered in close to a Killwing and fired. The Dominion gunship had no chance to maneuver away, the attack was too sudden, the IF-7 was turned into drifting rubble.

"Damn it," the leader showing emotional distress as he witnessed the kill. "Beta squad, work in teams of two, keep your wingman close to provide cover." "Bloody hell, I got one coming down on my tail," the leader saw out of the corner of his eye, through the canopy's overhead.

They were all flying manually because their human inborn

instincts could react faster than their sensors could, the elapse time of seconds could mean the difference between life and death.

The ground war raged on, impervious to the second battle raging beyond the planet's atmosphere. Laser bolts, from the sky, which rained down on the tawaquan warriors came only from the pair of cyclodrones that continued to carry out dive attacks. They would swoop down and barrage the technological inferiors with hell fire, and the only source that caused the aeroships to falter slightly, were the pulse weapons in the hands of the two off-worlders.

Joshua and Jackie had nowhere to hide for cover, they were on flat and open terrain and had a sense of defenselessness against the advantage the brigands had, at the moment. The legionnaires fought fiercely though, evading death and providing offense against the well-armored brigands. The crossfire, between sides, shortened as the opposing sides continued to march constant into each other, before the well discipline column formations turned into an all out rumble. The bodies, which fell victim to the energy bolts, turned the battlefield into a no-man's land of twisted metal and torn flesh.

"They're coming again," Josh shouted.

The cyclodrones were attacking in a pair as they proceeded with another dive attack, toward the legionnaire's position. Josh and Jackie made a quick split apart, distance from each other, and dropped low to the ground again to avoid open fire, from the flying birds of prey. As the cyclodrones fired down, at an angle of descent, their main guns blazed leaving a trail of smoke and turned over dirt following the riveted chain of blasts.

When the blasts reached dangerous closeness to the off-worlders, as they were still lying flat to the ground, they pushed themselves up by their hands and made a belly-flop evasion to duck the trail of fire. The legionnaires, though they did not lose their grip of their weapons or their nerve, kept flat to the ground until the danger flew pass them again.

Another couple of blasts, which sounded more like explosions, did not seem that they came from the cyclodrones' nose turrets but from the cyclodrones themselves. After Josh looked up and his eyes widened when he saw nothing but fallen debris, of what used to be a structurally sound pair of aeroships. The cyclodrones' destruction came from a series of discharged weapons, which origin came from the first squadron of Killwings, and led by the Cauldron.

As the Cauldron of metallic gray, and its following of a small grouping of Killwings, did a fly pass Josh sprung to his feet in an excited state. The roar of their engines was an inviting intrusion amidst the other chaotic sounds of the battle. While Joshua remained standing, for a second at least, he waved his arms in victory at his friends; and particularly Jagaba, as he piloted the starcruiser in a flyby.

The marshal jerked his head to the side, in sync and keeping his eyes affixed on the squadron, as they did their valiant pass. "Go get 'em boy's," the marshal said loudly. "Those are my boys up there," when he turned to Jackie's direction.

No response came from her; she was still lying on her belly with her face to the ground and a little bit unbalanced, she lost count of how many close calls that she had. Josh rushed to her and hoped her condition was well, shifting his attention from the legionnaire gunships for only a moment.

"Jackie, you ok," he asked as he slowly helped her to an almost sitting position. He gently brushed the snow off her garb.

"Can we go home now?" she responded being facetious. She than clenched the snow out from under her lapel and than sat motionless, for a second to catch her breath, but she was obviously uninjured. Josh was relieved again that she was unharmed; they were now more than just comrades, because of their shared experience the previous night.

But he brushed those feelings aside for now and concentrated on more critical matters. The marshal focused at the horizon, beyond the battlefield, and as he squinted he saw tiny dots in the distant sky, which appeared to him to be a flock of birds, and than he knew better.

His lizard friend knew it to when he turned the nose of the Cauldron around to head back toward the marshal's direction. Joshua turned and saw as the Cauldron decreased its acceleration enough to maneuver back around. He also saw as Jagaba tilted the wings; so that the body, wing tip to wing tip, was near vertical as it spun back for a pick-up.

"C'mon, it's time to go," the marshal said as he helped Jackie to her feet.

They were several meters from the front lines; and with their weapons poised, they turned and ran toward the Cauldron, as the triangle-shaped craft made its landing. The artillery unleashed from the HAVIC tanks became more numerous and intense as the legionnaires made their withdraw. Red streaks of lasers erupted into orange and yellow fireballs; but the tank's artillery wasn't within range of them yet.

The Cauldron's repellors slowed her descent and the after-exhaust dusted the area, turning the stagnant snow into a kicking frenzy, as her landing gear protracted down. When the starcruiser eventually touched securely to the ground the legionnaires wasted no time to hurry toward it, as its gangplank opened.

Out from the shadowy interior of the ship, and down the extended incline of the ramp, Crimson made himself visible. With his pumplaser subrifle in his hands he would provide cover as the two made their way toward the gangplank, to retreat inside.

They quickly sought refuge inside the cruiser, as well as their 'maton, which tagged not too far behind in flight mode. Crimson stayed to the side on the gangplank to allow a clear path for his friends to make their hasty retreat. The cybernetic kept his pumplaser aimed toward the battle, which still raged on in the background as he waited, but not for long.

Without undue wasted motion, and time, they quickly made a run up the metallic incline and passing Crimson, who stood midway, as they did so. The two, and their medicorp unit, were now at the threshold of the belly's cargo bay, and with apprehension, made use of it glancing back as they ducked for cover to see if danger was approaching.

A tank drover must have noticed their retreat, or maybe it was sheer chance, when the artillery bombardments drew closer to their position. The front lines haven't broken yet; the two opposing forces were still focused on each other and in a state of collision. But Crimson kept his pump aimed, as a mere defensive posture, as the three vanished inside. Crimson quickly followed their withdraw as the ramp slowly raised, and not turning his back from the enemy, until he was completely under the protection of the ship's safe covering.

"Man the rear turret," the marshal ordered Jackie as he swung himself through the ingress to exit the cargo bay.

Jackie clutched the above handle grips also and swung herself through the opening but they were heading in opposite directions. Jackie hurried to take control of the rear gun, as she did before, while Josh went for the bridge.

Crimson stepped through the wall's opening and proceeded toward the bridge as well, to assumed his station. As the crew took their positions the half sized 'maton stayed in the cargo bay; it was smart enough to know to stay clear, when reason submits to emotional stress, from its human masters.

Glad to be back on the bridge of his proud vessel, and as he assumed his pilot seat, Josh had a sensation that he was finally back within his element. Jagaba waited for him as he stayed at his station to serve as copilot, to operate the secondary support systems. As the two commenced preparations for take-off Crimson entered the bridge shortly thereafter, securing himself within the reciprocal's embracing arm guards, to augment the ship's controls.

"Yes Jag, I'm happy to see you to," the marshal picked up on the reptilian's cerebral converse. "We have no time for pleasantries, enemy ships moving in fast."

As Crimson plugged his coupling into the Cauldron's system's grid the pilots seemed ready for action. "Initiate repellor lift," the marshal issued his first order.

As the Cauldron ascended the discharge of the ship's ionized exhaust, and the fanning of the repellors' turbines, churned the surrounding loose snow into an uplift. And after the ship reached take-off suspension, from the ground, Joshua raised the craft's nose up toward the enemy's swarm and than he plunged ahead to intercept them.

The tawaques were now only seconds away from beginning

a second frontal assault, a charge, against the brigand line. Even though they have lost a good number of their warriors their spirit wasn't sapped, because of their combined numbers and the arrival of legionnaire air support, their confidence remained firm.

The two opposing armies were meters away from each other and the distance, between them, was quickly shortening to a clash. Pulse weapons still continued to discharge, against the disadvantaged tawaque line, and the artillery blasts continued also. The deafening and reverberating sounds of the brigands' arsenal was matched only by the thermal lasers overhead, which came from Joshua's alpha squad.

From the right flank, and closing in, a hover assault tank's long barrel cannon recoiled as it fired. The tank's under-hull stimulators left a trail of clouding snow debris from its path as it moved offensively closer, attempting to cut off a possible tawaque retreat. As both of the HAVIC tanks moved in, with a plan to snare its prey, the muzzle amplifiers lit up seconds before it shot out intense bursts of energy.

One tank in operation, the tank gunner had to adjust the range because he missed his main purpose, which was to destroy the ballista positions during his progression of flanking the enemy's rear. The ground shook from the tank fire as the determined tawaque operators stretched the spike as far back as it would go, while adjusting the tracking aim. When they finally pulled the release lever the short spear shot out from the cross-section and it hit its mark. A fallen cyclops, sparks flickering from its chest from the inflicted wound, came as a result.

As the tank lowered its long cannon, and right before the armored vehicle was about to fire a second time, the main turret blew off its mount. The source, of the tank's end, came from a Killwing when it swooped down and turned the artillery weapon into useless junk. The cannon, nearly severed from the main body, hung down and seemed to be still connected by just a scant of its armor. The cannon's muzzle weighed into the snow, and smoke escaped out from the blast opening as cheers were made from some of the Khalidanians, who stood near enough to be witnesses.

The tawaques quickly brushed aside those feelings of victory as they begun to load a second spike into the release track. Because they were outnumbered and outgunned they will savor their victory after the battle was won.

Shot after shot the ballistae units fired, each on their own accord, shooting the spikes through the cool air that than struck their targets. At least two of the cyclopes dropped on their knees at the momentum, of the pointed shafts, pierced through their armor. They did not scream as they were struck down, since 'matons felt no pain, only splintered metal and short-circuited sparks told of their malfunction. With sudden ferocity the tawaque cavalry than charged in a secondary assault, which eventually broke the brigand's spearhead column of robotic destroyers.

It was hard to tell the tawaques apart since they all averaged about the same height and they were discombobulated amidst the armor and their fellow warriors, fighting in a frenzy of movement. The state of confusion seemed to spread to the brigand attackers as well, the pushing ahead lines of assault seemed to be fading.

Some were struck down from pulse fire but most of the cavalrymen made it pass the cyclopes. One of the tawaques, with wild fury, made a charging pass with his spear extended. As he passed speedily by one of the destroyers the point of his shaft penetrated into and through the cyclops' chest cavity. With his, almost superhuman strength, the tawaque lifted the bulky 'maton off the ground, it being impaled at the end of his spear. As soon as the land dweller perceived it as being dead he discarded the robotic corpse, allowing the dead weight to slide off his spear, and than he sought out new game.

The footsoldiers continued to march toward the close-knit band of warriors, hampered only by their mechanical bodies. They moved, not as agile as their tawaque opponents, but they did not falter before their cunning foe. Their horizontal, oval-shaped, blue optic visors maintained a point of sight on their enemy as they made controlled bursts of pulse fire, wherever their killing aim was straight.

The tawaque cavaliers quickly broke into the brigands' infantry of footsoldiers, turning the white clad army's set pattern of attack into disarray. The tawaque's interposing clash into the brigand assault line both discombobulated and confused the cybernetics.

Regenerative alterations; even though they were partly human, were nothing more than programmed machines, their reaction time to sudden changes of events had a short delay. This gave the tawaques the advantage, since true organic life forms can react faster intuitively, but they still faced the disadvantage of competing against superior weaponry.

Firing at will; unaccustomed to such a strategy, the footsoldiers were scattered among the cavaliers. Their pulse fire lasers crisscrossed the battle's arena, since the front lines dissolved into nothing more than a clamoring clangorous mob.

The sounds of war cries could be heard as a few of the tawaques had the good luck of making their kill, to them it was like hunting carcasons in the open flatlands. As the footsoldiers fought for their mission the tawaques fought for their lives and livelihood, which gave the primitives more of a willing edge against the alien invaders.

As a tawaque charged toward a white clad he was unfortunately being aimed at by another footsoldier, who stood nearby across from his right side, and the mighty tawaque was struck down by the soldier's pulse rifle. The pulse laser ripped through his right rib cage, which pushed him off the side of his saddle and to the ground, and to his death.

His compatriot avenged his death by charging toward the footsoldier's rear and clubbing the cybernetic, across the head plate, with his throw ax. The footsoldier dropped, and not knowing if he was dead, without checking the body the vengeful cavalier went off searching for another worthy adversary.

The HAVIC reduced its artillery bombardment, in fear that they might hit one of their own; instead they concentrated their fire on the ballista positions. The ballista operators reduced their fire as well dreading that they might do also, of whom were immersed in infighting with the opposing army. When they were about to abandon their throwing devices, to join in with their countrymen, the HAVIC succeeded when it maneuvered behind their position.

A laser bolt discharged from the tank's cannon, one who took notice of the danger, warned the others to evade. As they quickly jumped clear from the incoming threat some were not so lucky, as the explosion engulfed the apparatus in fire, splintered fragments shot away from the projectile device and mortally wounded the unlucky few.

Josh piloted his prototype craft toward and into the mouth of the lion. The Cauldron streaked through the sky into the head-on winds, which shook the outer hull a little. But the craft was battle tested and proven sturdy enough to cope with even the most adverse conditions. All long-range sensory receivers were left off, since the enemy was in plain view, as well as other ancillary devices, except for targeting systems.

"Lieutenant, stay alert and prepare to fire at will," Josh said to his squad leader.

"Roger that," Jon Darvus responded.

He left two of his squaddies behind, to help take out the brigand's ground artillery, while he provided support at his marshal's side. Jon was at Josh's portside stern and another pilot was positioned starboard; in a conjoining effort them, and the others that followed their lead, flew in a V formation toward their enemy.

The Cauldron, its wing defense and the rest of the squadron tailing them, pierced through the center of the storm as the HEL-bomber ships scattered pass them. The brigand ships flew passed the legionnaires at all angles in linear approach, as though the Dominion gunships entered a whirlwind of steel and thermal light. The brigands discharged their weapons as they shot pass them, which at this beginning stage of the first air battle, was more to confuse and shock the legionnaire pilots than to make hits with precision.

"Spread out and take 'em out," Josh shouted. "Make sure they don't climb up to your zero, I'd like to avoid depth charges." Than he switched thoughts for only a second, "Jackie, are you strapped in?"

Jackie flexed her ball turret, which was protected by the hull's housing, and she pivoted the ball-turret's arm from side to side to warm-up her handling of it. And warming herself up for the shooting gallery to begin she stayed vigilant, "I'm ready, let's get this on."

"Alpha squad, transmit targeting to front visual," Josh ordered his men.

With a click of a switch the light dimmed a little, probably from a slight power drain, as Josh transferred some of his navigational power to a separate operating system. A red-checkered graph image, with crosshairs overlaying it, appeared on his frontal windscreen in a form of a hologram. The crosshairs were linked in perfect alignment and coordination with the Cauldron's top and under-wing thermal guns.

To follow suit the lieutenant switched his front targeting screen on and than he climbed way up, almost vertically, toward the heavens in pursuit of a HEL-bomber. He will attempt to intercept and destroy his first enemy target, before the brigand pilot could arrive at his opportunity to make use of his depth charge weapon. Climbing and climbing they hurled up, one chasing the other, as Jon attempted to match his ship with the one he was chasing, procuring the HEL-bomber between the crosshairs.

Accelerating up, following the HEL-bomber's contrail, Jon maneuvered slightly as needed to achieve a clean shot. The enemy was now within the crosshairs, of his twin cannons, so he quickly fired without a second thought. His twin cannons recoiled as energy bolts struck out converting the HEL-bomber into smoke and ruin.

"First target away," the lieutenant said excitingly.

The rest of the main group was in disarray, above the topography of icecaps below, as Jon quickly descended to join them. Accelerating in a drop Jon rushed to assist his comrades in the fight as the g-force pressed his back against his pilot seat; and his eyes were fixated to the battle, which laid below and to his anterior.

When he reached the dog-fighting group his cannons recoiled again, destroying another enemy ship, as he dropped down and repositioned, parallel, to take on the aggressors. "Second target away," he shouted a second time.

"Good shooting," Josh commended, "but don't get too cocky. Stay alert," he said while still keeping focus on his own steering.

John Deleo Custer

"What?" Jagaba warned him of an approaching bogey, "Uh oh," the marshal said under his breath as an enemy ship attempted to cut in front of him. The reptilian's cerebral cognition seemed to be attuned to the battle, and surely Josh valued his ability.

After the brigand ship became a barrier in Josh's flight path the HEL-bomber fired. Josh banked the Cauldron's wings slightly to duck the blast, which missed by a centimeter, nearly scraping the paint. After the marshal tilted his bird back he fired his thermal guns, destroying his first target, before the HEL-bomber had the chance to do an overhead pass.

"Your like an auxiliary defense my old friend," Josh thanked his copilot.

Jackie tracked her ball turret from left to right, and in all other directions, as she tried hopelessly to lock on to an enemy ship. The remaining HEL-bombers were taking the offensive in a frenzy, in disorder it seemed, and they fired at the Dominion gunships sporadically as she made an effort to keep up with their unpredictable maneuvers. As Joshua's piloting, and laser barrages, was jostling her around you could vaguely glimpse at her through the cross-slit of the ball covering she was in and armor housing.

"These vermin don't stand still," she shouted her protest. She eyeballed her prey, or potential prey, and fired but her targeted HEL-bomber was too quick as it veered northeast from her position and evaded her blast. "Damn it."

That same HEL-bomber was now near topside of the Cauldron when it fired, the blast struck the starcruiser's top fuselage. The impact pushed Jackie down and against the side of her turret chamber, she was both battered and startled from the sudden strike. As she dropped to the side she whaled out a sound of exasperation before she regained her seat.

"Don't worry, the repulsion shields are holding," Josh calming Jackie's nerves and his own.

Through his main port view the marshal saw the attacking HEL-bomber and he made quick readiness to fire upon it. Resting his palm against the control console he thumbed his firing peg, tracking his gun turrets in the direction of the brigand ship. When he had self-confirmation he fired but missed, the brigand was just too swift as it shot around, out of his sight and it seemed to be returning to the back quarter.

"Jackie, heads up," the marshal jolted her attention, "You got another shot at this one, don't miss."

When the HEL-bomber circled into her view again she jumped into readiness, and kept her wits about her, as she loosely gripped the gun handle. As the brigand ship was about to loop around the Cauldron for a second time Jackie followed it with her gun turret.

The barrel protruded out, from her ball turret, through the covering's glass shielding. A rubber conical, designed to flex and contort, was installed where the barrel extended out through the glass. This allowed the thermal gun's quick mobility while at the same time keeping her turret chamber pressurized.

As the brigand begun to pass her position it was finally locked on within Jackie's kill zone. She quickly fired upon it, governed by instinct, and obliterated her first kill; the entire sequence had an elapse of mere seconds only.

The U.S.S Intercede stood static, as the Coronation did, with all those aboard at their battle stations. There was much activity surrounding the starcarrier, as in a storm of laser fire from the multiples of war machines, which were in a combative fervor. The flight deck seemed to have only a skeletal sum of starfighters in dock; most of the pilots were within the surrounding parameter of space, and were fully engaged in the encircling battle.

A small infantry transport clung to the side of the Intercede, affixed to an umbilical, which was just one of the two groups of commandos waiting to transport down to the planet's surface. Aboard the shuttle bus the commandos who wore full white battle fatigues sat on opposite sides, on long bench rests, facing each other as they waited to disembark. They were geared with communicators and standard issue weaponry, as in pulse pistols and rifles, and a few specialists carried pulse bows. There was another identical transport waiting for separation as well, which was positioned tail to nose from the other, attached to the same umbilical framework.

Meanwhile, as the two-group task force awaited their drop, the mission operation control room was in a state of organized chaos. Most of the personnel there faced their TASC telemetry units whose job it was to monitor each detail of the battle. Both sides of the battle, which raged on outside, were identified and their maneuvers tracked on hologram computers. A few analyzed their computers on an elevated platform and some were stationed at the lower level of the control room. Their troops were engaged in three major battles at once and they needed to be apprised, in real time, of the most updated status.

The MOCR was a big facility chamber but made small from the abundance of equipment, which was emplaced everywhere to facilitate the MOCR's function. There was enough light throughout for the occupants within to see their way through, light from the overhead plasma lamps and that which emanated from the initiator lights. The initiator lights illumined from the array of electrical equipment that was in use, shining dots of green, red, and orange.

"Sir, IF-10 destroyers approaching steadily," an ensign said with urgency in his tone. He turned to his superior to inform him as blue light, which radiated from the computer's hologram, made a cast of its brilliance on his face.

"How many and how far?" he responded as he leaned in close and looking over the ensign's shoulder.

As the higher officer moved in close for a better look the ensign turned back to face the hologram screen, to make assessments in order to give his superior a quick reply. The blue screen was blue only on the edges, like a picture frame, but the central square was black, depicting space, with a digital interpretation of Khalidan and the surrounding activity. The ensign touched the part of the screen, where the IF-10s were detected, which enhanced the visual view of the threat along with coordinates.

"Two bogies, five hundred meters and closing," his quick reply was.

"Inform third squadron leader to escort safe passage for the incursion teams," the ensign's CO said as he leaned in even closer to the hologram screen. As he stood close to his younger subordinate he also said, "but only until the shuttle cars safely reach orbital entry."

"Yes sir."

And than to more pressing matters, "I need all my pilots up here." Moving away back to a standing position he concluded, "Get who you can to take those IF-10s out."

The ensign, still seated, than reached for the transceiver dial and leaned to the side, his face close to the console, and spoke into the mike. "Gamma one, two incursion teams are deploying to the surface. Provide escort for safe passage but do not enter the orbital field, just make sure their in the clear and regroup with the others."

"Copy that," the squad leader transmitted back.

At an instant the umbilical clamps released their hold on the first transport. Slowly the torpedo looking transport drifted down and away from the carrier's side, and than the stern thrusts ignited fully, the incursion was now underway.

The second transport quickly followed the same disembark procedures; the clamps released and the transport dropped away from the carrier fortress. After there were a few meters of spacing, between them and the Intercede, the thrusters lit up, and the second transport was ready to shadow the first. You could see the soldiers moving about through small portholes, topside, as the transport accelerated at a angle of descent.

A HEL-bomber, detecting an easy target he thought, swooped down on the second shuttle with his thermals firing. Blasts struck the nose causing serious but not critical damage, only interlink communications were severed, and some of the structural integrity had been weakened. The red streaks of lasers caused burnt and shard metal and the whole of the transport shuddered violently, as though it crashed into a magnetic field.

As the brigand ship made a sharp ascent, to prepare for another attack run, a pair of intercepting thermal bolts thwarted that prospect. An explosion over the transport resulted, one less brigand ship to deal with, but the approaching few ships from Gamma squadron knew that further attacks would be expected.

The opposing forces' quick and sharp dog fighting maneuvering, and the firing of their weapons, congested the path to orbital entry, which made an uneasy obstacle for the escort ships. A crisscross storm of blue and red lasers, from both of the opposing sides, would be a taunting challenge to overcome for planetary approach. But even so the commando assembly was undeterred from their mission, they knew their comrades and allies were depending on them as reinforcements.

"Gamma 10-13-34, move into standard escort formation and pay attention to your sensors," Gamma One ordered. "Give those HEL-bombers an incentive to move off, the incursion teams needs safe passage to the planet's surface."

"Copy."

"Copy that."

"Understood," the final pilot acknowledged.

As the four Killwings moved into a diamond cover formation their piston-action wing cannons commenced firing, as quick as their eyes could detect an enemy craft. They tried, with success, to not hit one of their own as the four escorts, and the two guided transports, navigated through the myriad of steel and crossfire. The four-legionnaire banked a little and made adjustments as they maneuvered in to take their positions, and as they unleashed warranted firepower.

The front position moved briskly, as the other three did, and as this Killwing took station it fired and destroyed a brigand ship, which had been engaged with a separate adversary and in the way of the escort's flight path. That adversary swerved away to face-off with another opponent, "Thank-you Gamma One," the Killwing pilot acknowledged his gratitude.

The four escorts, after enduring much resistance, were now in a solid diamond configuration and succeeded their task thus far. The closer they approached Khalidan's orbit the further away from the battle they were, hence, the less flak they had to cope with. Even though that was the case the Killwing pilots were afar from ease, even if the two transports made it safely, they would have to return back to the fighting.

While they still kept their nerve, and their eyes sharply

observant, a HEL-bomber appeared above them and it prepared to swipe down upon them in an offensive manner. Gamma One, who held the front, pivoted his medium gun turret upward, in the direction of the fast approaching opposition, and he fired. But the HEL-bomber's dive attack was so brisk it made Gamma One's attempt inconsequential.

As the HEL-bomber swooped down to target the leading transport it released a chain of rapid fire, with unfortunate good aim. The brigand's double cannons released a succession of double thermal blasts, which made grating penetrations across the transport's topside. One of those pairs of energy struck and breached one of the portholes, which violently depressurized the interior.

The commandos, almost oblivious to the hale storm, jumped out of their seats and cried out and than was silenced. The entire interior of the transport became engulfed as an exploding fireball, like a tidal wave, blasted through from the passenger hold to the bridge, which was quickly followed by the transport's ending explosion. The four escorts, unable to react fast enough to prevent the destruction, made quick evasive reactions to avoid the shooting fragments.

"Thirteen, he's moving in closer to you. Take that sucker out," the squad leader said with payback in his tone.

The HEL-bomber banked left to turn, to avoid the disgruntled legionnaire pilots who would obviously want to pursue a counterattack. The rear position, reacting to his leader's order, shot up at an angle to intercept the fleeing ship.

Only a few meters away from the destruction, the evading brigand had caused, the enemy detected the approaching retaliatory Killwing. Wishing to be the predator rather than the prey the brigand ship banked right, to turn back around to head toward the opposite direction, into the legionnaire's line of attack. At almost the exact second they both fired upon each other, when they were close enough, red thermals slicing through airless space between them. The brigand struck the Killwing's auxiliary engine, maiming the ship's backup propulsion, as the brigand HEL-bomber exploded from the legionnaire's retaliation.

The last commando transport progressively made distance further away from danger as its elongated hull, of the craft, steadily made its descent toward orbital entry. The passengers aboard felt fear and apprehension but they knew that the dangers, as soon as they made it to the surface, would be just as extreme as they're facing now.

The transport could be seen from a distance from where the legionnaire defenders were serving as watchdogs, where they stayed to ward off anymore attacks against her. Gamma leader sat in his cockpit seat while keeping an attentive eye on the transport, as sure as the rest of the escorts did. As he kept his ship static he remained focused on his ship's sensors, while keeping his God given senses acute to his surroundings.

"Sir, you got two sneaking up on you," Gamma Ten called out.

"What-," the leader snapped into his defensive mode as he sharply jerked his head to look behind. Straining his neck to achieve a glimpse of the two attackers he was warned about, "I see them."

The two HEL-bombers seemed to show little interest, to the leader's position, as they both flew passed him. But the one following the other, who was closest to Gamma One's portside, fired off a couple of shots to discourage interference. The heat emitting lasers missed his Killwing entirely, but they were enough to give him a jolt of alarm. Quickly after, he never took his eyes of the two enemy ships as they begun to initiate an attack run against the transport.

The leader fired off a few shots of his own but he gripped the control stick too late to make an accurate enough aim, to hit anything. "They flew pass me too quick, intercept them," not waiting until after those words were spoken to take action.

The HEL-bombers were heading straight toward the commando team, as their transport was about to enter Khalidan's gravity field. The brigand pilots showed little regard to their pursuers, who were bent on their demise. The separatist rebels' only single-mindedness was to prevent this commando team from reaching the legionnaire forces below.

All four of the patrols, a temporary duty for now, engaged their thrusters to intercept the brigand attack ships. Tails of thermal exhaust spat out from their exhaust ports, which accelerated their speed. Gamma 10, 13, 34, and the leader himself quickly shortened the gap between them and their targets.

The Killwings were spread out, unceremoniously, but they lessened the span between them as they zeroed in closer toward their intended targets. The HEL-bombers were almost in range from their objective as the four-pilot patrol team was about to derail the brigand attack.

"We're almost in range," the leader dispatched as he banked his craft to the left a little. "Don't take your time to shoot, get rid of these bad boys."

When it would seem as though the Killwing pilots were about to fully converge they ceased to maintain some distance apart; their close reach, of their targets, was a free hand to destroy the two brigand ships without prejudice. They were now near the brigands' topside; the leader loomed over his hopefully precise hit, which was slightly below the squad leader. Gripping his control stick he thumb-pressed the firing button, his main twin guns recoiled, as a barrage of laser bolts were unleashed.

The shots were fired too quickly, from Gamma One, which might of had a little too much zeal behind it. But as he approached closer to the first targeted brigand ship Gamma 10, to his left, banked as he swerved into his leader's line of fire. What his leader was unable to accomplish in time Gamma 10 obliged, he made a direct hit, which left only one enemy interceptor remaining.

"Good shot Gamma Ten," the leader praised as he saw Ten bank away from his flight path.

"No problem," Ten replied. "Anytime you need a helping hand just let me know."

"Roger that, I got the last one," the leader jumped ahead with the added thrust.

The last brigand interceptor was within range again of the surviving transport, as the transport was about to enter Khalidan's gravitational pull. But the leader was in place to prevent certain disaster for the commando team. You could almost see a flicker of light from the HEL-bomber's main gun, as it was about to discharge, but the squad leader fired within the same second the brigand attempted. The thermals, from squad leader, struck the brigand's top-central fuselage of which caused a shock wave of scattering debris.

The crew of the shuttle car grew at ease, for the time being, now that they had safe passage to the planet below. As they descended they finally entered the planet's exosphere, but the crew aboard knew that further dangers await them on the planet's surface.

As the leader watched the transport disappear into the outer region of the planet he stated, "Let's return to the main group, the fight ain't over yet."

The battle, for orbital supremacy, was still in full swing and both sides took heavy losses. The Intercede maintained its static posture with its bow; overlooking the planet, which laid ahead and below its massive hull. The carrier was still standing amidst the swarm of angry fighters hoping with confidence that their IF fighters, as part of their fleet, will protect her from the opposing side.

As the Intercede remained motionless two IF-10 destroyers snuck toward it slowly, like a pair of cats on the prowl. The IF-10s seemed to have covertly made it passed the legionnaires, even after the alert was given. The IF ships resembled a capital U; its bowl-like bow had an elongated, arrow-spread fashioned windscreen that was near topside. And its twin tail thrusters protruded out at aft, which engaged the two ships with propulsion.

From a conserved speed the IF-10s came to a casual halt, once they were within attack range from the Intercede. At the bows' undersides existed round shaped release hatches, which were the ships' launching portals. To launch what was the question until that question was answered, when the hatches snapped open and released almost-spherical objects, which shot toward their intended target. Small bended wiry protrusions were showing; so the spheres weren't completely rounded, the objects resembled balls of twisted yarn.

Within vantage point, from the enemy destroyers, one legionnaire was too busy engaging his opposition to take notice right away. Immediately following a counterstrike, he executed, he than noticed the impeding threat several meters from his position.

"Heads up, we got problems," he gave a general warning through dispatch, "arachnobots."

The fighting around him was intense, and after he subdued his latest target, he prepared to maneuver his ship. The spheres were quickly approaching the Intercede as he pulled his ship into slight reverse and than lunged toward them, at a downward angle. He made the first initiative assuming his dispatch alerted a few others to join him.

The pair of IF-10s stood poised as they launched a few more spheres; the ejections caused a shrilling aftereffect sound when they were spat out from the bow. One IF-10 shot out a couple and the other launched just one, for now. Even if the Legion's pilots were able to blast away a few of the spheres one of them would eventually slip through their defenses.

Beta Nine, who gave the heads up, was quickly within striking distance. He banked left, in a swooping action, as his twin guns recoiled barrages in rapid succession. The concentrated barrage of laser fire destroyed the last three, previously launched, sphericals.

The three remaining spheres, which were launched at the outset, were now within contact of the Intercede's hull. When the metallic objects struck the carrier's superstructure they opened up, like a beetle stretching out its outer shell, exposing eight needle-like legs and their spherical outer shells seem to have folded in, like soft tissue.

The IF-10s maneuvered their big and heavy bodies into hard reverse to counterattack Beta Nine's offense. Quickly thereafter Beta Nine was joined by a few of his squadron buddies, before the brigand configurators had the chance to fire.

One of Nine's fellow pilots zoomed in behind one of the IF-10s when the brigand was about ready to engage Beta Nine. The legionnaire's thermal bolts struck the IF-10's back quarter, nearly missing the exhaust port and super-cylinders. The top back cover of the brigand ship seemed to have blown off, from the impacts, followed by exploding fire and energy sparks.

As the two IF fighters, and Beta team, fought each other the arachnobots crawled up the carrier's hull, using prickly robotic legs. Since they were 'matons, each of the three with their own individualistic programming, they moved with unpredictability as to their heading. Their motion was consistent with that of real spiders, their metal make-up didn't seem to clumsy their movements at all.

The IF-10 that was hit was hit seriously; the blasts caused severe damage to the stern thruster engines, forward steering and propulsion was lost. Unable to maneuver much the brigand pilot still had use of his gun and he would use it, if or when a target became easily accessible to him.

One legionnaire ship was within his reach but not directly into the brigand's kill zone, but the IF-10 pilot fired anyway. The kill zone was an imaginary boundary, from a targeting scanner, which anyone within the zone was susceptible to the gun turret. As the legionnaire swerved in too close the IF-10 fired but missed, the thermal laser shot passed the gunship's stern.

Even though the discharge was a near hit it was an incentive, for the legionnaire to keep some distance away from the maimed IF-10, which still had the ability to fight. Even though the drifting IF-10 lacked maneuverability the enemy ship still had enough bite to cause a problem.

The IF-7 pilot dived into an attack mode and barraged the other enemy ship with unrestrained laser fire, striking the bow's topside. One of those thermals breached the windscreen causing the interior to depressurize and implode. The force of the escaping life-support was so violent that it made the structural soundness of the ship collapse in on itself, like squashing a tin can, which was than followed by the explosion.

Evading surrounding ships followed the shockwave so that the pilots could avoid the propelling shrapnel. The vacuum of space quickly snuffed out the fire from the destroyed brigand ship as the fragments, which were the remains of the IF-10, scattered apart.

One IF-10 remained but it seemed ill fated since it was outnumbered and damaged. Most of the brigand HEL-bombers were heavily engaged in their own fight, and trying to survive, thus the IF-10 was alone and it was not designed to outmaneuver Dominion gunships, even if the pilot wanted to. The IF-7s, a small few from beta team, held the advantage and they seized the opportunity with haste.

Tremendous strain agitated the IF-10 pilot and his ship as he attempted to maneuver, using retronic counterthrust, into a striking posture. When he had a desired target in his sights he ceased all motion as he prepared to fire his weapon.

"The arachnobots made contact with the Intercede," the legionnaire pilot apprised his fellow flyboys. "If you can take them out without hitting any of the vital areas of the carrier, do it."

The legionnaire pilot was positioned overhead the remaining IF-10 destroyer, looking down at the bow, and his attention was swayed only for a second to utilize his transceiver, but now he was ready to fire. But the IF-10 fired first with red streaks that flashed out from their apertures. These brigand destroyers had two small openings, above the launching portals, emplaced aligned and close together.

Too late to evade the Killwing pilot let out a scream before him, and his ship, were destroyed. The enemy's weapon fire sent fragments of the Killwing's front-top fuselage toward his cockpit, which shattered through his windscreen and killing him instantly. Fire spewed out from within as sparks flickered from the blast wound, and as his ship drifted. After only seconds the IF-7 eventually exploded long enough for everybody else around to maneuver away from the fireball.

"Damn it, keep alert Beta Twelve," Beta Nine said in distress. Loosing a fallen comrade was a demoralizing experience, for even the most hardened pilot, but grief will come later.

The IF-10 ignited its retronics again to avoid remnants of the Killwing, he destroyed, and to distance himself from an inevitable retaliation. The destroyer's attempt to retreat was futile because the brigand ship lost forward propulsion. When the IF-10's right retronic spun its hull to its portside only its dormant afterburners were eventually visible to the Dominion pilots.

The closest Killwing pilot, outraged by the death of his buddy, fired first at the disabled ship. The thermal's struck the brigand's exhaust port that caused severe damage to the fuel line, which still fed the ship's counterthrust. An explosion quickly resulted as the heat from the thermal lasers ignited its hydrofusion fuel causing the IF-10's instant destruction. The legionnaire, who perpetrated its demise, watched on until airless space stifled the flames out.

"Beta One," Nine transmitted as he piloted his ship toward the Intercede.

"What is it, I'm a little bit busy right now," One shouted his response. The inside of his cockpit was shuddering as he steered randomly, with laser fire all around him. His tone was that of exasperation for he was in the middle of a dogfight, and he had to deal with that for now.

"Beta Twelve," Nine determined, "We're on our own."
"Copy that," the dispatch reply was.
"Do a parameter sweep," Nine outlined his purpose. "If you see anything that has more than two legs, take it out."
"Received and understood," the final responding transmission.

Without a coordinated pattern the two IF-7s, Beta Nine and Twelve, sought out the arachnobot destroyers of which made direct contact with the Intercede. The starcarrier stood still as the crew and staff aboard continued to coordinate battle operations; while at the same time, they clung on the hope that Beta team will dissolve the threat that they were assigned to.

A few meters below the bow's rim an arachnobot moved briskly on its spidery legs until it stopped, to nestle in and to release its own venom. As soon as it was over the bow's edge it achieved a secure footing on the carrier's flattop.

The arachnobot's main weapon was its pulse armament, which was emplaced in the frontal head and had a power cable underneath that fed a link to the weapon's power cells. The pulse weapon's barrel was thin and it had an over covering; a broad shaped triangle with its points bent downward diagonally along the seam lines, which served as the weapon's housing.

When the 'maton utilized it, it sent fragments of the flight deck up and away from the percussion and heat from the blasts. The arachnobot was attempting to breach the flight deck's hull, which it was programmed and designed to do, to cause depressurization and massive damage.

Aboard the carrier and within the hangar bay sirens blared and the assigned crew there quickly begun to evacuate the vicinity, just in case a breach would occur. As they were running to escape possible harm the senior staff officer would perform his leadership role by prompting his crew to hurry, before the firewall had the chance to close completely and seal the bay off from the rest of the ship.

"C'mon guys we have to move, hurry," the staff officer yelled as he stood on the opposite side of the firewall's threshold. As the curtain wall slowly rolled to seal the passage of escape, which was their only way out, the egress gradually narrowed as time pressed on.

The crew moved feverously to make their escape before they were and would remain trapped, the firewall slowed down for no one. The staff officer, as he spurred everyone on and flagged them out, he looked up and saw smoke. Where the arachnobot stood topside, amidst the outer side elements, the robotic crawler made deep penetrations with its laser. The heat of which caused smoke to develop inside the bay, gradually, at the opposing point of contact from the ceiling's surface.

As he watched for a quick second, the smoke as it begun to fume as a breaching approached, the staff officer knew it would be only moments before the arachnobot would break through the only barrier that kept him and his crew alive. He than quickly looked ahead at his crew to spur them on even more, the wall was now passed half way.

As the wall continued to close, like a sliding curtain, he edged along with it but keeping the passage clear for his men to hurry passed him. Flailing his hand to flag his people to exit quickly he was in a state of urgency but he remained calm, as any true leader would, to keep his crew from panicking. As the mechanics, environmental maintenance, and a few pilots made their escape, through the quickly narrowing passage, they were almost climbing over each other. Almost, the staff officer succeeded in keeping the escape process done in a semi-orderly fashion.

As the smoke developed even more the urgency increased. The sirens continued to sound off loudly as the warning flashers, and emergency lights, radiated the inside hangar bay to a dim red.

Finally the firewall was nearly shut, only the staff officer's head and chest was exposed as he stood just right outside the wall's closing. Eventually, still coaching his men to hurry, he led the last crewmember out before the firewall sealed shut.

As the arachnobot continued to chew away at the deck, with its laser mount, it was quickly spotted by Beta Nine. The IF-7 pilot Flew toward it, from overhead and slightly behind, and when the Killwing's nose was upon it he fired and banked right as he did so. Before the arachnobot had the chance to breach the hangar bay it was destroyed, only tiny remnants remained. The IF-7 pilot reacted at first sight of his target, which was only one of three arachnobots eliminated. And as he flew elsewhere, to seek out the other two, the tiny remnants were like drifting stardust.

Near the starboard stern a second arachnobot crawled into view successfully still clinging to the carrier's superstructure. The end points of the arachnobot's eight legs were sharp and needle-like; of which made driven penetrations into the metallic surface it walked on, with piston action reflexes as it utilized its mobility, leaving a trail of pit marks behind.

Being secured to the structure's surface with each step, its appendagers affixed to the under deck, the 'maton crawled a few meters away and up from the super exhaust ports and than it stopped. Its sensors detecting no threat imminent, at least for now, the 'maton unleashed its piercing rapid fire. Its protruding barrel shot out broken streaks of red thermal blasts into the hardened plating of the near starboard side. The arachnobot was blasting away shards of metal to breach the exterior and gain entry.

Within the bridge, of the Intercede, the situation was stressed at best. The personnel who were bustling with activity consisted of weapons, communications, engineering, and sensor detection specialists, The control tower, otherwise know as the island, led the Legion's combatants in the initial ground and dog-fighting battle including the Intercede's on-board crew that disembarked to engage in such as these activities. But the bridge was responsible, singularly, for the conditions aboard the carrier. The bridge crew and officers had to keep order out of chaos by keeping the communication lines open to each of the battle stations, and to the crew who were manning them.

And not only to monitor the operations aboard but also to monitor any threats that might be imposed upon them from outside. Such was the responsibility of the sentry staff, of who manned the sensory devices, which took up a mere part of the elongated concave design of the operations console. The operation specialists had only digital display computers at their service.

"Sir, we have a breaching in progress," an ensign informed his security officer. He sat at his station monitoring the outside sensors until an alarm lit up, at onc of his control panels, alerting him to an intrusion.

"Where?"

"Near the starboard stern," the ensign answered.

"Inform Beta team."

"Yes sir," he leaned toward the transceiver mike after his reply. "Beta team, we have a breaching in progress. At the starboard stern just above the intake's super-cylinders," the ensign dispatched.

"Copy that," Beta Twelve responded as he than swerved his ship toward the designation that was given.

A the engineering sector within a narrow passageway, which was just one of the large group of corridors, danger was near and coming. A labyrinth of these corridors linked and made passage possible from one sector of the carrier to another.

The arachnobot destroyer, which was still clung to the outside of the carrier, was making sufficient progress. People who were near the vicinity at the opposite interior were scrambling to get away, attempting to do so in single file because of their constraints of their surroundings. Sirens and red alert flashers were in full showing, as was the same of the hangar bay, while just a few crewmembers were trying to escape the vulnerable section of the corridor, which was in the process of being penetrated. During their evacuation they made their withdraw trying not to climb over themselves as they did so.

The penetration point was beginning to turn red hot and than white as full breach was about to be made. When the vacuum of space, and the pressurized interior, came into contact calamity occurred. A full breach was made but only the size of a pinprick, which was enough to cause a good part of the corridor's siding to blow out into space.

One crewmember stood just right inside of an adjoining corridor, clutching close to the side and holding on to some power cables, as the pressure hatch was closing. "C'mon guys, their closing the pressure doors."

A few crewmembers, who were still within the danger zone, were clinging on to whatever they could to keep themselves from being sucked out. A couple of those unlucky few clung to the sides, holding on to cable or tubing emplacements while their bodies were suspended horizontally, which was caused by depressurization that pulled at their bodies.

A third victim of circumstance was low to the floor and holding on to the grid work of the grate paneling, which was one of many screen fittings that covered the floor well. His body was suspended and being pulled at, but slightly at an angle since he was low to the floor. The ear pounding sounds of the suction made all other sounds indistinguishable while he remained trapped in the throes of the breach opening.

The arachnobot was in view and free to move inside. The suction of depressurization seemed to have no consequence to the mechanical driven robot that stepped in, tempered and in ominous fashion. Its controlled spring action, needle-like toes, nailed and released itself from the floor with each pressing step for secured mobility.

The arachnobot was half way in until suddenly the pressure became too much for the individual, who clung to the floor. The suction picked his body up, along with the grid plate he was still holding on to, and it drew his body rapidly toward the breach opening. At the same time his body was about to be ejected out into space he found himself gouged in the 'maton's sharpe pointed weapon covering and barrel. The arachnobot quickly swung the nearly impaled victim to its side to allow the currents of depressurization to discard the corpse. The drawing currents violently released the crewmember's mangled body, from the 'maton's pointed snout, and into the depths of space.

Suddenly, and before the arachnobot had the chance to completely enter the corridor, a laser struck toward and demolished the robot into fragments. The laser originated from Beta Twelve as he flew passed the breach point, his ship was but a blur as he flew by the blast opening.

The two occupants, of who clung to the side of the corridor, were still holding on and snaking their way toward the adjoining side of the walkway, as the pressure hatch continued to close centimeter by centimeter. The crewmember, who stood just on the other side of the closing hatch, seemed to be the elected leader for now as he yelled and spurred the two on. The pressure hatch continued its closing momentum, but slow and sustaining, not varying in speed leaving little or no time for any escape.

The occupant, tailing the other behind, lost his grip and was at the mercy of the elements. While shouting out cries of help and attempting to hold on to something he gripped, with his fingers, the sharpe shard of metal at the blast opening to keep himself from being sucked out. He held on for a second, which seemed like an eternity to him, but to know avail, he was gone.

"Don't look back, keep going," the one pressing against the pressure hatch yelled out.

Braced against the closing of the hatch he yelled, muffled by the whooshing sounds of the high pressure. The last remaining survivor still clung to the side and he pulled himself as he held on to the cable tubing, hand over hand, toward the one who continued to coach him providing encouragement. The cable tubing provided insulation protection, to the many power cables in its interior, which were several in array and snaked along the entire wall and surrounding compartments.

He was near the hatch but the pressure hatch was nearly closed, only a quarter of spacing for him to squeeze through. "Quick, take my hand," the other at the adjoining side reached out. The remaining occupant, who was still clinging and pulling himself toward safety, was now close enough to reach out and grab the outstretched hand. When he grabbed the other's hand the other pulled him through the narrow spacing before the pressure hatch completely sealed shut.

And now tranquility replaced chaos as the whirlwind of drawing pressure was isolated behind the sealed hatch. The two survivors, one leaning on the side of his butt and the other in a repose position took a few moments to catch their breath.

Standing at attention, with tensions high, the sentry guards kept a watchful eye at the drive deck. Full facial helmet visors to keep the light, from the symmetry drive's binary energy links, from blinding them, shielded their eyes. With the exception of their dark visors the rest of their garb was white and the only deviance in color were that of their blue insignias, which they wore as patches on their upper sleeves.

At least two sentries were standing guard, across from each other shoulder-to-shoulder, with their backs facing the control booth. A sheet of slanted tinted glass shielded the staff behind it, within the control and monitoring housing, from the blinding light. There were more than just two sentries at their posts, they to were stationed about at the drive deck, and aimed to guard one of the most vital areas of the carrier.

Just outside the drive section tensions remained the same, with that of the rest of the ship. Guards were posted at opposite sides of the entry hatch, standing parallel to the entry's threshold, and standing at attention with their pulse rifles held erect to their sides.

Red flasher bulbs were gyrating and the sounds of the sirens remained the same, bothersome and deafening as that of everywhere else aboard the Intercede. The walkway floor was smooth but gray and mechanistic in appearance, which matched the surroundings. And ventilation pipes, which wormed along manifolds and bulkheads of the vicinity, were mounted paralleled and patterned a centimeter from touching the wall's surface.

Tensions increased abruptly when a big section of the side bulkhead blasted in and than out and away. And emerging from the other side was the third, and hopefully the last arachnobot. The smoke and flames that quickly ensued quickly stifled out, disappearing the same as the blasted fragments from the depressurization, which the 'maton spawned at each turn destroying everything in its path.

The two sentries were forced to let go of their weapons to grab on to whatever they could to keep themselves from being pulled out. One of them attempted to grab on to the ventilation manifold, which was near the entry hatch. He held on for seconds only, with his fingers, struggling to acquire a better hold. But the drawing resistance was to intense for his hold slipped and he immediately attempted to acquire a secondary anchor on the manifold's piping, his body suspended and directed in line with the breach opening. But the shock and surprise was so sudden his attempts were futile and lasted long enough for him to know that he was gone, gone with the depressurization currents, and his fellow guard quickly followed.

Everything that wasn't fused into the bulkheads and ceiling was caught in the whirlwind of the sucking pressure. The two sentries, almost immediately, were picked up off the floor and sucked toward the breach trail; hopefully the breach will be quartered off before they reach airless space. The arachnobot employed its mobility effortlessly though, since it was designed and equipped to do so, being well anchored and prepared to make the final blow.

At the same time the bridge officers and staff continued, despite the chaos aboard and off-ship, tried to maintain some control against the multiple threats that seemed to be mounting up. And now one more threat added to their worries as an alert flashed on the console and the ensign, seated at the security station, took notice.

"Sir, we have an intrusion alert at drive section," the ensign warned.

"What," the senior said and than turned to inform the same news to his captain.

"What," the captain stood up who was seated just a few paces behind. "Comm the crew to evacuate the ship," the captain ordered as he stepped a few until he reached the ensign's rear. The captain now stood directly behind his younger subordinate, looking over the ensign's shoulder, and watching the alert flash near the base of the monitor.

Along the rim of the starcarrier's superstructure was a built-in umbilical ring of which all ejector pods were linked to be released in a free fall. The ring, which was literally a walk through shaft, was specifically to be used at hand for the Intercede's crew in times such as these.

"All hands, sounding general evacuation," was announced over the intercom.

Crew of all ranks and specialists hurried within the shaft, not staling to gaze at the starlit backdrop, which was visual through the pockets of portholes along the way as they ran. The strain of their anxiety quickened their steps as their mind set determined them to hurry to their escape pods to be jettisoned, to safety. No fixtures of any kind were evident in the evacuation shaft; just smooth white walls patched with portholes and than there were the hatches, for them to gain quick entry to their pods.

From outside, the Intercede remained still almost in the heart of the battle that still raged on. The fighting, encircling the carrier and near orbit, didn't seem to be decreasing in its ferocity. At the outer side of the shaft ring suddenly had protrusions of stub-like arms, serving as support booms, that were activated to extend out. At the ends were the escape pods that quickly detached from the arms' clamps. When several pods were released; and after gaining some distance, the pods ignited their back thrusters to flee away from a possible disaster.

Up and over the starcarrier's flight deck, and quickly flying passed the island, Beta Nine made his retreat increasing thruster power to his stern. "Beta Twelve, get away from her," Nine dispatched. "The Intercede is about to blow."

"Copy," Twelve's reply relayed through Nine's transceiver.

At the same time the arachnobot moved toward the entry hatch, to gain entrance to the symmetry drive. As the 'maton approached closer to the hatch a thermal cannon, mounted above the hatch and to the right of it, tracked its barrel down and aimed at the approaching threat. The sub-cannon unleashed a couple of laser bolts striking the arachnobot's side and midsection, but the robotic's armor seemed to have resisted the impacts. The spidery robot countered with a couple of blasts of its own, turning the defensive weapon into dangling junk.

Now that there was no resistance in impede the arachnobot's purpose it closed in on the hatch. The arachnid pointed its weapon at the access and than fired sending fragments in; and before the metal shards and pieces rested on the floor, withdrew out with force, by the drawing out currents of escaping air pressure.

And now that a cleared and unhindered opening was made the mechanical unit was free to crawl inside. Approaching steadily, and with alarming spindly-like quickness, the arachnobot neared the symmetry drive and, not blinded by the light, when the automaton was close to near point blank range it fired.

At this present a lot of the escape pods were still being jettisoned and several fighters, from both sides, were making quick headings as far away from the carrier as possible. Until suddenly, and without warning, a cataclysmic explosion erupted that quickly enveloped the Intercede. The pods that had long been launched achieved enough distance to avoid the shockwave. But the close proximity ships, in the process of their evasiveness, and escape pods that hadn't jettisoned yet weren't that fortunate. The matter-antimatter chain reaction was automatically isolated, know as a blowoff, to avoid the cascading effect of critical mass. But this was of no comfort to the indiscriminate number of ships that succumbed to the shockwave and shooting fragments.

Aboard the Coronation, and at the bridge, the crew felt the shudder from the percussion; as sure as the crew did at all sections of the carrier. The captain braced himself against a nearby rail as he stood, or trying to, close to his seat. Anxiety surely consumed him and while he was still holding on to his balance, enduring the rocky tumble caused by the cataclysm, he gave an order before he would assess his own casualties.

"Prepare to mount a search for any surviving pods," the captain said to the communication's officer. "But wait for my order, just make preparations." And with a quick change of thought he stated, "Give me an instant damage and casualty report of my crew."

"Yes sir."

And than the captain uttered to himself, "We need to minimize resistance and clear this battle field."

The ground battle was whining down and the resilient task force, who survived the planetary approach, had long made touchdown. The brigand raiders were running out of steam, and now with the arrival of reinforcements, victory seemed assured for the Legion and tawaque inhabitants. The commandos' torpedo-looking shuttle was vacant, with the ramp door left open, as the occupants engaged against any resistance.

The tawaque engagement diminished much as well since a good number of them were killed or wounded during the fighting. And those who weren't were attending their wounded or removing their dead to be taken back to the village. The last of the HAVICs was put out of action several moments ago and it was now just lying dormant in the snow while smoldering smoke ascended in the air. And nearby, standing close to a couple of stood-still boadors, Jepheth gave attention to the injuries of one of his brother at arms.

Some parts of the battle still had enough ferocity left for the legionnaires to take heed. Isolated incidents of periodic laser fire crisscrossed between opposing enemies as the participating combatants ducked or weaved to avoid getting shot. There were only a few standing footsoldiers left and they stood in a concentrated and uneven line and they faced-off the commandos without faltering, they were programmed to do nothing less.

Keeping some distance apart, and in a slightly broken column as well, the commando team pushed their way across the battlefield while picking off any resistance they encountered. With their empty shuttle behind them they moved ahead with their weapons poised to kill and their awareness attuned to their enemy's every movement.

The footsoldiers fired in short controlled bursts as fast as their sights could direct their aim. They were programmed to react to the most threat firstly and right now the commandos were their chosen first. The white armor plated cybernetics advanced unstopping and apathetic as they utilized their pulse weapons. Not all of the brigands standing zeroed in on the commando team just a small grouping of them made the offensive action against their opposite. The other off-world raiders took the offense, futilely though, against Joshua's alpha squadron, or part of it.

Lasers from the commandos' side, shot out shooting down two enemy brigands. One footsoldier was struck in the middle chest near the collarbone, and at the same time, the other got struck to the side of the shoulder and chest as well.

Instantly a third party brigand, who stood close enough to his fallen comrades, counterattacked. Reacting to the threat, rather than seek emotional vengeance, its sensors targeted his perpetrators for termination. The retaliatory footsoldier fired a few shots in responsive action.

One of those lasers, in the succession of fire, struck down the culprit legionnaire who made the initial attack, but maimed him only. The legionnaire who was hit was now lying nearly flat in the snow-covered ground as he clutched his wounded shoulder. He than sat up a little bit to look up at his offender as his offender aimed to finish the job.

But before the footsoldier had the chance to fire a laser bolt shot across, passing the injured commando, and penetrated the footsoldier's chest plate before he had the chance to fire his weapon again. Although, immediately following the impact, the end discovery revealed that it wasn't a laser bolt at all but an arrow ejected from a pulse bow. The arrow was heated by the bow, and when accelerated through the air, the arrow's energized heat intensified. The end advantage was for the arrow to penetrate hard objects, such as the footsoldier's armor, which was just demonstrated.

In the commando offensive line there were two archers that made use of their bows as a few more footsoldiers replaced the three that were put down. A few, meaning three from the broken column of the brigand line, directed their visoroptics toward the commando assault force and they stepped in a second following the ones they lost.

As the legionnaires, who wielded their pulse rifles, continued to discharge short controlled bursts of attack the two archers prepped into their stances to fire their weapons. They controllably retrieved the arrows from their back quivers and, both of them acting together and slightly in sync, placed their arrows on the arrow rests. They than drew their bows up as they pulled down on the bowstrings, using the best means of counter-resistance to pull down against the strings' resistance. As they did so, retracting the arrows, they slowly lowered the points to their firing aim.

A series of micron components allowed for the practicality of the pulse bow. A small pulse generator, which was located at the lower end of the bow frame, generated thermal energy that was fed up through a fiber wire, which was imbedded in the trigger bar. And next to the pulse generator was a metastabilizer, which gave additional power so that the heated arrow was energized enough to reach its target with deadly consequence.

When the arrows were completely retracted to the strings' maximum resistance, and when the nocks of the arrows pressed against the trigger bars, a reaction occurred. At the back ends of the retracted arrows blinding arcs of amplified light energized the arrows to heat.

They than released and the microsecond of acceleration caused light to envelope the arrow shafts, which made them look like a couple of laser bolts streaking through the air. Two of the three-footsoldier replacements met their end when the arrows pierced half way through their armor and electrical innates, nearly passing through their bodies entirely.

As the archers pressed forward a few steps and stopped to reload the other legionnaires continued their push against the brigand line. The Legion's riflemen covered the archers with rapid and additional firepower; and now much of the enemy's attention was shifted to them, while the archers reloaded. The entire commando assembly had the end desire; only, to push the brigands back to submission and surrender.

And as the ground campaign continued the air cover proceeded with the same amount of purpose and determination. The two IF-7 Killwings, which the marshal left behind for aerial support, were in a state of heightened reaction. The Legion pilots maneuvered their gunships with nimbleness and tactical prowess. Even though the odds were much in their favor the few brigand footsoldiers, which were left, still had enough strength and firepower to cause harm to the commando team.

A row of four or five footsoldiers looked up to face the speedily approaching Killwings, moving in to fly over them. They pointed the end sights of their pulse weapons up at the advancing gunships; but before the cybernetics had the chance to fire they were stopped in their tracks, by the recoiling armament of one of those fighters. A spray of laser fire left a trail of overturned dirt, which the footsoldiers were in the path of. After the Killwing's dive attack the gunship swooped back up in search of more opposition.

"Darvus, you and the others regroup with the two we left behind," the marshal said throwing a little sigh of relief. Their situation seemed to be less sporadic and dangerous and it would seem alpha squadron became the victors in their air battle. "I'll pursue the three who are bugging out," he said as he went off after them.

Joshua piloted his ship with steady ease, because at this moment, no thermal discharge threatened him. Right now no enemy HEL-bombers were opposing him but retreating, or maybe to redeploy to attack him again, Josh couldn't take that chance. Jackie abandoned her rear turret once the marshal's message went out through dispatch; the cruiser wasn't swarmed with fighters, which made a rear defense unnecessary for the moment. She, being slightly weary, approached and sat in the rear seat slightly behind to the marshal's right.

After a second of catching her breath, "What's up," she asked as she stood up and braced herself against the marshal's backrest of his chair.

"We only have three left who seemed to be throwing in the towel," the marshal gathered and hoping that was the case. "I dismissed my boys, I think we can handle it from here."

From moderate push the marshal increased speed to gain close distance on the fleeing enemy crafts, which were dead ahead and in clear enough view through the Cauldron's main windscreen. Structural shuddering and an increase in g-force pressure followed the added acceleration. Jackie coped with the effects, for the strains of the ship were still with tolerable levels, so she remained on her feet for now but holding on to the marshal's backrest to keep herself steady against the bumps.

"Better strap yourself in, this could get ugly," the marshal advised as he progressively closed in on his three targets.

As she sat herself behind the marshal, to do as she was told, the marshal added even more expenditure to the stern thrusts. The Cauldron quickened and the targets were becoming more visible as he closed in on them and so was the mountainous impasse in the forefront, which the brigand ships, seemed to be heading toward.

"I know Jag," the marshal responding to the copilot's mindlink. "I'm trying to intercept them before they reach the ridgeline, we can search for them for hours and never find them."

Cruising in the air overhead a valley they were near and guided by a rock wall toward a separate but linking mountain chain, but they weren't close enough to the wall to even brush the snow off the landings. The mountain ranges were many and scattered and separated only by ravines and valleys, like the one they're in right now but not for long.

Josh sat at his command console, as well as his copilot did, as they both gazed out their windscreen while gaining closeness quickly to their adversary. But before their Cauldron was close enough to achieve a direct assault the brigands veered around the bend and they disappeared into a mountainous corridor. Two of the brigand gunships banked to the right and one spilt off to the left, the Cauldron followed the two.

The chase continued midway below the jagged icecaps and now

cruising between two facing rock walls of a deep mountainous gorge. While supersonic speeds were implemented the thrusts of their exhausts, and the currents of their velocity, whisked the snow off the lower rock landing. The gorge where the Cauldron's crew unsuspectingly ended up in was truly a no-man's land, the bottom of the floor bed was obstructed and congested with boulders in snow waist-deep.

The two evading ships were at a distant but they were still within the marshal's view. He increased added fuel to his stern to gain further closeness as he navigated straight and steady, thus it was smooth sailing from projected rock or other hindrances.

Not close enough to lock on their heat exhaust the marshal fired anyway as the gorge quickly narrowed. Red bolts shot out from the marshal's cannons as all three ships banked vertically to avoid collision, not decreasing in speed as the gorge narrowed to a tight pass. As they shot through the tapered passing they leveled off the marshal fired another short succession of blasts missing the enemy entirely, but instead, he blasted down a large shard fragment of rock. The marshal tailing the two speeding ships were unyielding; as the chunk fragment crashed to the ground, which caused a reverberating echo and a kick up of snow followed.

As the Cauldron closed in on the brigands, approaching target range, the two HEL-bombers increased their altitude for the purpose of evasion. Hollands promptly followed suit as he ascended as well, along sight the enemy's stern. Exiting and leaving the gorge at their backs all three ships swerved up, and now, navigating above the land-laden mountain peaks and ridges. The visual beauty of the landscape beneath them was vividly clear on that clear day.

Once free from the gorge's claustrophobic confines the pursuit continued in uninhibited skies, what was above was nothing but blue with mere scant patches of clouds. If it were not for the battle some would call it a beautiful day.

Abruptly the two brigands separated; one turned off into the distant, out of sight, and the other maneuvered in the marshal's opposing direction as if it were about to attack the Cauldron. The HEL-bomber that was in the marshal's front banked vertically to an inverted position, as the ship made its turn-around. The brigand pilot increased his afterburner thrust as he engaged, but this time with added speed and head-on against the starcruiser. The marshal fired in defense but because of the bomber's compact body, and quick maneuverability, Hollands was unable to make any sort of hit. The HEL-bomber counter-fired but only to sway any further attacks as the brigand pilot veered away from the cruiser and heading toward the marshal's right flank.

Reacting to the attack the marshal veered right also to follow by tilting the wings as he steered toward the bomber's direction, the maneuver would seem as though it would be hard to execute because of the cruiser's heavy body but the marshal manned his controls as though it was as light as a feather. To follow the marshal decreased altitude, as the HEL-bomber did, as he steered starboard bound and they both accelerated as they lowered toward another range of mountains.

They were now flying across the central median of another mountain chain as both ships continued their high-speed chase. Not slowing down any and veering starboard they neared the base of the chain and their momentum, and the push of their exhaust, brushed away any loose snow off the ridges as they shot passed a single standing monolith.

"He's trying to get himself lost in these mountains," Josh said as he followed the HEL-bomber's trail. "Let's see if we can bring this chase to a close," as he approached even closer on his target in view.

Josh could hear Jackie wail as she stayed buckled in her seat behind the marshal but was still being jostled around, by Joshua's dog fighting maneuvering. When will this come to an end," she said as she gasped.

The ships sped through the air, the cruiser tailing the fighter, passing by the various ripples and ridges of the mountainside. They were now approaching, with great impulse, another natural formation of what one might expect to see in such a surrounding. The obstacle they were approaching were two pillars of rock, deeply rooted in the ground, and they stood erected and closely adjacent.

Since, between the two standings, was a tight fit the HEL-bomber banked vertical as it begun to breeze through between them. But before the fighter had the chance to pass through a laser bolt struck out and impacted the topmost part of the right pillar, the one nearer to the mountain's rock face. The force of the blow caused falling slates of rock to crash down on the unsuspecting brigand ship; hence it was only midway from passing the twin monoliths. The crashing down of the avalanche of rock had enough impact force to cause the bomber to dive down into a flaming explosion, as the Cauldron shot passed the fallen debris without a scratch.

Looking out the bridge's overview windscreen for the two remaining HEL-bombers, both seemed to be in hiding right now, the marshal relaxed his grip on the steering stick while he commenced to probe his parameter. Jagaba sat at his side, and attentive as well, to aid in the marshal's efforts. When their eyes weren't on the ship's scouting sensors they would look out for visual assessment, but all they saw was barren terrain ahead of them.

"Let's gain some altitude Jag," the marshal directed, "We don't want them to have the advantage of higher ground." The marshal focused again on his navigation controls and reinitiated vectoring thrusts, "Besides we can probe better if we're higher up."

And now for the moment, since the ship's activity was at the least, Jackie relaxed a bit as she leaned back in her chair and hung her arms to the sides and sighed. Not much was spoken from her; words to Joshua's ears would have been pointless anyway.

The marshal angled his vectoring thrusters slightly up and ignited them to marginally drop the tail end down. He than engaged his main afterburners to ascend into a launch. The Cauldron climbed up at a near vertical rise with the ground extending away as he gained a higher advantage point. Even though vectoring and thrust was a series of small complex operations, know as micronics, the cruiser utilized its steering with natural control.

When the marshal, from his own intuitiveness, had reached his desired elevation he leveled off to reassume his forward search. He hovered still momentarily though for just enough time to decide his next plotted course, after he would read what his ship's sensors had to say.

"The photoscopes are no good, if he's hiding in some cave," the marshal assessing with a momentary look at his instrumentation. "The acoustics aren't picking up any exhaust vibrations." Joshua than turned away from the sensor relays to look out the windscreen and than he proposed a possibility, "Let's check out those channels over there, thirty degrees starboard."

The Cauldron was now descending again but propelling thirty degrees right toward a network of interconnecting valleys. The Cauldron shot down, like a ballistic, heading toward a labyrinth of connecting lowlands as his ship's afterburners arced intensely to give the desired acceleration. The area that he was heading toward, Joshua thought, would be an ideal place for an enemy to hide.

The Cauldron descended into a tight stretch of passage, an area for which Joshua thought would be a good starting point for a search. Once the cruiser was in and between the gorge's rock walls it lingered motionless for a while, while Josh glanced at his sensors to read any detections if any. While the marshal checked his instruments he maintained his ship's idle hovering position.

"Still nothing," looking at the video feed as the sensor's carrier waves transmitted back. He than looked out his windscreen again, "Let's see where this gorge takes us."

The combat cruiser was now accelerating speedily across the narrow strip of land. The sinuous passing of the rock walls' ridges, as his ship elapsed the various breaks and ripples of the opposing walls' surfaces, were an animate projection as the Cauldron's speed played a part in the impression. The rock walls weren't entirely planes of slated ice though, on occasion, sloping landings protruded out he would pass by.

The Cauldron had now reached the end of the gorge and exited into open land as it shot out from the confined space it traveled through. The open land was not exactly flatland but a span of hilly terrain and with a scattering of snow covered rocks. The blocks of stone and boulders were once part of the mountain's structure and left behind by the last continental collision milliniams ago.

Joshua piloted his ship at low altitude while his reptilian counterpart kept his eyes on the sensors, probing the reaches for possible threats. The triangulated shape of the Cauldron sliced through the air and crosscurrents of wind as it was heading toward another range of mountains and channel networks. The speed, in addition to the ship's aft push, created an upsurge of loose snow leaving a trail behind visible. The terrain of which they flew over was rough, bricks of layered stones and big boulders accompanied by smaller rocks.

"I think we should just let these two go, we're heading too far away from the main group," the marshal pondered showing some concern.

"Sounds good to me," Jackie couldn't argue and was pleased to hear it. She didn't even lean forward when she made her acknowledgement, she was too battle weary and was probably thinking the same thing.

Jagaba turned to his fellow pilot, looking just as natural as he usually would, but he was in fact exchanging converse. Jag took his thoughts off the ship's sensors long enough to reply with a mindlink.

"I know, I don't want them thrown back into circulation either, but the battle is nearly won," Josh held his tongue long enough to formulate a decision. "Ok, we'll probe one more channel up ahead and than we'll turn back," the marshal reasoned and than ordered, ".300 degrees to port."

The Cauldron had been flying over the same type of rugged terrain it had been, since it exited the last of the many channels through the mountains. But this time the starcruiser changed its route heading toward a specific end point; only to return back if nothing was found, over the same ground they were now crossing. The hand-glider shaped ship tilted slightly to veer left; the protuberance design of the top fuselage, and broad windscreen, was visible as the ship made its heading adjustment. The cruiser now leveled off once the new direction was made and they cruised at the maximum most speed, to cover the distance they need to. Some might consider this open terrain to be a meadow, but because of a lack in foliage and an abundance of ice and snow in this wintry world, it was hardly that.

From nothing but open and airy space of land to a sense of closing in and as the mountain, which they were approaching, got taller the land narrowed. They were about to enter another artery of the mountains' channel system but gradually since the entrance, two facing cliff sides, curved in and the spacing between them was broad and lengthy, like an anti-chamber to the main corridor. The two mountain structures had smooth rock face cliffs as their base line, which were almost geometrically even; as though water that once was, was the architect.

The Cauldron shot between and through the opposing cliffs, which were several meters apart. Once the starcruiser was through Josh decreased his speed to begin probing the various potential hiding places, which an enemy might use for safe haven or an ambush. The anti-chamber they were now in was wide and several meters in length before they would reach the main artery, between the two elevations. The starcruiser slowed to a stop and it was now just hovering in a fixed position, and eyeballing the lone ship, were a few scattered pockets of caves hollowing the cliff sides.

"We'll stop here for a sec, begin your probe, start with those caves," the marshal stated methodically reaching his immediate intention.

Jagaba complied by casually, and carefully, tapping his keypad of his sensors' transceiver controls. With his scaly webbed hand he vectored the wave impulses, for both sound and visual, toward the aforementioned directions. The only cumbersome facets of his anatomical make-up were his claws, which could be bothersome for such a dexterity of jobs.

The Cauldron maintained its static position while its relay sensors continued to probe the surrounding caves and landings; and not until now, no movement was astir, not even a breath of wind. Cradled inside a nearby impact crater arose one of the two surviving HEL-bomber ships, which movement broke the stillness. Hovering up from the depth startling near as the cruiser stayed still, for the moment, like a sitting duck.

At that instant Jagaba jerked his head to the alert beacon the moment the Cauldron's sensors noticed the brigand's presence. The marshal didn't need to wait to sense the worries of his copilot; the beeping sound of the intrusion alert was enough.

The HEL-bomber pilot spun his ship ninety degrees to port

so that the beak of its bow was pointing toward, and aiming its guns at, the starcruiser. The pilot used his right thruster only, initiating single pulses of thermal exhaust, to pivot his ship to his now aiming position.

Quick thinking enabled Josh to kick on his ship's underbelly repellors for vertical lift, to evade an inevitable cannon fire. That quick second as the repellors initiated, churning the snow into a drizzling mist, the Cauldron sharply lifted as the brigand fired. The laser blast shot under and passed the cruiser missing the under fuselage by a fraction and impacting, instead, the rock wall at the other side.

The brigand didn't wait for the marshal to track the ship's turret guns to his position; he commenced to push off. Powering up his afterburners, and underbelly turbine propulsions, he lifted the nose of his HEL-bomber to a launching position as he rose slightly from the ground. The brigand pilot than shot up at an angle to evade, what would more likely be, a continuing chase.

The Cauldron rose up to as the brigand ship gained a distance a few meters away. The bomber was higher than the cruiser still and nearing a rock wall; which tapered with it adjacent counterpart wall at the opposing side, which was the lateral part of the gorge narrowing. But before the HEL-bomber had the chance to fly over the rock wall a thermal blast, from the Cauldron's side armament impacted the evasive ship. Not destroyed as yet the blast damaged the HEL-bomber's navigation's input controls, severing the command cable feeds, and as a consequence the brigand was unable to gain a high enough altitude to clear the rock wall's rim. His ship was decimated when the brigand, unable to do anything, slammed into the wall's side, as the Cauldron was now higher and closer to where his target fell.

Before the starcruiser had the chance to leave the area, Josh keeping his bird still for a moment as his thoughts were drawn in on the exploding ship, a sudden and unpleasant surprise snuck behind him. The last HEL-bomber ship was revealed and took the marshal's .180 position, which was at the rear, and fired. The laser struck the top-central fuselage but caused no sever external damage; internal breakage had yet to be determined, as the brigand ship swerved up and away to avoid the cruiser's counterattack.

Aboard the bridge the three-seated occupants were jarred from the hit but nothing else, shaken nerves was all that they suffered from. "Systems check out?" the marshal inquired a damage report. And than the marshal sensed the reptilian's reply, "Good, the repulsion shields are still holding."

The last of the three enemy HEL-bombers flew over the funneling rock walls, which were ahead, and higher as the Cauldron quickly followed. The brigand swerved up, after his attempted attack, and than gained altitude by rising skyward at a sharp angle of ascent. The cruiser also asserted a 22.5-degree line of flight, shadowing the HEL-bomber.

Joshua saw his enemy clearly through the windscreen, looking up at the bomber's stern. The brigand was still attempting to get away from the marshal's grasp by continuing rapid thrust at an angle, near vertical, lift. Josh was affixed to the enemy's rear flank and continued to climb as his adversary did.

"Looks like he's attempting to break orbit," the marshal stated while he maintained pressure on the stern thrusts. He also kept a tight grip on the steering arm, keeping the nose up at the same angle as his opponent.

They continued to climb, one chasing the other, and breathable air in the atmosphere dissipated the higher they gained. Through the broad windscreen Joshua could still see the tail end of the brigand ship but they still maintained the same distance apart, even though Josh strained his ship to the most to outrun her. Through their windscreens, the Cauldron's crew and the brigand both saw the blue atmosphere slowly fade into darkness as they exited the exosphere, the final atmospheric layer of the planet.

Now that they were in open space they leveled off but the chase still continued, not diminishing in speed any. They were well away from the main accumulation of warships; some still in a fight but minor scuffles only, the conflict was whining down to a dead closure.

"Let's see if we can end this right now, launch ampliphone," the marshal instructed his copilot. Jagaba casually looked down at his controls and complied as Jackie stood up from her rear vantage point and approached the marshal to stand behind him, looking over his shoulder, and leaning in to look out at the evading ship.

"You're a determined little bugger aren't you," she griped as she leaned in even closer. "You can see the battle from here, it's over for them."

"It could be Kreed aboard," Josh replied but with doubt to the contrary, "Besides, they don't have any transports out here, I don't think. Let's see where he's going." The brigand sat at his cockpit; his brown padded covering of his arm, as part of his uniform, was visible through the canopy as he kept his hands on his controls and seemingly didn't care about his pursuers.

"You think he'll give it up?"

And than abruptly the HEL-bomber kicked further ahead after the brigand increased added power to his stern, which answered Jackie's question. All three at the bridge saw the brigand ship through the main viewer getting smaller the further it drew away from them; too late for Jagaba to eject the marshal's ampliphone.

'I would say no," the marshal wearingly replied.

The Cauldron's twin side cannons recoiled some fire but the enemy ship was too far away for the laser blasts to make any significant slight of change in the bomber's withdraw. Right away the marshal increased stern thrust, to near sub-light speed, to match that of his escaping potential prisoner.

What was visible, of the brigand ship, became invisible as the HEL-bomber entered the Angelica nebula. Joshua maintained his speed until he would reach the point of entry, because speed wouldn't be advisable when blinded by gaseous clouds. All three crewmembers continued to stare out the overhead windscreen as they were about to enter the nebula themselves, following the same path as their brigand friend.

"Great, not this again," Jackie uttered a protest to herself.

Only a minute elapsed when the starcruiser entered the nebula. Enveloped by white clouds nothing was visible to them, least of all the brigand ship, but the three continued to look out their windscreen for pockets of clearing in the ionized fog. When the Cauldron entered the Angelica Josh slowed his momentum and now, with its wide wingspread, the triangulated ship looked like it was merely gliding on a gaseous drift.

"I think we should head back, I don't want to get lost in this mess," the marshal reasoned and received no protests from his two shipmates.

As the cruiser turned to look for a way back the Cauldron was faintly visible, distorted by thick obscurity and only distinguishable where the clouds were less dense. The ship resembled a ghostly apparition as it pushed frontward, on moderate power, as it searched for a clearing to transmit and receive the fleet's location. The nebula was widespread and sending out transmissions would be useless, because of the ionizing effect of the gas, which surrounded them. One could easily get lost in such a mass and the marshal, who piloted the controls, would have had no idea how far off he might have strayed.

"There's a pocket of clearing over there, I see stars," the marshal pointed slightly ahead and to the left and making adjustments to that direction. And after he turned and headed toward that opening he made additional thrust to his stern, to shorten the distance for his exit.

The cruiser had eventually reached the clearing, and at the outer edges of the opening, ribbons of the white gas drifted outward as though it was showing the way out, which certainly seemed to be a welcome sight. But even the outer remnants drifted still as part of the nebulosity's formation. The opening was like a window to the stars, and the closer the Cauldron came to it, the less concentrated the ionized gas became.

And now, being completely withdrawn from the cloudy envelopment, they stunningly made a discovery that surprised them to the core. They were hoping, a few minutes before, to find their fleet and countrymen but instead of that they found something else to their terror.

Jackie was the first one to notice it, pointing portside, she stunned the marshal with a nudge to prevail upon him to look in that direction. "Oh my God, look over there," she pointed.

"Oh my, we're in trouble," the marshal said stunned after he saw what it was Jackie was pointing to. And they both sensed mixed feelings of fear and awe in the copilot as Jagaba also turned to look. "A concenter."

What they saw was a spectacle that would even rival the Regalia. What loomed was a huge and metallic gray sphere, about the size of a small moon, with soaring antenna tower arrays mounted into the top central crown. And at the bottom central point a single starpole antenna extended down, with a couple of navigation beacons near the bottom's end. Many HEL-bomber ships were present outside the base in column boarding formations, seemingly preparing to board and use the concenter as their means of escape.

"Should we warn mission control?"

"To do what, they don't have the manpower left to plan an assault on a mobile attack base," the marshal replied but all three never took their eyes off the behemoth.

The strands of the multiple count of HEL-bomber ships were in discipline columns, and well spaced apart, as they made their entry through the docking bay doors. Despite the criticalness for their leaving they maintained a safe speed as they boarded. The docking entrances, which were pentagon in shape, were many that pocketed almost the entire structure of the sphere, like honeycombs, and they were right above the launching tubes.

The marshal finally snapped out of his awe-struck state and determined, "That's how they were able to attack my escort squadron without alerting the defense grid, that thing can navigate on its own without the need of centralnet's mainframe." Josh looked away from the base only for a second to give Jackie the last piece of what puzzled him.

Finally the last ship docked aboard the concenter, and now, no activity was present around the outside of the station. Suddenly pulsating light illumined from the matrix crystals, which were affixed inside their orifices atop and below the sphere. Eventually the chain reaction of matter-antimatter light increased and engulfed the entire shape of the concenter, and after a shotgun sound that sounded more like a volcano blowing its top, the light seemed to implode in and the base was gone. Gone but not destroyed, the mobile attack base was now traveling through an open door between the stars.

"I thought the mobile attack bases were dismantled after the Colonial Wars," Jackie drawing on the historical records that were made public.

"Well I guess they missed one."

"What's going to happen now?"

Josh, still looking but looking at empty space where the concenter used to be, answered her, "Things just got complicated."

THE REMAINING STARCARRIER, THE Coronation, poised still even after the fighting had just been over and now their job was simply casualty and damage assessment, from the opposing side also. The flattop seemed deserted, most of the starfighter force haven't extracted from the battle zone yet. The super fortress maintained its static position near Kwidon's orbit amongst scattered mangled messes of lifeless spacecrafts and floating debris, which was just a mere acceptance of war's aftermath.

The first that seemed to be making a landing approach was the Cauldron when Josh maneuvered to a proper alignment to the landing strip. Josh made the necessary adjustments in altitude and direction as he teetered the ship's wings, in order to stay within the borders of the narrow length of strip. The span of the starcruiser seemed to effortlessly sail toward its final destination as it approached speedily.

The marshal saw, through his windscreen, the length of the flight deck, the angle of which was designated for landings. As the guidance markers, landing lights to serve as a visual guide, got closer and closer the further he advanced he sent out a transmission, "Control tower, I'm on approach, you better send someone topside to direct this bird."

"Copy that, you have a signalman on standby," the receiver sent the reply through Josh's transceiver speaker.

It was several meters from the bow's edge and swiftly, as it lowered, was only a few meters from touching down. At a moderate angle of descent the Cauldron sharply passed the bow, and as it lowered, flew along the landing strip.

Still a few meters from touching the hard dock, and several from passing the amidships, Josh lowered his landing gear. Like a flat stone skimming across a river the Cauldron made a smooth accelerated landing, retronics spewing out exhaust to slow her down. The marshal sped passed the control tower and was close to ready to being directed by the signal operator and stationing assistants, of whom were also on standby.

Near the island tower a hollow block of bulkhead concealed a propulsionlift, and from within, the signalman exited. Leaving the safety of his ship the operator stepped out and he walked toward the Cauldron hampered by zero gravity and his magnetic boots that resisted the absence of such forces.

Now at a stand still the Cauldron was now waiting for signal directions from the operator, who was close to taking position. Moving slowly to the point from where he could face the nose of the starcruiser, so that Josh could clearly see the signalman's flares, for which its gestures and movements could be rightfully interpreted. As the S.O took point the Cauldron was static but its engines were running and ready for the ship to be guided toward its designated station. Eventually the signal operator was where he had to be, with his guidance flares in hand, who stood a few meters away and whose head was lower than the Cauldron's windscreen as he looked up at the marshal.

Josh increased engine thrust only a little, enough to follow the S.O's lead. The marshal followed the same signal codes as the other pilots did, before and during the battle, and using the stern thrusts he vectored as he steered.

The marshal pushed forward as the S.O took some steps back, leading the Cauldron to follow. Than the signal operator motioned Josh to stop, which he did, and quickly thereafter the S.O prompted the Cauldron to pull in starboard. With smooth directional control Josh backed into his given station to dismount.

Now that the starcruiser was still Joshua severed off power to the engines and its afterburners were no longer burning. Joshua also checked to see if the remaining systems were turned off except for the ship's internal heaters, to keep the Cauldron warm until launched again.

While the marshal, aboard, was making final system checks a couple of the landing crew approached the motionless ship. Approaching steadfast they neared the bow section's underdeck. They wore the usual environmental protection gear; their bulky helmets with affixed utility lights showing off their bright beams, made them look more robotic than human.

Once they were under the Cauldron's hull the two stationing attendants crouched down, one across from the other, to unclamp a ring or some sort that was flush against the hard dock. Once the ring was unfastened they lifted it toward the cruiser's underhatch.

The ring was simply the end rim of an elastic foam shaft, which could be stretched until the ring reached the contact point of that of the ship. The access shaft was called the portway and it was a means for the fighter pilot to dismount his craft, through the underhatch and through the extended foam shaft, to gain entry into the carrier's stronghold.

When the portway was fully extended, so that its end ring was fully aligned and against the circular catch around the bow's underhatch, they begun to secure it. One crewman held the end up while the other turned over, which was a lever through a buckle, to tightly close the thumb clamp, one of a few more. As soon as the loop's teeth of the clamps were tightly pressed into the inner groove of the circular catch, and the portway was secure, the two crewmen backed away and they headed back, from where they came from, to board the carrier themselves.

Within the portway the bow's underdeck single-entry hatch snapped open and the marshal revealed himself. Josh had discarded his wintry garb exposing his gray environmental suit, which he wore underneath, commonly worn by starfighters as fatigues. Josh pushed away from the hatch and he dropped slowly down, evidently caused by being in zero gravity, toward the carrier's entry hatch at the bottom.

The decompression bay had a shop-looking interior accompanied by boisterous and mechanized sounds of noise, which matched what one would expect in such a surrounding. A line-up of environmental suits and helmets were hung in their retainer holds for proper storage. The floor was solid with gray coating and was at room temperature to the touch. The trims of the surrounding baseboard, personnel lockers, and a few other objects inside the bay had sort of a murky red in color but the bright plasma lamps above counteracted the dreary pigmented shades.

A convex long narrow door, which was black, smooth and shiny, reflected the scenery that was around inside the bay. Behind the convex door, which was one of several, were block chambers for decompression.

One of those curvature doors revolved open, the inside standing platform and the revolving door was that of a one-piece utility, molded and fused. As the door revolved .180 degrees so did the occupant who stood on the door's base. The occupant was Josh who now stepped off and away from the decompression hatch.

The decompression bay was mostly for the flight deck crew, those who coordinate launching and landing, fire and damage control or maintenance management conducting close proximity space walks. The decom's chamber's pressure equalizers kept the marshal's biochemistry balanced; with the change in barometric pressure aboard the carrier, because its composition was slightly heavier than that of his cruise. Although the marshal didn't have to go through it, he could have lowered himself along with his ship to the hangar bay by superlift, but he might have to push off again at a moment's notice. He was a well seasoned pilot so he was used to slight change in pressure, as most of the Legion pilots were, he was well able to launch out again should the need arise.

While the marshal searched for the nearest propulsionlift two of the extravehicular crew sat on a bench disrobing their environmental gear, their boots and lower dress. They were sweaty and tired but they still seemed to maintain a sense of humor; one of them looked down and smiled after his friend, who sat next to him, cracked a joke. But they were both anxious, as sure as those around them, to retreat back to their quarters for a little rest.

After several minutes had passed, since the marshal had boarded the Coronation, he eventually exited the lift once he reached the bridge. He saw two superior officers, above him in rank, standing on the upper balcony and one of them was Murius. Joshua walked over toward them passing by the lower stations, called the pits, as he neared the short and wide staircase that lead to those he had to answer to.

Once he made it to the top of the stairs he quickly stood between the two commanding officers as they turned to look at the marshal. "Commander, captain," the marshal respectfully gave his greetings.

"Marshal, welcome aboard," the captain greeted back.

"Marshal, excellent performance. I know this was a dangerous mission for you," the General Commander gave his marshal his gratitude.

"Thank-you Commander, but I think I'll wait for the final report before I relish a victory," Josh held back the Commander's tribute.

"Your feelings are understandable, for all we know Kreed could have escaped aboard the concenter of yours," Murius said being quite bothersome if the finding holds true.

"It be nice if his body is scattered among the remains of that refinery we blew."

"We'll soon know, I have an investigative team with DNA print finding equipment below rummaging through the remnants right now," Murius said hoping.

The marshal stood with his arms hung down at his sides but he still stood a slight stand at attention as he conversed with his superiors. Even though he was drained of every ounce of energy he may have had left he still wanted to show an attentive and concerning demeanor.

"Where's the rest of your crew?" Murius wondered.

"Well, my robot is at Maintenance getting powered and cleaned. The cybernetic is at Armature Machining downloading any of his received databit files that might be pertinent from the mission," Josh paused for a breath and continued, "and Jagaba is probably somewhere getting a snack, where's Jackie?" Josh turned to his captain to ask.

"She went down in a shuttle, shortly after you left decom, to help search and rescue teams recover pod survivors," with an authoritative tone the captain was referring to those who escaped the Intercede's destruction.

Than Josh turned to his Commander and submitted, "I wish to join her."

"By the way," the captain broke in before Murius had the chance to reply. The marshal jerked his head to the captain, "Your reassignment orders came in, congratulations, your now a permanent resident here aboard the Coronation."

Josh looked back at the Commander, "Sir."

"Its all been arranged and approved my me," Murius calming the marshal's feelings on the matter. "We received word that

Jahdiir station was attacked during the beginning commencement of this battle."

Which didn't do much to calm the marshal's feelings, "Sir?"

"It gets worse, most of the prisoners were let out of their cryotubes and escaped," the Commander sensing the strain and seriousness he put on Josh with the news. "You've been reassign here as scout to track them down."

"Yes sir," Josh said sharply but with a slight pause. The marshal knew; with their nanocell replacements, the prisoners' genetics being altered, their strength would be formidable and his task daunting.

"Welcome aboard," the marshal looked at the captain when he gave his formal greeting.

He than looked back at his Commander, "Your going down, but to help the investigators, she can take care of herself," Josh listened while Murius continued, "Just find me a body, I need to know if Kreed is dead or is still a fugitive."

"Yes sir," the marshal dutifully replied.

"Prepare a preliminary report before the next shuttle disembarks," Murius gave his final instruction.

"Aye sir," Josh snapped his reply and walked away to carry out his orders.

The wreckage from the blast of the processing station was no longer smoldering and only burnt fragments remained. Some pieces of the twisted and shard remains were too big and cumbersome to move and other pieces were pebbled and scattered. Only the base of the foundation was standing, or at least most of it anyway, a foundation that once supported an eye-popping structure that had once advanced above the snow.

Scavenger teams and investigators, surrounded by palisade high cliffs, scoured through the chaos that's been at their feet. They all had on their winter fatigues, which made them look about the same despite their rank and specialty insignia patches. A few of the men there were the scanning crew, of whom operated the bigger pieces of equipment that were present, probing and laser scanning DNA strands. The other searchers; some were volunteers giving assistance, combed through the rubble to find, distinguish or identify body parts.

Most of the enemy casualties though were footsoldier cybernetics, and as a result pertaining to them, they would be harder to identify if their serial numbers and bar codes were indistinguishable. The regenalts, those who were charred and scattered from the blast, would need to be taken for autopsy for careful examination to determine their cerebrospinal donors, and consequently, the manufacturer.

Closer to the foundation remained two crewmen; one who had his hands on his hips and the other his arms folded, continued their inquiry as the others did, as Joshua appeared approaching them. The marshal had thrown on his winter garb and head dress again, his cloak fluttering by the wind as he neared.

"Hey guys, what a mess," the marshal said to the two once he was close enough for casual verbal exchange.

"Yup," one of the replied, who was a sergeant, "you sure did do a good job," he concluded with a tenor of sarcasm.

"Do you think their commander was abouts when it blew, did you find anything reptilian," the marshal hoped.

"Negative, not as yet," the other crewman who was silent spoke out.

Before anything further was said the sergeant's interlink broke in, "Sergeant come in, do you copy?"

The crewman, of whom the message was addressed to, pulled his communicator away from its retainer clip and he raised it to acknowledge the dispatch. "I read you, over."

"Most of the pod survivors have been located and recovered."

"Any wounded?"

"Just a few scrapes and broken bones, nothing terminal," the dispatcher informed. The sergeant stood silent for a spell after that, showing a tad of fidgety of impatience, waiting for any other relevant information that he might deem noteworthy. And than temporary silence was interrupted as the dispatcher continued his transmission, "A storm is moving in from the east, looks pretty bad."

"Roger," the sergeant understood.

"We're gonna cleanup here and than evacuate." The dispatcher was now no longer addressing the sergeant but he still had his finger on the transmission button, Joshua and the two crewmen listened in on the chatter. "...Are all parties accounted for?"

"...Negative sir, we're missing one," another who was present there with the dispatcher replied back. "...Corin."

"What?" the marshal alarmed and hoped he misinterpreted the cross chatter.

"Say again, over," the sergeant asked the dispatcher to clarify.

"It would seem like we're missing someone," the dispatcher now addressing the sergeant.

"Who?"

"The hired gun, who volunteered to help us," the marshal was stunned and angered by this news as he overheard. The dispatcher continued, "The storm is moving in rapidly, if she doesn't evacuate soon she doesn't stand a chance."

"Where are they?" the marshal insisted.

"What's your location, over," the sergeant transmitted back.

"About sixty clicks north-east from you."

"I'm on my way," Josh said and than quickly turned to leave.

"Marshal, I can't vouch for the transport to pick you up in time before the storm hits," the sergeant shouted as Josh gained distance away. The sergeant was literally hollering at the marshal's back for Josh was several feet away from where he once stood, and the sergeant's warning fell on the marshal's deaf ears.

The daylight, that was, was short lived as Josh skimmed across near surface in his desperate search for Jackie. Him, being strapped in his scudder craft, was faintly visible as he bolted through his search parameter. The thick clouds seemed to have moved in swiftly, blanketing the sun, which laid a cast of still shade accompanied by turbulent winds.

The high pitch whine of the back engines was still easy to discern even though the beating currents of the rising storm drowned much of it out. The sight of the craft's afterburners was also easily visible, for the time being, as the orange burn at the aft propelled the marshal onward.

Wearing clothing that was highly protective, against the thrusting elements, Joshua kept his sash tightly pressed to most of his face, the ends of which fluttered behind; only his eyes were exposed behind a pair of goggles. His hood, which helped keep his ears warm, was fixed to his head by his field cap. Though adequately geared to endure the merciless developing situation he was in he still went through a lot of discomfort; while he kept his hearing attuned to the craft's sensor alert, in case any signs of life were detected.

A shadowy figure, of who was hard to distinguish through all the whiteout and dark cast of the heavy clouds, was present and alone and at the mercy of the storm. Only one who was in arm's reach of the distressed would know that it was Jackie, who appeared stranded and lost. She buried her head in her given overcoat to cover her face from the whirling snowfall and the churning loose snow, carried by the violent winds. The whirlpool effects of the spiraling snow debris were like tiny pellets eating away at her wintry garb, and if she doesn't seek shelter soon, her flesh to.

And soon came rather than later as a faintly audible sound of engines seemed to be drawing near, but Jackie hadn't heard it at the moment. A silhouette pattern of an individual atop a bulky frame drew nearer as its sounds died down, but Jackie was still ignorant of its presence, the whistling waves of the air currents kept her busy as she held her thermulated coat over her head to keep her face covered.

"Jackie," a voice rang out but muffled by the thrashing wind. It was the marshal's voice calling out to her as he ran, in nearly knee deep in snow to approach her.

Jackie suddenly felt a hand gripping her arm as Josh pulled her close to him, and at that instant, the spiraling snow twist subsided if only for a second. They need a means of escape, which to their hope should be immediate, because on Khalidan snow squalls were in consort with many snow twists, like small cyclones. The brief ease of the temporary passing, because twists move erratically and the same one could veer back toward them, did not remove the unease they felt. Though the other elements of the storm were still punishing the brief passing allowed her to look up, from under her coat, to see the welcomed intrusion.

"Josh," she said trying to be coherent. Her teeth clattering and her face being numb from the exposure made speech difficult. "You found me."

"Yea, I found you," he said softly since he was within hair's breadth from her face. Hollands noticed her trembling and he enveloped her in his cloak, as he wrapped his arms around her. To ease her discomfort somewhat from the bitter cold Joshua stayed close to Jackie to pass on some of his body heat.

Abruptly a sudden rush of air passed over them followed by an upsurge in snow volley. Though they did not see it as yet an obscured bird-like image flew pass them, which was several meters above their heads. Another rush of snow followed again, which flailed at their sides, from the direction the shadowy shape, flew toward. Only than did they realize what it was as they looked that way through the blizzard to glimpse, it was the Cauldron making a landing. As they stood at the mercy of the snowstorm eyeing the starcruiser, the rush of whiteout and snowfall dotted against their faces, they knew it was their ship from its shape and detection lights.

The Cauldron was completely settled on its landing gear now, and was slightly distorted from a distance by the whipping waves of the agitated snow furry, but Josh easily recognized his ship. It was even more familiar to him when Jagaba initiated the ship's flood beams; two blue brilliant rays piercing through the blizzard, like beams from a spotlight, so that the couple could find their way toward it.

Than Joshua turned to Jackie, and quickly afterwards, Jackie also looked away from the ship to meet his gaze and the marshal comforted, "We found you."

...The story ends

About the Author

It was 1980, two years before moving off to high school, when my grade school teacher had an assignment. There were cardboard strips with make up titles on them that she would stuff in a container and we would have to draw one out, like drawing straws. Any whatever title we get we would have to write a brief story on that titled, whatever it would be. In the end my teacher, Mrs. Conner, said I was a butting author so I guess it strarted out from there. Than, that same year, the Empire Strikes Back was released and it blew me away. That was the first Starwars movie I saw, I was only twelve. In the opening sequence when they had the intro scroll up the screen and than the magic began I told myself that I wanted to do a story like that. Well, it took all this time but I finally did it. To brainstorm story concepts, character ideas to come up with this adventure that I hope you'll enjoy.

-sincerely, John Deleo Custer